I0542432

From the Valley
of the Missing

Grace Miller White

From the Valley of the Missing

Copyright © 2020 Bibliotech Press
All rights reserved

The present edition is a reproduction of previous publication of this classic work. Minor typographical errors may have been corrected without note, however, for an authentic reading experience the spelling, punctuation, and capitalization have been retained from the original text.

ISBN: 978-1-64799-234-7

CHAPTER ONE

One afternoon in late October four lean mules, with stringy muscles dragging over their bones, stretched long legs at the whirring of their master's whip. The canal-man was a short, ill-favored brute, with coarse red hair and freckled skin. His nose, thickened by drink, threatened the short upper lip with obliteration. Straight from ear to ear, deep under his chin, was a zigzag scar made by a razor in his boyhood days, and under emotion the injured throat became convulsed at times, causing his words to be unintelligible. The red flannel shirt, patched with colors of lighter shades, lay open to the shoulders, showing the dark, rough skin.

"Git—git up!" he stuttered; and for some minutes the boat moved silently, save for the swish of the water and the patter of the mules' feet on the narrow path by the river.

From the small living-room at one end of the boat came the crooning of a woman's voice, a girlish voice, which rose and fell without tune or rhythm. Suddenly the mules came to a standstill with a "Whoa thar!"

"Pole me out a drink, Scraggy," bawled the man, "and put a big snack of whisky in it—see?"

The boulder-shaped head shot forward in command as he spoke. And he held the reins in his left hand, turning squarely toward the scow. Pushing out a dark, rusty, steel hook over which swung a ragged coat-sleeve, he displayed the stump of a short arm.

As the woman appeared at the bow of the boat with a long stick on the end of which hung a bucket, Lem Crabbe wound the reins about the steel hook and took the proffered pail in the fingers of his left hand.

"Ye drink too much whisky, Lem," called the woman. "Ye've had as many as twenty swigs today. Ye'll get no more till we reaches the dock—see?"

To this Lem did not reply. His shrewd eyes traveled up and down the girlish figure in evil meaning. His thick lips opened, and the swarthy cheeks went awry in a grimace. Before the hideous spasm of his silent merriment the woman who loved him paled, and turned away with a shudder. She slouched down the short flight of steps, and the man, with a grin, malicious and cunning, lifted the tin pail to his lips.

"It's time for her to go," he muttered as he wiped his mouth, "it's time for her to go! Git back here, Scraggy, and take this 'ere drink cup!"

1

This time the woman appeared with a fat baby in her arms. Mechanically she unloosened the pail from the bent nail on the end of the pole and put it down, watching the man as he unwound the reins from the hook. Again the long-eared animals stretched their muscles at his hoarse command. He paid no more attention to the woman, who, seated on a pile of planks, was eying the square end of the boat. She drew a plaid shawl close up under the baby's chin and threaded her listless fingers through his dark curls. Scraggy's thin hair was drawn back from her wan face, and her narrow shoulders were bowed with burdens too heavy for her years; but she hugged the little creature sleeping on her breast, and still kept her eyes upon the scene. Beyond she could see the smoke rising from the buildings in the city of Albany, where they were to draw the boat up for the night. On each side of the river bank, behind clumps of trees, stood the mansions of those men for whom, according to Scraggy Peterson's belief, the world had been made. Finally her gaze dropped to the scow, where little rivers of water made crooked paths across the deck. Piles of planks reared high at her back, and edged the scow with the square-ness of a room. Scraggy knew that hauling lumber was but the cover for a darker trade. Yet as she glanced at the stolid, indifferent man trudging behind the mules a love-light sprang into her eyes.

Later, by an hour, the mules came to a halt at Lem's order.

"Throw down that gangplank, Scraggy," stammered Crabbe, "and put the brat below! I want to get these here mules in. The storm'll be here in any minute."

Obediently the woman hastened to comply, and soon the tired mules munched their suppers, their long faces filling the window-gaps of the stable.

Lem Crabbe followed the woman down the scow-steps amid gusty howls of the wind, and the night fell over the city and the black, winding river. The man ate his supper in silence, furtively casting his eyes now and then upon the slender figure of the woman. He chewed fast, uttering no word, and the creaking of the heavy jaws and the smacking of the coarse lips were the only sounds to be heard after the woman had taken her place at the table. Scraggy dared not yet begin to eat; for something new in her master's manner filled her with sudden fear. By sitting very quietly, she hoped to keep his attention upon his plate, and after he had eaten he would go to bed. She was aroused from this thought by the feeble whimper of her child in the tiny room of the scow's bow. Although the woman heard, she made no move to answer the weak summons.

She rose languidly as the child began to cry more loudly; but a command from Lem stopped her.

"Set down!" he said.

"The brat's a wailin'," replied Scraggy hoarsely.

"Set down, and let him wail!" shouted Lem.

Scraggy sank unnerved into the chair, gazing at him with terrified eyes. "Why, Lem, he's too little to cry overmuch."

"Keep a settin', I say! Let him yap!"

For the second time that day Scraggy's face shaded to the color of ashes, and her gaze dropped before the fierce eyes directed upon her.

"Ye said more'n once, Scraggy," began Lem, "that I wasn't to drink no more whisky. Whose money pays for what I drink? That's what I want ye to tell me!"

"Yer money, Lem dear."

"And ye say as how I couldn't drink what I pay for?"

"Yep, I has said it," was the timid answer. "Ye drink too much—that's what ye do! Ye ain't no mind left, ye ain't! And it makes ye ugly, so it does!"

"Be it any of yer business?" demanded Lem insultingly, as he filled his mouth with a piece of brown bread. After washing it down with a drink of whisky, he finished, "Ye ain't no relation to me, be ye?"

The thin face hung over the tin plate.

"Ye ain't married to me, be ye?"

And, while a giant pain gnawed at her heart, she shook her head.

"Then what right has ye got to tell me what to do? Shut up or get out—ye see?"

He closed his jaw with a vicious snap, resting his half-dazed head on his mutilated arm. Louder came the baby's cries from the back room. Thinking Lem had ended his tirade, Scraggy made a motion to rise.

"Set still!" growled Crabbe.

"Can't I get the brat, Lemmy?" she pleaded. "He's likely to fall offen the bed."

"Let him fall. What do I care? I want to tell ye somethin'. I didn't bring ye here to this boat to boss me, ye see? Ye keep yer mouth shet 'bout things what ye don't like. Ye're in my way, anyhow."

"Ye mean, Lemmy, as how I has to leave ye?"

Crabbe regarded the appealing face soddenly before answering. "Yep, that's what I mean. I'm tired of a woman allers a snoopin' around, and a hundred times more tired of the brat."

"But he's yer own," cried the woman, "and ye did say as how ye'd marry me for his sake! Didn't ye say it, Lem? He ain't nothin' but a baby, an' he don't cry much. Will ye let me an' him stay, Deary?"

"Ye can stay tonight; but tomorry ye go, and I don't give a hell where, so long as ye leave this here scow, an' I'm a tellin' ye this—" He halted with an exasperated gesture. "Go an' get that kid an' shet his everlastin' clack!"

Scraggy bounded into the inner room, and, once out of sight of the watchful eyes of Lem, snatched up the infant and pressed her lips passionately to the rosy skin.

"Yer mammy'll allers love ye, little 'un, allers, allers, no matter what yer pappy does!"

She whispered this under her breath; then, dragging the red shawl about her shoulders, appeared in the living-room with the child hidden from view.

"An' I'll tell ye somethin' else, too," burst in Lem, pulling out a corncob pipe: "that it ain't none of yer business if I steal or if I don't. I was born a thief, as I told ye many a time, and last night ye made Lon Cronk and Eli mad as hell by chippin' in."

"They be bad men," broke in the woman, "and ye know—"

"I know ye're a damn blat-heels, and I know more'n that: that yer own pappy ain't no angel, and ye needn't be a sayin' my friends ain't no right here—ye see? They be—"

"They be thieves and liars, too," interrupted Scraggy, allowing the sleeping babe to sink to her knees, "and the prison's allers a yawnin' for 'em!"

"Wall, I ain't a runnin' this boat for fun," drawled Lem, "nor for to draw lumber for any ole guy in Albany. Ye know that I draw it jest to hide my trade, and if, after ye leave here, ye open yer head to tell what ye've seen, ye'll get this—ye see?" He held up the hooked arm menacingly. "Ye've seen me rip up many a man with it, ain't ye, Scraggy?"

"Yep."

"And I ain't got nothin' ag'in' rippin' up a woman, nuther. So, when ye go back to yer pa in Ithacy, keep yer mouth shet.... Will ye let up that there cryin'?"

Suppressing her tears, Scraggy shoved back a little from the table. "I love ye, Lem," she choked, "and, if ye let me stay, I'll do whatever ye say. I won't talk nothin' 'bout drink nor stealin'. If I go ye'll get another woman! I know ye can't live on this here scow without no woman."

"And that ain't none of yer business, nuther—ye hear?" Lem grunted, settling deep into his chair, with an oath. "I'll get all the women in Albany, if I want 'em! I don't never want none of yer lovin' anymore!"

During this bitter insult a storm-cloud broke overhead, sending sheets of water into the river. The wind howled above Crabbe's words,

4

and he brought out the last of his sentence in a higher key. Suddenly the shrill whistle of a yacht brought the drunken man to his feet.

"It's some 'un alone in trouble," he muttered. But his tones were not so low as to escape the woman.

"Ye won't do no robbin' tonight, Deary—not tonight, will ye, Lem? 'Cause it's the baby's birthday."

Crabbe flung his squat body about toward the girl. "Shet up about that brat!" he growled. "I don't care 'bout no birthdays. I'll steal, if the man has anything and he's alone. I'll kill him like this, if he don't give up. Do ye want to see how I'd kill him?"

His eyes blazing with fire, he lifted the steel hook, brandished it in the air, and brought it down close to the thin, drawn face.

Scraggy, uttering a cry, sprang to her feet. "Lemmy, Lemmy, I love ye, and the brat loves ye, too! He'll grin at ye any ole day when ye cluck at him. And I teached him to say 'Daddy,' to surprise ye on his birthday. Will ye list to him—will ye?"

In her eagerness to take his attention from the shrieking yacht, now close to the scow, Scraggy advanced toward the swaying man. She tried to lift brave eyes to his face; but they were filled with tears as they met his drunken, shifting look.

"Lem, Lemmy dear," she pleaded, "we love ye, both the brat an' me! He can say 'Daddy'—"

"Git out of my way, git out! Some'n' be a callin'. Git out, I say!"

"Not yet, not yet—don't go yet, Deary.... Deary! Wait till the kid says 'Daddy.'" She held out the rosy babe, pushing him almost under Lem's chin. "Look at him, Lemmy! Ain't—he—sweet? He's yer own pretty boy-brat, and—"

Her loving plea was cut short; for the man, with a vicious growl, raised his stumped arm, and the sharp part of the hook scraped the skin from her hollow cheek. It paused an instant on the level of her chin, then descended into the upturned chest of the child. With a scream, Scraggy dragged the boy back, and a wail rose from the tiny lips. Crabbe turned, cursing audibly, and stumbled up the steps to the stern of the boat. The woman heard him fall in his drunken stupor, and listened again and again for him to rise. Her face was white and rigid as she stopped the flow of blood that drenched the infant's coarse frock. Then, realizing the danger both she and the child were in, since in all likelihood Lem would sleep but a few minutes, she slid open the window and looked out upon the dark river in search of help. Splashes of rain pelted her face, while a gust of wind caused the scow to creak dismally. Scraggy could see no human being, only the lights of Albany blinking dimly through the raging storm. Another shrieking whistle

5

warned her that the yacht was still near. Sailors' voices shouted orders, followed by the chug, chug, chug of an engine reversed.

But, in spite of the efforts of the engineer, the wind swung the small craft sidewise against the scow, and, stupefied, Scraggy found herself gazing into the face of another woman who was peering from the launch's window. It was a small, beautiful face shrouded with golden hair, the large blue eyes widened with terror. For a brief instant the two women eyed each other. Just then the drunken man above rose and called Scraggy's name with an oath. She heard him stumbling about, trying to find the stairs, muttering invectives against herself and her child.

Scraggy looked down upon the little boy's face, twisted with pain. She placed her fingers under his chin, closed the tiny jaws, and wrapped the shawl about the dark head. Without a moment's indecision, she thrust him through the window-space and said:

"Be ye a good woman, lady, a good woman?"

The owner of the golden head drew back as if afraid.

"Ye wouldn't hurt a little 'un—a sick brat? He—he's been hooked. And it's his birthday. Take him, 'cause he'll die if ye don't!"

Moved to a sense of pity, the light-haired woman extended two slender white hands to receive the human bundle, struggling in pain under the muffling shawl.

"He's a dyin'!" gasped Scraggy. "His pappy's a hatin' him! Give him warm milk—"

Again the yacht's whistle shrieked hoarsely, drowning her last words. As the stern of the little boat swung round, Scraggy read, stamped in black letters upon it:

HAROLD BRIMBECOMB,
TARRYTOWN-ON-THE-HUDSON,
NEW YORK

The yacht shot away up the river, and was lost to the dull eyes that continued peering for a last glimpse of the phantom-like boat that had snatched her dying treasure from her. Then, at last, the stricken woman turned, alone, to meet Lem Crabbe.

"Where's that brat?" he demanded in a thick voice.

"I threwed him in the river," declared the mother. "He were dead. Yer hook killed him, Lem. He's gone!"

"I'll kill his mammy, too!" muttered Crabbe. "Git ye here—here—down here—on the floor!"

His throat worked painfully as he threw the threatening words at her; they mingled harshly with the snarling of the wind and the

6

sonorous rumble of the river. So great was Scraggy's fright that she sped round the wooden table to escape the frenzied man. Taking the steps in two bounds, she sprang to the deck like a cat, thence to the bank, and sped away into the rain, with Lem's cries and curses ringing in her ears.

CHAPTER TWO

Five years later the *Monarch* was drawn up to the east bank of the Erie Canal at Syracuse. It was past midnight, and with the exception of those on Lem Crabbe's scow the occupants of all the long line of boats were sleeping. Three men sat silently working in the living-room of the boat. Lem Crabbe, Silent Lon Cronk, and his brother Eli, Cayuga Lake squatters, were the workers. At one end of the room hung a broken iron kettle. Into this Eli Cronk was dropping bits of gold which he cut from baubles taken from a basket. Crabbe, his short legs drawn up under his body, held a pair of pliers in his left hand, while caught firmly in the hook was a child's tiny pin. From this he tore the small jewels, threw them into a tin cup, and passed the setting on to Eli. The other man, taciturn and fierce, was flattening out by means of strong pressers several gold rings and bracelets. The three had worked for many hours with scarcely a word spoken, with scarcely a recognition of one another.

Of a sudden Eli Cronk raised his head and said, "Lem, Scraggy was to Mammy's t'other day."

"I didn't know ye'd been to Ithacy?" Lem made the statement a question.

"Yep, I went to see Mammy, and she says as how Scraggy's pappy were dead, and as how the gal's teched in here." His words were low, and he raised his forefinger to his head significantly.

"She ain't allers a stayin' in the squatter country nuther," he pursued. "She takes that damn ugly cat of her'n and scoots away for a time. And none of 'em up there don't know where she goes. Hones' Injun, don't she never come about this here scow, Lem?"

"Hones' Injun," replied Lem laconically, without looking up from his work.

7

Presently Eli continued:

"Mammy says as how the winter's comin', and some 'un ought to look out for Scraggy. She goes 'bout the lake doin' nothin' but hollerin' like a hoot-owl, and she don't have enough to eat. But she's been gone now goin' on two weeks, disappearin' like she's been doin' for a few years back. Scraggy allers says she has bats in her head."

"So she has bats," muttered Lem, "and she allers had 'em, and that's why I made her beat it. I didn't want no woman 'bout me for good and all."

Lem Crabbe lifted his head and glanced toward the small window overlooking the dark canal. He had always feared the crazy squatter-woman whom he had wrecked by his brutality.

"I says that I don't want no woman round me for all time," he repeated.

The third man raised his right shoulder at that; but sank into a heap again, working more assiduously. The slight trembling of his body was the only evidence he gave that he had heard Crabbe's words. Snip, snip, snip! went the bits of gold into the kettle, until Eli spoke again.

"Ye can't tell me that ye ain't goin' never to get married, Lem?"

Crabbe lifted his hooked arm viciously. "I ain't said nothin' like that. I says as how Scraggy can keep away from my scow."

"Don't she never come here no more?" asked Eli in disbelief.

"Nope, not after them three beatin's I give her. She kept a comin', and I had to wallop her. I'd do it again if she snoops 'bout here."

"Ye beat her up well, didn't ye, Lem? And she told Mammy that yer brat were drowned one night in the river. Were it, Lem?"

There was an expectant pause between his first and last questions, and Lem waited almost as long before he grunted:

"Yep."

"Did ye throw it in when ye was drunk?"

"Nope, he jest fell in—that's all."

"I guess that last beatin' ye give Scraggy made her batty. Mam says that she ain't no more sense than her cat."

"Let her keep to hum then, and she won't get beat. I don't do no runnin' after her!"

Again there came a space of time during which Eli and Lem worked in silence. From far away in the city there came the sound of the fire whistle, followed by the ringing of bells. But not one of the men ceased his clipping to satisfy any curiosity he might have had.

Suddenly Lem Crabbe spoke louder than he had before that evening.

"Women ain't no good, nohow! They don't love no men, and men don't love them. What's the good of havin' 'em round to feed and to bother a feller 'bout drinkin' an' things? Less a man sees of 'em the better!"

The third man, Silent Lon Cronk, sunk lower at his work, even more fiercely flattening the gemless rings under the pressers. After a few moments he laid down his tools and began to stretch his long legs, scraping into a cup the bits of gold from his lap.

"I've been goin' to ask ye fellers somethin' for a long time. Might as well now as any other night, eh?"

"Yep," replied Eli eagerly.

"'Tain't nothin' that will take any money out yer pockets; 'twill put it in, more likely. We've been stealin' together for how long, Lem? How long we been pals?"

"Nigh onto ten years, I'm thinkin'. It were that year that Tilly Jacobson got burned, weren't it?"

"Yep, for ten years," replied Lon, ignoring Lem's last query, "and we've allers been hones' with each other. I've been hones' with both of ye, and ye've been hones' with me. Eh?"

"Yep."

"Lem, do ye want all the swag in this here room, only a sharin' up with Eli, without havin' to share and share alike with me?"

A small jewel bounded from the steel hook, and the pliers fell from Lem's fingers. Eli dropped back upon his bare feet.

"What's in the wind?" demanded Lem.

"Only want ye to help me with a job some night that won't be nothin' to nuther of ye. But it's all to me. Will ye?"

Lem wriggled nearer on the floor. "Ye mean stealin', Lon?" he demanded.

"Yep."

"And we ain't to share up with it?"

"Nope; but ye're to have all that's in this here room. If I tell ye, will ye help?"

Crabbe looked at Eli, and a furtive look was shot back. Each was afraid of the other; but for the big, gloomy man before them they had vast respect.

"What be ye goin' to steal, Lon? Tell us before we say we'll help."

"Kids," muttered Lon moodily.

"Live kids?" asked Eli, in great surprise.

"Yep, live ones. What do I want with dead ones? Will ye help?"

"Can't see no good a swipin' kids. What do ye want with 'em?"

"I'll tell ye if ye sit up and listen to me."

Crabbe dropped his hooked arm and leaned against the wall. Eli lighted a pipe. A mysterious change had passed over Silent Lon's face.

9

The blue eyes glowed out from under a massive brow, and a mouth cruel and vindictive set firm-jawed over decayed teeth.

"I'll tell ye this much for all time, Lem Crabbe: that ye lied when ye said that no woman could love no man—ye lied, I say!"

So fierce had he become that the man with the hook drew back into the corner and sat staring sullenly. Eli puffed more vigorously on his pipe.

Lon went on:

"I had a woman oncet," said he, "and she were every bit mine. And she were little—like this."

The big fellow measured off a space with his hand and, straightening again, stood against the wall of the scow, his head reaching almost to the ceiling.

"She were mine, I say, and any man what says she weren't—"

"Where be she?" interrupted Lem curiously.

"Dead," replied Lon, "as dead as if she'd never been alive, as dead as if she'd never laid ag'in' my heart when I wanted her! God! how I wanted her!"

"But were she a woman?" asked Lem meditatively.

"Yep, she were a woman, and I married her square, I did!"

Lon stirred his dank black hair ferociously, standing it on end with horny fingers. "I loved her, Lem Crabbe," he continued hoarsely. "I loved her, that I know! And ye can let that devilish grin ride on yer lips when I say it and I don't give a hell; but—but if ye say that she didn't love me, if ye so much as smile when I say that she died a callin' me, that she went away lovin' me every minute, I—I'll rip offen yer hooked arm and tear out yer in'ards with it!"

He was leaning against the wall no longer. As he spoke, he came closer to the crouching canal-man, his eyes straining from their sockets in livid hate. But he halted, and presently began to speak in a voice more subdued.

"But she's dead, and I'm goin' to get even. He killed her, he did, 'cause he wouldn't let me see her, and he's got to go the same way I went! He's got to tear his hair and call God to curse some 'un he won't know who! He's got to want his kids like as how I've been wantin' mine—"

"Ye ain't had no kids, Lon," his brother broke in scoffingly.

"I would a had if he'd a kept his hands to hum and let me see her. But she were so little an' young-like an' afeard, and I told her that night—I told her when she whispered that she were a goin' to have a baby, and said as how she couldn't stand bein' hurt—I says, 'Midge darlin', do it hurt the grass to grow jest 'cause the winds bend it double? Do it hurt the little birds to bust out of their shells in the

10

springtime?' And she knowed what I meant, that not even what she were a thinkin' of could hurt her if I was there close by."

His deep voice sank almost to a whisper, a hard, heavy sob closing his throat. He shook himself fiercely and continued:

"I took her up close—God! how close I tooked her up! And I told her that there wasn't no pain big 'nough to hurt her when I were there—that even God's finger couldn't tech her afore it went through me. And she fell to sleep like a bird, a trustin' me, 'cause I said as how there wasn't goin' to be no hurt. And all the time I knowed I were a lyin'—I knowed that she'd suffer—"

His voice trailed into silence, the muscles of his dark face twitching under the gnawing heart-pain; but after a time he conquered his feelings and went on:

"Then they comed and took me away for stealin' jest that there week and sent me up to Auburn prison, and they wouldn't let me stay with her. And I telled the state's lawyer, Floyd Vandecar, this; I says, 'Vandecar, ye be a good man, I be a thief, and ye caught me square, ye did. My little Midge be sick like women is sick sometimes, and she wants me, like every woman wants her man jest then, an' if ye'll let me see her, to stay a bit, I'll go up for twice my time.' But he jest laughed till—"

Lon stopped speaking, and neither listener moved. For a moment he lowered his head to the small boat window and gazed out into the vapors hanging low over the opposite bank.

Turning again, he backed up to the scow's side and proceeded in a lower voice:

"When they telled me she were dead, they had to set me in the jacket, buckled so tight ye could hear my bones crack. The warden ain't got no blame comin' from me, 'cause I smashed his face afore he'd done tellin' me. And I felled the keeper like that!" He raised a knotty fist and thrust it forth. "But it were all 'cause I wanted to be with her so, 'cause I couldn't stand the knowin' that she'd gone a callin' and a callin' me!"

He was quiet so long that Eli Cronk drew his sleeve across his face to break the oppressive stillness. Here, in the dead of night, his somber brother had been transformed into another creature,—a passionate creature, responding to the call of a dead woman, a man whose hatred would carry him to fearful lengths.

The hoarse voice broke forth again:

"Midge darlin', dead baby, and all that ye had belongin' to me, I do it for you! I'll steal his'n, and they'll suffer and suffer—"

He tossed up his great head with a jerk, crushing the sentiment from his voice.

11

"But that don't make no matter now," he muttered. "I'm goin' to take his kids! He's got two, an' he's prouder'n a turkey cock of 'em. I'll take 'em and I'll make of 'em what I be—I'll make 'em so damn bad that he won't want 'em no more after I get done with 'em! I'll see what his woman does when she finds 'em gone! Will ye help, Lem—Eli?"

"Yep, by God, you bet!" burst from both men at once.

"I'll take 'em to the squatter country, up to Mammy's," Lon proceeded, "and, Eli, if ye'll take one of 'em on the train up to McKinneys Point, I'll take t'other one up the west side of the lake. I'll pay all the way, Eli; it won't be nothin' out o' yer pocket. We'll tell Mammy the kids be mine—see? And ye can have all there be in this here room. Be it a bargain?"

"Yep," assured Eli, and Lena's consent followed only an instant later. After that there were no sounds save the snip, snip, snip of the pliers and the occasional low grating from a jeweled trinket as the steel hook gouged into the metal.

CHAPTER THREE

As Eli Cronk said, Scraggy Peterson left her lonely squatter home two weeks before with no companion but her vicious black cat. The woman had intervals of sanity, and during those periods her thoughts turned to a dark-haired boy, growing up in a luxurious home. In these rare days she donned her rude clothing, and with the cat perched close to her thin face walked across the state to Tarrytown. Several times during the five years after leaving Lem's scow she walked to Tarrytown, returning only when she had seen the little boy, to take up her squatter life in her father's hut. So secretive was she that no one had been taken into her confidence; neither had she interfered with her child in any way. Never once, hitherto, had her senses left her on those long country marches toward the east; but often when she turned backward she would utter forlorn cries, characteristic of her malady.

At eight o'clock, four hours before Lon Cronk opened his heart to his companions, Scraggy, footsore and weary, entered Sleepy Hollow

Cemetery and seated herself on the damp earth to gather strength. By begging and stealing she had managed to reach her destination; but now for the first time on this journey the bats were in her head, sounding the walls of her poor brain with the ceaseless clatter of their wings. Still the mother heart called for its own, through the madness—called for one sight of Lem's child and hers. At length after a long rest she turned into a broad path which she knew well, and did not halt until she was staring eager-eyed into the window of Harold Brimbecomb's house which stood close to the cemetery.

To the left of the Brimbecomb's was the mansion, belonging to the orphans of Horace Shellington. The young Horace and his sister Ann were the favorite companions of Everett Brimbecomb, now six years old. He was a strong, proud, handsome lad. Many conjectures had been made concerning him by the Tarrytown people, because one day five years before the delicate, light-haired wife of Mr. Brimbecomb had appeared with a dark-haired baby boy, announcing that from that day on he would take the place of her own child who had died a few months before. No person had told Everett that the millionaire was not his father, nor was he made to understand that the mother and the home were not his by right of birth. His bright mind and handsome appearance were the pride of his adopted mother's life, and his rich father smiled only the more leniently when the lad showed a rebellious spirit. In the child's dark, limpid eyes slumbered primeval passions, needing but the dawn of manhood to break forth, perhaps to destroy the soul beneath their reckless domination.

Everett was entertaining Ann and Horace Shellington at dinner, and after the repast the youngsters betook themselves to the large square room given to the young host's own use. Here were multitudinous playthings and mechanical toys of all descriptions. For many minutes the children had been too interested to note that the shadows were grown long and that a somber gloom had settled down over the cemetery that lay just beyond the windows.

Ann Shellington, a delicate little creature of eight, looked up nervously. "Everett, draw down the curtain," she said. "It looks so ghostly out there!"

Ann made a motion toward the window; but the boy did not obey her.

"Isn't that just like a girl, Horace?" he asked. "I'm not afraid of ghosts. Dead people can't walk, can they, Horace?"

The other boy answered "No" thoughtfully, as he started a miniature train across the length of the room.

"Then who is it that walks in the night out there?" insisted the girl. "Lots of town people have seen it. It's a woman with shaggy hair, and sometimes her eyes turn green."

"Pouf!" scoffed Everett. "My father says there aren't any such things as ghosts. I wouldn't be a fraidy cat, Ann."

"I'm not a fraidy cat," pouted the girl. "I always go upstairs alone, don't I, Horace?"

Another answer in the affirmative, and Horace proceeded to roll the train back over the carpet.

"If you had any mother," said Everett, "she'd tell you there weren't any ghosts. My mother tells me that."

"I haven't any mother," sighed the little girl, listlessly folding her hands in her lap.

"Nor any father, either," supplemented Horace, with seemingly no thought of the magnitude of his statement. "I don't believe in ghosts, anyhow!"

He glanced up as he spoke, and the train fell with a bang to the floor. Everett Brimbecomb dropped the toy he held in his hand, and Ann bounded from her chair. A white face with wide eyes, staring through scraggly gray hair, appeared at the window. For only an instant it pressed against the pane, then vanished as if it had never been.

"It was a woman," gasped Horace, "or was it a—"

"It wasn't a ghost," interrupted Everett stoutly. "I dare follow it out there. Look at me!"

He straightened his shoulders, threw up his dark head, and opened the door leading to the narrow walk at the side of the house. In another moment the watching boy and girl at the window saw him dart into the hedge and a minute later emerge through it, picking his way among the ancient graves. Suddenly from behind a tall monument stole a figure, and as it approached the solemn eyes of the apparition smiled in dull wonder on Everett Brimbecomb.

Scraggy held out her hands. "Don't run away, little 'un," she whispered. "There be bats flyin' about in my head; but my cat won't hurt ye."

She passed one arm about the snarling creature perched on her shoulder; but the cat with a hiss only raised himself higher.

"Don't spit at the pretty boy, Kitty—pretty pussy, black pussy!" wheedled the woman. "He won't hurt ye, childy. Come nearer, will ye? This be a good cat."

"Are you a ghost?" demanded Everett, edging into the light.

"Nope, I ain't no ghost. I love ye, pretty boy. Ye won't tell no one that I speak to ye, will ye? I ain't doin' no hurt."

"What do you carry that cat for, and what's your name?"

14

demanded Everett insolently; for the proud young eyes had noticed the disheveled figure. "If any one of our men see you about here, they'll shoot you. I'd shoot you and your cat, too, if I had my father's gun!"

Scraggy smiled wanly. "Screech Owl's my name," said she. "They call me that 'cause I'm batty. But ye wouldn't hurt me, little 'un, 'cause I love ye. How old be ye?"

"Six years old; but it isn't any of your business. Crazy people ought to be locked up. You'd better go away from here. My father owns that house, and—don't you follow me through the hedge. Get back, I say! If I call Malcolm—"

Everett drew back through the box-hedge, and the boy and the girl at the window saw the woman squeeze in after him. In another moment the young heir to the Brimbecomb fortune bounded through the doorway. His face was white; his eyes were filled with fear.

"Did you see that old woman?" he gasped. "She tried to kiss me, and I punched her in the face, and her cat did this to my arm."

He pulled up his sleeve, and displayed a long scratch from wrist to elbow.

"Are you sure it wasn't a ghost, Everett?" asked Ann, shivering.

"Of course, it wasn't," boasted Everett. "It was only a horrid woman with a cat—that's all."

As he closed the door vehemently, there drifted to the children from the marble monument and waving trees the faint wail of a night-owl.

CHAPTER FOUR

On a fashionable street in Syracuse, Floyd Vandecar, district attorney of the city, lived in a new house, built to please the delicate fancies of his pretty wife. His career had been comet-like. Graduated from Cornell University and starting in law with his father, he had succeeded to a large practice when but a very young man. Then came the call for his force and strength to be used for the state, and, with a gratified smile, he accepted the votes of his constituents to act as district attorney. Then, as Lon Cronk had told, it came within the duty

15

of the young lawyer to convict the thief of grand larceny committed three years before. After that Floyd married the lovely Fledra Martindale, and a year later his twin children were born—a sturdy boy and a tiny girl. The children were nearly a year old when Fledra Vandecar whispered another secret to her husband, and Vandecar, lover-like, had gathered his darling into his arms, as if to hold her against any harm that might come to her. This happened on the morning following the night when Silent Lon Cronk told the dark tale of suffering to his pals.

Just how Lon Cronk came to know the inner workings of the Vandecar household he never confided; but, biding his time, waited for the hour to come when the blow would be harder to bear. At last it fell, fell not only upon the brilliant district attorney, but upon his lovely wife and his hapless children.

One blustering night in March, Lem Crabbe's scow was tied at the locks near Syracuse. The day for the fulfilment of Lon Cronk's revenge had arrived. That afternoon Lon had come from Ithaca with his brother Eli to meet Lem.

"Be ye goin' to steal the kids tonight, Lon?" asked Lem.

"Yep, tonight."

"Why don't ye take just one? It'd make 'em sit up and note a bit to crib, say, the boy."

"We'll take 'em both," replied Lon decisively.

"And if we get caught?" stammered Crabbe.

"We don't get caught," assured Lon darkly, "'cause tonight's the time for 'em all to be busy 'bout the Vandecar house. I know, I do—no matter how!"

Wee Mildred Vandecar was ushered into the world during one of the worst March storms ever known in the western part of New York. As she lay snuggled in laces in her father's home, a tall man walked down a lane, four miles from Ithaca, with her sleeping sister in his arms. The dark baby head was covered by a ragged shawl; two tender, naked feet protruded from under a coarse skirt. Lon Cronk struggled on against the wind to a hut in the rocks, opened the door, and stepped inside.

A woman, not unlike him, in spite of added years, rose as he entered.

"So ye comed, Lon," she said.

"Course! Did Eli get here with the other brat?"

"Yep, there 'tis. And he's been squalling for the whole night and day. He wanted the other little 'un, I'm a thinkin'."

16

"Yep," answered Lon somberly, "and he wants his mammy, too. But, as I telled ye before, she's dead."

"Be ye reely goin' to live to hum, Lon?" queried the old woman eagerly.

"Yep. And ye'll get all ye want to eat if ye'll take care of the kids. Be ye glad to have me stay to hum?"

"Yep, I'm glad," replied the mother, with a pathetic droop to her shriveled lips.

Just then the child on the cot turned over and sat up. The small, tear-stained face was creased with dirt and molasses. Bits of bread stuck between fingers that gouged into a pair of gray eyes flecked with brown. Noting strangers, he opened his lips and emitted a forlorn wail. The other baby, in the man's arms, lifted a bonny dark head with a jerk.

For several seconds the babies eyed each other. Two pairs of brown-shot eyes, alike in color and size, brightened, and a wide smile spread the four rosy lips.

"Flea! Flea!" murmured the baby on the bed; and "Flukey!" gurgled the infant in Lon's arms.

"There!" cried the old woman. "That's what he's been a cryin' for. Set him on the bed, Lon, for God's sake, so he'll keep his clack shet for a minute!"

The baby called "Flea" leaned over and rubbed the face of the baby called "Flukey," who touched the dimpled little hand with his. Then they both lay down on a rough, low cot in the squatter's home and forgot their baby troubles in sleep.

The kidnapping of the twins was discovered just after Fledra Vandecar had presented her husband with another daughter, a tiny human flower which the strong man took in his hands with tender thanksgiving. The three days that followed the disappearance of his children were eternal for Floyd Vandecar. The entire police force of the country had been called upon to help bring to him his lost treasures. So necessary was it for him to find them that he neither slept nor worked. He had had to tell the mother falsehood after falsehood to keep her content. The children had suddenly become infected with a contagious disease, and the doctor had said that the new baby must not be exposed in any circumstances. After three long weeks of torture it devolved upon him to tell his wife that her children were gone.

"Sweetheart," he whispered, sitting beside her and taking her hands in his, "do you love and trust me very much indeed?"

The wondering blue eyes smiled upon him, and small fingers threaded his black hair.

"I not only love you, Dear, but trust you always. I don't want to

17

seem obstinate and impatient, Floyd, but if I could see my babies just from the door I should be happy. And it won't hurt me. I haven't seen them in three whole weeks."

During the long, agonizing silence the young mother gathered something of his distress.

"Floyd, look at me!"

Slowly he lifted his white face and looked straight at her.

"Floyd, Floyd, you've tears in your eyes! I didn't mean to hurt you—"

She stopped speaking, and the pain in his heart reached hers.

"Floyd," she cried again, "is there anything the matter with— with—"

"Hush, Fledra darling, little wife, will you be brave for my sake and for the sake of—her?"

His eyes were still full of tears as he touched the bundle on the bed.

"But my babies!" moaned Mrs. Vandecar. "If there isn't anything the matter with my babies—"

"I want to speak to you about our children, Dear."

"They are dead?" Mrs. Vandecar asked dully. "My babies are dead?"

At first Vandecar could scarcely trust himself to speak; but, curbing his emotion with an effort, he answered, "No, no; but gone for a little while."

His arms were tightly about her, and time and again he pressed his lips to hers.

"Gone where?" she demanded.

"Fledra, you must not look that way! Listen to me, and I will tell you about it. I promise, Fledra. Don't, don't! You must not shake so! Please! Then you do not trust me to bring them back to you?"

His last appeal brought the tense arms more limply about his neck. She had believed him absolutely when he said they were not dead.

"Am I to have them tonight?"

"No, dear love."

"Where are they gone?"

"The cradles were empty after little Mildred—"

"They have been gone for—for three weeks!" she wailed. "Floyd, who took them? Were they kidnapped? Have you had any letters asking for money?"

Vandecar shook his head.

"And no one has come to the house? Tell me, Floyd! I can't bear it! Someone has taken my babies!"

18

She raised herself on her arm wildly, fever brightening the anguished eyes. The husband with bowed head remained praying for them and especially for her. Another cry from the wounded mother aroused him.

"Floyd, they have been taken for something besides money. Tell me, Dearest! Don't you know?"

Faithfully he told her that he could think of no human being who would deal him a blow like this; that he had thought his life over from beginning to end, but no new truth came out of his mental search.

"Then they want money! Oh, you will pay anything they demand! Floyd, will they torture my baby boy and girl? Will they?"

"Fledra, beloved heart," groaned Vandecar, "please don't struggle like that! You'll be very ill. I promised you that you should have them back someday soon, very soon. Fledra, sweet wife, you still have the baby and me—and Katherine."

"I want my little children! I want my boy and girl!" gasped Mrs. Vandecar. "I will have them, I will! No, I sha'n't lie down till I have them! I'm going to find them if you won't! I will not listen to you, Floyd, I won't ... I won't—"

Each time the words came forth they were followed by a moan which tore the man's heart as it had never been torn before. For a single instant he drew himself together, forced down the terrible emotion in his breast, and leaned over his wife.

"Fledra, Fledra, I command you to obey me! Lie down! I am going to bring you back your babies."

He had never spoken to her in such a tone of authority. She sank under it with parted lips and swift-coming breath.

"But I want my babies, Floyd!" she whispered. "How can I think of them out in the cold and the storm, perhaps being tortured—"

"Fledra, sweet love, precious little mother, am I not their father, and don't you trust me? Wait—wait a moment!"

He moved the babe from her mother's side, called the nurse, and in a low tone told her to keep the child until he should send for her. Then he slipped his arms about the wailing mother, lay down beside her, and drew her to his breast.

During the next few hours of darkness he watched her—watched her until the night gave way to a shadowy dawn. And as she slept he still held her, praying tensely that he might be given power to keep his promise to her. When she started up he gathered her closer and hushed her to sleep as a mother does a suffering child. How gladly he would have borne her larger share, yet more gladly would he have convinced himself that by morning the children would be again under his roof!

19

At last Mrs. Vandecar awoke, calmer and with ready faith to acknowledge that she believed he would accomplish his task. At her own request, he brought their tiny baby.

"Will you see Katherine, too, Fledra," ventured Vandecar. "The poor child hasn't slept much, and she can't be persuaded to eat."

Misery, deep and pathetic, flashed in the blue eyes Mrs. Vandecar raised to his. At length she faltered:

"Floyd, I've never loved Katherine as I should. I'm sorry.... Yes, yes, I will see her—and you will bring me my babies!"

Vandecar stooped and kissed her; then, with a tightening of his throat, went out.

Five minutes later a small girl followed Mr. Vandecar in and stood beside the bed. Fledra Vandecar took the little girl-face in her hands and kissed it.

CHAPTER FIVE

The years went on, with the gap still left wide in the Vandecar household. As month after month passed and nothing was heard of her children, Mrs. Vandecar gradually gave up hope. Her despair left a shadow of pathetic pleading in her blue eyes. This constant silent appeal whitened Floyd Vandecar's hair and caused him to apply himself to business more assiduously than ever. Never once in all those bitter years did he connect Lon Cronk with the disappearance of his babies.

Meantime two sturdy children were growing to girlhood and boyhood in the Cronk hut on Cayuga Lake. So safely had the secret of the kidnapping been kept from Granny Cronk and the other squatters in the settlement that the twins were regarded by all as the son and daughter of the squatter.

The year following Flea's and Flukey's fourteenth birthday the boy was taken into his foster-father's trade of thieving. At first he was allowed only to enter the houses and deftly unbar the door for an easier egress for Eli Cronk and Lem Crabbe. Later he was commanded to snatch up anything of value he could. Many were the times he wept in boyish bitterness against the commands of Lon, revealing his sorrows to Flea, who listened moodily.

"I wouldn't steal nothin' if I was you," she said again and again. But Flukey one day silenced this reiteration by confiding to her that Pappy Lon had threatened to turn her to his trade if he rebelled.

One afternoon in late September, Flea left the hut and went out to the lake. Flukey, Lon Cronk, and Lem Crabbe had gone to Ithaca to buy groceries, and it was time for them to return. A chill wind swung the girl's skirt about her knees, and for some minutes she squatted on the beach, keeping her eyes upon the lighthouse in the distance.

For the last year Flea had been rapidly growing into a woman. Granny Cronk had proudly noted that the fair face had grown lovelier, that the ebony curls fell about her shoulders. The one dream the girl had had was a dream of long hair, ankle dresses, and girl's shoes. Until that year Lon had insisted that her hair be kept short, and had himself trimmed the ebony curls every month. Now, in the damp air, they twisted and turned in the wildest profusion. The coming of womanhood had thrown new light into the clear-gray, brown-flecked eyes. At this moment she was wondering what she and her brother would do if Granny Cronk died. She shivered as she thought of life in the hut without the protecting old woman.

Suddenly, from above the Lehigh Valley tracks, she heard the sound of horses' hoofs. Her attention taken from her meditations, she lifted her pensive gaze from the lake, wheeled about, and looked for the horseman. Flea knew that it was not a summer cottager; for many days before the last of them had taken his family to Ithaca. Perhaps some chance wayfarer had followed the wrong road. Just below the tracks she caught a glimpse of a black horse, and as it came nearer Flea noted the rider, a young man whose kindly dark eyes and white teeth dazzled her. His straight legs were incased in yellow boots, his fine form in a tightly fitting riding-coat. Flea had never seen just such a man, not even in the infrequent visits she made to Ithaca. Something in his smile, as he drew up his steed and looked down upon her, affected her with a curious thrill.

"Little girl, will you tell me if I am on the right road to Glenwood?"

Flea's tongue clove to the roof of her mouth. His voice, cultivated and deep, made her forget for a moment the question he had asked her. Then she remembered; but instinctively she did not reply in her usual high squatter tones.

"Nope, ye got to go back, and turn to the right at the top of the hill. Ye can't go round the shore from here; the water's too high."

21

This impulsive desire to choose her words and to modulate her voice came from a sudden realization that there lived another class of people outside the squatter settlement of whom she knew little.

"Thank you very much," replied the questioner. "Now I understand that if I ride to the top of the hill and turn to the right, I'll reach Glenwood?"

"Yep," answered Flea.

Her embarrassment caused her lips to close over the one word. Wonderingly she watched the man ride away until the sight of his dark horse was lost in the trees above the tracks.

"It were a prince," she stammered in a low tone, "a real live prince!"

Flea contemplated the darkening hills with moody eyes. She counted slowly one by one the towers of the university buildings. This she did merely from habit; for the expression remained unchanged on her melancholy face. At length the gray eyes dropped to the water and fixed their gaze upon a fishing boat turning toward the shore. A few moments before it had been but a black speck near the lighthouse; but as it came nearer Flea distinctly saw the two men and the boy in it. Upon the bow of the boat was perched Snatchet, a yellow terrier, his short ears perked up with happiness at the prospect of supper. When the craft touched shore the girl rose and ran toward it. Almost in fear, she searched the face of the youth at the rudder with eyes so like his own that they seemed rather a reflection than another pair. She said no word until she took her position beside the boy on the shore, slipping her hand into his as she walked by his side toward the hut.

"Be ye back for the night, Flukey?" she asked.

"Nope."

"Where ye goin' after supper?"

"To Ithaca."

"Air ye leg a hurtin' ye much?"

"Yep."

"Granny Cronk says as how yer pains be rheumatiz. If ye stay in out of the night air, ye'll get well."

"Pappy Lon won't let me," sighed Flukey.

He sank down on the cabin threshold, and as he spoke drew a blue trouser leg slowly up.

"Damn knee!" he groaned. "It gets so twisted! And sometimes I can't walk."

"Be ye goin' to steal again tonight?" asked the girl, bending toward him.

"Yep, with Pappy Lon and Lem. I hate it all, I do!" he cried impetuously.

22

"What makes ye go? Take a lickin', an' I bet ye'll stay to hum. I would!"

With a spiteful shake of the black curls, she rubbed a bare toe over Snatchet's yellow back.

"I wish I was a boy," she went on. "While I hate stealin', I'd do it to have ye stay to hum, Flukey; then ye'd get well. And—"

She broke off abruptly and lowered her eyes to the shore, where Lem and Lon were in earnest conversation. At the same moment Lon looked up and shouted a command:

"Flea gal, Flea gal, come down here to me!"

Flea dropped the hand of her brother, moved directly to the water's edge, and stood quietly until Lon chose to speak.

Lem Crabbe's eyes devoured the slight young figure, his smile contorting the corners of his whiskered mouth. One hand rested on the bow of the boat, while the long, rusty hook, sharp at the point and thick ironed at the top, protruded from the other coat-sleeve.

At last Lon Cronk began to speak deliberately, and the girl gave him her attention.

"Flea, ye be a woman now, ain't ye?" he said "Ye be fifteen this comin' Saturday."

"Yep, Pappy Lon."

"And yer brother be fifteen on the same day, you bein' twins."

"Yep, Pappy Lon."

"Yer brother's been taken into my trade," proceeded the squatter, "and it ain't the wust in the world—that of takin' what ye want from them that have plenty. It's time for ye to be doin' somethin', too. Ye'll go to Lem's Scow, Flea."

"To Lem's scow?" exclaimed Flea. "That ain't no place for a kid, and nobody ain't a wantin' me, nuther! I know there ain't!"

"Ain't there nobody a wantin' her in yer scow, Lem Crabbe?" grinned Lon.

"Ye bet there be!" answered Lem, with an evil leer.

Flukey, who had approached the group, placed himself closer to his sister. "Who—who be wantin' Flea, Lem Crabbe?" he demanded.

"It's me, it's me!" replied Lem, wheeling savagely about.

For a short space of time nothing but the splash of the waves could be heard as they rolled white on the shore. A change passed over Flea, and she clutched fiercely at her brother's fingers. It was as if she had said, "Help me, Flukey, if ye can!" But she did not speak the words; only stared at the hook-armed man with strained eyes.

"Flea ain't no notion of goin' away right yet, Pappy Lon," burst out Flukey, catching his breath after the shock. "She's perferrin' to stay with us; and I'll work for her keep, if ye let her stay."

23

"Nope, I ain't no notion o' marryin'," repeated Flea, encouraged by her brother's insistence.

"Who said as how Lem wanted ye to marry him?" sneered Lon, eying her from head to foot. "Yer notions one way or nother ain't nothin' to me, my gal. Ye'll go with the man I choose for ye, and that's all there be to it!"

Dazed by his first words, she whispered, "I hate Lem Crabbe!"

As if by its own volition, the hook rose threateningly to within a short distance of the fair, appealing face. But it dropped again, as Lon repeated:

"That ain't nothin' to do with the thing, nuther, Flea. A man ain't a seekin' for a lovin' woman. He wants her to take care of his shanty and what he gets by hard work, he does, and he gives her victuals and drink for the doin' of it. That's enough for you, or for any gal what's a squatter."

So well did Flea realize the powerlessness of the rigid boy at her side to help her, that she dropped his hand and alone went nearer to the thief.

"Can't I stay with you and with Granny Cronk for another year? Can't I stay? Can't I, Pappy Lon?"

"Nope, I wouldn't keep ye in the shanty if ye had money for yer keeps. Ye go on a Saturday to Lem's boat to be his woman, ye see?"

The iron hook by this time was hanging loosely by Lem's side; but a cruel expression had gathered on the sullen face. A frown drew the crafty eyes together, bespeaking wrath at the girl's words.

That he would have her at the bidding of her father, Lem never doubted. During the last three years he had been resolved to take her home in due time to be his woman. To subdue the proud young spirit, to make her the mother of children like himself,—the boys destined to be thieves, and the girls squatter women,—was his one ambition. That he was old enough to be her father made no difference to him.

He was watching her as she stood in the darkening twilight, gloating over the thought that his vicious dreams were so near their fulfillment.

Flea was looking into the eyes of her father, and he looked back at her with an impudent smile.

"Ye don't like the thought of this comin' Saturday, Flea—eh?" he asked slowly. "But, as I said before, a gal hain't nothin' to do with the notions of her daddy. And Granny Cronk'll give ye a pork cake to take to Lem's, and he'll let ye eat it all to yerself. Eh, Lem?"

"Yep," grunted Lem. "She eats the pork cake if she will; but after that—"

Suddenly Lon silenced Lem's words with a wag of his head

toward the girl. "Flea," he said, "I telled Lem as how ye'd kiss him tonight."

The words stunned the girl, they were so unexpected, so terrible. She turned her eyes upon Lem and fearfully studied his face. He was gazing back, his open lips showing his discolored, broken teeth. The coarse, red hair sprinkled with gray gave a fierce aspect to his whole appearance, and from the emotion through which he was passing the muscles under his chin worked to and fro. With a grin he advanced toward her. Flea fell back against Flukey. The boy steadied the trembling, slender body.

"I ain't a goin' to kiss ye," she muttered. "I hate yer kisses! I hate 'em!"

"Ye'll kiss him, jest the same!" ordered Lon.

Closer and closer Lem came toward the girl; then suddenly he sprang at her like a tiger, crushing the slim figure against his breast. For a moment Flea was encircled by his left arm. Then she turned fiercely to the ugly face so close to hers, and in another instant had bitten it through the cheek. He dropped her with a yelling oath, and Flea sprang back, turning flashing eyes upon Lon.

"That's how I kiss him afore I go to him," she screamed, "and worser and worser after he takes me!"

Lon laughed wickedly. He had not expected such a display of spirit. "I guess ye'll have to wait, Lem," he said; "fer—"

Flea did not hear the rest of the sentence; for she and Flukey were hurrying toward the hut.

Lem stood wiping the blood from his face. "The cussed spit-cat!" he hissed. "When I take her in hand—"

"When ye take her in hand, Lem," interrupted Lon darkly, "ye can do what ye like. Break her spirit! Break her neck, if ye want to! I don't care."

The children found Granny Cronk with bent shoulders and palsied hands toiling over the supper. About the withered neck hung a red handkerchief, and on top of the few gray whisps of hair rested a spotless cap. She grunted as the children entered the room like a whirlwind and climbed the long ladder to the loft, where for some time the low voice of Flukey and the sobs of Flea could be heard in the kitchen below.

It was not until her son had entered and hung his cap upon the peg that the old woman ventured to speak.

"Be Flea in a tantrum, Lon?"

"Yep, ye bet she be!"

"Have ye been a beatin' her?"

"Nope, I never teched her," replied the squatter; "but I will beat her, if she don't do what I tell her. No matter how she kicks ag'in' my notions, she has to do 'em, Granny!"

"Yep, I know that; but I asked ye what she was a blubberin' about."

"'Cause I says as how on Saturday she's got to go and be Lem's woman—that's what I says."

"Lem's woman! Do ye mean that she's got to go away?"

"Yep, with Lem Crabbe," replied Cronk; "he's to be her man on her next birthday. I bet he brings the kid to his likin'!"

"Lem's a bad man, Lon," replied Mrs. Cronk, "and ye be one, too, if ye be my own son, and Flea's your own flesh and blood, and I like her. It would be a good thing if ye let her stay to hum while I be a livin'; and I mean what I say, and I'm yer mammy, and that's the truth!"

"Mammy or no mammy," answered Cronk sullenly, "Flea goes to Lem, and ye makes her a pork cake, which she can hog down at one gulp, for all I care—the damn brat! I say it, and Lem says it. He'll dry her tears after she's left hum, I'm a guessin'!"

Seeing the futility of arguing the question, Mrs. Cronk placed the fish and beans on his plate and, with a shrill cry to Flea and Flukey, sat down to eat.

As he stumbled along the rocks to the scow, Lem Crabbe uttered dark threats against the girl who had bitten him. Her temper and the spontaneous deed that had marked his face did not lessen his longing to call her his woman, nor did it take the fever of desire from his veins. It had strengthened his passion to such a degree that he now determined to permit nothing to interfere with his plans. For at least three years he had lived on the promise of Lon Cronk that he should have the girl for weal or woe. Six months before he had offered Lon anything within his power to set the day of Flea's coming to him nearer; but the thief had shaken his head with the thought that Flea as a girl would not suffer through indignities as she would as a woman. He felt no remorse for the other girl that he had ruined so many years back; but he kept out of the way of the crazy woman who sometimes crossed his path.

Tonight Lem entered the living-room of his boat, muttering an oath that ended in a groan, dropped the basket on the table, and struck a match. He was touching it to the candle, when a sound in the corner startled him. He turned as he finished his task and saw the brilliant eyes of Scraggy's cat as the animal sat perched on the woman's shoulder. The presence of Screech Owl surprised him so that he did not move for a moment, and she spoke first:

"I hain't seed ye in such a long time, Lem, that I thought I'd come and let ye see my new kitty. He ain't but two years old."

Lem took a long breath. At first he thought that this must be Scraggy's wraith come to haunt him after some horrible lonely death. He had far rather deal with a living Scraggy than a dead one, and at once recovered his composure.

"I hain't sent for ye, have I?" he asked, hanging up his coat. "And if I ain't sent for ye, then ye needn't be sneakin' round."

"I've a lot to say to ye," sighed Scraggy mournfully, "and I thought as how the night was better than the day. It's dark now."

"Then ye'd better trot hum," put in Lem, "if ye don't want another beatin'."

"I ain't goin' to get no beatin' tonight," assured the woman, throwing one arm over the bristling cat, "'cause I comed to tell ye somethin'."

Lem turned on her sharply; for Scraggy seemed to speak sanely.

"The bats be gone from my brain, Lem, and I want to tell ye somethin' 'bout Flea—Flea Cronk—and to tell ye that I be hungry."

"What about Flea?" snapped Lem. "Ye're bein' hungry ain't nothin' to do with me. If ye got somethin' to tell me that I want to hear, lip it out, and then scoot; for I ain't no time to bother with ye. My time's precious, Scraggy—see?"

"Yep; but I ain't goin' to tell ye nothin' till ye give me somethin' to eat."

She cast ravenous eyes on the small bundles Lem was placing on the table.

"I'll give ye a piece of bread an' 'lasses," was the grudging answer. "And mind ye, I wouldn't do that but I want to hear what ye say 'bout Flea."

Avidly the woman ate the thick slice of bread and treacle, offering a bit now and then to the cat. When she had devoured it Lem spoke:

"Now wash it down with this here water and tell me yer tale—and if ye lie to me I'll kill ye!"

"I ain't a goin' to lie to ye—I'll tell ye the truth, I will!"

They both drank, the man from the bottle, the woman from a tin cup. Presently she asked:

"Be ye goin' to marry Flea Cronk?"

"Who's been carryin' tales to ye?" shouted Lem, bounding from his chair. "Ye better be a mindin' yer own affairs, or ye'll be havin' nothin' but bats in yer head till ye die. Scoot for hum! Ye hear?"

"Yep; but I ain't goin' jest yet. Ye want to hear 'bout Flea, don't ye?"

27

"Yep."

"Then set down an' I'll tell ye."

Lem, growling impatience, seated himself.

"Flea Cronk ain't for you, Lem!"

"Who said as how she ain't?" demanded Lem, starting up. The cat spat viciously, startled by the sudden movement. "I wish ye'd left that damn cat to hum! I hain't no notion to be bit by no cat."

"Kitty won't bite ye if ye let me alone—will ye, Kitty? I ain't never afeard of nothin' when I got him with me—be I, Kitty, pretty pussy?"

"Stop a cooin', ye bughouse woman," snarled Crabbe, "and tell me what ye got to!"

"I said Flea wasn't for you."

"Ye lie!"

He made a desperate move toward her; but the cat rose threateningly, its hair standing on end in a mound upon the humped back. Lem fell away with an oath, and Scraggy, smiling wanly, petted the vicious brute.

"I said ye was to keep away, Lem. Wait till I get done. Flea's got to be some 'un else's, not yers."

"Who's?" Lem's voice rose; but he did not advance toward her.

"I dunno; but I seed him. He rides a black horse, and has a fine, big body and wears yeller boots. This afternoon when the day was darkenin' I saw him from the railroad bed, and I saw Flea's spirit a travelin' with him. I know that ye cared for her this long time back; but ye can't have her."

"Who be the feller?" demanded Lem, frowning.

"I said I didn't know, and I don't."

"Were Flea with him?"

"Nope; not in her body, but jest in her spirit."

"Rats! Scoot along with ye, and take yer cat and get out!"

Scraggy had not noticed the blood oozing from Lem's, cheek until she had received her dismissal. She passed a long, red, bare arm about the animal and asked:

"Who bit yer cheek, Lem?"

"Who says it were bit?"

"I say it. I see white teeth a goin' in it. And I see red lips ag'in' it with deadly hate."

Lem glanced forbiddingly at the woman. "The bats be a comin' again," he muttered, "and there ain't no tellin' what she'll do. If it wasn't for that blasted cat, I'd chuck her in the lake!"

But he dared not carry out his threat; for Scraggy was muttering to herself, the cat rebuffing her rough handling.

28

In another minute she rose and made toward the steps. Her eyes fell upon Lem, and sanity flashed back into them.

"I gave the boy to the woman—with golden hair," she stammered, as if some power were forcing the words from her. "Ye would have killed him. Yer kid be a livin', Lem!"

Truth rang in her statement, and the man got to his feet abruptly. He had almost forgotten the black-haired little boy. Only when Scraggy's name was mentioned to him did he remember. But the woman's words awoke a new feeling in his heart, and mentally he counted back the years to the date of his son's birth. Scraggy was still looking at him in bewilderment, scarcely realizing that her story had been told to the enemy of her child. She battled with a desire to blurt out the whole truth; but the man's next words silenced her.

"Who be the golden-haired woman, Scraggy?" he wheedled.

"What woman—what golden-haired woman?"

"The woman who has our brat."

Like lightning a sudden joy filled Scraggy's heart. Her benumbed love for Lem Crabbe grew mighty in a moment and rushed over her. His words were softly spoken with an old-time inflection. She sank down with a cry. She was so near him that the cat rose and spat venomously. Lem's curses brought Scraggy out of her dreams.

"Chuck that damn cat to the bank," ordered Lem, "if ye want to stay with me! Do ye hear? Chuck him out!"

"Nope, I ain't a goin' to! I'm goin' hum."

"Not till ye tell me where the boy is. Didn't ye throw him in the river?"

"Nope."

"What did ye do with him?"

"Gived him away."

"Ye lie! That winder was open, and the river was dark as hell. Ye throwed him in, I tell ye!"

"Nope; I gived him to a woman—"

She stopped and edged toward the stairs, all her old fear of him returning. Reaching the short flight, she bounded up, the cat clinging to her sleeve. Lem did not follow; for the crazy woman had frightened him. He stood with hushed breath, holding grimly to the wooden table. A voice from the deck of the scow came down to him.

"I gave him to a rich woman on a yacht. He's rich with mints of money. Yer kid's a gentleman, Lem Crabbe!"

He sprang after her to the deck; but nothing greeted him save the cry of an owl from the ragged rocks and the glistening green of the cat's eyes as Scraggy hurried away.

CHAPTER SIX

After eating his supper, Lon, sullen and moody, looked out upon the lake, reviewing in his mind the terrible revenge he was soon to complete. He took his pipe slowly from his pocket and filled it with coarse tobacco. Soon gray rings lifted themselves to the ceiling and faded into the rafters. As the smoke curled upward, his mind became busy with the past, and so vivid was his imagination that outlined in the smoke rings that floated about him was a girlish face—a face pale and wan, but a loving, sweet one to him. He could see the fair curls which clung close to the head; the eyes, serious but kind, seemed to strike his memory in unforgotten glances. To another than himself the smoke-formed face would have been plain, perhaps ugly, the weakness of her race showing in every feature; but not to him. So intent was he with these thoughts that the present dissolved completely into the past, and beside him stood a small, fond woman. In his imagination she had risen from that grave which he had never been able to find in the Potter's Field. The personality of his dead wife called upon his senses and made itself as necessary to him then as in the moment of his first rapture when she had placed her womanly might upon his soul.

His revenge upon Floyd Vandecar would be finished when the gray-eyed Flea, so like her own father, went away with the one-armed man, to eke out her destiny amid the squalor of the thief's home.

For months he had been enthralled with the satisfaction of the last act in the one terrible drama of his life; for it had played with his rude fancy as a tigress does with her prey, inflaming his hatred and keeping alive his desire for retaliation. Flukey was a good thief, although obeying him at the end of the lash, and Flea would receive her portion of hate's penalty on her fifteenth birthday.

Cronk did not heed the pitter-patter of his mother's feet as she cleared the table, nor did he hear the droning of the twin's voices in the loft above. He was thinking of how the dead woman with her child—his child, the one small atom he would have loved better than himself—would be well avenged when Flea went away with Lem.

Lon had kept track of the doings of the young district attorney. He knew that he had gone to the gubernatorial chair but the year before. The squatter smiled gloomily as he remembered the words of a newspaper friendly to Vandecar, in which he had read that Syracuse was full of painful memories for the new governor, and that Floyd Vandecar had taken his family down the Hudson, to make another home at Tarrytown, where Harold Brimbecomb, a youthful friend, resided. Another expression of dark gratification flitted over Lon's heavy features as he reviewed again the purport of the article. It had plainly said that in the new home there would be fewer visions of a lost boy and girl to haunt the afflicted parents. Lon realized in his savage heart that the change of scene would not lessen the grief of the stricken family. It was his one satisfaction to brood over the bereaved father and mother, delighting in his part of the tragedy and enjoying every evidence of it. Never for a moment did he think gently of the children, but only of the woman sacrificed. On this night she stood so close that, with a groan, he put out his hand. His flesh tingled; for he felt that he could almost touch her, and his heart clamored for the warmth of the tender body he had never forgotten.

"God!" he moaned between his teeth, "if I could tech her once, jest for once, I'd let Flea stay to hum!"

"Did ye speak, Lon?" asked Granny Cronk.

"Nope; I were only a thinkin'."

"Have ye changed yer mind 'bout Flea?"

"Nope, Mammy, and ye keep yer mouth shet if ye want me to stay to hum! See?"

Granny Cronk grunted a reply, and passed into the back room. Five minutes later the rope cot creaked under her weight.

Wrapped in his somber musings, Lon did not hear Flea approach him until she was at his elbow. With her coming, the sweet phantom, to which he grimly held in his moments of solitude, fled back to its unknown grave. Never had his loved one been so near, so real; never before had she touched his writhing nature in all its primeval strength. The girl before him was so like the man who had withstood his agony that he clenched his fist and rose from his chair. Flea was looking at him in mute appeal; but before she could speak he had lifted his fist and brought it down upon the lovely, beseeching face. The blow stunned her; but only a smothered moan fell from her lips.

"I hate ye!" growled Lon. "Get back to the loft afore I kill ye!"

Slowly Flea was regaining her senses, and the squatter's curses struck her ears like a whiplash. Bitter, scalding tears blinded her as, holding her thin skirt to her bleeding nose, she stumbled up the ladder. With anger unappeased, Lon, staggering like one drunken, took his cap from the peg and went out.

When Lon called Flukey, Flea followed her brother into the night, while he arranged the thief's tools in the boat. There was a dull roar and rush of the wind, as it tossed the lake into gigantic whitecaps, which added to the girl's suffering. Her young soul was smarting beneath the scathing injustice. As she watched Lem and Lon pull away, with Flukey at the rudder, Flea squatted on the beach, bent her head, and wept long and wildly.

A gentle, sympathetic touch of a warm tongue made her put out her arms and draw Snatchet into them. It comforted her to feel the faithful heart beating against her own. That Lon disliked to have her and Flukey about him, she knew; but she had not known until today that he hated her. He had never before told her so. Flea caught her breath in a gasp, and turned her eyes to a rift in a rock where the scow lay. Only a dark line distinguished it in the shadows. At the thought that it was to be forced upon her for a home, she cried again, and Snatchet, from his haven of rest, lifted his pointed yellow nose and wailed dismally, striving with all his dog's soul to assuage her unusual grief.

The distant sound of a hoot-owl startled Flea from her tears. It was a familiar sound to her and came as a call from a friend.

Creeping into the low woodshed, Flea took up a bundle of fagots from the corner, and, closing the door on Snatchet that he might not follow her, mounted the hill with the wood under her arm. Once at the top of the lane, she opened her lips and echoed the hoot. She passed through a thicket of sumac into a clearing where a number of sheep were huddled together in the cold night air. An answer came back almost instantly from the ragged rocks, and, squatting in a hollow, Flea sat patiently until the branches broke below her. A woman with tangled hair came creeping cautiously forward.

"Who be there?" she whispered.

"It's Flea, Screech Owl. Be the bats a runnin' in yer head?"

"Yep, child," the woman answered mournfully. "The fagots be given out, too, and I'm a huntin' of 'em. The night's cold."

"I was lookin' for ye this afternoon, Screechy," said Flea. "Set down."

The lean, half-starved woman dropped beside the girl. Flea put out her hand and smoothed down the rough hair on Scraggy's black cat. The animal, usually so vicious, purred in delight, rubbing his nose against the girl's hand.

"Air the little Flea wantin' the owl to tell her somethin'?"

"Yep," replied Flea doubtfully.

"And ye brought yer old Screechy a little present?"

"Yep."

"What?"

"Some fagots to keep ye warm, Screechy."

"Where be they?"

"Here by my side."

"Ye be a good Flea," cackled Screechy. "Be ye in trouble?"

"Yep. So be Flukey. Can ye tell me anything 'bout Flukey?"

The woman frowned. "Flukey, Flukey, yer brother," she repeated. "I ain't a likin' boys, 'cause they throw stones at me."

"Flukey never throwed no stones at ye, Screechy, an' he's unhappy now. He'll bring ye a lot more fagots sometime to heat yer bones by."

"Aye, I'm a needin' heat. My bones be stiff, and my blood's nothin' but water, and my eyes ain't seein' nothin'."

"Don't they see things in the dark," asked the girl, superstitiously, "ghosts and things?"

"Aye, Flea; and the things I see now I'll tell ye if they be good or bad—mind ye, good or bad!"

"Good or bad," repeated Flea.

At length, after a silence, the girl broke forth. "Air Flukey in yer eyes, Screechy?"

"Yep, Flea, and so be you; but there ain't much for ye, savin' that ye go a long journey lookin' for a good land."

Bending her head nearer, Flea coaxed, "What good land, Screechy dear?"

"Yer's and Flukey's, Flea."

"Where air it?"

"Down behind the college hill, many a stretch for yer short legs from the squatter's settlement, and many a day when bread's short and water's plenty, many a night when the cold'll bite yer legs, and many a tear—"

"Be we leavin' Pappy Lon?" demanded the girl.

"Yep."

"Forever and forever?"

"For Flukey, yep; but for yerself—"

Flea stared in speechless wonder and fright. "I don't want to stay without Flukey!" she cried.

"I ain't a tellin' ye what ye want to do; only how the shadders run. But that's a weary day off. The good land be yers and Flukey's for the seekin' of it."

"Air Flukey goin' to be catched a thievin'?"

"Yep, some day."

"With Pappy Lon?"

"Nope, with yerself, Flea."

"I ain't no thief," replied Flea sulkily. "I ain't never took nothin', not so much as a chicken! And Flukey wouldn't nuther if Pappy Lon didn't make him."

From behind Screech Owl's shrouding gray hair two black eyes glittered.

"The good land, the good land!" whispered the madwoman. "It be all comin' for yerself and Flukey."

"Be I goin' to—" Flea sat back on her bare toes, her face suddenly darkening with rage. "I won't go with him! I won't, Screechy, if he was in every old eye in yer head! I won't, so there!"

The darkness hid from Screech Owl the glint in Flea's eyes.

"Who be it Lon said you was goin' with, Flea?"

Scraggy must have forgotten her conversation with Lem but an hour or two before; for she evinced no knowledge of any man interested in Flea.

"A one-armed man. Pappy says I'm to be his woman. Be I, Screechy?"

"Nope; but I see a hook a whirlin' in the air into the good land, a whirlin' and a whirlin' after ye. I see it a stealin' on ye in the night when ye think ye're safe. I see the sharp p'int of it a stickin' into yer soft flesh—"

"Don't, don't!" pleaded Flea in a smothered voice. "Ye said as how I were goin' with Flukey to a good land down behind the college hill."

"So ye be," assented the Owl; "but after ye get to the good land the sharp p'int of the hook'll come and rip at ye. I see it a haulin' ye back away from them what ye loves—"

Flea grasped the woman's arm between her fingers and pressed nearer Scraggy with a startled cry. The cat, hissing, lashed a bushy tail from side to side. His eyes flashed green, and a cry came from Flea's lips. In another instant she was speeding away down the rocks.

CHAPTER SEVEN

At three o'clock the next morning a boat left the lighthouse at the head of Cayuga Lake and was rowed toward the western shores. As before, two men and a boy were in it. The lad was still at the rudder, while the men swiftly cut the water stroke by stroke. For three miles down the lake no one spoke; but when the boat scraped the shore in front of his hut Lon broke the silence.

"It weren't a bad haul tonight, were it, Lem?" he said almost jovially. "And tomorry ye come up to the shanty for the dividin'. Ye know I wouldn't cheat a hair o' yer head, don't ye, Lem?"

"Yep, ye bet I know it! And I'm that happy 'cause I'm to take yer gal a Saturday that I could give ye the hull haul tonight, Lon."

"Ye needn't do that, Lem. I give ye Flea 'cause I want ye to have her, and I know that you'll make her stand round and mind ye, and if she don't—"

"Then I'll make her!" put in Lem darkly. "She'll give back no more bites for my kisses when I get her! I had a woman a long time ago, and when she didn't mind me I beat her, and beat her and beat her hard! That's the way to do with women folks!"

"Ye had Scraggy, didn't ye, Lem?" asked Lon, heaping his arm with his clothing.

Flukey stood silently by, his pale face ghastly in the thin, yellow moonlight.

"Yep; but Scraggy wasn't no good. I didn't like her. I do like Flea, and I'd stick to her, too. I'd marry her if ye'd say the word."

"Nope, I ain't a askin' ye to marry her. Yer jest make her stand around, and break her spirit if ye can. Flea ain't like Flukey; she's hard to beat a thing out of."

"I know how to handle her!" answered Lem. The silent laughter in his throat ended in a grunt. He slung a small basket over the hook and went off up the rocks to his scow.

"Ye can go to bed, Flukey," said Lon. "Ye've done a good night's work—and mind ye it ain't wicked to take what ye want from them havin' plenty."

Lon hesitated before proceeding. "And, Flukey, if ye know what's good for Flea, don't be settin' her up ag'in' my wishes, 'cause if she don't do what I tell her it'll be the worse for her!... Scoot to bed!"

The boy stood for a moment, opened his lips to plead with the big, sullen squatter for his sister; but, changing his mind, limped off to the cabin.

When the shanty was quiet a girl's figure shrouded in black curls crawled across the hut floor to the loft ladder. Flea ascended quickly; but halted at the top to catch her breath. She could hear from the other side of the partition the sound of Lon's heavy snores, and from the corner came the lighter breathing of her brother. Through the small loft window the moonbeams shone, and by them Flea could see the boy's dark head and strong young arm under the masses of thick hair.

35

She began to crawl toward the cot, wriggling like a huge worm across the bare boards. Several times she paused, trying to suppress her frightened heartbeats. Then, lifting her hand, she placed it over Flukey's mouth and whispered:

"Fluke, Fluke, wake up! It's Flea!"

Flukey made no movement to dislodge his tightly pressed lips from the trembling fingers. The gray eyes flashed open; but the lad lay perfectly still.

"Fluke," breathed Flea, "I'm goin' to the cave. Slip on yer pants, and don't wake Granny Cronk nor Pappy Lon!"

If it had not been that the boy pressed his fingers on the blanket, Flea would have wondered if her brother had heard.

The lithe form had crept back to the ladder and had disappeared before Flukey slipped quietly from his bed and drew on the blue-jeans overalls. As he stole through the kitchen, he could hear the snorts of Granny Cronk coming from the back room. The outside door stood partly open, and without hesitation he passed through and closed it after him that the wind might not slam it. Then he limped along under the shore trees, up a little hill, and dropped out of sight into an open cavern, where Flea, a candle in her hand, sat in semidarkness.

The cave had been the children's playground ever since they could remember. Here they had come to weep over indignities heaped upon them in childhood; here they had come in joy and in sorrow, and now, in secret conclave in the early hours of the morning, they had come again.

"Ye're here!" said Flea in feverish haste. "I feared ye'd go to sleep again."

"Nope; I allers come when ye want me, Flea."

"Did ye steal tonight?"

"Yep."

"What did ye get?"

The boy shuddered, and a strange, hunted expression came into his eyes. "Spoons, knives, clothes, and things," said he; "and I'd ruther be tore to pieces by wild bulls than ever steal again!"

His voice was toned with an unnatural ring. Wonderingly, Flea drew closer to him, the candle dripping white, round drops hot on the brown hand.

"But Pappy Lon says as how ye must steal, don't he?" she asked presently.

"Yep, and as how you must go with Lem."

"I won't, I won't! Pappy Lon can kill me first!"

She said this in passionate anger; but, upon holding the candle close to Flukey's face, she exclaimed:

"Fluke, don't look like that—it scares me!"

He was piercing the dark ends of the cave, his eyes colored like steel. They were softened only by shots of brown, which ran like chain lightning through them. The girl's gaze followed her brother's timidly; for he looked ahead, as if he saw something that threatened her and him. In spite of her soft touch, the boy looked on and on in his unyielding fierceness at the fast approaching inevitable, which he had not been able to stem. That day a change had been ordered in their lives, and it had come upon him in the shape of a mental blow that hurt him far worse than if Pappy Lon had flogged him throughout the night.

"If Pappy Lon sends me next Saturday to Lem," Flea ventured in an undertone, "then ye can't help me much, can ye, Fluke?"

The muscles of the boy's face relaxed, and he drew his knee up to his chest. "When my leg ain't lame I'm strong enough to lick Lem, if—if—"

"Nope; I ain't no notion for ye to lick him yet, Fluke. Do ye believe in the sayin's of Screech Owl?"

"Ye mean—"

"Do ye believe what she says when the bats be a flyin' round in her head, and when she sees the good land for you and myself, Flukey?"

"Did she say somethin' 'bout a good land for us, Flea?"

"Yep."

"Where's the good land?"

"Down behind the college hill, many a stretch from here—and, Flukey, I ain't a goin' to Lena's, and ye ain't likin' to be a thief. Will ye come and find the good land with me?"

"Girls can't run away like boys can. They ain't able to bear hurt."

Flea dropped her head with a blush of shame. She knew well that Flukey could perform wonderful feats which she had been unable to do. Grandma'm Cronk had told her that her dresses made the difference between her ability and Flukey's. With this impediment removed, she could turn her face toward the shining land predicted by Scraggy for Flukey and herself; she could follow her brother over hills and into valleys, until at last—

"I could wear a pair of yer pants and be a boy, too, and you could chop off my hair," she exclaimed. "All I want ye to do is to grow to be a man quick, and to lick Lem Crabbe if he comes after me. Will ye? Screechy says he's goin' to follow me."

"I'll lick him anywhere," cried the boy, his tears rising; "and if ye has to go to him, and he as much as lays a finger on ye, I'll kill him!"

His face was so rigidly drawn during his last threat that he hissed the words out through his teeth.

"Then ye'd get yer neck stretched," argued Flea, "and I ain't a goin' to him. We be goin' away to the good land down behind the college hill."

"When?" demanded Flukey.

"Tonight," replied Flea. "Ye go and get some duds for me,—a shirt and the other pair of yer jeans. Crib Granny's shears to cut my hair off. Then we'll start. See? And we ain't never comin' back. Pappy Lon hates me, and he's licked ye all he's goin' to. Git along and crib the duds!"

She rose to her feet, nervously breaking away the little rivers of grease that had hardened upon her hand and wrist.

"Ye've got to get into the hut in the dark," she said, "and then ye stand at the mouth of the cave while I put on the things."

"How be we goin' to live when we go?" asked Flukey dully, making no move to obey her.

"We'll live in the good land where there be lots of bread and 'lasses," she soothed; "the two dips in the dish at one time—jest think of that, ole skate!"

He tried to smile at her forced jocularity; but the hunted expression saddened his eyes again. To these children, brought up animal-like in the midst of misery and hate, their world revolved round their stomachs, too often empty. But this new trouble—the terror of Flea's going with Lem—had made a man of Flukey, and bread and molasses sank into oblivion. He was ready to shield her from the thief with his life.

"Get along!" ordered Flea.

Instead of obeying, the boy sat down on a rounded stone. "I'd a runned away along ago, if it hadn't been, for you, Flea."

"I know that you love me," said the girl brokenly; "I know that, all right!"

"I couldn't have stood Pappy Lon nor Lem nor none of the rest," groaned Flukey, "and I was to tell ye tonight to let me go, and I would come back for ye; but if ye be made to go with Lem—"

"That makes ye take me with you," gasped Flea eagerly. "Huh?"

"Yep, that makes me take ye with me, Flea; but if we go mebbe sometimes we have to go without no bread."

There was warning in his tones; for he had heard stories of other lads who had left the settlement and had returned home lank, pale, and hungry.

"I've been out o' bread here," encouraged Flea. "Granny's put me to bed many a time, and no supper. Get along, will ye?"

"Yep, I'm goin'; but I can't leave Snatchet. We can take my dorg, Flea. Where's he gone?"

38

"We'll take him," promised Flea. "He's in the wood-house. Scoot and get the duds and him!"

The boy toiled up the rocks to the top of the cave, and Flea heard his departing steps for a moment, then seated herself in tremulous fear.

Flukey pushed open the cabin door, listened a moment, and stepped in. No sound save of loud breathing came from the back room where the old woman slept. At the top of the ladder he could hear Lon snoring loudly. Flukey crawled upon his knees to a small box against the wall. He pulled out a pair of brown overalls and a blue shirt, and with great caution crept back. Almost before Flea realized that he had gone, he was in the cave again with Snatchet in his arms, displaying his plunder.

"Put 'em on quick!" ordered Flukey. "Here, hold still!" As he spoke, he gathered Flea's black curls into his fingers and cut them off boylike to her head. "If Pappy Lon catches us," he went on, "he'll knock hell out of us both."

The girl, having surrendered her spirit of command, crawled into the trousers and donned the blue shirt. After extinguishing the candle, which Flukey slipped into his pocket, they clambered out of the cave, leaving the rocky floor strewn with locks of hair, and stole softly along the shore toward the college hill.

CHAPTER EIGHT

Horace Shellington, newly fledged attorney and counsellor-at-law, sat in his luxurious library, his feet cocked upon the desk in true bachelor fashion. He was apparently deep in thought, his handsome head resting against the back of the chair, when his meditations were broken by a knock at the door.

"Come in. Is it you, Sis?" he said.

"Yes, Dear," was the answer as the girl entered. "Everett wants us to go in his party to the Dryden fair. Would you like to?"

Horace glanced up quizzically and smiled as the blush mounted to her fair hair. "The question, Ann dear, rests with you."

"I never tire being with Everett," Ann said slowly.

"That's because you're in love with him, Sis. When a girl is in love she always wants to be with the lucky chap."

"And doesn't he want to be with her?" demanded Ann eagerly.

"Of course. And, Ann, I shouldn't ask for a better fellow than Everett is, only that I don't want you to leave me right away. Without you, Dear, I think I should die of the blue devils!"

"Do you want me to stay at home until you, too, get ready to marry?" Ann asked laughingly. "I'm afraid I should never have a chance to help Everett make a home if you did; for you simply won't like any of the girls I know."

"I want to get well started in my profession before I think of marrying. I am happy over the fact that I have been able to enter Vandecar's law office. He's the strongest man in the state in his line, and it means New York for me some day. Vandecar is even more powerful than Brimbecomb."

"I'm glad for you, Horace, because it seems to me that you have an opportunity that few men have. Nothing can ever keep you back! And you are so very young, Dear!"

"No, nothing can keep me back now, Ann. Sit down, do."

"Not now, Dear; I'll run away from you, and tell Everett that you will go to Dryden with us—and I do hope that the weather will be fine!"

Ann tripped out, her heart light with contentment. Her star of happiness had reached its zenith when Everett Brimbecomb had asked her to be his wife. Rich in her own right, of the bluest blood in the state, soon to marry the man who had been her ideal since their childhood days, why should she not be happy?

After leaving Horace, Ann went to the side window and tapped upon it. Receiving no response, she lifted the sash and called softly to her fiance. Hearing her voice, Everett Brimbecomb appeared at the opposite window. The girl's heart thrilled with happiness as he smiled upon her.

"Run over a minute, Everett," she called.

"All right, dear heart."

His voice was so vibrantly low and rich that the girl experienced a feeling of thanksgiving as she stood waiting for him at the door. When he came, the lovers went into the drawing-room, where a grate fire burned dim.

"Horace says he'll go to Dryden, Everett," Ann announced, "and I'm so glad! I thought he might say that he was too busy."

Everett smiled, slipped his arm about the girl's waist, and for a moment she leaned against him like a frail, sweet flower.

Presently Ann noticed that a shadow had settled on her lover's face. Womanlike, she questioned him.

"Is there anything the matter, Dear?" she asked, drawing him to the divan.

"Nothing serious. I've been talking with Father."

"Yes?"

She waited for him to continue; but he sat silent, wrapped in thought for a long minute. At last, however, he spoke gloomily:

"Ann, I wish I knew who my own people were."

"Aren't you satisfied with those you have, Everett?" There was sweet reproof in the girl's tones.

"More than satisfied," he said; "but somehow I feel—no I won't say it, Ann. It would seem caddish to you."

"Nothing you could say to me would seem that," she answered.

Everett rose and walked up and down the room. "Well, it seems to me that, although the blood of the Brimbecomb's is blue, mine is bluer still; that, while they have many famous ancestors, I have still more illustrious ones. I feel sometimes a longing to run wild and do unheard-of things, and to make men know my strength, to—well, to virtually turn the world upside down."

A frightened look leaped into the girl's eyes. He was so vehement, so passionate, so powerful, that at times she felt how inferior in temperment she was to him. Her heart swelled with gratitude when she realized that he belonged to her and to her alone. How good God had been! And every day in the solitude of her chamber she had thanked the Giver of every gift for this perfect man—since he was perfect to her. In a few moments she rose and walked beside him, longing to enter into the hidden ambitions of his heart, to read his innermost thoughts. Everett appreciated her feeling. Again he passed his arm around her, and for a time they paced to and fro, each thankful for the love that had become the chief thing in life.

"I have an idea, Ann," began Everett presently, "that my mother will know me by the scar on me here." He raised his fingers to his shoulder and drew them slowly downward as he continued. "And I know that she is some wild, beautiful thing different from any other woman living. And I've pictured my father in my mind's eyes a million times, since I have found out I am not really Everett Brimbecomb."

"But Mr. and Mrs. Brimbecomb have done everything for you—"

"So they have," broke in Everett; "but a chap wants to know his own flesh and blood, and, since Mother told me that I was not her own son, I've looked into the face of every woman I've seen and wondered if my own mother was like her. I don't want to seem ungrateful; but if they would only tell me more I could rest easier." A painful pucker settled between his brows.

"Sit down here, Everett," Ann urged, "and tell me if you have ever tried to find them."

"I asked my fath—Mr. Brimbecomb today." His faltering words and the change of appellation shocked Ann; but she did not chide him, for he was speaking again. "I told him that, now I was through college and had been admitted to the bar, I insisted upon knowing who my own people were. But he said that I must ask his wife; that she knew, and would tell me, if she desired me to know. I promised him long ago that I would register in his law office at the same time that Horace went to Vandecar's. Confound it, Ann!—I beg your pardon, but I feel as if I had been created for something more than to drone over petty cases in a law office."

"But, Everett, it has been understood ever since you went to Cornell that you should enter Mr. Brimbecomb's office. You would not fail him now that he is so dependent upon you?"

"Of course not; I intend to work with him. But I tell you this, Ann, that I am determined to find my own people at whatever cost!"

"Did you ask Mrs. Brimbecomb about them?"

"Yes; but she cried so that I stopped—and so it goes! Well, Dear, I don't want to worry you. It only makes a little more work for me, that's all. But, when I do find them, I shall be the proudest man in all the world."

Ann rose to her feet hastily. "Here comes Horace! Let's talk over the fair—and now, Dear, I must kiss away those naughty lines between your eyes this moment. I don't want my boy to feel sad."

She kissed him tenderly, and turned to meet her brother.

"I was tired of staying in there alone," said Horace. "Hello, Everett! It was nice of you, old chap, to ask me along to Dryden. That's my one failing in the fall—I always go. Let me see—you didn't go last year, did you, Everett?"

"No; but I knew that Ann wanted to go this year, and I thought a party would be pleasant. I asked Katherine Vandecar; but her aunt is such an invalid that Katherine can scarcely ever leave her."

"Mrs. Vandecar is ill," said Ann. "I called there yesterday, and she is the frailest looking woman I ever saw."

"She's never got over the loss of her children," rejoined Everett. "It's hard on Vandecar, too, to have her ill. He looks ten years older than he is."

"Yes; but their little Mildred is such a comfort to them both!" interjected Ann. "They watch the child like hawks. I suppose it's only natural after their awful experience. Isn't it strange that two children

42

could disappear from the face of the earth and not a word be heard from them in all these years?"

"They're probably dead," replied Horace gently, and silence fell upon them.

CHAPTER NINE

Flea and Flukey Cronk, followed by the yellow dog, made their way farther and farther from Ithaca. They had left the university in the distance, when a dim streak of light warned them that day was approaching. It was here that Flea lagged behind her brother.

"Ye're tired, Flea," said Flukey.

"Yep."

"Will ye crawl into a haystack if we come to one?"

"Yep."

They spoke no more until, farther on, a farmhouse, with dark barns in the rear, loomed up before them.

"Ye wait here, Flea," said Flukey, "till I see where we can sleep."

After an absence of a few minutes he returned and in silence conducted the girl by a roundabout way to a newly piled stack of hay.

"I buried a place for us both," he whispered. "Ye crawl in first, Flea, and I'll bring in Snatchet. Lift yer leg up high and ye'll find the hole."

A minute later they were tucked away from the cold morning, their small faces overshadowed by the new-mown hay, and here, through the morning hours, they slept soundly. Then again they set forth, and it was late in the afternoon when they drew up before the high fence encircling the fair-grounds at Dryden. The fall fair was in full blast. Crowds were passing in and out of the several gates. With longing heart, first Flea, then Flukey, placed an eye to a knothole, to watch the proceedings inside. Rows of sleek cattle waved their blue and red ribbons jauntily in the breeze; fat pigs, with the owners' names pasted on the cards in front, grunted in small pens. For a time the twins stood side by side, wishing with all their might that they were possessed of the necessary entrance-fee.

"If I could get a job," said Flukey, "we could get in."

"I could work, too," said Flea, her hands dug deep in her trousers pockets.

Just then a man hailed them. "Want to get in, Kids?" he asked.

"Yep!" bawled Flea and Flukey in unison, their hunger forgotten in this new delight.

"Then help me carry in those boards, and then you can stay in."

Flukey looked apprehensively at Flea.

"Ye ain't a boy—"

"Shet up!" snapped Flea. "My pants're as long as your'n, and I be a boy till we get to the good land. Heave a board on my shoulder, Fluke."

They slid through the opening in the fence made to pass in the lumber, and for ten minutes aided their new friend by carrying plank after plank into the fair-grounds. When the work was done they stood awe-stricken, looking at the gorgeous surroundings. Flags waved aloft on each building; yards of bunting roped in exhibits of all kinds. Everywhere persons were walking to and fro. But still the squatter children stood motionless and stared with wide-open eyes at such an array of good things as had never before gladdened their sight. Then, after the strangeness had somewhat worn off, they wandered on, bewildered. Snatchet was hugged tight in Flukey's arms; for other dogs laid back their ears and growled at the yellow cur.

Suddenly they came upon the athletic field. Here, reared high in the air, was a slender greased pole, on the top of which fluttered a five-dollar bill. Several youngsters, dressed in bathing suits, awaited the hour when they should be allowed to try and win the money. One after another they took their turn, and when an extra spurt up the pole was made by some lucky boy the crowd evinced its delight by loud cheers. Time and again the breeze fluttered the coveted money, and yet no boy had won the prize.

"I'd like to try it," said Flukey.

"If we couldn't get it with bathing suits, you couldn't climb that pole with them long pants," retorted one of the contestants who stood near. "Look! that kid's goin' to get it, after all!" There was disappointment in the tones; but the words had no sooner died away than the climber slipped to the ground.

Flea pinched Flukey's arm. "Be yer knee so twisted that ye can't try, Flukey?"

"Nope, my rheumatiz ain't hurtin' me now."

"Then shinny up it, Fluke—ye can climb it! Get along there!"

She took the dog from his arms, and the boy went forward when the call came for another aspirant.

"I'm goin' to get that there bill!" said Flukey, shutting his teeth firmly.

He advanced and spoke in an undertone to a man, who, with a grin, shouted out the name, "Mr. F. Cronk."

The dignity of the prefix made Flukey spit upon his hands before he started to climb the pole. Flea came closer and stood almost breathless. Her parted lips showed small, even, white teeth, her eyes glistened, and flashes of red blood crimsoned her face. One suspender slipping from her shoulder, the vicious dog in her arms, the beautiful upturned face, was as interesting a spectacle as the onlookers had ever seen. It was with breathless interest that she watched her brother laboriously ascend the pole.

Flukey was indeed making a masterful climb. But at last he halted; and then, a moment later, he climbed desperately. The girl on the ground saw him falter, and knew that he was becoming faint-hearted. To encourage him, she lifted a voice broken by emotion and shouted:

"Go it, Fluke, go it!... Aw! damn it, he slid!... Go it, ole feller! Git there, git there! Ye're almost there, Fluke—git it! It's a dinner—it's a bone for Snatchet, and we'll eat!... Damn it! he slid again!... Aw! hell!"

Flukey gained the space he had lost in his last slide. Halfway up, he began again, the men cheering and the women waving handkerchiefs. But the boy had heard only the words from the little figure under the pole. The five dollars did mean a good dinner, and a bone for lean Snatchet. Up, up, and still up, until his fingers grasped the pole very near the top.

There he rested for breath. For a few seconds his head drooped on his shoulders, and absolute quiet reigned below. His slender legs encircled the pole, and finally, with a painful effort, he lifted out the pin stuck in the bill, grasped the money in his fingers, and instantly slid to the ground. Laughs and cheers roared into the air. Flea had backed away from the pole, still holding the small dog; but, before she could get to Flukey, other boys were surrounding him, asking how he had done it.

A sudden shouting came from hundreds of throats. One voice raised above the clamor:

"Anyone catching the greased pig, Squeaky, can have him. He's a fine roaster! After him, Boys!"

Over a knoll, his tiny nose swaying in the air, and four short legs kicking the dust into clouds, skurried a small pig, coated from head to tail with lard. Deftly he slipped for his life through many youthful hands stretched out to grasp him, and time and again he wriggled from

45

under a small boy crouched to stop his progress. He passed the danger-mark, and in the new stretch of ground, where the spectators were standing, discerned a chance to escape.

Flea saw him coming and could detect the terror in the flying little beast. Her heart leaped up in answer to the call from something in distress—something she loved, loved because it lived and suffered through terrible fear. She dropped Snatchet and caught the greased pig in her arms. She hugged him up to her breast and, turning flashing eyes upon the people staring at her, said:

"Poor little baby piggy! He's scared almost to death."

"You've caught the greased pig!" somebody shouted. "You can have him—he's yours!"

"Ye mean mine to keep?" Flea demanded of the man who had cheered on the boys.

"Yes, to keep," was the reply, "and this five-dollar gold-piece because you caught him."

"I didn't try to catch him," she said simply. "He jest comed to me 'cause he were so afeard. His little heart's a beatin' like as if he's goin' to die. I'll keep him, and I thank ye for the money.... Golly! but ain't me and Flukey two rich kids? Where's Fluke?"

Just then somebody stepped up behind the girl and touched her on the arm. Flea turned her head and found herself gazing into the kindly eyes and earnest face of her prince.

Instantly she lost all thought of her brother and Snatchet. The voice she had dreamed of was speaking.

"Little boy," it said, "I've purchased every year the greased pig of the youngster who caught him. May I buy him of you? I'll give you another gold-piece for him."

Words stuck in Flea's throat, and she only clung closer to the suckling. At last she murmured, "What do ye want with him?"

The man threw back his head and laughed. "Why, to eat him, of course. We always have roast pig for dinner the day after the fair."

Flea dug her toe into the dust and flung up a cloud of it, as her face drew into a sulky frown. "Well," she drawled, "ye don't hog down this 'un! He's mine!"

"But the money, Boy! Don't you want the money?"

Her heart was beating so fast that she dared not lift her eyes again to his. Then a lady spoke in a soft voice, and Flea glanced at her.

"This is Mr. Horace Shellington," she said, "and if he did not have the pig he would be disappointed. You'll let him buy it, won't you?"

Flea looked into the questioning face of her prince, the face of her dreams, looked again into his smiling eyes, and stood hesitant. Her

46

thoughts flew fast. She remembered the terrified pig, how she had pitied him, and how much he wanted to live, to frisk in the sunshine. She thought of the cruel knife that would reach the tiny heart tapping against her own, and threw back her head in defiance.

"Ye may have e't all the greased pigs in this here country," she said to Shellington; "but ye don't eat this 'un! Ye see, this 'un's mine, and he's goin' to live, eat, and be happy, that's all!" Although she had spoken emphatically, her eyes dropped again before the keen gaze bent upon her. To relieve her embarrassment, she turned and shouted, "Flukey, Flukey, come along! Where's Snatchet?"

So great had been Flea's excitement at the catching of the pig that she had given no heed to the dog. Flukey had handed the little fellow to her, and she had let him go.

Suddenly an appalling spectacle rose before her. On an elevated spot, a few feet from the greased pole, Snatchet stood poised in view of hundreds of curious eyes. His short stubby tail had straightened out like a stick. His nose was lowered almost to the ground. Each yellow hair on his scarred back had risen separate and apart from one another, while his beady eyes glistened greedily. Directly in front of him, staring back with feathers ruffled and drooping wings, was a little brown hen, escaped from her coop. She was eying Snatchet impudently, daring him to approach her by perking her wee head saucily first on one side and then on the other. Snatchet, pressed on by hunger beating at his lean sides, slid rigidly a pace nearer. A cry went up from a childish voice.

"He'll kill my Queen Bess! Father—Oh! Father!"

Flukey's voice, calling to his dog, rose high above the clamor. Suddenly the little hen turned tail and flew across over the soft earth, uttering frightened cackles; but her flight was slow compared to Snatchet's. He came scurrying behind her, snapping a tail feather loose with each onward bound, utterly oblivious of the two strong voices calling his name.

The little hen wove a precarious path through coops of chattering chickens, and Snatchet, bent upon his prey, added to the din. He had no way of knowing the twists and turns to be taken by his small brown victim, and it was only by making sharp corners that Queen Bess kept clear of the snapping teeth. Men were running to and fro for something to beat off the yellow invader. The girl's voice had settled to a cry, and, just as Flukey, panting and tired, reached the dog, Snatchet snapped up the hen, shook her fiercely, and settled down to his meal. In an instant Flukey had dragged the beating body from his teeth, kicked him soundly with his bare foot, and held out the dead hen to a man whose

47

face was darkened by anger. The young mistress of the feathered queen was clinging, sobbing, to his hand.

"Is that your dog?" Flea heard the man ask, pointing to Snatchet under the squatter boy's arm.

"Yep."

"Do you understand that he killed my little girl's prize hen?"

"The dog ought to die, too!" cried a voice from the people.

Her brother's sorrowful attitude made Flea press Flukey's arm soothingly.

"So he ought to die!" said another.

"He were hungry," explained Flukey, turning on Snatchet's accuser. "Mister, if ye'll let my dorg live—"

Before he could finish the child had interrupted him. "That dog ought to die for killing my Bess!"

Flea pushed past Flukey and stood before the little girl. "Kid, I don't blame ye for cryin' for yer hen," she began; "but my brother ain't got no dog but Snatchet, an' if ye'll let him live I'll give ye this bit of gold I got for catchin' the pig."

A murmur followed her words, and the tears dried in the blue eyes looking up at her.

"Here little 'un, chuck it in yer pocket," said Flea, straightening her shoulders, "and it'll buy another hen."

So the jury which had sat for a moment upon the precious life of Snatchet brought in a verdict of "not guilty," and the squatter children turned to find something to eat for the quartet of empty stomachs. Out of sight of Dryden, they sat down beside the road, and Flea looked the pig over.

"Ye has to tie a piece of cord to his leg, Kid," cautioned Flukey; "'cause he'll get away if ye don't. Ain't he fine?"

"The finest pig in this here world," responded Flea. "Ye ain't got no rag what'll wipe off some of this grease, have ye, Fluke?"

"Nope; but ye can scrape it off with a stick or a rock. Here, ye hold him tight while I dig at him."

For about twenty minutes they busied themselves with cleaning the suckling, laughing at his wriggles and squeaks.

"What'll we call him?" asked Flea.

"Squeaky," said Flukey, "that's what the man called out."

"Aw, that ain't nice enough for me! I'll call him Prince, and ye call him Squeaky—Prince Squeaky," she ended, knotting the cord Flukey had given her about the short hind leg of the animal.

"And we be rich," she declared later, "'most five dollars, a pig, and Snatchet, and yer leg's well. It don't hurt a bit, do it?"

"Nope, not now; but when I were at the top of that pole I got a damn good twist. It's better now."

"Then let's mog along," said Flea, "'cause we can eat all we want, now we got money."

CHAPTER TEN

For two weeks Flea and Flukey lived on the fat of the land. The country afforded them haystacks, and the brooks, clear water. The children were never happier than when Squeaky's nose was hidden in a tin can of buttermilk, and the precious five dollars bought countless numbers of currant buns, sugar cakes, and penny bones for Snatchet. Now Flukey lifted his head proudly and walked with the air of a boy on the road to fortune, and Flea kept at his side with the prince hugged close in her arms. Through the long stretch of houseless roads Snatchet was allowed to rove at will, and Flukey relieved his sister of her burden. By the third day out toward the promised land the two little animals had become firm friends, and the queer quartet walked on and on, as straight as the crow flies, through the valleys and over the hills, wading the creeks and ferrying the rivers, until they awoke one morning without money or breakfast. The warm hay at night, much sunshine, and the absence of rain had reduced the swollen joint in Flukey's knee to normal size; but that day, as they trudged along, Flea noticed that he limped more than at any time during their journey from Tompkins County. Even now, with hunger staring wolf-eyed at them, there was no desire to return to Ithaca, no thought of renewing their life in the squatter's settlement; for, unknown to themselves, they were being swept on by a common destiny.

"Ye're gettin' lame again," said Flea after awhile, the mother-feeling in her making her watch Flukey with concern. "Last night a-laying' in the field didn't do ye any good. Let me lug Prince Squeaky."

Without remonstrance, the boy surrendered the wriggling burden, and they started out once more.

"I wish we could find a nice, warm haystack," Flea commented; "it'd warm up yer bones. Will we get to one, Fluke, after awhile?"

"Nope, 'cause we're comin' to a big city."

As he spoke, he motioned to where Tarrytown lay on the banks of the Hudson River, several miles distant. Then they were silent a time; for each young life was busy with the tragedy of living. Just what they would do for a place to sleep Flea could not tell, since under the compact made in the rock-cavern they would steal no more.

In the gathering twilight the two came upon the cemetery of Sleepy Hollow, and here, tired, hungry, and despondent, they sat down to rest.

"It's gettin' night," said Flukey drearily. "I wonder where we'll sleep?"

"Can't we squirm in this dead man's yard 'thout nobody seein' us?" asked Flea, casting her eyes over the graves. "Ye can't walk no more tonight. I ain't hungry, anyhow."

"Ye lie, Flea!" moaned Flukey. "Yer belly's as empty as Squeaky's or Snatchet's. I've got to get ye somethin' to eat."

Nevertheless, without resistance, he allowed her to help him through the large gate, and they struck off into the older part of the cemetery. All through the night they lay dozing in the presence of the dead, Squeaky tied by the leg to a tree, and Snatchet snuggled warmly between the two children. The dawning of day brought Flukey new anguish; for both knees were swollen, and he groaned as he turned over.

Flea was up instantly. "Be ye sick?"

"Only the twist in my legs. I wish it wasn't so cold. If the sun would only get warm!"

"We'll get to the good land today, Fluke," soothed Flea, "and ye can eat all ye want, and sleep with a pile of covers on—as big—as big as that there vault yonder."

"But we ain't in the good land yet, Flea," groaned Flukey, "and we're all hungry. I wish I could 'arn a nickel. If ye didn't love the pig so much, Flea, we could sell him. He's a growin' thinner and thinner every minute, and Snatchet be that starvin' he could eat another mut bigger'n himself."

The girl made no answer to this, but tucked Squeaky's pink nose under the blue-shirted arm and sat mute.

Flukey, encouraged, went on. "Nobody'd buy Snatchet—he's only a poor, damn, shiverin' cuss."

"If we selled Prince Squeaky, some'un'd eat him," mourned Flea. "He ain't goin' to be e't, I says!"

So forceful were her tones that Flukey offered no more suggestions; but stared miserably at the sun as it rose up from the east,

50

dispersing the cold, gray morning fog. Presently Flea stood up and said decisively:

"We've got to eat. Ye stay here while I hunt for somethin'."

She darted away before Flukey could remonstrate. For a long time the boy lay on the damp ground, his face drawn awry with pain, watching the wagons going back and forth on the road below. The pangs of hunger and the night of rheumatism had told upon his young strength. His mind went back to the hut on Cayuga Lake, and he thought of how when their absence had been discovered Granny Cronk had cried a little, and how Pappy Lon had cursed and grown more silent than ever. The tender heart of the sick boy yearned toward the old squatter woman, who had been the only mother he and Flea had ever known. In his loneliness he stroked Squeaky on the snout and muttered tender words to the lean dog lying under his lame leg. After a short time he saw Flea, with a small bundle in her hand, picking her way among the graves. Flukey lay perfectly quiet until his sister offered him a bun.

"I could only buy four, 'cause I only had a nickel."

"Give Squeaky and Snatchet one, will ye, Flea?" ventured Flukey.

"Yep. I said, when I buyed 'em, there'd be one apiece."

"Somethin' has made ye pale, Flea," said Flukey after each of the four had devoured breakfast. "Ye didn't—"

"I see Lem Crabbe's scow down by the river."

Flukey uttered an exclamation and sat up with a groan. "He's comin' after ye, Kid," he breathed desperately.

"Nope, he ain't," assured Flea; "he's takin' lumber down to New York. And he didn't see me. And we'll stay in this here graveyard till he's gone. He's waitin' for the steam tug to come. I guess he poled from Albany down when he couldn't use his mules."

"Were Pappy Lon with him?" asked Flukey, drawing up his knees.

"I dunno; I didn't wait to see. I had to 'arn this nickel."

"Ye didn't steal it, Flea?"

"Nope; I had it give to me for holdin' a horse. Ye believe me, Fluke?"

"Yep, I believe ye. And ye say as how we can't go on now to the good land? We has to stay here?"

"For awhile," replied Flea. "When Lem Crabbe goes to New York, then we go, too."

While hundreds of birds made ready for a long night in the elm trees, the twins turned silent. Flukey lay with his eyes closed in pain.

The girl broke the quietude now and then by muttering softly the names on the gravestones over which her eyes roved:

> "EVERETT BRIMBECOMB
> ONE YEAR OLD
> BELOVED SON OF AGNES AND HAROLD BRIMBECOMB.
> RESTING IN JESUS"

Flea read this over several times, and turned to Flukey.

"Who's Jesus, Fluke?" she asked.

The boy raised his head and opened his eyes languidly. "What? What'd ye say, Flea?"

"Who's Jesus?" she asked again, pointing to the inscription on the stone.

"I dunno. I guess he's some old feller layin' down in there with that kid."

Thus the day had passed and the night fell. Flukey dropped into a deep sleep, and Flea, huddling to the cold earth, settled closer to her brother in the sheltering darkness. Suddenly the girl aroused as if from a bad dream. She sat up, feeling for the pig and Snatchet, and placed her hand on Flukey's quiet body and lay down. Once more came the sound. It was the faint, distant hoot of an owl, stealing out through the tall trees. Nearer and nearer it came, until Flea sat bolt upright. Instantly into her mind shot the picture of a shriveled woman from the squatter country. A cold perspiration broke over her.

She turned her head slowly and looked off into the dark end of the cemetery, over which hung a mist. Through this veil the pale moon watched the earth with steady gaze. From among the monuments and time-scarred headstones, looming darkly in the forbidding silence, an apparition arose, and to Flea's vivid imagination it seemed as if voiceless gray ghosts were peopling God's Acre on all sides. She recoiled in horror as the strange, wild cry drew nearer.

A hysterical sensation burning in her throat tightened it so she could not speak to Flukey, nor could she drag her eyes from the thing moving toward her. Snatchet growled; but Flea pressed his jaws together with a snap, and the sound died in his throat. Squeaky moved slightly among the dead leaves, then became quiet again. The phantom-like figure passed almost near enough to touch the rigid girl. Its lips opened, and a hoarse, owl-like cry aroused the sleepy birds above.

"It's Screechy!" murmured Flea, dropping back in fear. "She's come seekin' Flukey and me! The bats be flyin' in her head!"

Screech Owl, ignorant of the children's proximity, went straight

52

on, gliding over the graves until she stopped before the stone mansion at the edge of the graveyard. A light shone from the room, and the woman stole directly under it. A tall, handsome young man, his gaze centered thoughtfully upon the dark aspect, stood in the window. Flea saw Screechy hold out her arms toward him with an appealing gesture. He lifted his hand suddenly and drew down the shade, and his broad shoulders were silhouetted against it in sharp, black lines. After that the breathless girl saw the woman turn and stumble past her without a sound.

"The bats left her head the minute that there winder got dark!" gasped the watcher. Tremblingly she drew closer to Flukey, until sleep overpowered her.

The next day passed slowly, the cold rain lasting until almost nightfall, and yet the children dared not venture into the town. Flea fumed and fretted; for the earning of the nickel had whetted her ambition to earn more. Now she dared not go near the river where work could be found; but she knew that as soon as the tug appeared Lem Crabbe would go to New York. Probably by this time the scow was far on its way down the river. This was the decision at which the squatter twins arrived after weary hours of waiting. So, when the twilight again fell over the dead, they rose stiffly from their hiding place and limped to the road.

"We'll go back to the graveyard tonight, if this ain't the good land," murmured Flea. "We'll be safe there from Lem, Fluke."

"Wish we was rich like we was that fair-day, Flea," replied the boy, scarcely able to walk.

"I wish so, too. If we had that yeller gold-piece we coughed up for that damn brown hen, we'd eat. But I'd ruther have Snatchet, Fluke."

"I'd ruther have him, too; but we need money—"

"And when we get it," interrupted Flea, "Snatchet'll have a hunk of meat, and Prince Squeaky a bucket of buttermilk, and ye'll have liniment for yer legs, Fluke."

"Ye'll eat yerself first, Flea," said Flukey. "I saw ye when ye give the pig a bit of yer biscuit yesterday mornin'."

"We'll all eat in the good land," replied Flea hopefully.

By this time they had come to the gateway and turned into the street. Harold Brimbecomb's beautiful home was brilliantly lighted. It appeared the same to Flea as on the night before, when she had seen Scraggy make her melancholy play before it.

Flea had refrained from speaking of her midnight fright to Flukey; for he would but tell her that, like all girls, she was afraid, and a slur from her brother was more than she could bear.

Flea and Flukey had never been taught to pray, "Lead us not into temptation." Now, with aching hearts and empty stomachs, they turned in silence to the richly lighted houses. Flukey dragged himself resolutely past Brimbecomb's as if he would avoid the desire that suddenly pressed upon him to ply the trade in which he had been darkly instructed. But he halted abruptly before the next house, the curtains of which were pulled up halfway. The long windows reached to the porch floor. Through the clear glass the children saw a table dressed in all the gorgeousness of silver and crystal. At the spectacle a clamor for food set up in both aching stomachs, and the two passed as if by one accord to the porch. As they peered into the window with longing eyes, Squeaky was held tightly under Flea's arm; but Snatchet, resting wearily on Flukey's, suddenly sat up. He, too, had scented something to eat, and thrust in and out a lean red tongue over pointed, tusky teeth.

"It's time for me to steal, Flea," whispered Flukey, turning feverish eyes toward his sister.

"If you do it, Flukey, I'll do it with ye."

With no more ado, Flukey's practiced fingers silently slid up the sash. Two youthful bodies stepped through the opening. In absolute quiet, they stood raggedly forlorn, savagely hungry, before the tempting table. There was plenty to eat; so without a word the squatter girl placed Squeaky before a glass dish of salad. His small pink nose buried its tip from sight, and the food disappeared into the suckling's empty stomach. Snatchet, squatting on his haunches, snapped up a stuffed bird. Flea began to eat; but Flukey, now too ill, leaned against the red-papered wall.

Just at this critical moment the door opened, and Flea, greatly frightened, started back to the window. She blinked, brushed a dark curl from her eyes, and saw her Prince advancing toward her. He saw her, too; but did not connect her with the bare-footed girl on Cayuga Lake, but only with the boy who had kept from him the greased pig at the Dryden fair. He glanced at Squeaky calmly eating the salad and smiled.

"Bless my soul, Ann!" he said, turning to a lady who had followed him in, "we have company to dinner, or my name isn't Horace Shellington! Why didn't you young gentlemen wait, and we should all have been seated together?"

There was a whirling in Flukey's head, such as he had never felt before; but Flea's ashen face brought back his scattered senses. He tried to lift his arm to throw it about her; but dropped it with a groan. Realizing the agony that had swept over her dear one, Flea gathered in a deep breath and took his fevered hand in hers.

"It weren't him," she cried, lifting her eyes to her questioner and sullenly moving her head toward the shivering boy at her side. "I e't yer victuals—he didn't. If one of us goes to jail, I do—see?"

"Let me think," ruminated Horace, eying her gravely. "Six months is about the shortest sentence given to a fellow for breaking into a house. And what about the pig? I see him in the act of theft. Shall he go with you?"

"He were hungry, that's why Prince Squeaky stealed," exclaimed Flea, dropping Flukey's fingers. There was something in the kindly eyes of the man that forced her forward a step. She thrust out her hand in appealing anxiety. "We was all hungry," she continued, a dry sob strangling her. "Flukey nor me nor the pig nor Snatchet ain't e't in a long time. We did steal; but if I knowed it were yer house—"

A quizzical expression flashing into Shellington's eyes stopped her words.

"You wouldn't have come in?" he queried.

Flea nodded just as Snatchet jumped to the floor with another plump bird between his teeth. Flukey staggered to his sister's side.

"Let me tell ye how it was, Mister," he begged, his eyes bloodshot and restless. "We be lookin' for a good land where boys don't have to steal, and when they get sick they get well again."

Here Flea burst forth impetuously.

"He has such hellish rheumatiz that he can't set in no dark prison. I can set weeks among rats and bugs what be in all prisons! I ain't afraid of nothing what lives!"

Flukey interrupted her by taking her arm and pushing her back a little.

"I'm a thief by trade," he said; "but my sister ain't. She ain't never stole nothin' in all her life, she ain't. Take me, will ye, Mister?"

"Sister!" murmured the gentleman, turning to Flea.

If nothing else had been said, the question would have been answered in the affirmative by the vivid blush that dyed Flea's dark skin. Her embarrassment brought another exclamation from Flukey.

"She's a girl, all right! She's only tryin' to save me. She put on my pants jest to get away from Pappy Lon. I'll go to jail; but don't send her!"

He swayed blindly, closing his eyes with a moan.

"The child is sick, Horace," said Ann. "I think he is very sick."

"Where did you sleep last night?" Shellington asked this of Flea.

"Out there," answered the girl, pointing over her shoulder, "down by a big monument."

"Horace Shellington," gasped Ann, "they slept in the cemetery!"

The sharp tone of the girl's voice brought Flukey back to the present.

"We run away 'cause Pappy Lon were a makin' me steal when I didn't want to," he explained, clearing his throat, "and he was goin' to make Flea be Lem's woman. And that's the truth, Mister, and Lem wasn't goin' to marry her, nuther!"

He rambled on in a monotone as if too sick for inflection. Flea placed one arm about his neck.

"I'm a girl! I'm Flea Cronk!" she confessed brokenly. "And Flukey's doin' all this for me! And he's so sick! I stealed from yer table—he didn't! Will ye let him lay in yer barn tonight, if I go up for the stealin'?"

Never had Horace Shellington felt so keenly the sorrows of other human beings as when this girl, in her crude boy clothes, lifted her agonized, tearless eyes to his. His throat filled. Somehow, his whole soul went out to her, his being stirred to its depths. He put out one hand to touch Flea—when voices from the inner room stopped further speech. A light step, accompanied by a heavier one, approaching the dining-hall, brought his thoughts together.

"Ann," he appealed, stepping to his sister's side, "you're always wanting to do something for me—do it now. Let me settle this!"

Speaking to Flukey, he said, "Pick up your dog, Boy!"

"And the pig from the table!" groaned Ann distractedly.

Flukey mechanically stooped to obey, while Flea captured Squeaky and tucked the suckling under her arm just as Shellington opened the door to admit his guests. When Flea lifted her embarrassed gaze to the strangers, she saw the same face that had peered at her over Horace's shoulder at the Dryden fair, the face to which Screech Owl had made her silent appeal. A graceful girl followed, whose eyes expressed astonishment as Horace spoke.

"These are my young friends, you will remember, Everett, from the fair, Flea and Flukey Cronk." Turning his misty eyes upon the children he continued, "This is Mr. Brimbecomb, and Miss Katherine Vandecar, Governor Vandecar's niece."

He went through this introduction to gain control of his feelings.

"They have changed their minds, Everett, and have brought me the pig," he exclaimed. "It was kind of you, child!"

He had almost said "boy"; but, remembering the admission Flea had made, he gazed straight at her, watching with growing interest the changes that passed over the young face.

"You see," he hurried on nervously, "they found out where I lived, and thought I might still want the pig—"

Ann Shellington admonishingly touched her brother's arm. "Horace!" she urged; but he stopped her with a gesture.

"I think it mighty nice of them to come all the way from Dryden with a pig—on my soul, I do, Ann!"

Taking a silver case from his pocket, he extracted a cigarette from it, while directing his attention to Flea.

"I want it now as much as I did then; but I don't believe that I shall ever roast and eat him."

Flea searched the speaker's face fearfully, her eyes lustrous with melting tenderness. He had promised her that Squeaky should live; but was he going to send Flukey away? It was slow torture, this waiting for his verdict, each second measured full to the brim, each minute more agonizing than the last.

Horace Shellington was speaking again. "You see, Katherine," he said, turning to the younger girl, "I know this puzzles you; but these two youngsters won the pig at the fair, and I tried to buy it of them for a roast. Just at that time this little—chap—" he motioned toward Flea, "didn't want to part with it. He's changed his mind. You see the pig is here."

Miss Shellington did not supplement her brother's statement; but the tall stranger with the brilliant eyes gazed dubiously at the table and then down into Flea's face.

"I'll bet my hat," he said in a tone deep and rich, "that you boys have been thieving!"

Before the frightened girl could respond, the master of the house stepped between them; but not before Flea had caught an expression that took her back to Screech Owl's hut.

"For shame, Everett!" chided Horace. "I have just told you that they were trying to do me a favor. The pig has come a long way, and I gave him some—salad. There's plenty more in the larder."

It was hard for Horace Shellington to lie flagrantly, and his explanation sounded forced. The music in his voice pierced the childish lethargy of Flea's soul, awakening it to womanhood. Intuition told her that he had lied for her sake.

"And you gave him the birds, too?" Everett asked sneeringly, glancing at the scattered bones.

"No, I gave the dog the birds," replied Horace simply. "It seemed," he proceeded slowly, "that just at that moment I felt for the hungry dog and pig more than I did for my guests."

He had backed to his sister's side with an imploring glance, and allowed his hand to rest lightly on hers. She understood his message, and met his appeal.

"And now these young people have been so good to us," she said, "we ought to repay them with a good supper. If you will come with me, Boys, you shall have what you need.... Oh! Yes, you can bring both the dog and the pig."

A tranquil smile, sweet and pathetic, erased the pain-wrinkles from Flukey's face. Supper at last for his dear ones!

Ann held out her hand to him, and dazedly the sick lad took it in his hot fingers. Then, remembering Everett's disapprobation of the boys, she glanced into his face; but, meeting a studiously indifferent, slightly bored look, she led Flukey away.

CHAPTER ELEVEN

Flukey was too ill, as he stumbled along, to dread the outcome of their act of theft. He realized only that a beautiful lady was leading Flea to a place where her hunger could be satisfied, and, as he felt the warmth of Ann's fingers permeate his own famished body, a great courage urged him forward. He would never again steal at Lon's command, and Flea would have to dread Lem no more! Something infinitely sweet, like new-coming life, entered his soul. It was the first exquisite joy that had come to Flukey Cronk. He stopped and disengaged his hand, to press it to his side as a pain made him gasp for breath. Then of a sudden he sank to the polished floor, still clinging to Snatchet.

"Missus," he muttered, "I can't walk no more. Jest ye leave me here and git the grub for Flea."

Flea turned sharply. "I don't eat when ye're sick, Fluke. The Prince says as how ye can sleep in the barn, and mebbe—mebbe he'll let me work for the victuals Snatchet and Squeaky stole."

Flea added this hopefully.

"Children," said Ann in a smothered voice, "listen to me! You're both welcome to all you've had, and more. The little dog and pig were welcome too."

Tears rose under her lids, and she turned her head away, that the twins might not see them. Ann Shellington, like her brother, had never

58

before seen human misery depicted in small lives. At the mention of his dog, Flukey opened his eyes and turned his gaze upward.

"Thank ye, Lady," said he, "thank ye for what ye said about Snatchet. Ain't he a pink peach of a dorg, Ma'm?"

Ann inclined her head gently, glancing dubiously over the yellow pup. She could not openly admit that Snatchet resembled anything beautiful she had ever seen, when the boy, his lips twitching with agony, held his pet up toward her.

"Ye can take him, Ma'm," groaned Flukey. "He only bites bad 'uns like Lem Crabbe."

Snatchet, feeling the importance of the moment, lifted his head and shot forth a slavering tongue. As it came in contact with her fingers, Miss Shellington drew back a little. She had been used to slender-limbed, soft-coated dogs; this small, shivering mongrel, touching her flesh with a tongue roughly beaded, sent a tremor of disgust over her. Flea stepped forward, took Snatchet from her brother, and tucked him away under the arm opposite the one Squeaky occupied.

"Ye'll go to the barn, Fluke," she said, "and ye'll go damn quick! The lady'll let ye, and Snatchet'll go with ye. Squeaky sleeps with me."

Ann coughed embarrassedly. "Children," she began, "we couldn't let the dog and pig sleep in the house; neither could we allow you to sleep in the barn. So, if you will let the coachman take your pets, I'll see that you, Boy, go into a warm bed, and you," Ann turned to Flea, "must have some supper and other clothes. Your brother is very ill, I believe, and I think we ought to have a doctor."

Flea pricked up her ears, and a sad smile crossed her lips. "Ye mean, Ma'm," said she, "that Flukey can sleep in a real bed and have doctor's liniments for his bones?"

Ann nodded. "Yes. Now then hurry!... Look at that poor little boy!"

Flukey was on his knees, leaning against the wall, his feverish fingers clutching his curls.

"Horace! Horace!" called Ann.

Shellington opened the dining-room door and went out hurriedly, leaving Everett Brimbecomb and Katherine Vandecar still surveying the disarranged table.

"It all seems strange to me, Katherine; I mean—this," said Everett, waving his hand. "I scarcely believed Horace when he said he had allowed it."

As he spoke, he approached the table and lifted the soiled cloth between his fingers.

"You can see for yourself," he said, "the marks of the pig's feet on the linen."

Katherine examined the spots. "But it really doesn't matter, does it?" she said. "The poor little animals were hungry, and Horace has such a big heart!" and she sighed.

Everett made an angry gesture. "But I object to Ann having anything to do with such—" he hesitated and finished, "such youngsters. There's no need of it."

"Oh, Everett—but those two children must be cared for! Horace will come back in a few minutes, and then we'll know all about it."

"In the meantime I'm hungry," grumbled Everett, "and if we're going to the theater—"

He had no time to finish his sentence before Horace, with a grave countenance, opened the door.

"I'm sorry, Katherine," he apologized, and then stopped; for he noticed Everett's face dark with anger. Shellington did not forget that his friends had come to dinner; but he had just witnessed a scene that had touched his heart, and he determined to make both of his guests understand it also.

"The evening has turned out differently from what Ann and I expected," he explained. "The fact is that sister can't go to the theater, and I feel that I ought to stay with her. So, we'll order another dinner, and then, Everett, if you and Katherine don't—" His fingers had touched the bell as he was speaking; but Everett stopped him.

"If the boy is too ill to be taken to a hospital," he said coldly, "Ann might be persuaded to leave him with the servants."

"Yes, I suggested that," answered Horace; "but she refused. The boy has somehow won her heart, and the doctor will be here at any moment."

A servant appeared, and in a half-hour the table was spread with another dinner. Ann's coming to the dining-room did not raise the spirits of the party; for her eyes were red from weeping, and she refused to eat.

"I've never known before, Everett," she said, "that children could suffer as that little boy does."

"And you shouldn't know it now, Ann, if I had my way," objected Brimbecomb. "There's a strong line drawn between their kind and ours, and places have been provided for such people. I really want you to come with us tonight."

In sharp astonishment, Ann turned on him.

"Oh, I really couldn't, Everett!" she said, beginning to sob. "I shouldn't enjoy one moment of the time, while thinking of that poor child. You take Katherine, and say to Governor and Mrs. Vandecar that we couldn't come tonight. Tell them about it or not as you please. They are both good and kind, and will understand."

Her tears had ceased during the latter part of her speech; for the frown had deepened on Everett's brow, bringing determination to her own. Never before had she been forced to exercise her wish above his, and Brimbecomb was not prepared for it. Something new had been born in the large, sad eyes turned to his, something he did not comprehend, and he inwardly cursed the squatter children.

At eight o'clock Everett handed Katherine into the carriage and gloomily took his place beside her. They were late at the theater by several minutes, when he brushed aside the curtain and ushered Miss Vandecar into the Governor's box. Mrs. Vandecar was seated in the far corner, her attention directed upon the play. Vandecar rose quietly, and before resuming his seat waited until his niece had taken her place. Then they were silent until the curtain fell after the first act.

"Where are Horace and Ann?" asked Mrs. Vandecar of Everett. "Ann telephoned me at dinner-time that she would be here."

Everett inclined his head toward Katherine, and the girl explained the situation. When she had added pathos to the story by telling of Flukey's illness, Mrs. Vandecar broke in.

"I'm glad Ann stayed, dear girl! It's like her to nurse that sick child." She said no more; but turned away with misty eyes.

During the next act the Governor drew near her, and amid the shadows of the darkened box, took up the slender fingers and held them until the lights flashed upon the falling curtain. Both had gone back in memory to those dreadful days when tragedy had cast its somber shadows over them.

The doctor had predicted a serious illness for Flukey. Ann and Horace held an earnest conversation about it. Miss Shellington's maid had been instructed to relieve Flea of her boy's attire and clothe her in some of Ann's garments. Horace led his sister to the room where Flukey lay, and suggested that Flea be called.

A servant appeared at the touch of the bell.

"Tell the boy's sister to come here," said Horace.

When Flea knocked at the door a few minutes later, he bade her enter. Suppressing her pleasure and surprise at the girl's loveliness, Ann walked forward to meet her; but the little stranger backed timidly against the door and flashed a blushing glance at the man.

The mauve dressing-gown, reaching to the floor, displayed to advantage the girl's lithe figure, accentuating its long, graceful lines. The bodice, opened at the neck, exposed the slender white throat, around which the summer's sun had tanned a ruddy ring. Her hair had been parted in the center and twined in adorable curls about the young head.

The transformation drew an untactful ejaculation from Horace, and he stared intently at the sensitive face. Flea's gray eyes, after the first hasty glance at him, sought Flukey.

"Flukey ain't so awful sick, be he?" she questioned fearfully.

Ann passed an arm tenderly around her. "Yes, child, he is very ill. My brother and I want to speak to you about him."

"But he ain't goin' dead?"

Her tone brought Horace nearer. In spite of Flea's somberness, the bouyancy of her youth obliterated the memory of every other girl he knew. He was confounded by the thought that a short time before she had stood as a ragged boy before him. She had been transformed into womanhood by Ann's clothing.

Flea bent over Flukey and hid her face. Even when Horace had discovered the pig in the salad, her embarrassment had been of small moment to this. After an instant, she lifted her eyes from her muttering brother and allowed them to fall upon her Prince. There was an unmistakable smile upon his lips; nevertheless, a great fear possessed her. If Flukey were allowed to stay there because of his illness, she at least would be taken away; for she had never heard of a theft being entirely overlooked, and she believed that her imprisonment must be the penalty.

She stooped a little and lovingly touched Flukey's shoulder, looking first at Ann, then at Horace. Straightening up, she burst out:

"Mister, if ye're goin' to have me pinched for stealin', do it quick before my brother knows about it, and—I'd rather go to prison in Fluke's pants—please!"

Still the master of the house did not speak. Flea was filled with suspicion, and thought she divined the cause of his quietness and smile. He was ridiculing her dress, perhaps making sport of the way her curls were arranged. She thrust one hand upward and tumbled the mass of hair into disorder.

"Yer woman put these togs onto me," she said, "and I feel like an old guy—dressed up this way!"

Anger forced tears into her eyes, and her two small brown hands clenched under the hanging lace at her wrists. Her words and the spontaneous action deepened the expression on the face of the silent man, and she cried out again:

"Ye needn't be making fun of me, Mister! I can't help how I look."

But a feverish exclamation from the sick boy so increased her anxiety for him that her own troubles were overwhelmed. She was

62

rendered unmindful that Ann had softly called her name; nor did she realize that Shellington had spoken quietly to her.

She flung out her hands in eloquent appeal.

"Oh, I thank ye for covering my brother up so warm! He didn't need no sheets nor piller-slips; but his bones did need the blankets—sure. I say as how he'd thank ye, too, if he weren't offen his head."

Horace gently took the girl's hands in his, and Flea lowered her sun-browned face.

"I know he would, child," he said in moved tones. "He's more than welcome to all we can do—and you are to stay here, too, little girl."

Horace had done what Ann had been unable to do. The words had soothed the squatter girl, and the savage young heart was softened. The long, dreary country marches were over; the cold nights and bare fields were things of the past. For Flukey, there were tender hands that would ease his pain; for her, a home unmenaced by Lem. She had looked her last upon horrors that had bound her to a life she hated.

Shellington spoke to her.

"Look at me, child!" said he. "I want to tell you what the doctor said."

She lifted an anxious gaze filled with the emotion of a woman's soul. It was her dawning womanhood that Horace saw, and toward it his manhood was unconsciously drawn.

Ann spoke quietly:

"The doctor says that your brother will be ill many weeks, and we have decided to keep him here with us, if you consent to our arrangements."

"Ye mean," gasped Flea, snatching her hands from Horace, "ye mean that Flukey can lay in that there bed till he gets all well and all the misery has gone out of his bones?"

Ann's answer meant much to Flea. The girl had realized the import of the speech; but, that she might better understand the words, she had sent them questioningly back in her vernacular for further confirmation.

"If you are willing to stay with us," Horace was saying, "and will help us take care of him—"

He could not have offered anything else that would so have touched her. How she had longed to do something for Flukey those last hours in the graveyard! But Flea wanted no mistake. Did the gentleman understand how terribly poor they were?

"We ain't got no money, and we only own Squeaky and Snatchet."

Shellington smiled at the interruption.

"You will still own your dog and pig, child, if you ever wish to go away. My sister and I are anxious to have your brother grow strong and well. He has rheumatic fever, which is sometimes very stubborn, and if we don't work hard—"

He paused, tempted to pass one arm about the girl as his sister had done; but the womanliness of her forbade.

"Ye think Flukey mightn' get well?" Flea breathed.

Ann turned anxious eyes upon the boy, who was muttering incoherently.

"Poor little child! May Jesus help him!" she whispered.

Flea rose to her feet.

"Jesus! Jesus!" she repeated solemnly. "Granny Cronk used to talk about him. He's the Man what's a sleepin' in the grave with the kid with the same name as that bright-eyed duffer who don't like Fluke nor me."

Ann, mystified, glanced at Horace.

Flukey turned slowly, opened his eyes, and murmured;

"'Gentle Jesus, meek and mild, look upon a little—'"

He sighed painfully as the last words trailed from his lips. Flea ended his quotation, saying:

"'A little child.' But, Flukey, Jesus is dead and buried."

"No, no, He isn't, child!" cried Ann sharply. "He'll never die. He will always help little children."

"Ain't He a restin' in the dead man's yard out there?" demanded Flea, lifting her robe as she moved toward Ann.

"No! indeed, no! He is everywhere, with the dead and the living, with men and women, and also with little children."

"Where be He?" Flea asked.

"In Heaven," replied Ann, leaning over Flukey. "And He's able even to raise the dead."

Flea grasped her arm.

"Then, if He's everywhere, as ye've jest said, can't ye—"

Flukey opened his eyes.

"If ye know that Man Jesus, well enough," he broke forth, trying to take her hand in his, "if ye ever sees Him to speak to Him, will ye say that, if He'll let my bones get well, and keep my little Flea from Lem, I'll do all He says for me to? Tell Him—tell—tell Him, Ma'm, that my bones be—almost a bustin'."

"Can He help Fluke any if ye ask Him?" Flea questioned.

Ann nodded; but Flea, not satisfied, asked the question directly of Horace.

"I believe so," he hesitated; "yes, I do believe that He can and will help your brother."

64

"Will ye ask Him?" Flea pleaded. "Will ye both ask Him?"

Ann answered yes quickly; and Flea was satisfied with the nod Horace gave her before he wheeled about to the window.

When Flukey was resting under the physician's medicine, Horace and Ann listened to the tale of the squatter children's lives, told by Flea. It was then that Shellington promised her that Squeaky should find a future home on their farm among other animals of the kind, and that he would make it his task to see that the little pig had plenty to eat, plenty of sunshine, and a home such as few little pigs had. Snatchet, too, Horace promised, should be housed in a warm kennel with the greyhounds and blooded pups.

When Flea leaned over Flukey to say goodnight to him, she breathed:

"This be the promised land, all right, Fluke! Ain't we lucky kids to be here?"

CHAPTER TWELVE

With infinite tenderness, Ann led Flea into the pretty blue bedroom. The girl drew back with an exclamation.

"It's too nice for a squatter! But I'm glad you put Fluke in that red place, 'cause it looks so warm and feels warm. But me—"

Ann interrupted hastily.

"You remember my brother saying that you were going to stay here with us until your brother was well?"

Flea assented.

"Then, as long as you are with us, you will be our guest just as though you were my sister. Would you like to be my sister?"

Flea dropped her gaze before the earnest eyes.

"Yep!" she choked. "But I'm a squatter, Missus, and squatters don't count for nothin'. But Fluke—"

"Poor child! She can't think of anyone but her brother," Miss Shellington murmured to herself.

But Flea caught the words.

"He's so good—oh, so awful good—and he ain't never had no

chance with Pappy Lon. If he gets well, we'll work together, and we won't steal nothin' ever no more."

"I feel positive you won't," assured Ann. "You remember, I told you tonight how very good God is to all His children, and you are a child of His, and you know that the Bible says that you must never take anything that doesn't belong to you."

"Nope, I ain't never seen no Bible," faltered Flea.

"Then I'm going to give you one, and you can learn to read it. Wouldn't you be happy if your brother should get well, and you knew that your prayers had done it?"

"It wouldn't be me, Ma'm; 'twould be you and your brother."

Ann considered how she should best begin to open the young mind to truth.

"Child, would you like me to tell you a story?" she asked presently.

"Yep," replied Flea eagerly. "Is it about fairies, or ghosts, or goblins what live near lakes?"

"No; it's about Jesus, who died to save the world."

Then gently and simply Ann told the story of the Passion to the wondering girl, and shortly after left her to sleep.

Miss Shellington went to her brother's study, and he met her with a quizzical smile.

"You've woven a net about yourself, Sis, haven't you?" said he.

"And about you, too, Dear," Ann retorted. "But, Horace, I shouldn't have thought of keeping them, if you hadn't consented."

She looked so troubled, her brow puckered up in thought, that he smiled again.

"Of course, you wouldn't—I know that. But I'm not in the least sorry. We've money enough to do a kindness once in awhile. And as long as you don't work yourself to death over them I sha'n't complain."

They were silent for a little while. Then presently Ann spoke musingly:

"Horace, do those children remind you of someone?"

"I don't know that they do. I'm not a fellow who notices resemblances. Why?"

"I can't tell. Only, when they stood there tonight by the table, looking so forlorn, there was something familiar about them."

"Your dear, tender heart imagined it," Horace declared.

"Possibly. Still, the feeling has been with me ever since. Horace, I've always wanted to do some real work, and don't you think this—"

"Hark!" Horace interrupted. "Wasn't that the bell?"

"Yes, it's Everett, I hope," said Ann, rising, "I thought perhaps he

66

would run in. Yes, I hear his voice! Shall I bring him in here for a few moments?"

"Yes."

When Everett came in, Horace noted that he had lost the frown. Brimbecomb good naturedly demanded if Ann intended to start a kindergarten. He recounted how Mr. and Mrs. Vandecar had received their excuses, and then said:

"Ann, Mrs. Vandecar thought you so charitably inclined. She seemed quite exercised over the story. But you don't intend to keep them here after tomorrow morning, do you?"

"Well, you see, Everett," Ann explained, "Horace and I have talked for a long time about doing some real charity work; so now we're going to try an experiment."

"These boys—"

Ann interrupted. "One of them is a girl."

Horace saw the change on Brimbecomb's face and said hurriedly:

"The girl had on her brother's clothes, that's all."

"Strange proceedings all the way through, though," snapped Everett.

He was showing himself in a new light, and Horace noted that the young lawyer's face bore sarcasm and unpleasant cynicism. He wondered that his gentle, obedient sister had gathered courage to stand against her lover's wishes; for Everett had expressed a decided objection to Ann's working for the squatter children. Suddenly he felt a twinge of dislike for the man before him, and his respect for Ann deepened. How many girls, he reasoned, would have the courage and desire thus to take in two suffering children? He rose quickly and left the room.

Everett took up the argument again with Miss Shellington:

"Ann, you're going very much against my wishes if you keep those children here."

"I'm sorry, Dear," she said simply; "but you know—"

"I know that you won't do anything of which I disapprove, Ann."

"You're mistaken, Everett," Ann contradicted slowly. "I could not allow even you to mark out my duty. And something makes me so anxious to help them! I don't want to go against your wishes; but—I must do as my conscience dictates."

"Surely you don't mean, Ann, that if you were my wife you would force—"

"Please don't, Everett! No, of course not; but this is Horace's home and mine, and, if we desire to share it with someone less fortunate than we are, you shouldn't object."

Everett took up no more time in vain argument; but registered a vow that he would make it warm for the beggars who had thrust themselves upon the Shellingtons. He would search for an opportunity! Impatient and unsettled, he left Ann. She, too, was unhappy; for it had been the first time her duty had ever clashed with her love. The shock of the collision hurt.

The next morning Flea crept into her brother's room and stood looking down at him. He opened his eyes languidly, smiled, and groaned.

"Ain't yer bones any better this mornin'?" asked Flea in an awed whisper.

"Yep; but my heart hurts me. The pains round it be worse than the misery in my knees, 'cause I can't breathe."

Flea bent lower.

"Did the pretty lady tell ye anythin' last night?"

"Nope; did she tell you anythin'?"

"Yep, all about the Jesus. Get her to tell you, Fluke. It's better than fairy stories. I can't remember all of it; but she says He jest loved everybody so well that He let 'em nail Him on a cross, and died there. But He got up again, and that's how He came to be up there."

Flea pointed upward.

"Did Miss—Miss Shellington tell ye that?"

"Yep, Fluke." She hesitated and whispered again, "Do ye believe it, Fluke?"

"Course I do, if she says it! Don't ye think what she says is so?"

"I don't believe all that," replied Flea. "I tried last night, and couldn't. You used to laugh at me when I said as how there was ghosts."

"Mebbe she don't believe in ghosts," sighed Flukey.

"It's almost the same. She believes in Jesus."

"He's all I believe in, too." Flukey closed his eyes wearily.

"Fluke," whispered Flea presently, "ye ought to see that room I slep' in! It were finer'n this one."

"This be the promised land, all right, what Scraggy speaked about," said Flukey. "There ain't no more places like it in this here world."

"I believe that, too," answered Flea, "and if we hadn't been hungry we'd never have stealed, and we wouldn't have found Mr. and Miss Shellington. Yet she says it's wicked to steal."

"So it be, Flea, and ye know it. All ye're tryin' to do now is not to believe about that Jesus. I bet somethin'll come that'll make ye believe it."

"Mebbe," mumbled Flea darkly; "but 's long 's 'tain't Pappy Lon or Lem, I don't care."

CHAPTER THIRTEEN

During the next two weeks, while Flukey was fighting with death, and the great Shellington mansion was as silent as a tomb, Scraggy Peterson was tramping back to the squatter country. When she reached Ithaca, she was almost too ill to start up the Lehigh Valley tracks toward her hut. The black cat clung to her tattered jacket, his wizard-eyes shining green, as Screech Owl passed under the gas-lamps. It was almost ten o'clock at night when she unlatched her shanty door and kindled a fire. The larder was bare, save for some crusts of hard bread. These the woman soaked in hot water and shared with the cat. Then, in a state of great exhaustion, she picked up Black Pussy, blew out the candle, and, for the first time in many days, slept in her own hut.

On the shore below Lem Crabbe's scow was drawn up near the Cronk hut. The squatter and scowman were conversing in the dim light of a lantern that swung from Lem's hook.

"Did ye make any hauls while ye was gone, Lem?" asked Lon.

"Nope, only sold the lumber. I ain't trying nothin' alone."

"It was cussed mean I couldn't go along with ye," Lon said; "but I had to stay to hum. Did ye know that Mammy were dead?"

"Nope!"

"Yep, and buried, too! She fretted over the brats, and kep' a sayin' they was dead in the lake. But I know they jest runned off some'ers."

"I know it, too," Lem grunted savagely. "The gal didn't have no likin' for me."

"I jest see Scraggy come hum," ventured Lon. "She's been gone for a long while. She were a comin' down the tracks."

Lem muttered a savage oath, and faced the scow preparatory to entering. Looking back over his shoulder, he asked:

"Be ye comin' in, Lon?"

"Nope; I'm goin' to bed. Say, Lem, while ye was away, ye didn't get ear of no good place to make a haul soon, did ye?"

"Yep; I tied up to Tarrytown goin' down. There be heaps of rich folks there. Middy Burnes what runs the tug says as how there be a feller there richer than the devil.... Hell! I've forgot his name!"

Lem halted on the gangplank and thought for a moment.

"Nope, I ain't; I jest thought of it!... Shellington! That's him, and he's a fine house, and many's the room filled with—"

Lon broke in upon Lem with a growl:

69

"Then we'll separate him from some of his jewjaws. I bet we has a little of his pile afore another month goes by!"

"That's what I bet, too," muttered Lem. "Night, Lon."

"Night," repeated Lon, walking away.

Lem placed the lantern on the table and sat down to think. Ever since the day Screech Owl had told him of the boy he had wounded so many years before his mind had worked constantly with the thought that he must find the home where his son was. Scraggy was the only human being to tell him. She must tell him! He would make her, if he had to choke the woman to death to get her secret! He remembered how she had mocked at him when she had told him that strange bit of news. Realizing that Scraggy's malady made her difficult to coerce, he decided to try cajolery at once.

Lent rose and took a bit of bread from the cupboard shelf. He slipped it into a bag, caught up the lantern with his hook, and left the scow. He halted in front of Scraggy's dark hut and pounded on the door. The cat, scrambling to the floor inside, was Lem's answer. He knocked again.

"Scraggy! Scraggy!" he called. "It be Lemmy! Open the door!"

Through her deep sleep came the voice Screech Owl had loved, and still loved. She sat up in bed, trembling violently, pushing back with a pathetic gesture the gray hair from her eyes. She had been dreaming of Lem—dreaming that she had heard his voice. But black pussy couldn't have dreamed also. He was perched in the small window, lashing his great tail from side to side. She slid from the bed, stretched out a bony hand, and clutched the cat.

"Did ye hear him, too, black pussy?"

"Scraggy!" called Lem again, "Open the door! I brought you something to eat."

It was the thought of the time when he had loved her so, and not of the food he had brought, that forced Scraggy to the door. She flung it open, and the scowman entered.

"I thought ye might be hungry, Scraggy; so I brought ye this bread," said Lem, lifting the hook and sending a ray from the lantern upon the woman. "Can I set down?"

Could he, this king among men to her, could he sit down in her hut? He could have had her heart's blood had he asked it! Had she not crowned him that day, when he had stood awkwardly by, as she tendered him a dark-haired baby boy? Scraggy's happiness knew no bounds. She forgot her fatigue and set forth a chair for Lem.

"Be ye glad to see me, Scraggy?" asked he presently, crossing his legs and watching her as she lighted some candles.

"More'n glad," she replied simply. "But what did ya come for, Lemmy?"

Lem remained silent for some seconds; then said:

"Do ye want to come back to the scow, Scraggy?"

"Ye mean to live?"

Lem shoved out his hairy chin.

"Yep, to live," said he.

"Did ye come to ask me back, Lemmy?"

"Yep, or I wouldn't have been here. I've been thinkin' our fambly oughter be together."

"Fambly!" echoed Screech Owl wonderingly.

"Yep, Scraggy. We'll get the boy again, and all of us'll live on the scow."

His swarthy face went yellow in the candlelight, and the huge goiter under his chin evidenced by its movements the emotion through which he was passing. Scraggy had sunk to the floor. Now she crawled nearer him, staring at his face with wonder-widened eyes.

"Do ye mean, Lemmy, that ye love yer pretty boy brat well enough to want him on the scow, and that he can eat all he wants?"

"That's what I mean," grunted Lem.

"And that ye mean me to tell him what ye says, Lemmy, and that ye want me to bring him back?"

"Yep."

Scraggy had drawn closer and closer to Lem, her sad face wrinkling into deeper lines. With each uttered word Lem had seen that he had conquered her. Suddenly he dropped his heavy left hand down on the gray head and kept it there.

For the first time in many weary years Scraggy Peterson was kneeling before her man. Now he wanted her! He had asked her to come again to that precious haven of rest, and to bring the child! Scraggy forgot that the babe she had passed through the barge window was grown to be a man, forgot that he might not want to come back to the scow with her and his father.

Lem drew her close between his heavy knees and touched her withered chin with his fingers.

"Where be the brat, Scraggy?" he wheedled.

Screech Owl lifted her head and drew back frightened. Something warned her that she must not tell him where his son lived.

"I'll get him for ye," she said doggedly.

"Where be he?" demanded the scowman.

"I ain't tellin' ye where he be now, Lem." Scraggy's tone was sulky.

"Why?"

71

"'Cause I'll go and get him. I'll bring him to the scow lessen—lessen—"

"Lessen what?" cried Lem darkly.

"Lessen a month," replied Scraggy, "and ye'll kiss the brat, and he'll call ye 'Daddy,' and he'll love ye like I do, Lemmy dear."

Lem was rigid, as the woman smoothed down his shaggy gray hair and patted his hard face. Suddenly he started to his feet.

"Ye say, Scraggy, that ye'll bring the boy lessen a month?"

"Yep, lessen a month. And, Lemmy, he be a beautiful baby! Ye'll love him, will ye, Lemmy?"

"Yep. And now ye take yer cat, Screechy, and get back to bed, and when ye get the boy bring him to the scow." He hesitated a moment; then said, "Ye don't know, do ye, where Flea and Flukey run to?"

Scraggy's face dropped.

"Be they gone?" she stammered, rising.

"Yep, for a long time; and Granny Cronk be dead."

"Then ye didn't get Flea, Lem?"

"Nope. And I don't want the brat, Scraggy; I only want the boy." He spoke with meaning, and when he stood on the hut steps he turned back to finish, "Ye'll bring him, will ye, Owl?"

"Yep, Lemmy love, lessen a month."

Scraggy greedily watched the shadowy form move away in the light of the lantern. "Pussy, Pussy," she muttered, as she closed the door, "black Pussy, come a beddy; yer ole mammy be that happy that her heart's a bustin'."

When Screech Owl, although the happiest woman in the squatter settlement, fell asleep with the cat in her arms, her pillow was wet with tears.

Through long days of anxious waiting for Flukey's recovery, Flea struggled with the Bible lessons Ann set for her each day. Yet she could not grasp the meaning of faith. She prayed nightly; but uttered her words mechanically, for the Savior in the blue sky seemed beyond her conception. In spite of Miss Shellington's tender pleading, in spite of the fact that Flukey believed stanchly all that Ann had told them, Flea suffered in her disbelief. Many times she sought consolation in Flukey's faith.

"Ye see, Flea, can't ye," he said, one morning, "that when Sister Ann says a thing it's so? Can't ye see it, Flea?"

"Nope, I can't. I don't know how God looks. I can't understand how Jesus ruz after he'd been dead three days."

"He did that 'cause He were one-half God," explained Flukey, and then, brightening, added, "Sister Ann told me that if He hadn't

72

been a sufferin' and a sufferin', and hadn't loved everybody well enough, God wouldn't have let Him ruz. 'Twa'n't by anything He did after He were dead that brought Him standin' up again."

"Then who did it?" queried Flea.

"God did—jest as how He said 'way back there when there wasn't any world, 'World, come out!' and the world came. He said, 'Jesus, stand up!' and Jesus stood up. That's as easy as rollin' off a log, Flea."

She had heard Ann explain it, too; but it seemed easier when Flukey interpreted it.

"If I could see and speak to Him once," she mourned, "I could make Sister Ann glad by tellin' her that I knowed He'd answer me."

"Ask Him to let ye see Himself," advised Flukey, "He'll do it, I bet! Will ye, Flea?"

"Nope! I'd be 'fraid if He came and stood near me. I'm 'fraid even now when I think of Him; but 'cause I can't believe 'tain't no reason why you can't, Fluke."

She turned her head toward the door and listened.

"Brother Horace ain't like Sister Ann," she whispered.

"Nobody ain't like her, Flea. She's the best ever!"

"Yep, so she is. But I wish as how—" She paused, and a burning blush spread over her face. "I wish as how Brother Horace had Sister Ann's way of talking to me. I could—"

"Brother Horace ain't nothin' to do with yer believin', Flea."

"Yep, he has, and when he says as how he believes like Miss Shellington, then I'll believe, too. See?"

Then Flea fell into a stubborn silence.

One afternoon in December, Ann and Horace sat conversing in the library.

"I don't see how Mrs. Vandecar can refuse to help you get that child into school, Ann."

"I don't believe she will; but Everett thinks she ought."

"Everett's getting some queer notions lately," Horace said reluctantly.

Ann's heart ached dully—the happiness she had had in her lover had diminished of late. Constantly unpleasant words passed between them on subjects of so little importance that Ann wondered, when she was alone, why they should have been said at all. Several times Brimbecomb had refused to further his acquaintance with the twins.

"I only wish he would like those poor children," said she. "I care so little what our other friends think!"

Shellington pondered a moment. He reflected on Flea's beseeching face as she pleaded for Flukey, and he decided that the censure of all his acquaintances could not take his protection from her.

73

"No, I don't care for the opinion of any of them," he replied deliberately. "I want only your happiness, Sis, and—theirs."

"Wouldn't it be nice if we could find respectable names for them?" Ann said presently. "One can't harmonize them with 'Flea' and 'Flukey.'"

After a silence of a few moments, Horace spoke:

"What do you think about calling them Floyd and Fledra, Ann?"

"Oh, but would we dare do that, Horace?"

"Why not? It wouldn't harm the Vandecars, and the children might be better for it. We could impress upon them what an honor it would be."

"But the Vandecars' own little lost children had those names."

"That's true, too; but I haven't the least idea that either one of them will take offense, if you explain that we think it will help the youngsters."

"Shall I speak with Mrs. Vandecar about it this afternoon?" asked Ann.

"Yes, just sound her, and see what she says."

"I might as well go to her right away, then, Horace. You talk with the little girl about going to school while I'm gone. You can do so much more with her than I can."

"All right," said Horace, "and I feel very sure that we won't have any trouble with her."

After seeing his sister depart, he returned to the library and, before settling himself in a chair, sent a summons to Flea.

When the girl appeared, Horace rose and cast smiling eyes of approval over her.

"That's a mighty pretty dress you have on," said he. "Was it Sister's idea to put that lacy, frilly stuff on it?"

Flea crimsoned at his praise, as she nodded affirmation.

"Sit here in this chair," invited Shellington. "I want to have a little chat with you this afternoon."

Unconsciously Flea put herself into an attitude of graceful attention and gazed at him worshipfully. At that moment Horace felt how very much he desired that she grow into a good woman.

"How do you think your brother is today?" he questioned kindly.

"He's awful sick," replied Flea.

"I fear, too, that he will be very ill for a long time. He was filled with the fever when he came here. Now, my sister and I have been talking it over—"

Flea rose half-hesitantly.

"And ye wants me to take him some'ers else?" she questioned.

Horace motioned again for her to be seated.

74

"Sit down, child," said he; "you're quite wrong in your hasty guess. No, of course, you're not to go away. But my sister and I desire that while you are here you should study, and that you should come in contact with other girls of your own age. We want you to go to school."

"Study—study what?"

"Why, learn to read and write, and—"

"Ye mean I have to leave Flukey, and—and you?"

She had risen and had come close to him, her eyes filled with burning tears. Horace felt his throat tighten: for any emotion in this girl affected him strangely.

"Oh, no! You won't go away from home—at least, not at night; only for a few hours in the daytime. I'm awfully anxious that you should learn, Flea."

She came even closer as she said:

"I'll do anything you want me to—'cause ye be the best ole duffer in New York State!" Then she whirled and fled from the room.

Ann Shellington rang the Vandecar doorbell, and a few minutes later was ushered upstairs. Mrs. Vandecar was in a negligee gown, and Katherine was brushing the invalid's hair.

"Pardon me, Ann dear," said Mrs. Vandecar, "for receiving you in this way; but I'm ill today."

"I'm so sorry! It's I who ought to ask pardon for coming. But I knew that no one could aid me except you in the particular thing I am interested in."

"I shall be glad to help you, if I can, Ann.... There, Katherine, just roll my hair up. Thank you, Girly."

Ann had seated herself, and now spoke of her errand:

"You've heard of our little charges who came so strangely to us not long ago?"

Mrs. Vandecar nodded.

"Horace and I wish to do something for them. It seems as if they had been sent to us by Providence. The lad is very ill, and the girl ought to go to school. We were wondering if you could have her admitted for special lessons to Madame Duval's. The school associations would do such a lot for her." As Ann continued, she marked Mrs. Vandecar's hesitation. "I know very well, Dear, that I am asking you a serious thing; but Brother and I think that it would do her a world of good."

Mrs. Vandecar thoughtfully received the shawl Katherine brought her. Then she looked straight at Ann and said:

"Everett doesn't approve of your work, does he, Ann?"

Miss Shellington colored, and fingered her engagement ring.

"No," she replied frankly; "but it's because he refuses to know

75

them. They're little dears! I've explained to him our views, and have promised that they shall not interfere with any plans he and I may make. I've never seen Horace vitally interested before, or at least so much so. Now, do you think that you would be willing to do this for us? Mildred's going to the school, and you being a patroness will make Madame Duval listen to such a proposal from you."

Mrs. Vandecar turned upon her visitor searchingly.

"Are you doing right, Ann, in taking these children into your home life? I appreciate your good-heartedness; but—"

"Horace and I have talked it all over," interjected Ann, "and we are both assured that we are doing what is right. Won't you think it over, and let us know what you decide? If you find you can't do it—why, we'll arrange some other way."

The plan of naming the children came into her mind; but she hesitated before broaching it. Mrs. Vandecar was a type of everything high-bred and refined. Would it offend her aristocratic sense to have the children named after her and her husband? Ann overcame her timidity and spoke:

"Fledra, there's another thing I wanted to speak of. The children came to us without proper names, and Horace suggested that we call them Floyd and Fledra. Would you mind?"

Mrs. Vandecar drew back a little, a shade passing over her face. A painful memory ever present seized her. Long ago two babies had been called after their father and mother—after her and her strong husband. Could she admit that she did not care? Could she consent to Ann's request? Ann noted her struggle, and said quickly:

"I'm sorry—forgive me, Dear!"

Mrs. Vandecar's face brightened, and she smiled.

"I thought at first that I didn't want you to; but I won't be foolish. Of course, call them whatever you wish. Floyd won't mind, either."

Horace met his sister expectantly.

"Did you ask her about the names, Ann?"

"Yes. At first she was not inclined to either of our plans; but she has such a tender heart."

"So she has," responded Horace.

"She consented about the names; but said that she would send me word about the school."

"And she didn't give a ready consent?"

"No; but I'm almost sure that she will do it. And now about Flea. Did you talk with her?"

"Yes. She consented to go to school, and said—that I was the best old duffer in New York State."

"Oh, Horace! She must be taught not to use such language. It's dreadful! Poor little dear!"

"It'll take sometime to alter that," replied Horace, shaking his head. "They've had a fearful time, and she's been used to talking that way always; she's heard nothing else. You can't alter life's habits in a day."

"But Madame Duval won't have her if she's impudent," said Ann.

"Oh, but she's scarcely that," expostulated Horace; "she doesn't understand. I'll try to correct her sometime."

But he felt the blood come up to his hair as he promised; for it seemed almost impossible to approach the girl with a matter so personal. For the present, he dismissed the thought.

"What about the names, Ann?" he asked.

"As you wish, Dear; Fledra doesn't care."

From that moment, the boy, struggling with fever, and the gray-eyed girl, so like him, were called Floyd and Fledra Cronk.

One morning in January, the day before Flea was to begin her school work, she was passing through the hall that led to the front door. Her face was grave with timidity; although for hours Ann had been trying to fortify the young spirit against the ordeal that was to confront her the following day. Only once had Flea faltered a request that she be allowed to stay at home; but Horace had melted her objections without expelling her fear. To Ann's instructions concerning conduct she had listened with a heavy heart.

Everett Brimbecomb opened the front door as Flea approached it. She stopped short before him, and he drew in a sharp, quick breath. Flea was uncertain just what to do. She knew that he was going to marry Ann, and was also aware that he hated her brother and herself. Ann, however, had taught her to bow, and she now came forward with hesitant grace, and inclined her head slightly. The beauty of Flea made Everett regret that his objections to the twins had been so strenuous; but he would immediately establish a friendship with her that would please both Ann and Horace. He vowed that at the same time he would get some amusement out of it.

"Well! You've blossomed into a girl at last," he said banteringly, "and a mighty pretty one, too! I swear I shouldn't have known that you were one of those boys!"

Flea threw her peculiar eyes over him; but did not speak.

"You're going to school tomorrow, I hear. How do you like that?"

Flea shook her head.

"I don't want to go," she admitted; "but my Prince says as how I have to."

"Your what?"

"My Prince!"

"Your Prince! Who's your Prince?" demanded Brimbecomb.

"Him, back in there," replied Flea, casting her head backward in the direction of the library.

"You mean Mr. Shellington?"

"Yep!"

Everett burst into a loud laugh. At the sound, Horace stepped to his study-door and looked out. His face darkened as he discerned Flea standing against the wall and Brimbecomb looking down at her. He came forward and stationed himself at the girl's side, placing one hand upon her shoulder.

"What's the matter?" he asked.

"Why, little Miss—I'm sure I don't know the child's name," cried Everett breaking into merriment again, "she says you're a—Prince, Horace."

Shellington lowered his eyes to Flea, who was gazing up at him fearfully. She did not look at Everett; but made an uneasy gesture with her hand toward Horace. She had never seemed so appealingly adorable, and inwardly Everett cursed the stupidity that had allowed so many weeks to pass by without his having become Flea's friend.

There was silence, during which the girl locked and unlocked her fingers. Then she relieved it with the frank statement:

"This man here didn't seem to know nothin' about ye; so I told him ye was a Prince."

Ann's voice from the drawing-room caused Everett to turn on his heel, leaving Horace alone with Flea.

For a moment they were both quiet. Flea considered the toe of her slipper. A tear dropped to the front of her dress as Horace took her hand and led her into the library.

"Fledra," he said, using the new name with loving inflection, "what are you crying for?"

"I thought you was mad at me," she shuddered. "That bright-eyed duffer what I hate laughed when I said ye was a Prince. I hate his eyes, I do, and I hate him!"

Shellington did not correct her mistakes in English as he had done so often of late. With shaded remonstrance in his tone, he said:

"Fledra, he is going to marry my sister, and he's my friend."

"He ain't good enough for Sister Ann," muttered Flea stubbornly.

"She loves him, though, and that is enough to make us all treat him with respect."

Turning the subject abruptly, he continued:

"I'm expecting you to work very hard in school, Fledra. You will, won't you?"

"Yes," replied Flea, making sure to pronounce the word carefully.

Horace smiled so tenderly into her eyes that she grew frightened at the thumping of her heart and fled precipitately.

CHAPTER FOURTEEN

Fledra Cronk's school days lengthened slowly into weeks. She was making rapid strides in English, and Miss Shellington's patience went far toward keeping her mind concentrated upon her work. At first some of the girls at the school were inclined to smile at her endeavors; but her sad face and questioning eyes drew many of them into firm friends. Especially did she cling to Mildred Vandecar, and raised in the golden-haired daughter of the governor an idol at whose shrine she worshiped.

One Saturday morning in the latter part of March, Mildred Vandecar persuaded her mother to allow her to go, accompanied by Katherine, to the Shellington home. They found Ann reading aloud to the twins, Flukey resting on the divan. Mildred was presented to him, and in the hour that followed the sick boy became her devoted subject.

The three young people listened eagerly to the story, and after it was finished Ann entered into conversation with Katherine.

Suddenly she heard Flukey exclaim, in answer to some question put by Mildred:

"My sister and me ain't got no mother!"

Miss Shellington colored and partly rose; but she had no chance to speak, for Mildred was saying:

"Oh, dear! how you must miss her! Is she dead? And haven't you any father, either?"

"Yep," said Flukey; "but he ain't no good. He hates us, he does, and worse than that, he's a thief!"

Mildred drew back with a shocked cry. Ann was up instantly; while Fledra got to her feet with effort. She remembered how carefully Ann had instructed her never to mention Lon Cronk or any of the episodes in their early days at Ithaca; but Flukey had never been thus warned.

"Mildred, dear," Ann said anxiously, "Floyd and Fledra were unfortunate in losing their mother, and more unfortunate in having a father who doesn't care for them as your father does for you." She passed an arm about Fledra and continued, "It would be better if we were not to talk of family troubles anymore, Floyd.... Fledra, won't you ask Mildred to play something for you?"

The rest of Mildred's stay was so strained that Miss Shellington breathed a sigh of relief when Katherine suggested going. For a few seconds neither Ann nor Fledra spoke after the closing of the door. It was the latter who finally broke the silence.

"Flukey hadn't ought to have said anything about Pappy Lon; but he didn't know—he thought everybody knew about us.... Are ye going to send us away now?"

The girl's anxiety and worried look caused Ann to reassure her quickly.

In describing the events of the afternoon to her mother, Mildred wept bitterly. When a grave look spread over Mrs. Vandecar's face, Katherine interposed:

"Aunty, while those children undoubtedly had bad parents, they will really amount to something, I'm sure."

It was not until she was alone with Katherine that Mrs. Vandecar opened the subject.

"I'm almost afraid I was incautious to allow a friendship to spring up between this strange child and Mildred. I wish I could see her."

"Ask her here, then. She's very pretty, very gentle, and needs young friends sadly, although the Shellingtons are treating the two children beautifully. If they don't grow up to be good, it won't be Ann's fault, nor Horace's."

"I'll invite the child to come some afternoon, then." With this decision the subject dropped.

That evening Ann went out on a charitable mission, leaving Fledra to deliver a message to Everett and to care for Floyd. The boy was in bed, his thin white hands resting wearily at his sides. For sometime he allowed his sister to work at her lessons. Then he said impetuously:

"Flea, why be these folks always so kind to you and me? They ain't never been mad yet, and I'm allers a yowlin' 'cause my bones and my heart hurt me."

Flea looked up from her book meditatively.

"They're both good, that's why."

"It's 'cause they pray all the time, ain't it?" Floyd asked.

"I guess so."

"I'd a died those nights if Sister Ann hadn't prayed for me, wouldn't I, Flea?"

"Yes," replied Flea in abstraction.

After a silence, Floyd spoke again:

"Flea, do you like that feller what Sister Ann's going to marry?"

The girl dropped a monosyllabic negative and fell to studying.

"Why?" insisted Floyd.

Before Flea could reply, a servant appeared at the door, saying that Mr. Brimbecomb wanted Miss Shellington.

Fledra closed her book and went to the drawing-room, where she found Everett standing near the grate. His brilliant smile made her drop her eyes embarrassedly. She overlooked his extended hand, and made no move to come forward. The girl had always felt afraid of him. Now his presence in the room increased her vague fears. Why she had felt this sudden premonition of evil, she did not know, nor did she try to analyze her feelings. Young as she was, Fledra recognized in him an enemy, and yet his attitude betrayed a personal interest. She had seen him many times during the last few weeks; but had managed to escape him through the connivance of Miss Shellington. Ann had tactfully explained to the girl that Mr. Brimbecomb did not feel the same toward her and Flukey as did her brother; but had added, "It's because he does not know you both, Dear, as Horace and I do."

Once alone with him, she knew only that she wanted to give him Ann's message and return quickly to Floyd. Before she could speak, Brimbecomb passed behind her and closed the door.

"Sister Ann won't be home for an hour," said Flea, turning sharply.

Everett smiled again.

"Sit down, then," he said.

"I can't; I have to study."

Something in the girl's tones brought a low laugh from Everett. He came closer to her.

"You're a deliciously pretty child," he bantered. "Won't you take hold of my hands?"

Placing her arms behind her, Flea answered:

"No, I don't like ye!" She backed far from him, her eyes burning with anger.

"You're a very frank little maid, as well as pretty," drawled Everett. "Ever since I first saw you as a girl, I've wanted to know something about you. Who's your father?"

"None of yer business!" snapped Flea.

"Frank again," laughed the lawyer ruefully. "Now, honestly, wouldn't you like to be friends with me?"

"No! I said I didn't like ye, and I don't! I want to go now. You can sit here alone until Sister Ann comes."

She looked so tantalizingly lovely, so lithely young, as she flung the disagreeable words at him, that Brimbecomb impulsively made a step toward her. He was unused to such treatment and manners. That this girl, sprung from some unknown corner, dared to flaunt her dislike in his face, made him only the more determined to conquer her.

"If I wait until Sister Ann comes," he said coolly, "I shall not wait alone. I insist that you stay here with me!"

"I have to go back to my brother. So let me go by—please!"

Fledra made an effort to pass Brimbecomb; but he grasped her deliberately in his arms. Drawing her forcibly to him, he exclaimed:

"I've caught my pretty bird! Now I'm going to kiss you!"

Flea's mind flashed back to the day when Lem Crabbe had tried to kiss her, and the thought came to her mind that she could have borne that even better than this. She squirmed about until her face was far below his arm, and muttered:

"If you try to kiss me, I'll dig a hole in yer mug!"

Half-mocking at the threat, half-inviting its fulfilment, Everett laughed. Then, with all his strength, he forced Flea's angry, crimsoned face up to his and closed his lips over her red mouth, kissing her again and again. The girl struggled until she was free. In an uncontrollable temper she thrust her hand to Everett's face, and he felt her fingernails scrape his cheek. He released her instantly, stepping back in a gasp of rage and surprise.

Pantingly the girl rubbed her lips with her sleeve.

"If Sister Ann weren't a lovin' ye," she flashed at him, "I'd tell her how cussed mean ye be! If ye ever try to kiss me again, I'll tear yer eyes out, Mister!"

She was gone before he could stop her, and, like a young fury bounded into the presence of Flukey.

"I know why I hate that feller of Sister Ann's," she muttered; "'cause he's bad—he's a damn dog! That's what he is!"

With a startled ejaculation, Floyd half-rose; but Ann's step in the hall sent him back on the pillow gasping.

Fledra sank down at the table, by effort repressing her breath. She heard the door open, and when Miss Shellington entered her red face was bent low over the grammar.

CHAPTER FIFTEEN

A few seconds before, when Miss Shellington had entered the house, she had seen Everett's shadow on the drawing-room curtain; but for the moment her habitual concern for Floyd overrode her eagerness to be with her lover, and she hurried to the sickroom. As was her custom, she took the boy's hand in hers and examined him closely. With her daily observance of him, she had learned to detect the slightest change in his appearance. Now his flushed cheeks and racing pulse told her he was laboring under great excitement.

"Floyd," she exclaimed in dismay, "you've been talking too much! Your face is awfully red!... Why, Fledra, I've cautioned you many times—"

At the girl's apparent unconcern, Miss Shellington left the reproach unfinished. She perceived the scarlet cheeks and flashing eyes peering at her over the open book.

"Is there anything the matter, Fledra?"

The girl let her gaze fall.

"You haven't been quarreling with Floyd?"

"Nope, Sister Ann; Flukey and me never have words."

"I should hope not," Ann replied sincerely; "but, Fledra dear, when I speak to you, please look at me."

With a shake of the black curls, Fledra lifted her face.

"Tell me what is the matter with you," said Ann.

A glint of steel shown in the gray eyes. Flea's lips opened to speak, and for one moment Ann's happiness was threatened with destruction. The girl was on the point of telling her about Everett—then Brimbecomb's voice rang out from the reception-room.

"Ann, dear! Aren't you ever coming?"

Fledra noticed Miss Shellington's face change as if by magic, and saw a lovelight grow in her eyes.

In silence, she received Ann's sorrowful kiss.

"Little sister, I really wasn't scolding you. I was only thinking of how careful we have to be of Floyd. I—I wish you would be kind to me!"

During the painful constraint that followed, Fledra allowed Ann to leave the room; but before she had more than closed the door the girl rose and bounded after her. Impulsively she grasped Miss Shellington's arm and thrust herself in front.

"Sister Ann," she whispered, "I lied to ye! I was mad at Floyd, as mad as—"

Ann placed her finger on the trembling lips.

"Don't say what you were going to, Dear—and remember it is as great a sin to get into such a temper as it is to tell a story."

"Ye won't tell anyone that I fibbed, will ye—Flukey or yer brother, either?"

Everett's voice called Ann again, and she replied that she was coming.

Softly kissing the girl, she said:

"If I loved you less, Fledra dear, I should not be so anxious about you. But I'm so fond of you, child! Now, then, smile and kiss me!"

Fledra flung her arms about the other.

"I keep forgettin'. I'll try not to be bad anymore." Flea turned back into the room, as Ann hurried away at another call from Everett, and muttered:

"If I loved ye less, Sister Ann, I wouldn't have lied to ye."

Floyd's eyes questioned her as she passed him.

"Fluke," said she, coming to a halt, "I told Sister Ann I was mad at you, and I wasn't. You won't tell her, will ye?"

"No," replied Flukey wonderingly, "I won't tell her nothin'."

Flea said no more in explanation, and sat again at the study table. She was still bent over her book when Shellington opened the door and glanced in. The boy's eyes were closed as if in sleep, and Horace beckoned to Flea. She rose languidly and walked to him.

"As your brother is sleeping, Fledra," he murmured, "come into the library and talk to me awhile."

There were traces of tears on Fledra's face when Horace ushered her into the study.

"Now, little girl, sit down and tell me about your lessons. I've been so busy lately that I haven't had time to show you my interest.... You've been crying, Fledra!"

"Yes, I got mad, and Sister Ann talked to me."

"Will you tell me why you became angry?" he queried.

Flea had not expected this, and had no time to think of a reason for her anger. Deliberating a moment, she placed her head on her arm. It would be dangerous to tell him about Brimbecomb. If the bright-eyed man in the drawing-room had only let her go before kissing her—if he had only remembered his love for Ann! She knew Horace was waiting for her to speak; but her mind refused absolutely to concoct a reasonable excuse, and she could not tell him a deliberate lie, as she had to Ann.

For what seemed many minutes Horace looked at her.

"Fledra," he said at length, "am I worthy of your confidence?"

His question brought her up with a jerk. Would she dare tell him? Would he be silent if he knew that Sister Ann was being perfidiously used? She was sure he would not.

"If I tell you something," she began, "you won't never tell anybody?"

"Never, if you don't want me to."

She leaned forward and looked straight at him.

"I just lied to Sister Ann," she said.

Horace's face paled and he grasped the arms of his chair. Presently he asked sharply:

"Why did you lie to my sister, Fledra?"

"I just did, and you said you wouldn't tell."

"Was it because you lied to her that you cried?"

She tossed his question over in her mind. She intended to be truthful to him, unless a falsehood were forced from her to shield Ann.

"I cried because Sister Ann was so good to me."

"Are you going to tell me what caused you to be untruthful?" he asked persistently.

Fledra shook her head dismally.

Immeasurable compassion for the primitive, large-eyed child flooded his soul, and his next words assumed a more tender tone.

"Of course, you don't mean that you are going to keep it from me?"

Her dark head suddenly dropped again, and a smothered storm of sobs drew him closer to her. In the silence of arrested speech, he reached for her fingers, which were twisting nervously in the webby lace on her dress. With reluctance Flea permitted herself to be drawn from her chair.

"Fledra, stand here—stand close to me!" said he.

Obediently she came to his side, hiding her face in one bended arm. He could feel the warmth of her bursting breaths, and he could have touched the lithe body had he put out his hand. And then—and not until then—did Horace know that he loved her. Yesterday she had seemed only a child; but at this moment she was transformed into a woman, and his sudden passion gave him a lover's right to pass his arm about her. In bewilderment Flea checked her tears and drew back. He had never before caressed her in any way.

Horace stood up, almost mastered by his new emotion.

"Fledra," he breathed, "Fledra, can't you trust me? Dear child, I love you so!"

Stunned by his words, Fledra stared at him. His voice had vibrated with something she had never heard before. His eyes were brilliant and pleading.

"Fledra, can't you—can't you love me?"

85

As if by strong cords, her tongue was tied.

"Listen to me!" pursued Horace. "I know now I loved you that first night I saw you—that night when you came into the room with Ann's—"

He stopped at the name of his sister—he had forgotten for the moment Flea's confession of the falsehood to her. Then the seeming injustice done Ann turned his mind to the probing he had begun at first for the cause of Flea's grief. Intermingled with this was a whirl of thought as to the things that the girl had accomplished. Her entire submission to Ann and himself, her devotion to Floyd, her desire to master the difficult problems of her new life, all persuaded him that for his happiness he must know the cause of her agitation. Spontaneously he pressed his open hands to her cheeks.

"Fledra, Fledra! Can I believe you?"

The girl lowered her head and nodded emphatically.

"Do you—do you love anyone else—I mean any man?"

His rapidly indrawn breath came forth with almost an ejaculation. Flea's eyes sought his for part of a minute. Then slowly she shook her head, a shadow of a smile broadening her lips. With effort she lifted her arms and whispered:

"I don't love anyone else—that is, no man! Be ye sure that ye love me?"

Like an impetuous boy he gathered her up, caressing her hair, her eyes, her lips. With sudden passion he murmured:

"Fledra! Fledra dear!"

"I do love ye!" she whispered. "Oh, I do love ye every bit of the day, and every bit of the night, jest like I did when you came to the settlement and I saw ye on the shore!"

Hitherto she had not told him that she had seen him in Ithaca, and he did not understand her allusion to a former meeting. To his astonished look, she replied by a question.

"Don't ye remember one day you came to the settlement and asked the way to Glenwood?"

Horace conjured up a vision of a child of whom he had asked his road, and remembered, in a flashing glance at the girl in his arms, that he had inwardly commented upon the sad young face. He had noted, too, the unusual shade in her eyes, and now he wondered vaguely that he had not loved her then.

"I remember—of course I remember! Oh, I want you to say again that you love me, little dearest, that you love me very much!" His lips roved in sweet freedom over her face as he continued, "You're so young, so very young, to have a sweetheart; but if you could only begin to love me—in a few years we could be married, couldn't we?"

86

Flea's body grew tense with tenderness. She had never heard such beautiful words; they meant that her Prince loved her as Ann loved Everett, as good men loved their wives and good wives loved their husbands. Instead of answering, she lifted a pale face intensified by womanly passion.

"Will ye kiss me?" she breathed. "Kiss me again on my hair, and on my eyes, and on my lips, because—because I love ye so!"

His strong avowal had opened a deep spring in her heart which overflowed in tears. The taut arms pressed him tightly. The words were sobbed out from a tightened young throat. The very passion in her, that abandonment which comes from the untutored, stirred all that was primeval in him, all the desperate longing in a soul newly born. His mouth covered hers again and again; it sought her closed white lids, her rounded throat, and again lingered upon her lips. After a few moments he sat down and drew her into his arms.

"Little love, my heart has never beaten for another woman—only for you, always for you! Fledra, open your eyes quick!"

The brown-flecked eyes flashed into his. Horace bent his head low and searched them silently for some seconds.

"I must be sure, Dear, that you love me. Are you very sure?"

"Yes, yes! That's why I felt so bad tonight, when I told ye about lying to Sister Ann." There was entreaty in her glance, and her figure trembled in his arms. Horace started slightly. He had again forgotten her admission.

"But you will tell me all about it now, won't you, Fledra? Then we can tell Ann and your brother about our love."

Flea stood up; but Horace still kept his arm about her. Her thoughts flew to Everett. How unfaithful he had been! Could she confide in Horace, now that she was absolutely his? No; for he would punish Everett even the more to the detriment of Ann. The thought set her teeth hard. Had she been Ann, and Horace been Everett, had the man she loved been unfaithful to the point of stealing kisses from another—She took a long breath.

But she was not Sister Ann, neither was Horace, Everett. In a twinkling everything that Horace had been to her since the first day in Ithaca flooded her heart with happiness. Her dreamy imagination, which had enshrined him king of her life, worked with a new desire that nothing should interfere with the love that he had showered upon her. He had said, "Do you love me, Dearest?"

The anxious question had thrilled her vibrant being to silence, had stilled her eager tongue with the magnitude of its passion. Horace was pleading with his eyes, imploring her to answer him. Suddenly he burst out:

87

"You will tell me, Dear, why you were untruthful to my sister?"

Fledra pondered for a moment.

"Something happened," she began, "and Sister Ann came in—I was mad—"

"Were you angry at what happened?"

"Yes."

Horace led her on.

"And did Floyd know what had happened?"

"No."

"And then?" he demanded almost sharply.

"And then Sister Ann asked me what was the matter, and I lied, and said I was mad at Floyd."

Horace still held her. This sweet possession and desire of her filled him with serious decision. He deliberated an instant on her confession.

"Now you've told me that much," said he, "I want to know what happened."

"I can't tell ye," she said slowly, "I can't, and ye said that ye wouldn't tell anybody about it."

Horace's arms loosened. Surely she could have no good reason for keeping anything from him! Suddenly he grasped her tightly to him and kissed her again and again.

"Of course you'll tell me, of course you will! Tell me all about it. I won't have this thing between us! I can't, I can't! I love you!"

It maddened her to hear him chide her thus, filled as she was with all the primeval qualities of the native woman to feel the strength of her man. How his pleading touched her, how gravely his dear face expressed an anxiety that she herself was unable to banish! Even should he send her from him, she could not be false to Ann. To this decision the strong, untutored mind clung, and again she refused him.

"No, I'm not goin' to tell you. Mebbe someday I will; but not now."

She heard him take a deep breath which tore savagely at all the best within her. It wrestled with her affection for Miss Shellington, for her duty to Floyd's friend. Not daring to glance up, she still stood in silence. Horace's voice shocked her with the sternness of it.

"You've got to tell me! I command you! Fledra, you must!" Then, tilting her chin upward, he continued reproachfully, "If you're going to keep vital things from me, you can't be my wife!"

The resistance against telling him grew faint in her heart in its battle for desirable things.

"Ye mean," she asked, with quick intaking of breath, "that I can't be your woman if I don't tell you?"

A flush crawled to his forehead as the rich young voice flung the question at him. She was so maddeningly beautiful, so young and clinging! But she must bend to his will in a thing like this! In his desire to set her right, he answered somewhat harshly.

"You must tell me; of course, you must!"

Fledra threw him a glance, pleading for leniency. She had expected him to importune, to scold, but in the end to trust. Suddenly, in the girl's imagination, Ann's gentle face bending over Floyd rose in its loving kindness.

"Then—then," she stammered, "if you won't have me, unless I tell you—then I'll go now—please!"

She left him with pathetic dignity, and her last glance showed his eyes, too, filled with a strange pain.

CHAPTER SIXTEEN

The next week held unutterable pain for Flea, each twenty-four hours deepening her unhappiness more and more. She made no effort to talk with Shellington, nor did she mention her sorrow to Ann. It did not seem necessary to her that she should again speak to Horace of going away. When she had last suggested it, he had said that nothing she could do would alter his decision about his home being hers until Floyd should be well. Nevertheless, an innate pride surged constantly within her. Any deprivation would be more welcome than the studied toleration that, she thought, she encountered in Horace.

One morning she stood looking questioningly down at her brother.

"How near well are ye, Fluke?"

"Ain't never goin' to get well!" he replied, shivering. "'Tain't easy to get pains out of a feller's bones when they once get in."

"If you do get well soon, I think we'd better go away."

"Why?" demanded Flukey.

"Because we wasn't asked to stay only till you got well."

"Don't ye believe it, Flea! Ye wasn't here last night. Brother Horace and Sister Ann thought I was to sleep, and I wasn't."

"What did they say?" broke in the girl, with whitening face.

"Sister Ann told Mr. Shellington about yer work at school, and he said—as how—"

Floyd waited a moment before continuing, and Flea crept closer to the bed. She was crying softly as she knelt down and bent her face over her brother. The boy passed his hands through the black curls.

"What's the matter, Flea?"

"I want to know what my Prince said to Sister Ann."

"Be ye crying about him?"

"Yes!"

"Ye love him, I bet!"

Flea buried her face deeper into the soft counterpane; but she managed to make an affirmative gesture with her head.

Floyd was silent, and sometime passed before he heard the girl's smothered voice:

"And I'm goin' to love him always—even after we go away!"

"We ain't goin' away," said Floyd.

"Who said so?"

"Mr. Shellington."

"When?"

"Last night."

Fledra lifted her head and grasped the boy's thin hands in hers.

"You're sure it was last night, Fluke?"

"Yep, I be sure. I was layin' here with my face to the wall. When Sister Ann comes in nights, if I don't say anything, she thinks I be asleep, and she kisses me, and I like her to do that. Last night, when she'd done kissing me, Mr. Shellington came in, and then they talked about us."

"And he didn't say we was to go away?"

"No."

Fledra rose in sudden determination, and in her excitement spoke with swift reversion to the ancient manner.

"Flukey, ye be the best da——"

Flukey thrust up a reproving finger which stopped the oath.

"Flea!" he cautioned.

"I were only goin' to say, Flukey," said Flea humbly, "that ye be the best kid in all the world. Don't tell anybody what I said about my Prince."

She went out quickly.

With her hand upon her heart, Flea halted before the library. She knew that Horace was there; for she could hear the rustling of papers. At her timid knock, he bade her enter. Her tongue clove so closely to the roof of her mouth that for a minute she could not speak. She held out her fingers, and Horace took them in his. His face whitened at her touch; but he gazed steadily at her.

"You've—you've something to say to me, Fledra—sweetheart?"

The hope in his voice rang out clearly. Fledra nodded.

"What?"

He was determined she should explain away the black thing that had arisen between them.

"I didn't come to tell ye about what happened," said she; "but to say that, if ye don't smile and don't touch me sometimes, I'll die—I know I will!" Her tones were disjointed with emotion, and she felt the hands holding hers tighten.

"I can't smile when I'm unhappy, Fledra. I can't! I can't! This past week has been almost unbearable."

"It's been that way with me, too," said Flea simply.

"Then why don't you make us both happy by being honest with me? If you didn't care for me, I should have no right to force your confidence; but you really do, don't you?"

"Yes; but I'm never goin' to marry ye, because mebbe I can't never tell ye. I think ye might trust me. It's easy when ye love anyone. I say, ye couldn't marry me without, could ye?" She seemed to suddenly grow old in her sagacious argument. Horace shook his head sadly.

"We'd never be happy, if I should," said he, "because—because I couldn't trust you."

"Oh, I want ye to trust me!" she wept. "I want ye to! Won't you once more? Please do! Won't ye forget that anything ever happened—won't ye?"

For a moment her supplication almost unnerved him; but he thought of their future, of the necessity of having unlimited faith and honor between them, and again slowly shook his head.

Suddenly the twisting hands worked themselves loose from his, and in another instant her feverish arms tightly encircled his neck. By the weight of Flea's body, Horace Shellington knew that her feet were no longer on the floor, each muscle in the rigid girl having so well done its part that she hung straight-limbed against him. Close to his face drew hers, and for a space of time, the length of which he could never afterward accurately measure, he forgot everything but the maddening expression in her face. Her eyelids were closed, and her breath came hot upon his lips.

"I want ye to kiss me like ye did that night—kiss me—please—please—" In her low voice was illimitable strength and passion.

Like burning rivers, his blood was driven through his veins. He

91

flung out his arms and crushed her to him. Just then his lips found hers.

"Dear God! How I—how I love you!" he breathed.

Fledra's arms relaxed and slipped from his shoulders.

"Then forget about what happened!" she panted.

All the bitter apprehensions of the last week swept over him at her words. His love battled with him, and he wavered. How gladly would he have dispelled every doubt and listened to her pleading!

"But I want you to tell me, Fledra."

Flea backed slowly from him.

"I can't.... I can't.... I can't tell anybody!"

The man ran his fingers across his forehead in bewilderment. In his bitter disappointment he turned away.

"When you come to me," his voice broke into huskiness, "when you tell me what happened that night before you saw my sister, I shall—I shall love you—forever!"

Then came a single moment of critical silence; but it needed only the thought of Ann for the girl to toss aside his plea and turn upon her heel.

"I don't want Sister Ann to know that I love ye," she said sulkily. "Ye won't tell her?"

"No, no, of course not—not yet!" He dropped into his chair, his head falling forward in his hands. "I wouldn't have believed," he said from between his fingers, "that my love for you—"

Flea stopped him with an interruption:

"Are ye trying to stop lovin' me?"

Horace shook his shoulders, lifting swift eyes to hers. He noted her expression irrevocable in its decision of silence. She was extraordinarily lovely, and he grew suddenly angry that he had not the power to change her, to draw from her unresistingly the story she had locked from his perusal.

"Don't be foolish, Fledra!" he said quite harshly. "A man can't love and unlove at will. I feel as if I should never know another happy moment!"

For several days Ann watched her brother in dismay. He had grown taciturn and gloomy. The boyish energy had left him. She ventured to speak to Everett about it.

"He doesn't seem like the same boy at all," she said sadly, after explaining. "I can't imagine what has caused the change in him."

Everett remembered Shellington's face as it had bent over Fledra, and smiled slightly.

"Have you ever thought lately that he might be in love?"

92

"In love!" gasped Ann. "No, I know that he isn't; for it was only at the time of the Dryden Fair that he told me he cared for no one."

"He might have changed since then," Everett said quizzically.

"But he hasn't met anyone lately," argued Ann. "I know it isn't Katherine; for—for he told me so."

"I know someone he met at the fair."

Ann, startled, glanced up.

"Who? Do tell me, Everett! Don't stand there and smile so provokingly. If you could only understand how I have worried over him!"

Brimbecomb put on a grave face.

"Haven't you a very pretty girl in the house who is constantly under his eye?"

Still Ann did not betray understanding.

"Don't you think," asked Everett slowly, "that he might have fallen in love with—this little Fledra?"

An angry sparkle gleamed in Ann's eyes.

"Don't be stupid, Everett. Why, she's only a child. It would be awful! Horace has some sense of the fitness of things."

Everett thought of the evening he himself had succumbed to a desire to kiss Flea.

"No man has that," he smiled, "when he is attracted toward a pretty woman."

"But she isn't even grown up."

How little one woman understands another! In his eyes Fledra had matured; for his masculinity had sought and found the natural opposite forces of her sex. These thoughts he modified and voiced.

"Not quite from your standpoint, Ann; but possibly from Horace's."

Pale and distressed, Ann got to her feet.

"Then—then, of course, she must go," she said with decision. "I can't have him unhappy, and—Why, such a thing could—never be!"

She could scarcely wait for Everett to depart; but suppressed her anxiety and delicately turned the subject out of deference to Horace. She listened inattentively as Brimbecomb explained some new cases that he was soon to bring to court, and kissed him when he bade her goodnight. Then, with beating heart, she sought her brother.

Unsmilingly, Horace asked her to be seated. His face was so stern that she dared not at once speak of the fears Brimbecomb had raised in her mind; but at last she said:

"Horace, I've been thinking since our last talk about the children—" His sharp turn in the desk-chair interrupted her words; but she paused only a moment before going on resolutely. "Don't you think that I might put Floyd in a good private hospital where he would be taken care of, and Fledra—"

His face turned ashen. Her fears were strengthened, and, although her conscience stung her, she continued, "Fledra's getting along so well that I would be willing to put her in a boarding school."

"Are you tired of them, Ann?"

"Oh, no—no, far from that! I love them both; but I thought it might be pleasanter for you, if we had our home to ourselves again."

Horace looked at his sister intently.

"Are you keeping something back from me, Ann?" he demanded.

"Scarcely keeping anything from you, Dear; but I want you to be happy and not to—" Horace rose in agitation, and quick tears blurred Ann's sight.

"Is there anything I can do for you, Dearest?" she concluded.

"No!"

Reluctantly she left him, troubled and perplexed.

CHAPTER SEVENTEEN

Lem Crabbe had cunningly planned to keep Scraggy under his eye and follow her to the hiding place of their son. He realized that the lad was a man now; but so much the better. He would obtain money from him, or he would bring him back to the scow and make him a partner in his trade. In spite of his wickedness, Lem had a strong longing for a sight of his child. Many times he had meditated upon the days Scraggy had lived in the barge, and, although he had no remorse for his cruelty to her, he had regretted the death of his boy. To be with him, he would have to tolerate the presence of Scraggy for awhile. He felt sure that Flea had gone from him forever, and the loneliness of his home made him shiver as he entered it a few nights after his conversation with Scraggy.

He had been in the boat but a few moments when he heard Lon's whistle and called the squatter in.

"I thought we'd make them plans for Tarrytown," Cronk said

presently. "We might as well get to work as to be lazin' about. Don't ye think so?"

"Well, I were a thinkin' of stayin' here for awhile," stuttered Lem.

"What for?"

"Nothin' perticular."

"Ye know where that rich duffer's house be what ye heard Middy Burnes speak about?"

"Yep. It ain't far from the graveyard. I thought as how we could crawl in there while we was waitin' for night."

A strange look passed across Lon's face.

"Ye mean to hide in the cemetray?" he asked.

"Yep. Be ye afeared?"

"I ain't got no likin' for dead folks," muttered Cronk.

He added nothing to this statement; but said after a moment's silence:

"Scraggy ought to go dead herself some of these days, 'cause she's allers a runnin' about in the storms. I see her ag'in tonight a startin' out for another ja'nt. She had her bundle and her cat and was makin' a bee line for Ithaca."

Lem glanced up quickly.

"I've changed my mind, Lon," he grunted. "I'll go to Tarrytown any day yer ready."

Accordingly, they took a week to prepare their burglar's kit, which they had not used for sometime, and ten days after the slipping away of Screech Owl, Lon Cronk and Lem Crabbe left the squatter settlement and made their way to Tarrytown.

The once happy household of the Shellingtons had turned into a gloomy abode. Ann was nonplused at the strange behavior of her brother and the unusual reserve of Flea. Floyd from his bedroom endeavored to bring the home to its former cheerfulness; but, with all Ann's energies and the boy's tireless tact, the change did not come. At length Miss Shellington gave up trying to bring things to their usual routine. She spent her day hours in helping Fledra with her school studies and giving Floyd simple lessons at home. Everett came every evening, taking Ann from the sickroom. This left Fledra free to study quietly beside her brother.

One Thursday, after dinner, Horace went by invitation to Brimbecomb's home to play billiards. Of late the young men had not passed much of their time together; for business and the presence of Fledra and Floyd in his house had given Horace less time for recreation. After a silent game they sat down to smoke. For many

95

minutes they puffed without speaking. Everett finally opened the conversation.

"It seems more like old times to be here together again."

"Yes, I've missed our bouts, Everett."

"You've been exasperatingly conservative with your time lately!" complained Everett. "A fellow can't get sight of you unless your nose is poked in a book or you're in court!"

Horace laughed.

"Really, I've been awfully busy since—"

"Since the coming of your wonderful charges!" finished Brimbecomb.

Horace scented a sneer. His ears grew hot with anger.

"Ann has done more than I," he explained; "although there is nothing I would not do."

"I can't understand it at all, old man! Pardon me if I seem dense, but it's almost an unheard-of thing for a fellow in your and Ann's positions to fill your home with—beggars." His voice was low, with an inquiring touch in it. Having gained no satisfaction from Miss Shellington, he was seeking information from Horace.

"We don't think of either one of them as beggars," interjected Horace. "Both Ann and I have grown very fond of them."

In former days the two young men had been on terms of intimacy. Everett presumed now upon that friendship by speaking plainly:

"Are you going to keep them much longer?" he asked.

Horace allowed his lids to droop slowly, and looked meditatively at the end of his cigarette without replying.

"I have a reason for asking," Everett added.

"And may I ask your reason?"

"Yes, I suppose so. The fact is, I'm rather interested in them myself. I thought—"

Horace lifted his eyes, and the man opposite noted that they had grown darker, that they sparkled angrily. Everett was desirous of satisfying himself whether Horace did, or did not, care for the young girl he was sheltering.

"They don't need your interest so far as a home is concerned," Horace said at last.

Everett's face darkened as he mused:

"They're lowly born, and such people were made for our servants, and not our equals. If the women are pretty, they might act as playthings."

Horace turned his eyes toward the speaker wrathfully. He

wondered if he had understood correctly what was implied by the other's words.

"What did you say, Brimbecomb?"

Everett drew his left leg over his right knee deliberately.

"I think the girl pretty enough to make a capital toy for an hour," said he.

Disbelief flooded Shellington's face.

"You're joking! You're making a jest of a sacred thing, Brimbecomb!"

Everett recalled former principles of the boy Horace, and a smile flickered on his lips.

"I can't concede that," said he. "I think with a great man of whom I read once. Deal honestly with men in business, was his maxim, keep a clean record with your fellow citizens; but, as far as strange women are concerned, treat them as you wish. It's a man's privilege to—to lie to them, in fact."

Without looking up, Horace broke in:

"Ann has an excellent outlook for happiness, hasn't she?"

"We weren't talking about Ann," snapped Everett. "I was especially thinking of the girl in your home, who belongs leagues beneath where you have placed her. I won't have her there! I think my position is such that I can make certain demands on the family of the woman I'm going to marry."

"To the devil with your position! I wouldn't give a damn for it, and I'll take up your first question, Brimbecomb. You asked me how long I intended to keep those children. This is my answer! As long as they will stay, and longer if I can make them!" His voice rang vibrant with passion. "Don't let your position interfere with what I am doing; for, if you do, Ann, friendship, or anything won't deter me from—"

Brimbecomb rose to his feet and faced the other.

"Threats are not in order," said he.

His deliberate speech made Horace turn upon him.

"I, too, intend to marry!" was his answer. "I intend to marry—Fledra Cronk!"

Brimbecomb ejaculated in anger.

"If you will be a fool," said he, "it's time your friends took a hand in your affairs. I think Governor Vandecar will have something to say about that!"

"No more than you have," warned Horace. "The only regret I have is that Ann has chosen you for her husband. I'm wondering what she would say if I repeated tonight's conversation to her—as to a man lying to a woman."

"She wouldn't believe you," replied Everett.

97

"And you would deny that you so believed?"

"Yes. I told you it was my right to lie to a woman."

"Then, by God! you're a greater dog than I thought you! Let me get out of here before I smash your face!"

Everett's haughty countenance flamed red; but he stepped aside, and Horace, shaking with rage, left the house.

"I think I've given him something to think about," muttered Everett. "He won't be surprised by anything I do now, and I've protected myself with Ann against him, too."

It was only when alone with Everett that Ann felt completely at her ease. Then she threw aside the shadow that many times dismayed her and looked forward to her wedding day, which was to come in May. This evening she was sitting with her betrothed under the glow of a red chandelier.

"You know, Ann, I haven't given up the idea of finding my own family," said Brimbecomb presently. "The more I work at law, the more I believe I shall find a way to unearth them. I told Mr. and Mrs. Brimbecomb that I intended to spend part of my next year looking for them. Mrs. Brimbecomb said she didn't know the name under which I was born. I'm convinced that I shall find them."

"I hope you do, Dear."

"You don't blame me, do you, Ann, for wanting to know to whom I'm indebted for life?"

"No," answered Ann slowly; "although it might not make you any happier. That is what I most wish for you, Dearest—complete happiness."

Everett lifted her delicate fingers and kissed them.

"I shall have that when you are my wife," he said smoothly.

Later he asked, "Did you speak with Horace of the matter that worried you, Ann?"

Miss Shellington sighed.

"Not in a personal way," she replied; "but I really think there is more than either you or I know. Fledra never puts herself in Horace's way anymore; in fact, they have both changed very much."

"Possibly he has told her that he cares for her, and she has—"

Ann shifted from him uneasily. "If Horace loves her, and has told her so, she could not help but love him in return. She is really growing thin with hard work, poor baby!"

"Does she love Horace?" sounded Everett.

"I can't tell, although I have watched her very closely."

A strange grip caught Everett's heart. He could not think of the small, dark girl without a pang of emotion. He had made no effort to

98

see Fledra; yet he was constantly wishing that chance would throw her in his path. Later, he intended in some way to bring about another interview. He dared not write her a letter, although he had gone so far as to begin one to her, but in disgust at himself had torn it up. The fact that Horace was unhappy pleased him, now that they had become antagonistic.

The mystery clinging to Fledra haloed her for Everett beyond the point of interest.

"Ann," he said suddenly, "you haven't told me much about those children—I mean of their past lives."

"We know so little," she replied reservedly.

"But more than you have told me. Have they parents living?"

"A father, I think," murmured Ann.

"And no mother?"

"No."

"Do you know where their father is?"

"He lives near Ithaca, so we're told." After a silence she continued, "We want them to forget—to forget, ourselves, all about their former lives. I asked Horace if he wanted to place them in schools; but he didn't want them to go away. As long as they are as good as they have been, they're welcome to stay. Poor little things, they're nothing more than babies, not yet sixteen!"

"The girl looks older," commented Everett.

"That's because she's suffered more than most girls do. I'm afraid it'll be a long time before Floyd is completely well."

The conversation then drifted to that happy spring day when they would be married.

CHAPTER EIGHTEEN

From the window of the drawing-room in his home Everett threw a glance into Sleepy Hollow and listened to the wind weeping its tale of death through the barren trees. The tall monuments were as spectral giants, while here and there a guarding granite figure reared its ghostly proportions. But the weird scenery caused no stir of superstition in the lawyer.

In hesitation, Everett stood for some seconds, the snow falling silently about him; for he was still under the mood that had come upon him during Ann's parrying of his curiosity concerning the squatter children. As he paused, the Great Dane, in the kennel at the back of the house, sent out a hoarse bark, followed by a deep growl. So well trained was the dog that nothing save an unfamiliar step or the sight of a stranger brought forth such demonstrations. Everett knew this, and walked into the garden, spoke softly to the animal, and, noting nothing unusual, ran up the back steps. The door opened under his touch, and he stepped in. The maids were in the chambers at the top of the house, and quietude reigned about him. The young master went into the drawing-room, stirred the grate fire, and sat down with a book. For many moments his eyes did not seek its pages. His meditations took shape after shape; until, dreaming, he allowed the book to rest on his knees.

Everett was perfectly satisfied with his success as a lawyer. He had proved to others of his profession in the surrounding county that he was an orator of no little ability and preeminently able to hold his own in the courtroom.

He could not have desired or chosen a better wife than Ann promised to be; but something riotous in his blood made him dissatisfied with affairs as they stood now. Manlike, he reflected that, if he had been allowed to caress Fledra as he had desired, he would have been content to have gone on his way. He wondered many times why his heart had turned from Ann to another. Something in every thought of Fledra Cronk sent his blood tingling and set his heart to leaping. His dreams melted into pleasurable anticipations, and he tried to imagine the windings of his future path. Chance had always been kind, and he wondered whether an opportunity to win the affections of the small, defiant girl in the Shellington home would be given him. A strain in his blood called for her absolute subjection—and, subdue her he would; for he felt that an invincible passion slept in her tempestuous spirit.

Suddenly, from the direction of the cemetery, an owl sent out a mournful cry, and a furious baying from the dog behind the house sounded. He rose, walked to the window, and surveyed the bleak view through the curtains. He again noted the tall trees threshing in the wind, and the looming monuments. Still under the spell of pleasant day-dreams, Everett silently contemplated the gloomy aspect. He had forgotten the owl and its harsh cry.

So deeply was he engrossed in his meditations that he did not hear the stealthy turning of the door-handle, and it was not until a distinct hiss reached his ears that he turned. A woman, dripping with water, her gray hair hanging in wet strings about a withered face, stole toward him. Everett was so taken aback by the sight of her and the hissing, cross-eyed cat perched on her shoulder that he could not speak. A newly born superstition rose in his heart that the woman was a wraith. Yet an indistinct memory made her black eyes familiar. He did not move from the window, and Screech Owl sank to the floor.

"Little 'un," she whispered, "I've comed for ye, little 'un!"

The sound of her hoarse voice stirred Everett's senses. He gave one step forward, and the woman spoke again:

"I telled yer pappy that I'd bring ye!"

Brimbecomb shook his shoulders, his dread deepening. What was the witch-like woman saying to him, and why was she calling him by the name he now remembered she had used before? She crept nearer on her knees, her thin hands held up as if in prayer, and, with each swaying movement of her the cat shifted its position from one stooped shoulder to the other.

Everett found his voice, and asked sharply:

"How did you get into the house?"

Scraggy put up her arm, drew the snarling cat under it, and looked stupidly at the man. She was so close that he could see the steam rising from her wet clothes, and the hisses of the animal were audible above his own heavy breathing. Screech Owl smoothed the cat's bristling back.

"Pussy ain't to hiss at my own pretty boy!" she whispered. "He's my little 'un—he's my little 'un!"

A premonition, born of her words, goaded Everett to action.

"Get up!" he ordered. "Get up and get out of here! Do you want me to have you arrested?"

Scraggy smiled.

"Ye wouldn't have yer own mother pinched, little 'un. I'm yer mammy! Don't ye know me?"

He moved threateningly toward her; but a snarl from the furious cat stayed him.

"You lie! You crazy fool! Get up, or I'll kick you out of the house! Get out, I say! Every word you've uttered is a lie!"

"I don't lie," cried Scraggy. "Ye be my boy. Ain't ye got a long dig on ye from—from yer neck to yer arm—a red cut yer pappy made that night I gived ye to the Brimbecomb woman? The place were a bleedin' and a bleedin' all through your baby dress. Wait! I'll show ye where it is." She scrambled up and advanced toward him.

Everett made as if to strike her.

101

"Get back, I say! I would hate you if you were my mother! You can't fool me with your charlatan tricks!"

The woman sank down, whimpering.

Again Everett sprang forward; but again the cat drove him back.

"Go—go—now!" he muttered. "I can't bear the sight of you!"

There were tones in his voice that reminded Scraggy of Lem, and her heart grew tender as she thought of the father waiting for his child.

"Ye won't hate yer pappy, if he does hate me. He wants ye, little 'un. I've come to take ye back to yer hum. He won't hurt ye no more."

Everett stared at her wildly. Was the delicious mystery that had surrounded him for so many years, which had occupied his mind hour upon hour, to end in this? He would not have it so!

"Get up, then," he said, his lips whitening, "and tell me what you have to say."

Scraggy lifted herself up. Her boy wanted to hear more about his father, she thought.

"I gived ye to the pretty lady with the golden hair when yer pappy hurt ye, and I knowed ye again; for the Brimbecomb's name was on the boat that took ye. Yer pappy didn't know ye were a livin' till a little while ago, and he wants ye now."

"Were you married to him, this man you call my father?" demanded Everett.

Scraggy shook her head.

"But that don't make ye none the less his'n, an' ye be goin' with me, ye be!"

Everett no longer hoped that the woman was either mistaken or lying. The stamp of truth was on all she had said. He knew in his heart that he was in the presence of his mother—this ragged human thing with wild, dark eyes and straggling hair. And somewhere he had a father who was as evil as she looked. For years Everett had struggled against the bad in his nature; but at that moment he lost all the remembrance of the lessons of his youth, of the goodness taught him by his foster father and mother. It flashed into his mind how embarrassed Mrs. Brimbecomb had been when he had constantly brought up the subject of his own family, and how impatiently Mr. Brimbecomb had waved aside his petitions for information. They should never know that he had found out the secret of his birth, and he breathed thanks that they were not now in Tarrytown. Neither Ann nor Horace should ever learn of the stain upon him; but the girl with the black curls should make good to him the suffering of his new-found knowledge! She came of a stock like himself, of blood in which there was no good.

Everett forgot the dripping woman before him as a dark thought

102

leaped into his mind. He could now be at ease with his conscience! Of a sudden, he felt himself sink from the radius of Horace Shellington's life—down to the birth level of the boy and girl next door. It dawned upon him, as his mind swept back over his boyhood days, that Horace had ever been better than he, with a natural abhorrence against evil.

When Scraggy again spoke, he turned burning eyes upon her. How he hated her, and how he hated the man who called himself his father, wherever he might be! He shut his teeth with a grit, and, unmindful of the cat, bent over Screech Owl. He forced her head so far back that she moaned and loosened her hold upon Black Pussy, who sprang snarling into the corner.

"If you ever repeat that story to anyone, that I'm your son, I'll kill you! Now go!"

Scraggy began to cry weakly, and Black Pussy howled as if in sympathy.

"Shut up, and keep that cat quiet! You'll draw down the servants. Now listen to me! You say you're my mother—but, if you ever breathe it to anyone, or come round here again, I shall certainly kill you!"

The thoughts began to scurry wildly in Scraggy's head. Everett's threat to kill her had not penetrated the demented brain, and his rough handling had been her only fright. She could think of nothing but that Lem was waiting for them at the scow.

She dragged herself away from Everett, and with a torn skirt wiped her ghastly face. She dropped the rag to grope dazedly for the cat, and whispered:

"Ye can do anything ye want to with yer ole mammy, if ye'll come back with me to Ithaca!"

"Ithaca, Ithaca!" Everett repeated dazedly. "Was that child you spoke of born in Ithaca?"

"Yep, on Cayuga Lake."

"Get up, get up, or I'll—I'll—" His voice came faintly to Screech Owl, and she moaned.

The man's mind went back to his Cornell days when he had been considered one of the richest boys in the university. His sudden degradation, the falling of his family air-castles, made him double his fists—and with his blow Scraggy dropped into a motionless heap.

His bloodshot eyes took in her prostrate form, guarded by the fluffed black cat, and his one thought was to kill her—to obliterate her entirely from his life. He stepped nearer, and Black Pussy's ferocious yowl was the only remonstrance as he stirred Scraggy roughly with his foot.

The thought that her boy did not want to go with her coursed slowly through the woman's brain. She knew that without him Lem

103

would not receive her. She longed for the warmth of the homely scow; she wanted Lem and the boy—oh, how she wanted them both! She half-rose and lunged forward. Brimbecomb's next blow fell upon her upturned face, stunning her as she would have made a final appeal. The woman fell to the floor unconscious, and Everett kicked Black Pussy into the hall. There was a snarling scramble, and when he opened the front door the cross-eyed cat bounded out into the night.

Everett returned hastily to the drawing-room after a covert search of the hall for disturbers. In the doorway he hovered an instant, and then advanced quickly to the figure on the floor. Lifting the limp woman, he bore her out of the house and down the slushy steps. With strength that had come through the madness of his new knowledge, he threw the body over into the graveyard and bounded after it. Once more then he took Scraggy up, and, stumbling frequently in the half-light, carried her to the upper end of the cemetery. Here he deposited the body in a snow-filled gully by a vault. Ten minutes later he was staring at his mirrored reflection in his own room, convinced that, if he had not already killed her, the woman would be dead from exposure before morning. The cat had disappeared, and all traces of the night's visitation had been removed.

Several hours before, Lem Crabbe and Lon Cronk had slunk into Tarrytown. The snow still fell heavily when they made their preparations to enter the home of Horace Shellington. About five in the afternoon they had worked their way against this sharp north wind to Sleepy Hollow Cemetery and had entered it. Until night should fall and sleep overtake the city, they planned to remain there quietly. Not far from the fence they took up their station in an unused toolhouse, smoking the next hours away in silence.

When ten o'clock neared, Lem stole out; but he came back almost immediately, cursing the wild night in superstitious fear.

"The wind's full of shriekin' devils, Lon," he said, "and 'tain't time for us to go out. Be ye afeard to try it, old man?"

"Nope," replied the other; "but I wish we had that cuss of a Flukey to open up them doors, or else Eli was here. This climbin' in windows be hard on a big man like me and you with yer hook, Lem."

Lem grunted.

"I'll soon have a boy what'll take a hand in things, with us, Lon," he said, presently. "I ain't sayin' nothin' jest yet; but when ye see him ye'll be glad to have him."

"Whose boy be he?" demanded Lon.

"Ain't goin' to tell."

Lon ceased questioning, dismissing the subject with a suggestion that he himself should reconnoiter the ground. He left Lem, groped his way among the gravestones for several yards, and brought up abruptly at the fence. From here he eyed the Brimbecomb mansion for some minutes; then he cast his glance to the steps of the Shellington home beyond. After a few seconds a young man ran down the stairs, and Lon slunk back to Lem in the toolhouse. An instant later both men were startled by the cry of an owl. Lem rose uneasily, while Lon stared into the darkness.

"That weren't a real owl, were it, Lon?" Lem muttered.

"Nope," growled Lon; "it sounded more like Scraggy."

He looked at the one-armed man with suspicion.

"Can't prove it by me," said Lem darkly.

"Do ye know where she ever goes to?" demanded Cronk.

Lem shook his head in negation.

Crabbe dared not venture out again alone; for apprehension rose strong within him. He knew that Scraggy had left the settlement to find their boy. Had she come to Tarrytown for him? The two men crouched low, and talked no more during some minutes. Finally, Lon, bidding Lem follow him, lifted his big body, and they left the toolhouse. The squatter led the way to the fence. They stood there for a time watching in silence. Two shadows appeared upon a curtain of the house before them. A man was lifting a woman in his arms, and the downward fall of her head gave evidence of her unconsciousness. As the front door opened, the squatter and the scowman retreated to their quarters. When Everett Brimbecomb threw the body of Screech Owl into the cemetery, both were peering out. They saw the man carry the figure off into the shadows, marking that he returned alone. Neither knew that the other was Scraggy; but, with a lust for mystery and evil, they slipped out with no word. Lon made off to view the Shellington home once more, and Lem disappeared in the direction from which Everett had come, easily following the tracks in the snow. Coming within sight of the vault, Lem rounded it fearfully. On the ground he saw the woman, and as he looked she rose to a sitting position.

Screech Owl was just recovering her battered senses. She was still dazed, and had not heard the scowman's footsteps, nor did she now hear the mutterings in his throat. Faintly she called to Black Pussy; but, receiving no response from the cat, she crawled deeper into the shadows of the vault and tried to think. Her fitful whining brought Lem from his hiding place.

"Be that you, Owl?" he whispered.

"Yep. Where be the black cat?"

"I dunno. Where ye been? And how'd ye get here?"

Scraggy leaned back against the marble vault in exhaustion.

"I dunno. Where be I now?"

Lem bent nearer her, shaking her arm roughly.

"Ye be in Tarrytown. Did ye come here for the brat?"

"What brat be ye talkin' 'bout, Lem?"

"Our'n, Screechy. Weren't ye here lookin' for him?"

Through the darkness Lem could not see the crazed expression that flashed over Scraggy's face. She thrust her fingers in her hair and shivered. The blow of Everett's fist had banished all memory of the boy from her mind; but Lem lived there as vividly as in the olden days.

"We ain't got no boy, Lem," she said mournfully.

"Ye said we had, Screechy, and I know we have. Now, get up out of that there snow, or ye'll freeze."

The scowman helped Screech Owl to her feet, and supported her back over the graves to the toolhouse.

"Ye stay here till I come for ye, Scraggy, and don't ye dare go 'way no place. Do ye hear?"

Screech Owl uttered an obedient assent, and Lem left her with a threat that he would beat her if she moved from the spot. Then he crawled along the Brimbecomb fence, and saw Lon leaning against a tree, some distance down the road.

CHAPTER NINETEEN

After Everett's departure, Ann tripped into Floyd's room in a happier state of mind than had been hers for several days. It had been her habit to kneel beside the boy at night and send up a petition for his recovery. Now she would thank God for his goodness to her,—Everett had come to be more like himself, and Floyd's welcoming smile sent a thrill of joy through her. As Ann entered, Fledra looked up from her book. Her pale, beseeching face drew Miss Shellington to her.

"Fledra dear, you study too late and too hard. You don't look at all well."

"I keep tellin' her that same thing, Sister Ann," said Floyd; "but she keeps mutterin' over them words till I know 'em myself."

106

Miss Shellington turned Fledra's face up to hers, smoothing down the dark curls.

"Go to bed, child; you're absolutely tired out. Kiss me goodnight, Dear."

Fledra loitered in the hall until she heard Miss Shellington leave Floyd; then she stole forward.

"Will you come to my room a little while, Sister Ann?"

Without a word, Ann took the girl's hand; together they entered the blue room.

Fledra wheeled about upon Miss Shellington, when the door had been, closed.

"Do you believe all those things you pray about, Sister Ann?" she appealed brokenly.

Ann questioned Fledra with a look; the girl made clearer her demand by adding:

"Do you believe that Jesus hears you when you ask Him something you want very, very bad?"

She looked so miserable, so frail and lonely, that Ann put her arms about her.

"Sit down here with me, Fledra. There! Put your little tired head right here, and I'll tell you all I can."

"I want to be helped!" murmured Fledra.

"I've known that for sometime," Ann said softly; "and I'm so happy that you've come to me!"

"It's nothin' you can do; but I was thinkin' that perhaps Jesus could do it."

Ann pressed the girl closer.

"Is it something you can't tell me?"

Fledra nodded.

"And you can't tell my brother?"

The girl's nervous start filled Ann with dismay; for now she knew that the trouble rested with Horace. She waited for an answer to her question, and at length Fledra, crestfallen, blurted out:

"I can't tell anybody but—"

"Jesus?" whispered Ann.

"Yes; and I don't know how to tell Him."

Ann thought a moment.

"Fledra, if you wanted someone to do something for you, about which that person knew nothing, wouldn't you have to tell it before it could be granted?"

Fledra nodded.

"Then, that's what you are to do tonight. You are to kneel down here when I am gone, and you are to feel positively sure that God will

107

help, if you ask Him in Jesus' name. Do you think you have faith enough to do that?"

"I don't know what faith is," replied Fledra in a whisper.

"I'll tell you what it is, Dear. Now, then, don't you remember how my brother and I prayed for Floyd?"

Fledra pressed Ann's arm.

"And don't you remember, Dear, that almost immediately he was helped?"

"You had a doctor," said Fledra slowly.

"Yes, for a doctor is God's agent for the good of mankind; but we had faith, too. And in something like this—Is your trouble illness?"

"Only here," answered Flea, laying her hand upon her heart.

Ann could not force Flea's confidence; so she said:

"Then if it is impossible to confide in Horace, or in me, will you pray tonight, fully believing that you will be answered? You must remember how much Jesus loved you to come down to suffer and die for you."

"I don't believe I thought that story was true, Sister Ann." Fledra drew back, and looked up into Ann's shocked face as she spoke, "I shouldn't say I believed it if I didn't, should I?"

"No, Darling; but you must believe—you surely must! You must promise me that you will pray first for faith, then for relief, and tomorrow you will feel better."

"I promise," answered Fledra.

For many minutes after Ann had left her, the girl lay stretched out upon the bed. Her heart pained her until it seemed that she must go directly to Horace and confess her secret.

She got up slowly at last, and, kneeling, began a whispered petition. It was broken by sobs and falling tears, by writhings that tore the tender soul offering it.

Fledra prayed for Horace, and then stopped.

After a time she rose, having done all a girl could do for those she loved, and, undressing, slowly crawled into bed. Through the darkness as she lay looking upward she tried to imagine what kind of a being God was, wondering if He were kindly visaged, or if, when His earthly children sinned, He looked as Horace had looked when she confessed the lie told to Ann. In her imagination, she framed the Savior of the world like unto the man she loved when he smiled upon her, and then she believed, and believed mightily. In likening Jesus to Horace—in bringing the Savior nearer through the lineaments of her loved one— she gathered out of her unbelief a great belief that He could, and would, smooth away all the troubles that had arisen in her life.

That night she turned and tossed for several hours, praying and weeping, weeping and praying, until from sheer fatigue she lay perfectly quiet. Suddenly she sat up and listened. The stupor of slumber dulled her hearing, and she struggled to catch again the sound that had awakened her. From somewhere across the hall she heard a faint click, click, which sounded as though some mechanic's tool were being used.

Fledra slipped from the bed and opened the door stealthily. She crept along the hall in her bare feet, terrified by the muffled sound, and stopped before the velvet curtains that were drawn closely across the dining-room doorway. Someone was tampering with the silver chest.

For a moment terror almost forced Fledra back to her room without investigating; but the thought that somebody was stealing Ann's precious family plate caused her to slip her fingers between the curtains and peep in.

The lock of the steel safe was lighted by the rays of a dark-lantern, and Fledra could see two shadowy figures on the floor before it. One held the light, while the other turned a small hammer machine containing a slender drill. The girl did not have the courage to scream a warning to Horace and the servants, and before she could move of a sudden one of the men whispered:

"The damn thing is harder'n hell, Lem. I guess I'll take a crack at this here hinge."

The name awoke the senses of the trembling girl, and instantly she knew the man who had spoken to be Lon Cronk. A chill gathered round her heart and froze the very marrow in her bones. She dropped the curtain and fled back to her room. Standing against the door, she pressed her hands over her face to stifle the loud breathing. Lem and Lon were robbing the house! She would be forced then to let thieves have the contents of the safe; for, if Pappy Lon knew that she and Flukey were housed there, he would take them away. But, if he made off with the plate, no one would ever know who had done it, and her sick brother would still be safe in Ann's care.

"I won't go to 'em. I won't! I won't! They can take the whole thing for all of me!"

She turned sharply as though she had heard a voice that had made answer to her. With her faculties benumbed by the terror of the men in the dining-room, and yet remembering that her grief had been subdued, she turned her face upward, and fancied she saw the Christ-man, so like Horace, descending into the room. But the face, instead of smiling at her, looked melancholy and sad.

It was the dawn of a lasting belief in the Son of God, her first real vision of Him. She gazed steadily at the beautiful apparition, and then said haltingly:

"I'm goin' back to stop 'em, and if Pappy Lon takes me back to the squatter settlement then help me if ye can, dear Jesus!"

The struggle was over, and with rigid desperation Fledra again opened the door and stepped into the hall. Gliding swiftly along to the entrance of the dining-room, she flung aside the curtains and appeared like a shade before Lem and Lon.

The squatter saw her first; but in the semidarkness did not recognize her. He lifted his arm, and a flash of steel sent her trembling backward.

"Don't open yer mug, Kid, or I'll shoot yer head off!"

Then he recognized her, and stepped back to Lem's side.

"It's Flea, it's Flea Cronk!" he gasped.

The girl advanced into the room.

"What do you want here, Pappy Lon? Did you come to steal?"

She saw Lem grimacing at her through the rays of the lantern. The scowman looked so evil, so awful, as he grinningly raised his steel hook, that her faith very nearly fled. Crabbe's heavy face was working with violent emotion. His full neck moved with horrid convulsions, while a discord of low noises came from his throat. The girl, clad in her white nightgown, under which he could trace the slender body, filled him again with passionate longing.

"By God! it's little Flea!" he exclaimed at last.

"Yep," threw back Lon. "We found somethin' we didn't expect—eh, Lem?"

"Did you come to steal?" Fledra demanded again, this time looking at the canal-man.

"Yep; but we didn't know that you was here, Flea."

"Then you won't take anything—now, will you?"

"We don't go till you come with us, Flea!" Lon moved nearer her as he spoke. "Ye be my brat, and ye'll come home with yer pappy!"

Fledra choked for breath.

"I can't go with you tonight," she replied, bending over in supplication. "Flukey's sick here, and I have to stay."

"Sick! Sick, ye say?" Cronk exclaimed.

"Yes, he's been in bed ever since we left home, and he can't walk, and I won't go without him."

"I'll take ye both," said Lon ferociously. "I'll come after ye, and I'll kill the man what keeps ye away from me! I'm a thinkin' a man can have his own brats!"

Fledra did not set up an argument upon this point. She wanted to

110

get the men out of the house, so that she might think out a plan to save her brother and herself.

"Ye'll have to let Flukey stay until he gets well, and then mebbe we'll come back."

"There ain't no mebbe about it," growled Lon. "Ye'll come when I say it, and Lem ain't through with ye yet, nuther! Be ye, Lem?"

Never, since the children had left his hut, had Lon felt such a desire to torture them. The dead woman seemed to call out to him for revenge. The wish for the Shellington baubles and the money he might find was nothing compared to the delight he would feel in dragging the twins back to Ithaca. Granny Cronk was there no longer, and everything would go his way! He put out his hand and touched Crabbe.

"We ain't goin' to steal nothin' in this house, Lem," he said sullenly; "but I'll come tomorry and take the kids. Then we be done with this town. Ye'll get yer brother ready by tomorry mornin'. Ye hear, Flea?"

"Yes," answered Flea dully.

"If Flukey be too sick to walk, he can ride. I've got the money, and all I want be you two brats, and, if ye don't come when I tell ye to, then it'll be worse for them what's harborin' ye. And don't ye so much as breathe to the man what owns this house that we was here tonight— or—I'll kill Flukey when I get him back to the shanty!"

His glance took in the beautiful room, and, unable to suppress a smile, he taunted:

"I'm a thinkin' ye'll see a difference 'tween the hut and this place—eh, Flea?"

"And between this and the scow," chuckled Lem.

"Yep, 'tween this an' the scow," repeated Lon. "Come on, Lem. We'll go now, an' tomorry we'll come for ye, Flea. No man ain't no right to keep another man's kids."

Fledra's past experiences with her squatter father were still so vivid in her mind that she made no further appeal to him; for she feared to suffer again the humiliation of a blow before Lem. She stood near the table, shivering, her teeth chattering, and her body swaying with fright and cold. To whom did she dare turn? Not to Ann or to Horace; for Lon had forbidden it. To tell Flukey would only make him very ill again. Lon was advancing toward her as these thoughts raced through her mind. She drew back when he thrust out one of his horny hands.

"I ain't a goin' to hit ye, Flea; but I'm goin' to make ye know that I ain't goin' to have no foolin', and that ye belong to me, and so does Flukey, and that, when I come for ye, ye're to have yer duds ready."

Lem neared the open window, and Lon turned to follow him.

111

For fully three minutes after they had gone, the girl stood watching the black hole through which they had disappeared, where now the snow came fluttering in. Then she crept forward and lowered the window noiselessly. With swift footsteps she ran back through the hall and into the bedroom. After turning on the light, she drew on a dressing-gown and slipped her feet into a pair of red slippers.

Somewhere from the story above came the sound of footfalls, and then the creaking of stairs. The girl stood holding her hand over her beating heart. A servant, or possibly Ann, had heard the noises and was coming down. Suddenly into her mind came the prayer Floyd loved.

"Gentle Jesus, meek and mild, look upon a little child."

She said the words over several times; but had ceased whispering when a low knock came upon her door. She opened it, and saw Horace standing in his dressing-gown and slippers. For a moment she looked at him with almost unseeing eyes, and her lips moved tremulously, as if she would speak and could not. Horace, noticing her agitation, spoke first.

"Fledra, I thought I heard you. I looked down and saw a light shining from your window. Is anything the matter?"

Fledra could not find her voice to reply. She had not expected him, and, locking her fingers tightly together, she stood wide-lidded and trembling.

"Were you speaking to someone?" asked Horace.

"Yes, I was. I was speaking to Jesus just before you came. I was asking Him to help me."

The man looked at the red gown hanging over her white nightrobe, the tossed black curls, and the pale, sensitive face before he said:

"Fledra, whatever is the matter with you? Surely, there is something I can do."

"Sister Ann said I would be happier, and we all would, if I asked Jesus; and I was askin' Him jest now."

Horace eyed her dubiously.

"It is right to ask Him to help you, of course; but, child, it isn't right for you to act toward me as you do."

Fledra was so desirous of his love and confidence that she made as if to speak. She took two steps forward, then hesitated. Remembering Ann and the care she had given Floyd, her hand fell convulsively on the door, and she tried to close it. She dared not tell him of Lon's midnight visit to the home, and wondered if he would give her up to her squatter father, and let Flukey be taken back to the settlement.

"I told ye the truth when I said I was prayin'," she said; "but I was

112

thinkin', too, if it was right for a father to have his own children, if he was to ask for 'em."

Horace, not understanding her enigmatical words, regarded her gravely.

"What a queer girl you are, anyway, Fledra!" he exclaimed. He spoke almost irritably. He felt like grasping her up and shaking her as one might an obstreperous child.

His moody silence made Fledra repeat her words.

"I'm sure I don't know what you mean," Horace answered; "but, I suppose, if a father's children were being kept from him, he could take them if he wished. Fledra, look at me!"

She raised her gaze slowly, her somber eyes smiting the watching man as might a blow. Her beseeching expression arrested the bitter speech that rose to his lips. As the memory of her hard work gripped him, he bent forward and took her slim, cold hand in his.

"Fledra, I want you to pay attention to what I am going to say. I feel sure that you want to be a good girl. If I were not, I could not bear it. Even if you don't trust me, I'm going to help you all I can, anyway."

"And pray," gasped Fledra, "pray, Brother Horace, that I can be just what you want me to be, and that I can stay with Floyd in your house!"

The girl closed the door quickly in his face, and Shellington moved slowly away, racking his brain for some solution of the problem.

With their minds in a perturbed state, Lem and Lon passed silently back into the cemetery. The shock of the girl's appearance had awed them both. They were nearing the toolhouse before Scraggy came into Lem's mind.

The whole situation was changed, now that Flea was coming to him. It was the same to him whether she wanted to come or not; nor did it matter that he had promised Screech Owl that she should be in the scow. He still wanted his boy to help him with his work; but Scraggy was a person wholly out of his life.

The two men halted in front of the shed.

"There be a woman in there," said Lem in a low voice.

"What woman?" asked Lon.

"Scraggy."

"Scraggy! How'd she come in here?"

"I took her in," said Lem. "She were the woman what that guy throwed over the fence."

Lon pushed his companion aside and pressed through the small doorway. He cast the light of the lantern about; but no Screech Owl was in sight.

"If Scraggy was over here, Lem," he said doubtfully, "then she's gone. We'd better scoot and get a place to stay all night."

CHAPTER TWENTY

When Fledra entered the breakfast room it was evident to both Ann and Horace that she had had no sleep. Dark rings had settled under her eyes. The girl had decided that Lon would make good his threat against the person who should try to keep his children from him, and, if she went to school, Lem and her father might come when she was gone. As they rose from the table, she said sullenly:

"I'm not goin' to school anymore. I don't like that place. I want to stay at home."

"Are you ill, Dear?" asked Ann, coming forward.

"No, I'm not sick; but I can't go to school."

Horace's brow darkened.

"That's hardly the way to speak to my sister, Fledra," he chided gently.

Ann glanced at him in appeal. Fledra was standing before them, and her eyes dropped under his words.

"If I asked you to let me stay home," she said in a low tone, "you'd both say I couldn't; so I just had to say that I won't go."

Fledra knew no other way to stand guard over the houseful of loved ones. If Lon were to come while she was gone, he might take her brother. If she told Horace that thieves had entered his home, and if she named them, that would draw fatal consequences down on Floyd. She could only hold her peace and let matters take their course. At any rate, she did not intend to go to school. Now she cast a quick glance at Ann; but kept her eyes studiously from Horace. Noting Miss Shellington's entreating face, Fledra flung out her hands.

"I didn't want to be mean," she said quickly; "but I want you to let me stay home today. Can I? Please, can I?"

"There! I knew that you'd apologize to my sister," Horace said, smiling.

At this, Fledra turned upon him. He had never felt a pair of eyes affect him as did hers. How winsomely sweet she was! It came over him in a flash that he had not dealt quite justly with her; so he smiled again and held out his hands.

During the morning Fledra crept ghostlike about the house. She strained her eyes, now at one window and then at another, for the first glimpse of Lon. The luncheon hour came and passed, and still the thieves gave no sign of coming. Horace had returned from his office

114

early in the afternoon, and was smoking a cigar in the library, when suddenly a loud peal of the doorbell roused him. Fledra, too, heard it distinctly. She was sitting beside Floyd; but had not dared to breathe their danger to him. Her cheeks paled at the sound, and she rested silent until presently summoned to the drawing-room.

"What's the matter?" asked her brother.

"Nothin', Fluke, lay down, and if ye hear anyone talkin' keep still. Somebody's coming."

"Somebody comes every day," answered Floyd. "That ain't nothin'. What ye doin', Flea?"

She was standing at the door with her ear to the keyhole. She heard the servant pass her, heard the door open, and Lon's voice asking for Mr. Shellington. Then she slid back to Flukey, trembling from head to foot.

"Ye're sick, Dear," said the boy. "Get off this bed, Snatchet! Lay down here by me, Flea and rest."

The girl dropped down beside him and closed her eyes with a groan. Floyd placed his thin hand upon her, and Fledra remained silent, until she was summoned to the drawing-room.

"Who wanted me?" Horace asked the question of the mystified servant.

"I didn't catch the name, Sir. I didn't understand it. He's a dreadful-looking man."

Horace rose, put down his cigar, and walked into the hall.

Lon Cronk was waiting with a shabby cap in his hand. He bowed awkwardly to Shellington, and essayed to speak; but Horace interrupted:

"Do you wish to see me?"

"Yep," answered Lon, glancing sullenly over the young lawyer. "I've come for my brats."

"Your what?"

"My kids, Flea and Flukey Cronk."

Horace felt something clutch at his heart. Fledra's radiant face rose before his mental vision, and he swallowed hard, as he thought of her relation to the brutal fellow before him.

"Walk in here, please," he said.

Then he bade the servant call his sister.

Miss Shellington obeyed the summons so quickly that her brother was indicating a chair for the squatter as she walked in. At sight of the uncouth stranger she glanced about her in dismay.

"Ann," said Horace, "this is the father—of—"

Ann's expression snapped off his statement. She knew what he would say without his finishing. She remembered the stories of terrible beatings, and the story of Fledra's fear of a wicked man who wanted her for his woman. The boy's words came back to her plainly. "And he weren't goin' to marry her nuther, Mister, and that's the truth." Nevertheless, she stepped forward, throwing a look from her brother to the squatter.

"But he can't have them—of course, he can't have them!"

Lon had come with a determination to take the twins peaceably if he could; he would fight if he had to. He had purposely applied to Shellington in his home, fearing that he might meet Governor Vandecar in Horace's office. As long as everyone thought the children his, he could hold to the point that they had to go back with him. He would make no compromise for money with the protectors of his children; for he had rather have their bodies to torment than be the richest man in the state. He had not yet avenged that woman dead and gone so many years back. At thought of her, he rose to his feet and smiled at Ann with twitching lips.

"Ye said, Ma'm, that I couldn't have my brats. I say that I will have 'em. I'm goin' to take 'em today. Do ye hear?"

"He can't have them, Horace. Oh! you can't say yes to him!"

Horace's mind turned back to Fledra, and he mentally blessed the opportunity he had to protect her.

"I don't think, Mr. Cronk, that you will take your children," he said, "even granted that they are yours. I'm not sure of that yet."

Lon's brown face yellowed. Had they discovered the secret that he had kept all the dark, revengeful years?

Horace's next words banished that fear: "I shall have to have you identified by one of them before I should even, consider your statement."

Cronk smiled in relief; and Ann shuddered, as she thought of Flukey's frail body in the man's thick, twisting fingers.

"That be easy enough to do. Jest call the gal—or the boy."

"The boy is too ill to get up," said Ann huskily; "and I beg of you to go away and leave them with us. You don't care for them—you know you don't."

"Who said as how I don't care for my own brats?"

"The little girl told me the night she came here that you hated her, and also that you abused them."

"I'll fix her for that!" muttered Lon.

"I don't believe you'll touch her while she is with me," said Horace hotly. "I shall send for the girl, and, if you are their father, then—"

"They can't go!" cried Ann.

116

"I haven't said that they could go, Ann. I was just going to say to Mr. Cronk that if they wanted to go of course we couldn't keep them. Otherwise, there is a remedy for him." Horace leaned over toward the squatter and threw out his next words angrily, "There's the law, Mr. Cronk! Ann, please call Fledra."

The girl responded with the weight of the world on her. Had some arrangements been made for her and Floyd between Horace and Lon? She knew that Ann was there, and that Mr. Shellington had been talking with the squatter long enough to decide what should be done. She walked slowly to the door, her head spinning with anxiety and fear. For one single moment she paused on the threshold, then stepped within.

Drop by drop, the color went from her cheeks, leaving them waxen white. She threw the squatter an unbending opposing glance.

"Did you come for Fluke and me, Pappy Lon?" she stammered.

Her lips trembled perceptibly; but she went forward, and, taking Ann's hand in hers, stood facing Cronk.

Lon looked her over from head to foot. First, his gaze took in the pretty dark head; then it traveled slowly downward, until for an instant his fierce eyes rested on her small feet.

"Yep," he replied, raising a swift look, "I comed for ye both—you and Flukey, too. Go and git ready!"

Fledra dared not appeal to Horace. He stood so quietly in his place, making no motion to speak, that she felt positive that he wished her to go away. She was too dazed to count up the sum of her troubles. Her face fell into a shadow and grew immeasurably sad. Lon was glowering at her, and she read his decision like an open page. The dreadful opposition in his shaggy brown eyes spurred Fledra forward; but Ann's arms stole about her waist, and the slender figure was drawn close. A feeling of thanksgiving rushed over the girl. How glad she was that she had kept the secret of Everett's unfaithfulness!

"Sister Ann," she gasped, "can't ye keep us from him? Fluke nor me don't want to go, and Pappy Lon don't like us, either. I couldn't go—I'd ruther die, I would! He'd make me go to Lem's scow! Ye can see I can't go, can't you?" She wheeled around and looked at Horace, her eyes filled with a frightened appeal. Shellington's glance was compassionate and tender.

"I not only see that you can't go," said he; "but I will see to it that you don't go. Mr. Cronk, I shall have to ask you to leave my house."

"I don't go one step," growled Lon, "till I get them kids! Where's Flukey?" He made a move toward the door; but Horace thrust his big form in front of him.

117

"The boy shall not know that you are here," said he. "I shall keep it from him because he's ill, and because a great worry like this might seriously harm him. It might even kill him."

Lon's temper raced away with his judgment.

"What do I care if he dies or not? I'm goin' to have him, dead or alive!"

Shellington noted the hatred and menace in the other's tones, and he smiled in triumph.

"It's about as I thought, Mr. Cronk. You care no more for these children than if they were animals. That statement you just made will go against you at the proper time, all right. Please go now, and remember what I've said, that you have the law. And remember another thing: if you do fight, I shall bring everything I can find against you, if I have to ask the aid of Governor Vandecar. I see no other course open to you. Good-day, Sir."

Cronk glared about until his gaze rested upon the two girls. His eyes pierced into the soul of Fledra. She shuddered and drew closer to Miss Shellington. The squatter walked toward the door, and once more looked back, an evil expression crossing his face and settling in deep lines about his mouth.

"Ye remember what I told ye, Flea, the last time I seed ye! I meant what I said then, and I say it over again!"

The emphasis upon the words struck terror to Fledra's sensibilities. But, with new courage in her eyes, she advanced a step, and, raising a set face, replied:

"Ye can't have us, Pappy Lon—you can't! I'll take care of Flukey, and Mr. Shellington'll take care—of—me."

CHAPTER TWENTY-ONE

Horace set his teeth firmly as he closed the door, upon Cronk. Through the door window he saw the squatter take his lumbering way down the steps, and noticed that the man paused and looked back at the house. The heavy face was black with baffled rage, and Lon raised his fist and shook it threateningly. If Horace had been determined in the first instant that the squatter should not get possession of the twins, he was now many times more resolute to keep to his decision. For his life, he could not imagine Lon Cronk the father of his young charges.

He returned to the drawing-room, and found Ann and Fledra still together, the girl's face hidden in Miss Shellington's lap.

"Horace," cried Ann, "there can't be any way in which he can take them, can there? He didn't tell you how he found out they were here, did he?"

"No, I forgot to ask him, and it doesn't matter about that. Our only task now will be to keep them from him. Fledra, when you have finished talking with Ann, will you come to me?"

Fledra raised her head. Something in Horace's eyes frightened her. She had never seen him so pale, nor had his lips ever been so set and white.

Ann rose quickly. Of late Horace's actions had aroused her suspicions. She was now fully convinced that Everett had been right. Moreover, she had come to feel that she would willingly overlook Fledra's birth, if her brother's intentions were serious.

"Go to him now, and trust—have faith that you will not have to go away!"

Fledra kissed Ann's hands and tremblingly followed Shellington into his study.

She sat down without waiting for an invitation; for her legs seemed too weak to hold her. Her attitude was attentive, and her poise was graceful. For some minutes Horace arranged the papers on his desk, while Fledra peeped at him from under her lashes. He looked even sterner than when he had ordered Lon to leave the house, and his silence terrified her more than if he had scolded her. At last he turned quickly.

"Fledra, I've asked you to come here, because I can't stand our troubles any longer. I believe in my soul that you love me; for you have told me so, and—and have given me every reason to hope it. We are facing a new danger, both for you and for Floyd, and I am sure you want to help me all you can." He paused a moment, and went on, "Your suffering is over as far as your own people are concerned. There is no law that can force a child as old as you are to return to such a hateful place, and I shall take it upon myself to see that neither you nor your brother is forced to leave here."

Fledra uttered a cry and half-rose to her feet; but, as Horace continued speaking, she sank down.

"I think it probable that we shall have to go to law, for Mr. Cronk looks like a very determined man; but he'll find that I will fight his

119

claim every inch of the way." Shellington bent toward her and rested a hand on the papers he had been sorting. "I'm very glad you didn't go to school today, and you must not go again until it is over. This man may try to kidnap you." He found it impossible to call Lon her father.

Fledra reached out and grasped his hands. At her touch, Horace flushed to the roots of his hair. Loosening his own fingers, he took hers into his. Finally he drew her slowly round the corner of the desk, close into his arms.

"Fledra, for God's sake, tell me what has made you so unhappy! Will you, child? Isn't it something that I ought to know? Poor little girly, don't cry that way! It breaks my heart to hear you!"

There was inexplicable weariness on the fair young face.

"I want to stay here," moaned Flea; "but what I have that hurts me is here." She drew his fingers close over her heart. "It isn't anything anybody can help—just yet."

"I could help you, Fledra," Horace insisted. "Every man has the power to help the woman he loves, and you are a'woman, Fledra."

"I want to be your woman."

Young as she was, Fledra was an enigma to him. There was but one way to make her his woman,—his wife,—that was to force her confidence, and, once obtained, keep it. But his longing to caress her was stronger than his desire to conquer her,—the warmth and softness of her lips he would not exchange for the world's wealth!

"Sweetheart, Sweetheart!" he said, reddening. "I'm sorry that I spoke as I did last night,—I was angry,—but I've had such awful moods lately! Sometimes I've felt as if I could whip you to make you tell me!"

A thrill ran over Fledra from head to foot.

"Beat me—will you beat me?" she murmured, drawing his hand across her moist lips. "I'd love to have you beat me! Pappy Lon always said that a woman needed beatin' to make her stand around. Then, when I saw you, I thought as how princes never beat their women; but now I know you have to."

If the young face had been less earnest, the gray eyes less entreating, Horace would have laughed despite his anger.

"Of course, I shan't whip you, child," he said; "only I want you to prove your love for me by trusting me. You're a woman, Fledra. It would be an outrage to punish you that way. Then, too, I love you too well to hurt you."

She watched him for one tense moment. She was quivering under his firm grasp like a leaf in the wind. Her eyes were entreating him to trust her, to take her, regardless of her seeming stubbornness.

"Fledra," he whispered, "if the time ever comes that you can, will you tell me all about it?"

"Yes."

"And you'll not lie again?"

"I've never lied to you!" came sullenly.

"Never, Fledra?"

"Never!"

"And you won't tell another untruth to Ann, either—not even once?"

Fledra's mind flashed to Everett. She might have to lie to keep Ann's happiness for her. She slowly drew her hand away, and turned fretfully with a hatred against Brimbecomb for bringing all this misery upon them.

"I'm not going to promise you that I won't lie to Sister Ann; but I'll tell you the truth, always—always—"

Because he did not understand a woman's heart, Horace opened the door, white and angered.

"It is beyond my comprehension that you should treat a woman as you have my sister. You take advantage of her generosity, and expect me to uphold you in it!"

There was a catch of genuine sorrow in his voice. Slowly Fledra looked back over her shoulder at him.

"You've promised me that you'd never tell anybody what I told you."

Horace supplemented his last rebuke with:

"Nor will I! But I insist that you come to me the next time you are tempted to lie. Do you hear, Fledra?"

"Yes," she answered.

Suddenly she began to sob wildly, and in another instant fled down the hall.

CHAPTER TWENTY-TWO

Not more than two weeks after Lon had demanded the twins from Horace, Everett Brimbecomb sat in his office, brooding over the shadow that had so suddenly darkened his life. The dream he had dreamed of a woman he could call Mother, of some man—his father—

of whom he had striven to be worthy, had dissolved into a specter with a shriveled face and shaggy hair, into a woman whom he had left in the cemetery to die. Although he was secure in the thought that he would not be connected with the tragedy, he shuddered every time he thought of her and of the coming spring, when the body would be discovered. He did not repent the crime he had committed; but the fear that the secret of his birth would be brought to life tortured him night and day. He remembered that Scraggy had said his father wanted him; that she had come to Tarrytown to take him back. Did his father know who and where he was? If so, eventual discovery was inevitable.

Everett's passion for Fledra only heightened his misery, and the girl's face haunted him continually. In his imagination he compared her with Ann, and the younger girl stood out in radiant contrast. He had daily fostered his jealous hatred for Horace, and, because of her allegiance to her brother, he had come to loathe Ann, although he was more than ever determined to marry her. The home in which he had been reared repelled him, and he could now live only for the fame that would rise from his talent and work, and for the pleasures that come to those without heart or conscience. Almost the entire morning had been consumed by these thoughts, when two men were ushered in to him.

"I'm Lon Cronk," said the taller of the two, "and this be Lem Crabbe, and we hear that ye're a good lawyer."

Everett rose frowningly.

"I am a lawyer," said he; "but I choose my clients. I don't take cases—"

"We'll pay ye well," interrupted Lon, "if it's money ye want. Ye can have as much as that Mr. Shellin'ton—"

Everett dropped back again into his chair. The mention of Horace's name silenced him. He motioned for the men to be seated, without taking his eyes from Lem. The scowman's clothes were in shreds, and, as he lifted his right arm, Brimbecomb saw the chapped red flesh, strapped to the rusted iron hook. Although Lem had not spoken, the young lawyer noted the silent convulsions going on in the dark, full throat, the unceasing movements of the goiter.

"State your case to me, then," said he tersely.

Lon Cronk settled back and began to speak.

"There's a man here in this town by the name of Shellington. He's a lawyer, too, and he's got my kids, and I want 'em. That's my case, Mister."

Brimbecomb's heart began to beat tumultuously. Chance was giving him a lead he could not have won of his own efforts, and he smiled, turning on Cronk more cordially.

"Have you demanded your children of Mr. Shellington?" he asked.

"Yep."

Everett bent over eagerly.

"What did he say to you?"

"He says as how I could go to the devil, and that I could git the law after him if I wanted 'em. Can I get 'em, Mister?"

The lawyer straightened up, and for many moments was deep in thought before answering Lon. The chance of which he could never have dreamed had come to him. This visit laid open a way for him to tear Fledra from Horace; in fact, he could now legally take her from him with no possibility of public discredit to himself. He narrowly observed the men before him, and knew that he should later be able to force them to do as he wished. He forgot his foster father and mother— aye, forgot even Ann—as all that was black in his nature inflamed his desire for the ebony-haired girl.

During several minutes he rapidly planned how he could bring the affair to a favorable climax with the least possible danger. But, whether by fair means or by foul, he resolved that Fledra should become his.

Presently, as if to gain time, he asked:

"Do you want them both?"

"Yep."

"The boy is ill, I hear," he said.

"That don't make no difference," cried Lon. "I want him jest the same. Can ye get 'em fer me, Mister?"

"I think so," replied Everett; "and, if I take the case, I shall have to ask you to keep out of it entirely, until I'm ready for you. We shall probably have to go into court."

"Yep, ye'll have to bring it into court, all right, I know ye will. How much money do ye want now?"

"Fifty dollars," replied Everett; "and it will be more if I have a suit, and still more if I win. Come here again next week Monday, and I'll lay my plans before you."

Lon clapped his shabby cap upon his head, and, with a surly leave-taking, moved to go. Lem lagged behind; but a glance at the lawyer's forbidding face sent him shuffling after the squatter.

Long after they were gone Everett sat planning a future course. He felt sure that Horace would not allow the children to be taken from him without a fight; he knew there were special statutes governing these things, and took down a large book and began to read.

123

Much to his satisfaction, Brimbecomb found a letter from Mr. and Mrs. Brimbecomb awaiting him at home that evening. In it his foster mother informed him that they had decided to return to Tarrytown immediately and make ready for a trip abroad, where they hoped that Mr. Brimbecomb would recover his health. In a postscript from the noted lawyer, Everett read:

I am glad that you are doing well, dear boy, and when my doctor   said
that I must have a complete rest I knew that I could leave you in charge of the office and go away satisfied.

There followed a few personalities, and after finishing the reader threw it down with a smile. He had hesitated a moment over the thought that his father would have a decided objection to the Cronk case. But his desire to work against Horace had overcome his irresolution. Now his way was clear! The sooner Mr. and Mrs. Brimbecomb were away, the better pleased he would be.

Floyd was suddenly taken worse.

"I think, if you were to come and speak with him, he might feel better," said Ann to Horace. "He wants to see you. Fledra is with him."

Floyd was quiet now, his large eyes closed with quivering pain.

"Floyd!" murmured Horace, touching the lad gently.

The lids lifted, and he put up his hand.

"I'm glad ye come, Brother Horace," he said in a whisper. "I've been wantin' to talk to ye. Will ye take Flea out, Sister Ann?"

Both girls left the room, as Horace drew a chair to the bed.

"I ain't goin' to get well," said Flukey slowly. "I know the doctor thinks so, too, 'cause he said there was somethin' the matter with my heart. And I have to go and leave Flea."

Shellington took the thin, white hand in his.

"You must not become downhearted, boy; that's not the way to get well. And you're certainly better than when you came, in spite of this little setback."

Floyd closed his eyes, and Horace saw silent tears rolling down the boy's cheeks. The young man bent over him.

"Floyd, are you worrying about your sister?"

Flukey nodded an affirmative.

"Why?"

"Because she ain't the same as she was. And she ain't happy anymore, and I can't make her tell me. Have ye been ugly to her—have ye?"

Horace racked his mind for a truthful answer. Had he been unfair to Fledra?

"Floyd," he said softly, "your sister and I have had some words; but we shall soon understand each other—I know we shall!"

"What did ye say to Flea?"

"I can't tell you, Floyd, because I promised her I would not."

The boy writhed under the warm blankets.

"She's always makin' folks promise not to tell things," he moaned. "It's because you're mad at her, that's what makes her cry so, and I can't do anything for her. Can't you, Brother Horace?"

"She won't let me, Floyd."

"Did ye ask her?"

"Many times."

"Would she let ye if I asked her?"

"No, Floyd, you must not! I promised her that I would not speak with you about her unhappiness." Horace ejaculated his reply so emphatically that Floyd looked at him curiously.

"But I can't die and leave her that way, and I'm a goin' soon. Sometimes my heart jest stands still, and won't start again till I lose all my breath. A feller can't live that way, can he, Brother Horace?"

"It will pass off; of course, it will—it must!" Horace looked into the worn, suffering young face, and a resolution took possession of him.

"Floyd," he said huskily, "Floyd, if I tell you something, will you keep it from my sister and yours?"

"Yes," murmured Flukey.

"I love Fledra, and want to make her my wife. Does that help you any, to know that I shall always watch her and care for her?"

Flukey searched the earnest face bent over him.

"Ye love her?"

"Very much, very much indeed. But she is young yet—only a little girl."

"Did ye tell her that ye loved her?"

"Yes."

"Did she say she loved you?"

"Yes."

Flukey groaned.

"Then it's something else than that, because I've known for a long time that Flea loved ye. What's the matter? What's the matter with ye both?"

"Floyd, when I tell you that I do not know," answered Horace, "will you believe me?"

"Did ye want her to tell ye somethin'—something that'll keep ye from takin' her now?" Horace's silence drew an outpouring from Flukey. "And I suppose she said she wouldn't—and ye won't take her unless she tells ye. Then ye'll never get her; for, when Flea says she won't, she won't, if she dies for it! Ain't ye lovin' her well enough to take her, anyway?"

Horace answered warmly, "Yes, of course, I am!"

By the dawn of day Floyd had become so much worse that a trained nurse was placed at his side, and the physician's verdict, that the boy might die at any moment, overshadowed the threats of the squatter father.

Lon Cronk had come alone to Everett's office on the hour set. Brimbecomb wondered vaguely where the other man was, and what was his concern in the affair.

After greeting Lon coldly, the young lawyer said:

"I should like to know about your life, Mr. Cronk, how long your children have been away from you, and all about it."

"They've been gone since September," replied Lon. "They runned away from hum, and I ain't seed 'em till I found out that they was at Shellington's."

"And how did you discover them?"

"Saw Flea goin' up the steps," lied Cronk. "I knowed her the minute I see her, in spite of her pretty clothes."

"Then you applied to Mr. Shellington for them?"

"Yep."

"And he refused to deliver them up?"

"Yep—damn him! But I'll take 'em, anyway."

"Don't say that outside my office," warned Everett. "The law does not want to be threatened."

Lon remained silent.

"We'll have to deal with Mr. Shellington very carefully," cautioned the lawyer; "for he is proud and stubborn, and has a great liking for your children. In fact, I think he is quite in love with the girl."

Lon started to his feet, his swart face paling.

"He won't git her!" he muttered. "I've got plans for that gal, and I ain't goin' have no young buck kickin' 'em over, I kin tell ye that!"

Brimbecomb's words put a new light upon the matter. That Flea would be protected by the young millionaire Lon knew; but that the young man thought of marrying her had never come into his mind.

"I don't believe as how he'd marry a squatter girl," he said presently. "He won't, if I get her once to Ithaca!"

The mention of Brimbecomb's college town and birthplace brought a new train of thought to the lawyer.

"Have you lived in Ithaca many years?" he demanded.

126

"Yep."

"The first thing I shall do," said the attorney deliberately, "is to make a formal demand upon Mr. Shellington in your name, and get his answer. Please remain in town where I can see you, and if anything comes up I shall write you."

Lon gave him the address of a man near the river, and Everett allowed his client to go. Some force within him had almost impelled him to ask the squatter concerning Screech Owl, and he breathed more freely when he thought that he had not given way to the temptation to learn something about his own people.

At eight o'clock that evening Everett met Mr. and Mrs. Brimbecomb at the station. He could not comprehend the feeling that his foster parents had become strangers to him. He kissed his mother, shook hands with Mr. Brimbecomb, and followed them into the carriage.

He went to bed content with the knowledge that their steamer would sail two days later, and that for six months he would be alone.

CHAPTER TWENTY-THREE

"I can't understand why Horace wants to keep those children indefinitely," said Governor Vandecar to his wife one evening. "It seems their own father has turned up and asked for them."

"Is Horace going to let him have them?"

"Not without a fight, I fear. He talked to me about it, and seemed perfectly decided to keep them. I told him to take no steps until papers were served upon him."

"Can they keep them, Floyd?"

Mrs. Vandecar had become suddenly interested in Fledra and Floyd.

"I'm sure I don't know," replied the governor. "Such things have to be threshed out in court, although much will depend upon what the youngsters wish to do. I fear, though, that Ann and Horace are making useless trouble for themselves."

127

"What process will the father have to take to get them?"

"Have *habeas corpus* papers issued. It will be a nuisance; but I did not try to change his mind, because he was so earnest about it."

"So is Ann," replied Mrs. Vandecar, "and then, Dear, I always think their kindness to those poor little children might make the little dears useful in life sometime. Mildred says they are very pretty and sweet."

"Well, as I said before, it's strange that such a case should be here in this peaceful little town, and I have promised Horace to advise him all I can, although I am too busy to take any active part in it."

"Oh, do everything you ought to, Floyd, if you discover that they have really been abused. It might be that they would be really harmed if they were taken back to their home. Did Horace tell you where they lived?"

"Yes, near Ithaca somewhere. I think he said they had a shanty on Cayuga Lake."

"One of the squatters?"

"Yes."

"I remember very well," remarked Mrs. Vandecar after a moment's thought, "when I went to Ithaca with Ann Shellington, and Horace and Everett were graduated from the university, that we went up the lake in Brimbecomb's yacht. The boys called our attention to numbers of huts on the west shore, near the head of Cayuga. I suppose it must be one of those places the children left."

"I presume so," replied the governor.

"Ann telephoned over that the boy was ill with a rheumatic heart. She seemed quite alarmed over it."

"He probably won't get well, if that's the case," murmured Vandecar. "It's a pernicious thing when it attacks the heart. Wasn't it rather strange that Ann and Horace should have used our names for them, Fledra?"

"You remember Ann asked me if I cared. She said that when they came they had some strange nicknames, and that they wanted to make them forget about their former lives, and it really pleased the poor little things to have our names. I don't mind; do you, Floyd?"

"No," was the answer. "I only wish—" He stopped quickly and turned to his wife.

Her eyes were filled with tears. Floyd Vandecar's wish had been her own, that she knew.

"I wish you had a son, too, Floyd dear!" she sobbed. "Oh, my babies, my poor, pretty little babies!"

"Don't Fledra, don't!" pleaded her husband. "It was God's will, and we must bow to it."

"It's so hard, though, Floyd, so awfully hard, and the days have been so long! Floyd, do you ever wonder and wonder where they are?"

The man shook his shoulders sharply.

"Do I ever wonder, Fledra? My hair is whitened, my life shortened, and many of my efforts of no avail, because of my sorrow and yours. If the days have been long to you, they have been longer to me; if your heart has been torn over their disappearance, mine has been doubly hurt, because—because you have depended upon me to return them to you, and I have not been able to."

He spoke drearily, shading his face with his hand.

"Floyd, dear Floyd, I'm not blaming you. I realize that if it had been possible you would have given me back my babies, and you must not say that your efforts have been of no avail. Why, dear husband, the papers are full of your great, strong doings. I'm immensely proud of you." She had leaned over him; but the despondent man did not take the hand from his eyes.

"Of all the strange cases, Fledra, ours is the strangest. You remember how I turned the state almost upside down to find those children. Yet, with all the power I could bring to bear, I made no headway."

"I did not realize that you felt it so deeply," whispered the wife. "I've been so selfish—forgive me! We'll try to be as happy as possible, and we have Mildred—"

"If we had a dozen children," replied the governor sadly, "our first babies would always have their places in our hearts."

"True," murmured the mother. "How true that is, Floyd! There is never a day but I feel the touch of their fingers, remember their sweet baby ways. And always, when I look at you, I think of them. They were so like their father."

Lon Cronk and Lem Crabbe had arranged between them that the scowman should return to Ithaca for some days, and so the big thief was alone near the Hudson, in a shanty that had been given over to him by a canal friend to use when he wished. When Lon decided to rob Horace Shellington, he had known that there would have to be some place to take the things thus obtained, and had secured the hut for the purpose. It was at this address that Everett came to him, upon his return from New York.

Lon admitted the lawyer, who found the hut reeking with the rank smoke from a short pipe that Cronk held in his hand.

"Have ye got the kids?" the squatter questioned.

Everett catechized the heavy face with a smile.

"Did you think for a moment it was possible to obtain them so quickly?"

"I hain't had no way of knowin'," grunted Lon, "and I'm in a hurry."

He seemed changed, and looked as if he had not slept. Everett wondered if his affection for the children had been so great that his loss of them had altered him thus. The lawyer did not know how Lon was tortured when he caressed the image of the dead woman, nor could he know the man's agony when her spirit left him suddenly.

"You'll have to curb your haste," said Brimbecomb, with a curl of his lip. "It takes time to set justice in motion."

"Have ye done anything?"

"Not yet. I was forced to go to New York."

"Hadn't ye better git a hustle on yerself?" snarled Lon.

"Yes, I intend to begin tomorrow; that is, to take the first steps in the matter. But I wanted to talk with you first. Are you alone?"

"Yep; there ain't nobody here. Fire ahead, and say what ye're wantin' to."

Everett bent over and looked keenly into Lon's face; then slowly he threw a question at the fellow:

"Are you fond of those two children, or have you other motives for taking them from Shellington?"

Cronk made no reply, but settled back in the rickety chair and eyed Everett from head to foot.

"Be that any of yer business?" he said at length.

The lawyer took the repulse calmly. He had not come to fight with Lon.

"It's my business as far as this is concerned. If you care for them, and intend to shield them after you have them—well, say from all harm—and do your best for them, then I don't want your case. I'm willing to return your money."

For a moment the elder man looked disconcerted; then he jumped to his feet with an oath.

"Put her there, Mister!" said he, with an evil smile. He thrust forth a great hand, and for an instant Everett placed his fingers within it.

"I thought I had not guessed wrongly," the lawyer quickly averred. "If that is how you feel, I can do better work for you."

"I see that, Mister," muttered Lon.

"Are those children really yours?" Everett took out a cigar and lighted it.

"Yep," answered Lon, dropping his gaze.

Everett decided that the man had lied to him, and he was glad.

"I think you said you had some plans for the girl," he broke forth presently.

130

"Yep; but no plans be any good when she's with Shellington."

"But after she has left him? Would you be willing to change your plans for her?"

Cronk did not reply, but centered his gaze full upon Everett.

"The question is, would you, for a good sum of money, be willing to give her to me?"

"Why give her to ye, Mister—why?" His voice rose to a shout.

"I want her," Everett answered quietly.

"What for?"

"I love her."

"Ye want to marry her?" muttered Lon vindictively.

"No," drawled Everett; "I am going to marry Miss Shellington."

"Good God! ye don't mean it! And yet ye take this case what's most interestin' to 'em? Yer gal won't like that, Mister."

"She loves me, and when I explain that it's all under the law she'll forgive me. There's nothing quite like having a woman in love with you to get her to do what you want her to."

"But her brother, he ain't lovin' ye that way. He won't forgive ye."

"He doesn't cut any ice," said Everett. "In fact, I hate him, and—"

"Be ye lovin' my Flea?" Lon's voice cracked out the question like a gunshot.

"I think so."

"Be Flea lovin' you, or him?"

"She loves him."

"Then it will hurt her like the devil to take her away from him, eh?"

The eagerness expressed in the squatter's tones confirmed Everett's suspicions. Cronk hated that boy and girl. Brimbecomb impassively overlooked Floyd; but Flea he would have!

"Yes," he said, "I think it will hurt them both."

"How much money will ye give if I hand her over to ye?" asked Cronk presently.

"How much do you want?"

"Wal, Mister, it's this way: Ye remember that feller I had with me t'other day?" Everett nodded. "I mean, the feller with the hook?" Again Everett inclined his head. "I said as how he could have Flea. Ye has to buy him off, too, and that ain't so easy as 'tis to settle with me— especially, as ye ain't goin' to marry Flea. I ain't goin' to give her to no man what's honest—ye hear?"

"I supposed as much," commented Everett, reddening.

"Lem's been waitin' for Flea for over three years, and I said as how ye'd have to buy him off, too."

"That's easy. Where is he?"

"Gone to Ithaca. He's went up to bring down his scow. It's gettin' 'long to be spring, and it's easier to lug the kids back by water, and we know that way, and it don't cost so much. I telled him when he went away that he could have the gal as soon as we got back to the settlement. Lem won't reason for a little bit of money."

"Money doesn't count in this," assured Everett. "Now, then, if I take this case, put it through without cost to you, and give you both a good sum, will you give me the girl?"

"If ye promise me ye won't marry her."

Everett laughed, his white teeth gleaming through his lips.

"Don't let that worry you, Mr. Cronk. I have no desire to place at the head of my home a girl like yours. I told you that I was going to marry Miss Shellington—and not even that damned brother of hers can prevent it!"

For a long time after Everett had left the hut Lon sat meditating over what he had heard. He wondered if Everett really loved Ann, and, if he did, how he could wish for Flea. How another woman could erase from any man's mind the picture of a loved woman, Lon with his loyal heart could not understand. He sat for an hour with his head on the old wooden table, and planned what he should do with Flukey, leaving it to the brilliant-eyed lawyer to dicker with Lem for Flea.

CHAPTER TWENTY-FOUR

Horace Shellington took a long breath as he entered his office one morning in the latter part of March. The blustering wind that had raged all night had almost subsided, and he felt glad for Floyd's sake; for, no matter how warm they kept the little lad, the sound of the wind through the trees and the dismal wail of the branches at night made him shiver and fret with nervous pain. Horace had scarcely seated himself when Everett Brimbecomb entered the room.

"Hello, Horace!" said the latter jovially. "I was going to come in yesterday, but was not quite ready to see you. Haven't been able to get a word with you in several days."

Horace offered a chair, and Everett sank into it.

"You are always so busy when I run in to see Ann," Brimbecomb went on, "that one would think you were not an inmate of that house."

"Yes," said Horace, "I've been studying up on an interesting case I expect to handle very soon."

Everett laughed.

"So have I," he said, narrowing his lids and looking at Shellington.

"When one is connected with offices as we are, Everett," remarked Horace uninterestedly, "there is little time for visiting."

"I find that, too," replied Everett.

During the last few weeks Horace had seen little of his sister's fiance; in fact, since their quarrel he had drawn away from the young man as a companion; but above everything else he desired his gentle sister to be happy, and the man before him was the only one to make her so. He thought of this, and smiled a little more cordially as he said:

"Is there anything I can do for you, Everett?"

"Well, yes, there is," admitted Brimbecomb.

"I'll do anything I can," replied Horace heartily.

Brimbecomb hesitated before going on. Shellington looked so grave, so dignified, so much more manly than he had ever seen him, that he scarcely dared open his subject.

"It's something that may touch you at first, Horace," he explained; "but—"

Horace, unsuspicious, bent forward encouragingly:

"Go ahead," he said.

Everett flushed and looked at the floor.

"A case has just come into our office, and, as my father is gone from home, I have taken it on."

Horace listened expectantly. Everett could have struck the man in the face, he hated him so deeply. He groaned mentally as he thought of Scraggy and her wild-eyed cat and of his endeavor to close her lips as to her relation to him. It was a great fear within him that soon his father would appear as his mother had. The time might come when this haughty man before him would have reason to look upon him with contempt. To make Horace understand his present power was the one thought that now dominated him.

With this in mind, he began to speak again:

"A man came to us with a complaint that you were keeping his children from him."

If Horace had received the blow the other longed to give, he could not have been more shocked.

"I believe his name is Cronk," went on Everett, taking a slip from his pocket; "yes, Lon Cronk."

Horace took his paper-knife from the table and twirled it in his

133

fingers. His face had grown ashen white, his lips were set closely over his teeth.

"I have met this Cronk," he said in a low tone.

"So I understand. He told me that he had been at your home, and had demanded his children, and that you had refused to give them up."

"I did!" There was no lack of emphasis in the words.

"And you said that he could not have them unless he went to law for them."

"I did!" said Horace again.

"And he came to me."

Horace rose to his feet, a deep frown gathering on his brow. Everett rose also, and the two men faced each other for a long moment.

"And you took the case?" Horace got out at last.

"Yes, I took the case," Everett replied.

"And yet you knew that Ann loved them?"

"I was—was sure that if you both understood—"

The speaker's hesitation brought forth an ejaculation from Shellington.

"What are we to understand?"

"That justice must be done the father," responded Everett quickly.

Horace squared his jaw and snapped out:

"Do I understand that, in spite of the near relationship of our family, you are willing to deal a blow to my sister and me that, if it falls, will be almost unbearable? You intend to fight with this squatter for his children?"

"I don't intend to fight, Horace, if you're willing to give them to me. I had much rather have our present relations go on as they are, without a breach in them. I think, if you and Ann talk it over, you will see that by giving the boy and girl into my hands—"

Horace came a step nearer, with darkening brow:

"You can go straight to hell!" he said, so fiercely that Everett started back. "And the sooner you go, the better I shall be pleased," his face reddened as he finished, "and so will Ann!"

"You're speaking for someone who has not given you authority," Everett sneered. "Your sister will give me at least one of those children—I imagine, the girl. I think the father is more particular about having her."

"I should think he would be, and you may take him this message from me: that, if he sneaks about my house at any time of day or night, I'll have him shot like a dog, for every man can protect his own; and if you—"

Everett, seeing his chance, broke in:

134

"He would be protecting his own, if he came to your home, for his own are there; and we are going to have those children before another month goes by!"

"Try it, and perhaps I may bring to your mind what you once said to me about that girl," muttered Horace, with set teeth. "Your errand being finished, Mr. Brimbecomb, you may go!"

Everett had received the worst of the encounter. He had expected that Horace would consider Fledra's and Floyd's case in a gentler way, would probably compromise for Ann's sake. He went out not a little disturbed.

Horace waited for a few moments after Brimbecomb left him before he took his hat and coat and went home. Ann was surprised to see him, and more surprised when he drew her into the drawing-room, where he mysteriously closed the door.

"Ann," he said solemnly, "I believe the turning point in your life has come. And I want you to judge for yourself and take your own stand without thinking of my happiness or comfort."

The young woman lifted startled eyes and searched his face.

"What is it, Horace—that squatter again? Has he made a move against us?"

Horace bent over and took her hands in his.

"He has not only made a move against us, as far as the children are concerned, but he has used an instrument you would never have dreamed of." Seeing his sister did not reply, he went on, "Just what legal procedure they will undertake I don't know; but that will come out in time. Cronk went to Everett Brimbecomb with the case, and I was notified this morning by Everett to give up the children."

"Everett!" breathed Ann, disbelieving. "My Everett?"

"Yes, your Everett, Ann. Don't, child, please don't! Ann, Ann, listen to me!... Yes, sit down.... Now wait!"

He held her closely in his arms until the storm of sobs had passed, and then placed a pillow under her head and went on gravely:

"Ann, I have come to this conclusion: you love Everett dearly, and I cannot understand his actions; but I'm not going to intrude upon your affection for him, nor his for you. I'm going to ask you not to take sides with either of us. I'm a lawyer, and so is he. Do you understand, Ann?"

Fearfully she clutched his fingers.

"But Fledra and Floyd—I can't let them go back, I can't! I can't!"

"They're not going back," said Horace firmly. "Mind you, Ann, even to renew my friendship with Brimbecomb, I shouldn't give them up."

"Renew your friendship!" gasped Ann. "Oh, have you quarreled with him, Horace?"

"Yes, and told him to leave my office."

Ann sobbed again.

"What a fearful tragedy is hanging over us!" she cried.

"It is worse than I imagined it could be," Horace declared; "much worse, for I never thought that the squatter could get a reputable firm to represent him. And as for Everett—well, he never entered my mind. I told him that he could not take those children, and that he might—"

He remembered plainly what he had said, but did not communicate it to his sister. She was so frail, so gently modest, that an angry man's language would hurt her.

"I told him," ended Horace, "to do whatever he thought best, and that, if Cronk came here again, I should shoot him down like a dog. I think we ought to tell Fledra, and then, too, I desire to speak to her of something else. Can you bring her to me, Ann, without frightening Floyd?"

It did not need Ann's quiet plucking at her sleeve to tell Fledra that the blow had fallen. She had expected it day after day; until now, when she faced Horace and looked into his tense face, she felt that her whole hope had gone.

Ann tiptoed out before her brother opened his lips.

For a moment the harassed man knew not what to say to the silent, trembling girl.

"Fledra," he began, "the first move has been made in your case by your father."

"Must we go?" burst from the quivering lips.

"No, no: not if you have told me the truth about your past life—I mean about your father being cruel to you."

The sensitive face gathered a deep flush:

"I've never lied to you, Brother Horace," she replied gently.

"If I could believe you, child, if I could place absolute confidence in your word, I should have courage to go into the struggle without losing hope."

"What's Pappy Lon done?"

"He has employed Everett Brimbecomb to take you back to Ithaca."

Fledra shrank back as if he had struck her. Swiftly into her mind came the smiling, handsome face of the lawyer whom Ann loved. His brilliant eyes seared her soul like fire. In all her life, even when facing Lem Crabbe, she had never felt as she did now. She saw Floyd fading into the graveyard beyond, while she was being torn from the only

136

haven of rest she had ever known. Lem Crabbe could not have taken her; but Everett Brimbecomb could! She felt again his burning kisses, the clasp of his strong arms, and her own disgust. He seemed a giant of strength, and Horace's white face and set lips aggravated her fear. Fledra's desire for comfort had never been so great as the desire she had at this moment to open her tired heart to Horace and reveal to him Everett's perfidy.

"Did you tell Sister Ann about Mr. Brimbecomb?"

She stumbled over the name.

"Yes."

"What did she say?"

"My sister loves him—you know that. She is heartbroken that he should have accepted this case. We must make it as easy as we can for her, dear child."

The girl saw Horace's lips twitch as he spoke, and thought of the love he had for his sister, and her desire to tell him what she knew died immediately.

"Do you want me to go with Pappy Lon and not make any trouble for her?" she whispered.

"No, no, not that! You can't go, Fledra, and they can't take you, if—you have told me the truth about the man your father wanted to give you to."

"Floyd and I told the truth," she said seriously, lifting her eyes to his face; "but for Sister Ann I'd go away with Pappy Lon, and with Lem, if you'd take care of Fluke till he—"

"Don't, Fledra, don't!" groaned Horace. "It would tear me to pieces to give you up. But—but you couldn't relieve my mind, Dear, could you?"

Fledra knew what he meant, and shook her head.

"No, not now," she replied.

If it troubled Ann to have Everett take part in their going back to the squatter country, how much worse she would feel if she knew what he really had done! Horace's appeal to shield Ann from overmuch burden strengthened Fledra's courage.

"Can you keep us?" she asked, after a moment's thought.

"I am going to try."

"If you love me well, Brother Horace," said Fledra, "won't you believe that I'd do anything for Sister Ann and you?"

He nodded his head; but did not speak.

When he reached Ithaca, Lem Crabbe found a flood besieging the forest city. The creeks of Cascadilla and Six Mile Gorge had overflowed their banks, and the lower section of the town was under water. He had

137

come back for the scow, and to find Scraggy. He was determined to force from her the whereabouts of his son. He wended his way toward the hut of one of his friends at the inlet, and hailed the boat that conveyed the squatters to and fro in flood-time. As the boat lapped the muddy water breaking into the weeds and brushes, Lem saw Eli Cronk perched in another boat, with a spear in his hand.

"Eli!" shouted Lem.

Eli greeted him with a wave of the pole.

The boats neared each other, and Lem shouted that he wanted to get into Cronk's craft.

"What ye doin'?" asked Crabbe, as the boat he had just left shot away toward the bridge.

"Catching frogs," replied Eli. "I sell a lot of 'em to the hotels, and this flood is jest the thing to make 'em thick." He lowered his spear and brought up a struggling frog. Throwing it into a covered box, he peered again into the water.

"Where's Lon?" he said, straightening again with another victim.

"To Tarrytown."

"What's he to Tarrytown fer?"

"He's a gittin' Flea and Flukey. That's where they runned to."

"He ain't found 'em, has he? Truth, now!"

"Yep, truth," answered Lem; "and he's got a fine-lookin' lawyer-pup to git 'em for him."

As Eli again and again thrust his spear into the water, Lem told the story of the finding of the twins. He refrained from speaking of his experience with Screech Owl; but said finally, as if with little interest:

"Ye ain't seen Scraggy, has ye?"

"Nope; and she ain't in her hut, nuther; or she wasn't awhile back, 'cause I stopped there, when I was a lookin' for Lon."

"When did ye git back to town?"

"I dunno jest what day it were," responded Cronk, spearing again.

"Can I git up the tracks, Eli?" inquired Lem presently.

"Ye'll have to wade in mud to yer knees fer a spell after ye leave the boat."

"I can take the hill over the tracks for a way. Will ye row me up as far as ye can?"

"Yep, I'll row ye up," replied Eli, proceeding with his work.

Late in the afternoon, Lem Crabbe, wet to his knees and covered with mud, entered the scow. He had stopped at Screechy's hut, knocked, and, having received no answer, clicked down the hill to the boat.

He made up his mind to stay there until Scraggy came back; then he would go back to Tarrytown and bring the twins to Ithaca. Every morning Lem mounted the hill, only to find that Screech Owl had not returned. But one day, just at dusk, as he appeared before the hut, he saw the flickering of a candle. He did not wait to knock, but entered, and found Scraggy stretched out on the old bed. She looked up as if she had expected him, noted his dark face, and lowered her head again.

"Black Pussy's gone, Lem. I've got a cold settin' on me here," she whispered, wheezing as she laid her hand on her chest.

"I hope it'll kill ye!" grunted Lem. "What did you leave the toolhouse fer, when I told ye to stay?"

"What toolhouse, Lemmy?" The dazed eyes looked up at him in surprise.

"Don't try none of yer guff on me. I want to know who ye went to see in Tarrytown, and who the man was that throwed ye over the fence, and then lugged ye off to that vault?"

Scraggy sat up painfully.

"I wasn't throwed over no fence."

"Ye was, 'cause I seed the man when he done it. I wish now that I'd a gone and settled with him. Who was he, Screechy?"

"I dunno," she answered.

Lem bent over her, his eyes blazing with wrath.

"Ye want to git yer batty head a workin' damn quick," he shouted, "or I'll slit yer throat with this!" The rusty hook was thrust near the thin, drawn face.

"I can't think tonight," muttered Screech Owl, "'cause the bats be a runnin' 'bout in my head. When I think, I'll tell ye, Lemmy."

"Where be that boy?" demanded Lem.

Scraggy shook her head. Every time she thought of Lem's questions, there was an infernal tapping of unnumbered winged creatures at the walls of her brain.

"There ain't no boy that I knows of," she said listlessly, sinking down again. "And ye wouldn't slit my neck when I ain't done nothin', would ye, Lemmy?"

"Ye has done somethin'," growled Lem. "Ye has kep' that brat from me these years past, and now he's big 'nough I'm goin' to have him! Ye hear?" Every word he uttered came forth with effort. The red mark under his chin moved relentlessly, preventing him from speaking with clearness.

Scraggy writhed beneath the tightening grasp of the man's wet fingers.

"I'll choke ye to death!" Lem gasped, between throaty convulsions.

139

"Lemmy, Lemmy dear—"

Another twist of Lem's fingers, and the woman sank back unconscious. Lem shook her roughly.

"Scraggy, Scraggy!" he cried wildly. "Set up! I Want to talk to ye! Set up!"

The silence in the gloomy hut, the whiteness of the seemingly dead woman, filled Lem with superstitious dread. He grasped his lantern and ran out, failing to close the door.

The frightened man made off up the hill, and, passing through the Stebbins farm by the Gothic church and dark graveyard, he tramped the Trumansburg road to Ithaca. The tracks were covered with water as they had been when Eli had given him the lift toward the settlement. But the flood had so receded that by drawing his trousers up over his boots Lem managed to get through the mud to the bridge. From there he sought the house of Middy Burnes, where he made an agreement with the tugman that the scow should be towed from Ithaca to Tarrytown.

CHAPTER TWENTY-FIVE

To usher Everett into her home with the same fond heart as hitherto was more than Ann could do. Dearly as she loved him, much as she desired to be his wife, it was hard to pardon him for casting aside her interests for those of the dark-browed squatter. But, womanlike, she felt that she could break down her lover's determination, and resolved that she would not hesitate to open argument with him.

Everett met her with a smile, and her lips trembled as they received his warm kiss. After they were seated he said:

"Horace has told you, no doubt, Ann, of the children's case." She nodded her head sorrowfully. "Your brother seems to feel," went on Everett, "that I should not have taken charge of it."

"Neither should you have done so, Everett, unless you've other motives than we know of."

She looked up; but lowered her eyes as Brimbecomb glanced at

140

her furtively. Had Fledra told her of his advances? No, or she would never have received his kisses. His fears were quieted by this thought, and he asked gently:

"What motives could I have other than that justice should be done the father? I took the case, first, because it came to me; then, because I think the man ought to have his children."

Miss Shellington's face darkened.

"Oh, Everett, you can't be so hard-hearted as to want those poor little things misused! They have been persecuted by their own people, and you certainly have more heart than to want that to happen again."

"It's not a case of feeling; it's a case of justice. I know how this man has struggled all his life to rear this boy and girl. They've had no mother, and then, as soon as they were old enough and had the chance, they ran away."

"Because he was cruel to them!"

"I don't believe it. I've had something to do with men, and I'm assured that he told me the truth. I believe, as he says, that they excused their leaving home by brazen lies. Have you never caught them lying to you, Ann?"

"No, no! They've always been truthful to me."

"And to Horace?"

"I haven't asked him. But, if they hadn't been, I am sure he would have spoken of it. Everett, let me plead with you. They have been with us a long time, and Horace and I have grown used to them. They need our care more than I can tell you. The boy is still very ill. Won't you let my love for you plead for them, and withdraw from the case? Do, Dear, and let me call Horace. Will you, Everett? He's so sad over it! Oh! may I call him?" She had risen from her chair; but a negative shake of the man's head made her resume her place again, and she continued, "It will be a dreadful thing for them, if they have to go back. Now, listen, Everett! If you will withdraw and let Horace settle it with that man, our arrangements," her face was dyed crimson,—"I mean your plans and mine for our wedding, shall remain as they are. Otherwise—"

"Otherwise, what?" breathed Everett, bending toward her.

"I—I shall have to postpone them." Her voice had strengthened as she spoke, and the last statement was clear and ringing.

"Oh, you couldn't, Ann! Because I take a perfectly legitimate case, which comes into our office, you propose to postpone our marriage?"

"But, Everett, think of what you are doing! It is as if you had taken my brother by the throat. You were the first one to suggest that he might love the girl. What if he does?"

"We will not talk of Horace, please." Everett turned from her as

141

he spoke. "You and I are the parties interested. If you will aid me, and you should, seeing that you love me, your brother need not be considered."

Ann rose, shuddering.

"You do not mean, Everett, that you wish to gain my consent that Fledra and Floyd should go back to Ithaca?"

Brimbecomb also rose.

"Fledra and Floyd!" he mimicked smilingly. "What a farce it all is! And how foolish to give them such names! I should think the governor and his wife would feel complimented that those kids were called for them! They are but paupers, after all!"

"Everett," stammered Ann, "am I just beginning to know you? Oh, you can't mean it! You're but jesting with me, aren't you, Dear?" Her love for him impelled her forward, and her slender hands fell upon his shoulders. He slipped them off, and gathered her fingers into his.

"Ann," he said earnestly, "I'm not jesting, and I ask you, by your love for me, to aid me in this, the first thing of importance I have ever asked you."

Miss Shellington drew reluctantly away.

"I can't, I can't! My very soul revolts at the idea." Then, gaining strength of voice, the girl, marble-white, exclaimed, "If you're not jesting, and are still determined to follow out your plans," she caught her breath in a sob and whispered, "then, like my brother, I shall have to ask you to leave, please."

A frown darkened Everett's face, followed by an expression of ridicule.

"Is this your love for me? You would let two strange squatter children come between us? Am I to understand it so?"

"You may understand this: that, after knowing that their father is wicked, that he would have sacrificed his daughter to a vile man, without marriage to lessen her suffering, after knowing that he tried to make a thief of his noble-hearted boy,—I say, after knowing all this, if you can still insist upon helping him, then I would not dare—to trust— my life with you!"

Everett's rage blotted out all remembrance of how he left the house; but there was a vivid picture in his mind of a woman, pale and lovely, opening the door and dismissing him coldly. He remembered also that she had shut the door as if it were never to be opened again to him. His only consolation was that before long he would be able to face Fledra Cronk and prove his power to her. With this thought came the satisfaction of knowing that he would be able to wring Horace Shellington's heart.

After closing the door upon her lover, Ann stood breathless. The light had suddenly gone from her sun—the whole living world seemed plunged into darkness. Everett was gone, gone from her possibly forever. His face had expressed a determination that proved he would not change his mind. Why had he reasoned himself into thinking that justice could be served in the squatter's cause? Everett must have a motive. Her judgment told her to accuse the man she loved; her heart demanded that she excuse him. For one instant her generous spirit balanced the squatter children's welfare and her own future. She had promised to protect Fledra and Floyd, promised them and Horace. Only a broken prayer escaped her lips as she turned and walked quickly down the hall. She did not wait to knock, but twisted the door-handle convulsively, and appeared before her brother without a plea for pardon for her unannounced entrance.

"He's gone forever!" she said brokenly. "Oh, oh, I can't—"

She swayed forward, and suddenly a merciful oblivion rested her turbulent spirit, during which her agonized brother worked, hoping and praying that she might soon know how he pitied and loved her.

At length, when she opened her eyes and gazed at him, Ann murmured under her breath, with a world of pleading:

"Don't speak of him—don't! Dear heart, I can't—I can't bear it!"

It was not until long afterward that Horace Shellington heard of the scene through which she had passed.

Everett Brimbecomb's card admitted him to the governor's home. Mrs. Vandecar welcomed him with outstretched hands.

"Strange, Everett," said she, "but I was thinking only this afternoon that I should ask you to dinner. I feel ashamed that I haven't before; but I've been such an invalid for a long time! You must be lonely, now that your father and mother are gone."

"I've been busy."

The other laughed understandingly.

"Ah! I had forgotten that a young engaged man has but few free evenings on his hands."

To this Everett did not reply.

"How is dear Ann?" asked Mrs. Vandecar.

"I left her quite well; but not in the best of spirits. In fact, dear little lady," and he bent over the white hand he held, "I've come to ask a favor of you."

"Is it anything about Ann? I can't have matters disarranged between you two. I've always said you were an ideal couple."

"Thank you," murmured Everett.

Her frank words somewhat shattered his courage; for he knew her to be kind-hearted. He did not expect to have her make any impression upon the Shellington brother and sister; but wished her assistance as far as her husband was concerned.

He kept his gaze so long upon the floor that Mrs. Vandecar spoke:

"I'm glad you came to me, Everett."

"Yes, I'm glad, too, and I need your help just now. The fact is, Ann and I have had words over a case I have taken charge of in the office."

"How very strange!" exclaimed the woman, mystified.

"It's no more strange to you than to me," went on Everett, after they were seated. "First, Horace and I quarreled, and then, thinking Ann would uphold me in my work, I went to her; getting about the same reception I had received from him."

"I should never have believed it of either of them," faltered Mrs. Vandecar. "But do tell me about it."

"Horace and Ann, as you know, have a boy and a girl in their charge."

The governor's wife sat up interestedly.

"I have heard of them," said she; "but have never seen them. I asked Ann over the telephone one day this week, if I sent Katherine for the girl, would she allow her to come and spend an afternoon with Mildred. But she said that—"

"Fledra, they call her," interrupted Brimbecomb, with a keen glance at his companion.

"Yes, so I've heard. Ann said that this Fledra was not going out at all."

"Do you know why?"

"Why, I supposed that it was because their father had asked for them and they feared some foul play."

"Foul play!" cried Brimbecomb. "Why, Mrs. Vandecar, don't you think that a father ought to have his own children?" Everett's eyes pierced her gaze until it dropped.

"Not if he is bad," murmured she, "and I heard he was brutal to them."

"It is not so; of that I am sure. That is the matter I have come about. I have accepted the father's case."

"Oh, Everett, was this necessary for you to do, as long as you know Ann's heart is set upon keeping them?"

Everett twisted nervously.

"She has no right to have her heart set upon them. Now, here is what I want you to do. Ann is wearing away her health with these scrubs of humanity, for which she won't even receive gratitude, and Horace looks like a June shad. The boy has been sick constantly since he's been there. If there were no hospitals in the town, it might be different. I must make a move to separate the girl I love from the burden she can't bear."

Everett averted his face. Until that moment this excuse had not come into his mind. If Mrs. Vandecar had any affection at all for Ann, the thought that the girl was making herself ill would tempt her to interfere.

"Everett, does Ann know why you want to take them away from her?"

"Of course not; I couldn't tell her that, nor Horace, either. They would have promptly told me to attend to my own affairs; but I could come to you."

"I'm so glad—I'm so glad you did! And poor Ann, I wish she would allow her friends to help her! She's such a darling in her charitable work, though, isn't she?"

"I don't agree with you," dissented Everett.

"But you must admit, boy, that a girl who will make a hospital of her home, who will wear out her strength for two little strangers, has the heart of Christ in her."

"I admit her goodness," said Everett slowly, "or I should not want her for my wife. But you can't blame me when I say that I desire her to be herself again."

Mrs. Vandecar rose.

"Well, come in to dinner, and we can still talk. Mildred has gone to her father in Albany with Katherine for a day or two, and I'm alone."

When they were seated, Everett pressed his plea again.

"I don't think Ann would have been so stubborn in the matter, if Horace had not insisted upon it. And I know that you will be surprised to hear that he is in love with the girl, a little pauper who uses bad English and swears like a pirate."

Fledra Vandecar dropped her fork and started back from the table.

"Everett, has Horace lost his mind, or what is it? What can there be in two children—for they are very young—to have such a hold upon a man like Horace and a woman like Ann?"

"I have asked myself that a dozen times, and more," commented Everett. "But now you understand why I want to do something to relieve these misguided young people—to say nothing of my love for Ann?"

"I do understand," replied Mrs. Vandecar, "and I can't blame you. But, really, I don't see what I can do, without incurring the enmity of both of my friends."

"Your husband," breathed Everett.

"Is pledged to Horace in this very matter, and, of course, I couldn't take a stand against him. Everett, why don't you drop the case and let time take its course? I fear that you're going the wrong way."

Brimbecomb bit his lip. He might have known that Horace would apply to the governor; but he had hoped to steal a march upon him and to keep the state's official from aiding him. But Everett also knew what an influence Mrs. Vandecar had over her husband, and now rejoined:

"I have gone too far with it; and, what's more, if I have to bear the brunt of the thing alone, I'll free Ann from a presence that has completely changed her! Have you seen her lately?"

Mrs. Vandecar shook her head.

"I haven't," she admitted slowly. "I haven't been well enough to go out, and she hasn't been here. I have heard from her only now and then on the 'phone. Poor child! I must try to get over there tomorrow."

Next day Ann met Mrs. Vandecar with open arms.

"Oh, Fledra," said she, "I've longed for you so many days! I do appreciate your coming!"

"I knew you would, Ann. You are the first acquaintance I have called on in weeks. But, honey girl, you don't look well."

Ann's eyes filled with tears. Fledra Vandecar was one of the many bright rays of sunshine in her past life, when she had been happy and contented, when Everett had been her lover, and Horace at ease. Now her life was all chaos. Misery, fright, and a troubled heart were her constant companions.

Mrs. Vandecar leaned over and gently brushed back a lock of hair from the girl's brow.

"Ann, dear, can't you tell me what is the matter?"

"There's so very much, it would weary you."

"Indeed, no! Mayn't I stay with you just a little while?"

Ann checked back her emotion and rose.

"Pardon, Dear; I didn't dream that you could."

"Of course I can. Mildred is in Albany. How happy I should be if I could help you!"

"Time only will do that, Fledra. It will take many weeks before Horace and I are running in our old home gait. But I love to have you here, especially as Horace has gone out for a long drive. He will be away all the afternoon."

"That's too bad," interjected Mrs. Vandecar. "I hoped to see him. And, Ann, I want also to see those children."

"The girl is riding with Horace today—she gets out so little, and Brother insisted upon taking her. The boy is still very ill."

"Is he too ill for me to see him?"

Ann hesitated.

"Well, his heart is affected, and anything unusual throws him into a new spell. We keep all trouble from him."

Mrs. Vandecar touched her friend gently.

"And you've had enough of his to bear, poor Ann!"

"We don't consider it a trouble to do anything for those we love. I wonder if you would like to peep at him—making no noise, remember! He is sleeping under a drug. Come, Dear, and I'll look at him first."

The governor's wife followed Ann to Floyd's door, and waited until a beckoning finger called her in. She entered the darkened chamber, and paused a moment to get her bearings. Miss Shellington was near the bed, her eyes calling.

"He's sound asleep," she whispered.

With his head thrown back a little, Floyd's face was turned toward the wall. His profile and thick black curls were sharply distinct upon the white pillow-slip. His broad brow was covered with beads of perspiration, and the lips were muttering incoherent words. Mrs. Vandecar leaned far over the bed, and peered into his face. Something so touched her in the thin, sunken cheeks, in the drawn mouth, whispering in an unnatural sleep, that she drew back weeping. Suddenly words formed on the sleeper's lips:

"Gentle Jesus, meek and mild," fell from them, "look upon—look upon—" Then the whisper trailed once more into incoherence.

Fledra Vandecar clutched at Ann's sleeve.

"He's praying, Ann! He's praying!" Miss Shellington bowed her head in assent. "Poor baby, poor little dear!" Mrs. Vandecar's voice was louder than before.

"Hush, hush!" breathed Ann. "Come away. He's so very ill!"

"Pity—pity my simplicity," murmured Floyd again, "and Lord prepare my soul a—place!"

Mrs. Vandecar straightened and flashed the rigid girl at her side an appealing glance. Ann touched her again, and the two women passed from the room, weeping.

"How very beautiful he is!" stammered Mrs. Vandecar. "Oh, Ann, dear, can't you do something for him? Can't I? Why haven't I tried before? You won't be offended, will you, Ann, when I say that until this moment I have never approved of your having him? But I've seldom seen such a face, and he was—he was praying, poor baby! Poor, little tormented boy! I wish that he had been awake, or that his sister were here—I want to see her, too."

"Yes, you should see her. She is very sweet," replied Ann so gravely that Mrs. Vandecar wept again.

Very soon she made ready for home, with no hint of the

conversation she had had with Everett, and no word of advice to Ann about giving up her charges.

CHAPTER TWENTY-SIX

A letter went that night from Fledra Vandecar to her husband in Albany. It was written after the woman had paced her room for several hours in inexplicable disquietude and unrest. Puzzled, the governor read:

Dearest.—

"I went today to see Ann Shellington, with my mind fully made up to speak to her about the boy and girl who have been with her for these last few months. Everett was here to dinner last night with me, and confided in me his trouble with Horace, which has finally culminated in a breach with Ann. It seems the difficulty arose over the case of the squatter from Ithaca who has demanded his children.

"Everett has taken the man's side, and until I called upon Ann I felt quite in sympathy with him. And still I cannot tell you, dearest Floyd, what changed my mind, unless it was the sight of that sick boy. He was sleeping when I went in, and was muttering over a babyish prayer, which quite touched me. I had no opportunity to talk with him, nor the girl either. She was riding with Horace, and Everett tells me that he (Horace) is quite infatuated with the child.

"I'm going to ask you, Floyd darling, to help Horace all you can, and if Everett comes to see you, as he said he was going to, I want you to know that it is my wish that you should keep to your policy with Ann and her brother. I cannot tell why I am writing you this, only that my heart aches for that boy, and that for years I have never felt so impelled to help a human being as I have him.

"I thought Everett might tell you that I was won to his way of thinking by his pleading how he wanted to remove Ann from contact with the boy and girl; so I hasten to write you. Kiss my precious Mildred for her mother, and, Floyd, dear, see to it that she doesn't stay up too late; for she is not strong. I cautioned Katherine about it; but I'm afraid she might yield to the child's entreaties.

"With fondest love to you, my darling, and to my baby and Katherine, I am,

"Your own loving wife,

"FLEDRA"

The governor read and reread the letter, especially the part in which his wife implored him to aid Horace Shellington. He laid it down with a sigh. He well knew that Fledra's heart was tender toward all little ones since the disappearance of her own. All hope that he would ever see his twin children had left him years before, and now, for some moments, with his hand on the envelop, his mind wandered into hidden places, where he saw a boy and a girl growing to manhood and womanhood, and he groaned deeply.

Later, when Everett Brimbecomb was ushered into his office at the capital, the governor was primed with the sympathy that he had gathered from his wife's letter.

"This is something of a surprise, my dear boy," he said. "I did not know you were coming to Albany so soon."

"I came with a purpose," replied Everett; "for, as you know, my father is away, and I need your advice in something."

Vandecar waited for his visitor to proceed.

"Do you see any reason," Everett stammered, "why two young lawyers should not be friends, even if they have to take opposite sides in a lawsuit?"

"No," replied the governor slowly.

"Then I'll lay the whole thing before you, and let you tell me what you think of it."

"Have a cigar while we talk," broke in Vandecar, offering Everett his case.

In silence they began to smoke, and both remained quiet until the governor said:

"Now, explain it to me, please."

Everett began the story of the children's running away, as the squatter had told it to him, and of their coming to Horace. He did not forget to add that he believed Shellington had lied to him the night he came into the dining-room and discovered Fledra and Floyd with the two little animals. When a shade passed over the governor's face, Everett quickly noted that he had made a mistake in the drawing of conclusions.

"Don't be too hasty, Everett," cautioned Vandecar, shaking an

149

ash deliberately from his cigar. "Horace is the soul of truth. If he did not tell it to you, he had good reasons."

Brimbecomb frowned. He could have bitten his tongue out for making that misstep.

"That's so," he admitted. "But, ever since last September, Horace, and I might say Ann, too, have drawn more and more away from me. For my part, I see no good that can come of their relations with squatters."

"It was the most charitable act I have ever heard of," replied Vandecar. "But you are straying from the case. Do I understand that you have taken up the side of the father?"

"Yes."

"And that you intend to make a move to return his children to him?"

"Yes."

"Why?"

As Everett looked at the stern, unyielding man before him, his excuse to Mrs. Vandecar seemed tame as it ran through his mind. The governor's eyes were scanning him critically, almost dazzling him with their steely gray. An expression in the steady gaze made him tremble; but he took heart as he thought of the friendship between the governor and his foster father.

"It's hardly fair to ask me why I took the case, which came to me in a legitimate manner," said he. "I can see no reason why the man, although poor, should not have his own children. Do you?"

It was a pointed question, and Vandecar waived it by saying:

"There are always circumstances surrounding these things, such as when parents are cruel to their children, which might make it advisable, almost imperative, to take the youngsters away and put them with reputable people. I think Horace is of the impression that this is true in the present case."

"Then is one man's opinion to be taken? Do you advise that?"

"No; but I do not yet understand why you should be interested against your friends. I should think that, rather than disagree with them, you would wish to have nothing to do with it."

Everett would have to use Ann again to convince the governor of his right to act. It had been far easier to explain his interest in Cronk to Mrs. Vandecar than to this quiet, powerful man opposite. The brown-flecked gray eyes looked unusually sober and truth-demanding.

"I won't have them any longer with Ann than I can help," Everett broke forth suddenly. "She is killing herself over them. Have you ever seen them, Mr. Vandecar?"

"No."

150

"If you had, then you would agree with me. The fact is, your wife thinks the way I do, but would not help me because you were pledged to Horace. Your influence over him is great, and I should like to keep this out of court, if possible. Mrs. Vandecar was rather exercised over Ann."

With a deliberation that baffled Everett, the governor put down his cigar and drew a letter from his pocket. He opened it in silence and glanced at it, while Everett stared uneasily at this unusual proceeding. Presently the governor looked up casually.

"You say that my wife is exercised over Ann?"

"So she told me. She—-"

"Well, just at this time," interjected Vandecar, "Mrs. Vandecar is very much in sympathy with the boy. She has seen him, since talking with you." Everett stood up abruptly. "She has changed her mind; so her letter tells me, Brimbecomb," went on the elder man, "and, as I am working with Horace, and this thing touches him so deeply, I shall have to ask you not to come to me for advice or help. You understand," and the governor rose also, "that, while I have a deep feeling of interest in you and your work, I must say that I think it would be better taste for you to withdraw while you can. It will be unpleasant all around, and, as your father is away, it is rather dangerous to connect your office with low people."

Everett went forth from the interview discomfited, but none the less firm in his evil purpose. Only a few days later, when Lem Crabbe's scow was slowly making its way from Ithaca to Tarrytown, *habeas corpus* papers were served upon Horace Shellington to produce the twins in court and to give reasons why they should not be given to their father.

Horace held a consultation with Ann, and it was decided that they should appeal to the court for time, procuring a doctor's certificate to prove that Floyd was too ill even to know of the proceedings. This having been done, it placed an unlooked-for stay upon Everett Brimbecomb; but he secured a court order instructing the sheriff to guard the children at the Shellington home until the boy was well enough to be taken out. So, a deputy was stationed in the house.

In the meantime Lon watched eagerly for the coming of Lem. When at last he espied the scow fastened in its accustomed place, he went down to carry the news to the owner. After explaining the matter as far as it had gone, he ventured:

"Lem, be ye carin' for Flea yet?"

"Why?" demanded Lem suspiciously.

"'Cause we can make some money outen her, if ye gives up yer claim on her."

"Ye mean to sell her?"

Lem's words sounded hoarse as he wheezed them out.

"'Tain't sellin' her," explained Lon. "A whollopin' good-lookin' feller wants her, and he says he'll buy yer off and give me money fer her. Will ye do it, Lem?"

"Nope, I won't! I want her myself. I been waiting long 'nough fer her."

"But wouldn't ye ruther have a pocketful of money? I would, I bet ye!"

"Lon, be ye goin' to do me dirt?" asked Lem darkly.

Lon straightened his shoulders.

"Nope, I told him ye had to be buyed off, afore I could say nothin'. But I thought ye liked money, Lem."

"So I do; but I like Flea better. I helped ye get 'em when they were babies, Lon, and ye said—"

Cronk flung out his arms.

"I said as how ye wasn't to mention aloud, even to me, that the kids wasn't mine. Ye has Flea, if ye say so, and I'll tell the lawyer—"

"Be it that good-lookin' feller what ye give the fifty dollars to what wants Flea?" Cronk nodded. "I thought ye wouldn't let me marry her," Lem cried, "and now ye be goin'—"

Lon interrupted the scowman fiercely:

"Nuther is he goin' to marry her—ye can bet on that! No kid of Vandecar's gets a boost up from me—a boost down, more like!"

"I'll kill the feller if he touches her," growled Lem, "and ye can make up yer mind to that, Lon!"

Lon Cronk shrugged his shoulders disdainfully.

"Take her if ye want her, Lem. I won't put no straw in yer way. But I never could see what ye wanted her fer. She's a big mouth to feed, let me tell ye!"

For some moments the two men sat in the darkening scow and smoked in silence. Suddenly Lem looked up.

"We couldn't get ahead of the nasty scamp, could we, Lon? I mean, could we git the money, and then keep the gal?"

"I don't want her," growled Lon; "she couldn't stay with me no more."

"We oughter make him pay the money, though," Lem insisted.

"Then, if ye has Flea, Lem," said Lon, looking keenly at the scowman, "and ye git yer share of money, ye has to share up yer half with me. See?"

"Yep," muttered Lem. "Will ye bring the feller down here some day, and we'll talk it over?"

Lon acquiesced by a nod of his head, saying only, "Come on out, and let's get a drink."

"When's he goin' to git 'em—Flea and Flukey, I mean?"

"I dunno. The boy's too sick to come to court. He's liable to die any minute."

Lem started forward at the unexpected word.

"If he croaks, be ye goin' to leave Flea there?"

"Not by a damn sight! We'll git her, and I don't care if the boy goes dead afore mornin'. I only want him to suffer, and die if he wants to. And, Lem," Lon smiled evilly, and, looking into the swart face of his pal, said, "and I guess ye can make the gal come to yer likin'."

Lem's throat worked visibly, his face reddened by the silent laughter that shook him.

"I only want the chance," he said. "Come on and let's git a drink."

CHAPTER TWENTY-SEVEN

Everett Brimbecomb had become impatient. He missed his evenings with Ann, and was tortured with the thought that Horace was with Fledra. Every day made his hatred for his former friend more deadly, more vindictive, and he not only desired to take the squatter girl away, but he felt impelled to separate Ann from her brother. He received a badly spelled note from Lon with a feeling of thanksgiving. Something had happened to make the squatter wish to see him. So, after dinner, he took the direction Lon had given, and reached the scow in a heavy rain. It was much more to his liking that the evening should be stormy; for no person of his own station in life would be apt to be abroad on such a night.

As he entered the living-room of the scow, Everett bowed frigidly to Lem Crabbe, and forgot to extend his hand to Lon.

"You sent for me," he said in a low tone, looking at the squatter.

"Yep. I knowed ye wanted to see Lem, and I thought as how ye'd ruther come here than have him come along to yer office. Ain't that right?"

"I believe I told you so," responded Everett coldly, as he took his place in a rickety chair.

"Ye said, didn't ye, Mister, that ye wanted the handlin' of Flea after we took her away from that meddlin' millionaire?"

"Yes."

"And I telled ye that ye had to make a bargain with Lem, 'cause he had first right to her. What ye willin' to give?"

"How much money do you want to withdraw your claim from the girl?"

"I ain't thought 'bout no price," replied Lem covertly.

"Then think and listen to me. I have an idea in my mind that we can take the girl away from that house, if not tomorrow, at least in a few days."

Lem's eyes glistened, and Lon placed his clay pipe carefully upon the table.

"Lip it out, then, Mister," said the latter; "and, if me and Lem's agreein' with ye, then we'll help ye."

Everett moved uneasily in the creaking chair. He did not desire to dicker with these ruffians; but it was necessary, if he wished to carry out his plans concerning Fledra.

"The boy is likely to die any moment. The girl is the only one who can help you, Mr. Cronk." Everett had meaning in his voice, and his words made Lem swallow hard.

"I was a thinkin' that myself," ruminated Lon.

"The girl idolizes her brother and Mr. Shellington. If you could make her understand that they would otherwise both be killed through your instrumentality, she would leave the house of her own free will, I'm sure."

Lon, grimacing with delight, bounded up and faced Lem.

"That be so! That comes of gittin' a lawyer what's got stuff in his head, ye see, Lem. I told ye that when ye said as how we could get them kids without spendin' no money."

"You will have to use great care, both of you," Everett urged, "and it only means for you to take the girl, as you first planned, to Ithaca; and I will come after her. You will both have your money, and our business together will be at an end." Lem laughed, but with no sound. "Just how to get this girl is more than I have figured out," Everett continued; "but it might be well for me to try and get a letter to her. I have been a steady visitor at Shellington's home for many years. We are hardly upon good terms now; but I could manage it, if one of you men would write it. Make the letter strong, and you will gain your

154

ends. You may bring it to my office tomorrow, Mr. Cronk." He rose, buttoned up his raincoat, and went out, leaving two gaping men looking after him.

Since the papers had been served upon him, Horace had had no peace of mind. The solemn deputy loitering about the home menaced the whole future. It sickened him when he forced his imagination to dwell upon Fledra's future, if she were dragged back to Ithaca, and he had rather place Floyd in his grave than give him into the hands of the squatter. Suddenly, one morning, he took a great resolution, and no sooner had he made up his mind to take the one step that would change his whole life than he called Ann to tell her about it.

"I'm going to marry Fledra," he said, catching his breath.

Ann dropped her hands fearfully; but intense interest gathered on her face.

"I can save her no other way," he went on, almost in excuse, noting her glance. "And you must have seen, Ann, dear, that I love the child. Sit down here and let me tell you about it."

He began at the beginning, telling her of his early growing love, of his desire to make the squatter child his wife. Ann allowed him to narrate his story impulsively, without interruption.

Then she said gently:

"Horace, dear, have you told her that you love her?"

"Yes; but I am going to tell her again this morning."

"Ask her now," suggested Ann eagerly, and she rose.

Horace found Fledra with Floyd, and she lifted her eyes confidingly to his with a smile. For a long time he had been so tender, so loving, that the specter bred and fostered by Everett Brimbecomb's kisses had nearly vanished.

"Floyd is so much better this morning!" she said. Her words were well chosen, and she pronounced her brother's new name carefully.

Floyd held out his hand and raised himself slowly up.

"Look, Brother Horace!" he cried eagerly. "Look—just this morning I've been able to stand up! Sister Ann says in a few days I can walk."

Horace held the thin, white fingers in his for an instant.

"So you will, boy. It won't be long before you can get out."

The words startled Fledra. Not until the trouble of Lon's coming had she wished that Floyd might linger in the sickroom. The man outside, watching every movement in the house, frightened her. She knew that when her brother was well enough he and she would be called away for the court's decision as to their future.

155

"Floyd, will you spare your sister just a few moments? I want to talk with her."

"Course I will, Brother Horace. Scoot along, Fledra!"

"This way, child," whispered Horace. "I've something—oh, such a dear something!—to say to you."

They quietly passed the deputy, who only raised his eyes, smiled at Fledra, and dropped his gaze again to his paper. When Horace's door was closed, Horace took Fledra into his embrace and kissed her again and again. She loved the warmth of his arms, and the delight of his kisses caused her to rest unresisting until he chose to speak.

"Fledra, dear, will you marry me—immediately?"

His question brought her to rigidity.

"You mean—"

"I mean that all our troubles are going away."

Fledra drew slowly from him.

"How can our troubles go away?" she asked.

"By your consenting."

"I told you once, and more than once, that I couldn't tell you. Won't you ever understand?"

But Horace did not loosen his hold upon her. He drew the dark head against him tenderly.

"You misunderstood, Fledra. I am going to trust you in everything. I am going to put all my faith in you, and to save you and your brother from a fearful life. I must make you my wife!"

Fledra drew a long breath. All the stumbling petitions she had made to Heaven were answered by those few words. At last, to be Horace's wife, to save Flukey, and to protect Ann, who would now have back her lover! It seemed to the young girl, in this flashing moment of thought, that all the clouds of the last few months had floated over their heads and away.

"It will take a few days before I can arrange our marriage," explained Horace. "One reason for not arranging today is that I have to run down to New York for two or three days; and then, too, I must be careful not to let anyone know of our plans. I want you to talk with my sister. I have told her that I love you."

"Was she sorry?" whispered Fledra.

"No—very, very glad!"

"And can I tell Floyd?"

"Yes, just as soon as you like. I have an idea your happiness will go far to make him well."

For an hour Horace refused to let her leave him, and when Fledra did go back to the sick brother her face was radiant with happiness.

Floyd was not prepared for the rush of words or the passionate appeal with which she met him.

Blinking his eyes, the boy waved his sister back.

"I can't make out what you're saying, Flea."

"I'm going to marry Brother Horace!" She stopped, and began again. "I'm going to marry Horace—oh, so soon, Fluke! And aren't you glad? And then they can't take us away!"

It was the first intimation Floyd had had of their danger. He rose up, standing upon his legs tremblingly.

"Has anybody been trying to take us away, Flea?"

Then Fledra realized what she had said, and hesitated in fear.

"I forgot, you weren't to know, Fluke. Will you wait till I call Brother Horace?... Fluke, don't be trembling like that! Sit down, Fluke!... Fluke!"

Floyd's face had paled, even to the tips of his ears. He realized now that danger had hung over the fair young sister and he had not known of it.

"It's Pappy Lon, and ye never told me, Flea, and that's why ye been so unhappy! He'll take ye away because yer his kid, and Brother Horace can't do anything."

"Yes, he can, Fluke—yes, he can! He loves me, and I love him, and he's going to marry me! Nobody can't take a wife away from her man!... Fluke, don't wabble like that! Brother Horace! Brother Horace!"

Fledra's voice reached the dreaming man, bending over his desk, and he bounded to answer her call. He found her supporting her brother, white and shivering, with eyes strained by fright.

"I told him," gasped Fledra looking up; "but I didn't mean to."

"Told him what?"

"Pappy Lon," muttered Floyd, "comin' for Flea!"

Horace caught the words in dismay.

He placed the suffering boy on the divan and bent close. In low tones he said that the squatter in some mysterious way had found where they were, and that he had come for them. He began at the beginning, explaining to the boy Lon's demand upon him. He refrained, however, from mentioning Everett, because of the pain to his sister. He had just finished the story, when Ann softly opened the door and came in.

"But I insist that you will place your faith in me, Floyd. I shall see to it that neither you nor your sister leave me—unless you go of your own free will," Horace concluded.

"If Pappy Lon takes one of us," muttered Floyd, as Miss

Shellington calmed him with sweet interest, "let him take me. I'm as good as dead, anyhow. I want Flea to marry Brother Horace."

"And so she will," assured Ann. "Now then, Dear, try and sleep."

During the rest of the afternoon Ann held conferences with her brother, fluttering back and forth from him to Floyd, and then to Fledra. She noted that the strained expression had gone from the girl's face, and uttered a little prayer of thanksgiving when she heard Horace's hearty laugh ring out once more.

CHAPTER TWENTY-EIGHT

Everett Brimbecomb took the letter Lon Cronk handed him, without rising from his chair.

"It be for Flea," said Lon, grinning, "and I think she'll understand it. It's as plain as that nose on yer face, Mister."

"May I read it?" asked the lawyer indifferently. Then, as Lon nodded, he slipped the letter deftly from the finger-marked envelope and read the contents with a smile. "It's strong enough," he said, replacing it. "I, too, think she'll succumb to that. If you'll leave this letter with me, I'll see that she gets it."

Everett put the envelop in a drawer and implied that the interview was at an end. But the squatter twirled his cap in his fingers and lingered.

"Lem says as how he'll take the gal and me in his scow to Ithaca. Ye can follow us when ye git ready."

The younger man stood up, nodding his approval.

"That'll be just the way to do it, and I shall look to you, Mr. Cronk, to keep faith with me. Frankly speaking, I do not like your friend. I think he's a rascal."

"Well, he be a mean cuss; but there be other cusses besides Lem, Mister."

Brimbecomb flushed at the meaning glance in the squatter's shrewd eyes.

"All you both have to do," said he bruskly, "is to spend the money I'll give you—and keep your mouths shut."

If Everett had noted the crafty expression on the squatter's face as the latter walked down the street, he would not have been so satisfied over his deal with Lon. After he was alone, he reread Cronk's letter. Later he wrote steadily for sometime. His communication also was for Fledra, and he intended by hook or crook to get it to her with the other.

There never had been greater rejoicing in the Shellington home than on the night when it was settled that Fledra was to marry Horace. It was decided that after the wedding the girl should have tutors and professors. A lovelight had appeared in the gray eyes when she promised Ann that she would study diligently until Horace and Floyd and all her dear ones would be proud of her advancement. How gently Ann encircled the little figure before she said goodnight, and how tearfully she congratulated Horace that he had won such a fond, faithful heart for his own! Even after kissing Floyd, and tucking the coverlet about his shoulders, the young woman was again drawn to Fledra.

"May I come in, Darling?" she whispered.

Fledra did not cease combing her curls before the mirror when she welcomed Miss Shellington.

"I simply couldn't go to bed, child," said Ann, "until I came to see you again. I feel so little like sleeping!"

Fledra turned a blushing, happy face upon her friend.

"And I'm not going to sleep tonight, either. I'm going to stay awake all night and be glad."

This brought Ann's unhappiness back to her, and she smiled sadly as she thought of her own tangled love-affair.

"I want you and my brother to be very happy."

Fledra dropped her comb and looked soberly at the other.

"I'm not good enough for him," she said, with a sigh; "but he loves me, and I love him more than the whole world put together, Sister Ann."

The young face had grown radiant with idealized love and faith, and through the shining gray eyes, in which bits of brown shaded to golden, Ann could see the girl's soul, pure and lofty. She marked how it had grown, had expanded, under great love, and marveled.

"I know that, Dearest. I wish I were as happy as you!"

The pathos in her tones, the sad lines about Ann's sweet mouth, made Fledra grasp her hands in girlish impetuousness.

"He'll come back to you, Sister Ann, some day," she breathed. "He thinks Pappy Lon ought to have us kids, and that's what makes him work against you and Brother Horace. He can't stay away from you long."

Ann shook her head mournfully.

"I fear he doesn't love me, Fledra, or he couldn't have done as he has. Sometimes it seems as if I must send for him; for he isn't bad at heart." She rested her eyes on Fledra's face imploringly. "You think, don't you, Dear, that when a woman loves a man as I love him her love in the end will help him?"

Fledra thought of her own mad affection for Horace, of his love for her, and of how her longing for him stirred the very depths of her soul, uplifting and refreshing it. She nodded her head.

"He'll come back to her, all right," she murmured after Ann had gone and she had thrown herself on the bed. "Floyd will get well, and Horace and I—" She dropped asleep, and the morning had fully dawned before she opened her eyes to another day.

Then, as Fledra sat up in bed, brushed back the curls from her face, and with the eagerness of a child thought over the happy yesterday, suddenly her eyes fell upon an envelop, lying on the carpet just beneath her window. It had not been there the night before. She slipped to the floor, picked up the sealed letter with her name on it, and climbed into bed again, while examining it closely. With a mystified expression upon her face, she tore open the envelop. Unfolding one of the two letters, inclosed, she read:

"*Flea Cronk.*—

"This is to tell ye that if ye don't come back with me and Lem, we'll kill that guy Shellington and Flukey. Flukey can stay there if he wants to, if you come. Make up yer mind, and don't ye tell any man that I writ this letter. Come to Lem's scow in the river, or ye know what I does to Flukey.

"LON CRONK."

Fledra folded up the letter and opened the other one dazedly. It was written with a masterly pen-stroke, and the girl, without reading it, looked at the signature. It was signed, "Everett Brimbecomb." Her eyes flashed back to the beginning, and she read it through swiftly:

"*Little Miss Cronk.*—

"I am delivering this letter in a peculiar way, because I know that you had rather not have anyone see it. It is necessary that you should think calmly and seriously over the question I am going to ask you. I am very fond of you. Whether or not you will return my

160

affection is a thing for you to decide in the future. Now, then, the question is, Do you want to protect your brother and your friends from the anger of your father? If so, you must go with him. I will answer for it that your brother stays where he is; but you must go away. Think well before you decide not to go; for I know the men who are determined to have you, and would save you if I could. I shall try to see you very soon. Destroy this letter immediately. Your friend,

"EVERETT BRIMBECOMB"

Fledra sat as if in a trance, her eyelids drooping over almost sightless eyes. The last blow had fallen upon her, and she knew that she must go. That she could ever be forced away thus without her brother, that Horace could be given no chance to help her, had never crossed her mind. Through her imagination drifted Lon's dark, cruel face, followed by a vision of Lem Crabbe. Feature after feature of the scowman came vividly to her,—the wind-reddened skin, the foul, tobacco-browned lips, the twitching goiter,—all added to the nervous chill that had suddenly come upon the girl. Lem and Lon represented all the world's evil to her, and Everett Brimbecomb all the world's influence. The three had thrust their triple strength between her and happiness. Her dear ones should not fall before the wrath of Lem and Lon, or before the unsurmountable power of Everett Brimbecomb! In her hands alone lay their salvation. Like one stunned, she rose from the bed and carefully destroyed the two letters. This was the one command she would obey promptly.

When Ann knocked softly at the door, and no answer came, she gently pushed it open. Fledra lay with her face to the wall as if asleep. Miss Shellington bent over her, and then crept quietly out to allow the girl to rest another hour. No sooner had the door closed than Fledra sat up with clenched fists, her face blanched with terror. She could not confront the inevitable without help. But not once did it occur to her that Horace Shellington would be able to protect not only her, but himself also. The path of her future life stretched from Tarrytown to Ithaca, straight into Lem's scow!

Through the entire day the girl was enigmatical both to Horace and to Ann. Weary hours, crowding one upon another, offered her no relief. The thought of Lon's letter shattered hope and made her desolate. She did not stop to reason that her relations with Horace demanded that she tell him of Everett's perfidy. Had not her loved ones been threatened with death, if she disclosed having received the letters? She spent most of the day with Floyd, saying but little.

161

In the evening Fledra waited wide-eyed and sleepless until the household was quiet, and while she waited she pondered dully upon a plan to escape. Toward night two faint hopes had taken possession of her: Everett Brimbecomb could help her; Pappy Lon might. Before leaving Floyd and severing her connections with Horace, she would appeal to the squatter and his lawyer. She opened the window and looked out. It was but a short drop to the path at the side of the house.

At half-past ten Fledra slipped into her coat and set a soft, light cap upon her black curls. In another minute she had reached the road and had turned toward Brimbecomb's. To escape any eyes in the house she had just left, she scurried to the graveyard. For an instant only did she halt, and, somber-eyed, glance over the graves. She could easily mark the spot where she had lain so long with Floyd, and tears welled into her eyes as she thought of him. How many things had happened since then! In hasty review came week after week of the time she had spent with Horace and Ann. How she loved them both! Turning, she scanned the gloomy Brimbecomb house. In the servants' quarters at the top several lights burned, while on the drawing-room floor a gas-jet shot forth its beams into Sleepy Hollow. If Mr. Brimbecomb were at home, then he must be in that room. Fledra crouched under the window.

"Mr. Brimbecomb! Mr. Brimbecomb!" she called.

Silence, as dense as that in God's Acre near her, reigned in the house. She called again, a little louder. Suddenly she heard a rapid step upon the road and crept back again to the corner of the building.

Everett Brimbecomb was passing under the arc light, and Fledra could see his handsome face plainly in its rays.

He stopped a moment and looked at Shellington's house, with a shrug of his shoulders. Again he resumed his way; but halted as Fledra called his name softly. From her hiding-place in the shadow of the porch she came slowly forward.

"Can I talk with you a few moments, Mr. Brimbecomb?" she faltered. "I know that you can help me, if you will."

Everett's heart began to beat furiously. Something in the appealing girl attacked him as nothing else had. How slim she looked, how lithe and graceful, and yet so childishly young! He compared her with Ann in rapid thought, and remembered that he had never felt toward Horace's sister as he did toward this obscure girl.

"Come in," he murmured; "we can't talk here. Come in."

"Let me tell you out here in the night," stammered Fledra.

Everett touched her arm, urging her forward.

"They may see us from the Shellingtons'," he said; and, in spite of her unwillingness, he forced her up the steps. Like the wind of a hurricane, a mixture of emotions stormed in his soul. He dared not do as he wished and take the girl in his arms. He checked his desire to force his love upon her, and motioned to a chair, into which Fledra sank. Like shining ebony, her black hair framed a death-pale face. The darkness of a new grief had deepened the shade in the mysterious eyes. For an instant she paused on the edge of tears.

"I don't want to go back with Pappy Lon!" she whispered.

Everett caught his breath. She was even more lovely than he had remembered. Inwardly he cursed the squatters. If he could eliminate them from his plans—but they were necessary to him.

"I don't like none o' the bunch of ye!" Fledra burst out in his silence. Brimbecomb's lips formed a slight smile. The girl pondered a moment, and continued fiercely, "And I hate Ithaca and all the squatters!"

"You speak very much like your father," ventured the lawyer. "I can't understand why you hate him. Your place is with him."

The girl bowed her head and wept softly. She realized that when she was excited she could not remember her English.

"I've been a squatter," she said, forlornly shaking her head, "and I s'pose Pappy Lon has a right to me; but I love—"

"You love whom?"

"Mr. Shellington. Oh, Mr. Brimbecomb, can't ye help me to keep away from Pappy Lon? Can't ye make him see that I don't want to go back—that I can't go back to Lem Crabbe ever?"

"There's no danger of your going to—what did you say his name was?"

"Lem Crabbe—the man with a hook on his arm. I hate him so!"

"I remember seeing him once. I don't think you need worry over going with him. Your father is not a fool."

"He promised me to Lem!" wailed Flea.

"And he—promised—you to—me!"

So deliberately did Everett speak that Fledra was on her feet before the sentence was finished. Horror, deep-seated, rested in the eyes raised to his. Oh, surely she had not heard aright!

"What did ye say?" she demanded.

"Your father has promised you to me."

"Oh, that's why you done it, was it? That's why ye fit Sister Ann and Brother Horace? 'Cause ye wanted me to go with ye! I hate ye like I hate—the devil!"

Her words, grossly coarse, struck and stung the man to action. He strode forward and grasped her arm roughly in his fingers.

"You little fury, what do I care how much you hate me? It's a man's pleasure to conquer a woman like you. You can have your choice between the other man and me."

Dumb with fright and amazement, his treachery driving every thought from her mind for the moment, Fledra looked at him.

"I'd rather go with Lem," she got out at last, "'cause I couldn't stand yer hellish pretty face nor yer white teeth. They look like them big stones standing over the dead men out yonder."

With a backward motion of her head toward the window, Fledra drawled out the last words insultingly. That she preferred Lem to him wounded Everett's pride, but made him desire her the more. He loved her just then so much that, if it had been in his power, he would have married her instantly. Her fine-fibered spirit attracted all the evil in him as a magnet draws a needle. Fledra brought him from his reverie.

"There ain't no use of my standin' here any longer," she said. "I might as well go and ask Pappy Lon. He's better'n you."

To let her go this way seemed intolerable.

"Wait," he commanded, "wait! When you came in, I didn't mean to offend you. Will you wait?"

"If ye'll help me keep away from Pappy Lon, and will promise nothin' will happen to Brother Horace or to Fluke."

"I can't do that; it's impossible. But I can take you away, after you get back to Ithaca."

"Can I come back to Brother Horace?"

"No, no; you can't go there again! Now, listen, Fledra Cronk. I'll marry you as soon as you'll let me."

Fledra's eyelids quivered.

"I'll stay with Pappy Lon and Lem, because I love Sister Ann too well to go with you."

"Oh, I thought that was the reason," said Everett. "All your hard words to me were from your tender, grateful heart. That only makes me like you the better."

Fledra turned to go.

"But I don't like you, and I never will. Let me go now, because I'm goin' down to the scow to Pappy Lon."

Brimbecomb threw out an arm with an impetuous swing; but Fledra darted under it.

"Don't—don't!" she cried brokenly. "Don't you never touch me, never—never! I don't want you to! Let me go now, please."

Everett stepped aside and allowed her to reach the door.

"I shall help you, if I can, child," he put in, as she sprang out. "Remember—"

But Fledra did not wait to hear. She was outside the door and flying down the steps.

The wind came sharply from the north as, dejectedly, the girl made her way to the river. She had decided to appeal to Lon, to beg her future of him. Before she reached the scow, she could hear the gurgle of the river, and the sound of the water came familiarly to her ears. Lem's boat lay like a silent, black animal near the bank, and she came to a stop at sight of it. How many times had she seen the dark boat snuggled in the gloom as she saw it now! How many times before had the candle twinkled from the small window, and the sign of life caused her to shiver in fear! But, thinking of what Lon's consent for her to remain with her dear ones meant, she mounted the gangplank and descended the short flight of stairs.

Lon was seated in a chair by the table, and Lem on a stool nearby. Crabbe rose as the pale girl appeared before him; but Lon only displayed two rows of dark teeth. It seemed to him that all his waiting was over; that his wife's constant haunting of his strong spirit would cease, if he could tear the girl from her high estate and watch the small head bend under the indignities Lem would place upon her. The very fact that she had come when he had sent for her showed the fear in which she held him.

Fledra unloosened her wrap from her throat as if it choked her.

"How d'y' do, Flea?" grinned Cronk. His delight was like that of a small boy who has captured a bright-winged butterfly in a net.

"I got yer letter, Pappy Lon," said Fledra, overlooking his impudent manner.

"And ye goin' to stay, ain't ye?" gurgled Lem.

Fledra snapped out "Nope!" to the scowman's question, without looking at him. Her next words were directed to the squatter:

"I've come to beg ye, Pappy Lon, to let me stay in Tarrytown. Mr. Shellington wants to marry me."

She was so frail, so girlishly sweet and desirable, that Lem uttered an oath. But Lon gestured a command of silence.

"Ye can't marry no man yit, Flea," said he. "Ye has to go back to the hut." Determination rang in his words, and the face of the rigid girl paled, and she caught at the table for support. "Ye see," went on Lon, "a kid can't do a thing her pappy says she can't. I says yer to come home to the shanty. And, if ye don't, then I'll do what I said I would. I'll kill that dude Shellington and—"

Before he could finish, Fledra burst in upon him.

"Ye mustn't! Ye mustn't, Pappy Lon! I love him so! And he's so good! And poor little Flukey is so sick, though he's gettin' better, and if I'm happy, then he'll get well! Don't ye love us one little bit, Pappy Lon?" She loosened her hold upon the table and neared the squatter.

Cronk brushed his face awkwardly. The presence of his Midge

filled the scow-room, and his dead baby, wee and well beloved, goaded him to complete his vengeance. For a few seconds he breathed hard, with difficulty choking down sobs that shook his whole body. In a haze, the ghost-woman wavered toward him through the long, bitter years he had lived without her. She thrust herself between him and Fledra. The image that his heated brain had drawn up held out a tiny spirit babe, and so real was the apparition that he put out a trembling hand. For a moment he groped blindly for something tangible in the nothingness before him. Then, with a groan, he let his arm fall nerveless to his side. The vision disappeared, and Lem's presence and even Fledra's faded; for Lon again felt the agonizing cracking of his bones under the prison strait-jacket, and could hear himself shrieking.

He started up and wiped drops of water from his face. He glared at Fledra, his decision remaining steadfast within him. Only exquisite torture for Vandecar's flesh and blood would appease the wrath of Midge and the pale-faced child.

"I love ye well enough to want ye to do my will," he brought out huskily, "and when Flukey gits well he'll come with me, too."

Fledra braced herself for the ordeal. Lon had promised her in his letter that sacrificing herself would mean safety for Floyd and her lover. She would not allow him to break that promise, however much he demanded of her.

Cronk spoke again:

"Ye'd better take off yer things and set down, Flea 'cause ye ain't goin' back."

She made no move to obey him.

"Yes, I'm goin' back to Flukey," she said, "even if you make me come here again. I haven't left any letter for him. But I'll come back to the scow, and go with you and Lem, if you let Fluke stay with Mr. Shellington. If you take him, you don't get me."

"How ye goin' to help yerself?" Lon questioned, with a belittling sneer.

"When I get hold of ye," put in Lem, "ye'll want to stay."

The squatter again motioned the scowman to silence. A fear, almost a respect, for this girl, with her solemn gray eyes and unbending manner, dressed like the people he hated, took root within him.

Fledra's next address to Lon ignored Lem's growling threat.

"I didn't come to fight with you, Pappy Lon. But you've got to let me go back and write a letter. I won't tell anybody that I'm goin' from home. Mr. Shellington's going to New York tomorrow, to stay four or five days. That'll give me a chance to get away, and I'll come to you again tomorrow night. But I'll go with you only when you say that Fluke can stay where he is. Do you hear, Pappy Lon?"

Her face expressed such commanding hauteur, she looked so like Floyd Vandecar when she threw up her head defiantly, that Cronk's big chest heaved with satisfaction. To take his grudge out upon her would be enough. He would cause her to suffer even more than had Midge. He waited for a few moments, with his eyes fastened upon her face, before he spoke. He remembered that she had never told him a lie nor broken a promise.

"Ye swear that, if I let ye go now, ye'll come back tomorry night?"

"Yes, I swear it, if you'll swear that you'll let Fluke alone, and that you won't ever hurt Mr. Shellington. Do you swear it?" Her voice was toned with a desperate passion, and she bent toward the squatter in command.

"I swear it," muttered Lon.

"And can I bring Snatchet with me? I want him because he's Flukey's, and because he'll love me. Can I, Pappy Lon?"

"Yep, damn it! ye can. Bring all the dogs in Tarrytown; but be back tomorry night."

"I'll come, all right; but I'm goin' now."

As the girl turned to go, Lem lumbered to his feet.

"I've got somethin' to say about this!" he stuttered.

"Sit down, Lem!" commanded Lon.

Crabbe stood still.

"That gal don't go back tonight! She's mine! Ye gived her to me, and I want her now."

Lem wriggled his body between Fledra and the stairs; but the girl thrust herself upon him with an angry snarl.

"Don't touch me with your dirty hands!" she gasped.

Lem caught his breath.

"Ye've let that rich pup of a Shellington kiss ye—ye don't move from here!"

Fledra crushed back against the cabin wall and eluded his searching fingers.

"I was goin' to marry Mr. Shellington; but I ain't now. I'm going back to him for tonight, and tomorrow, and I'm goin' to let him kiss me, and I'm goin' to kiss him."

She put forward her face until her breath swept Lem's skin.

"I'm goin' to kiss him as much—as much as he'll let me. And I'm goin' to write Fluke; and, if ye touches me afore I does all that—I'll kill ye!"

Lena drew back from her vehemence, leaving the way of the staircase clear, and in another instant Fledra was gone.

CHAPTER TWENTY-NINE

The following day Shellington left for New York, immediately after breakfast.

Fledra made no attempt to write her farewells until in the evening after she had looked her last upon Floyd, and Ann had seen her to bed. An hour passed before she got up softly and turned on the light. She fumbled warily about her table for writing materials, and after she had found them her tense face was bent long over the letters. When she had finished, she stole along the hall to Horace's study, and left there the tear-stained envelops for him and her brother.

Once back in her room, she donned her street-clothes rapidly, and, after taking a silent farewell of the surroundings she loved, climbed through the window and dropped to the ground. She crept stealthily to the back of the house and approached the dog-kennels. Through the dim light she could see the scrawny greyhounds pulling at their leashes as she fumbled at the wire-mesh door. Whines from several of the dogs made Fledra step inside, whence she glanced out misgivingly to see if she had been observed.

"Snatchet!" she whispered.

From a distant corner she heard the rattle of a chain.

"Snatchet!" she called again.

This time she spoke more loudly and advanced a step.

"Where are ye?"

A familiar whine gave her Snatchet's whereabouts. She felt her way along the right wall, and as she passed each animal she spoke tenderly to it. Upon reaching the little mongrel, Fledra placed her face down close to him. The glitter of his shining eyes, the warm contact of his wet tongue, brought tears from her. She told him gently that they were going away together, going back to the country where many of the evil persons of the world congregated. The girl took the collar from the dog's neck and, picking him up quickly, retraced her steps.

"We're going back to the hut, Snatchet," she told him again, "and Fledra's going to take you because Floyd won't care when he's got Sister Ann—and Brother Horace." At the mention of the man's name, the squatter girl bent her head over the yellow dog and sobbed.

Then she ran until she was far from the house; but her steps lagged more and more as she neared the river. Long before she reached it she stopped and sat down. How intensely she wished that her sacrifice was to wander alone with Snatchet the rest of her days!

Anything would have been preferable to Lem and his scow. But the bargain with her enemies had been the surrendering of herself to the canal-man, and shortly she rose and proceeded on her way to the barge. Before entering it, she raised her eyes to the sky. Everything was at peace with the Infinite, save her own little tortured soul. She dashed aside her tears and ascended the gangplank, halting at the top a moment to answer Middy Burnes' familiar call to her. She saw that Middy had his little tug under steam and was ready to tow the scow away. Shuddering, Fledra went down the stairs into the living-room, where Lem and Lon awaited her.

Neither man spoke when she put Snatchet down on the floor and threw back the lovely cloak she had received from Ann at Christmas. Lem's eyes glittered as he looked at it. Before Fledra entered, the scowman had been industriously tacking a sole on a big leather boot, held tightly between his knees. Now he ceased working; the rusty hook loosened its hold upon the heel of the boot, and the hammer was poised lightly in his left hand. From his mouth protruded the sparkling points of some steel tacks.

Lon was first to break the strained silence.

"We been waitin' a long time fer ye, Flea. Ye've kept the tug a steamin' fer two hours."

"I couldn't come before," replied the girl. "I had to wait till Fluke and Sister Ann went to bed."

Lon sneered as he repeated:

"Sister Ann!"

"She's the lady you saw when you were there, Pappy Lon. And she's the best woman in all the world!"

The squatter smiled darkly.

"Ye'd best put Snatchet in the back room, and then come here again and set down, Flea, 'cause it'll take a long time to get to Ithaca, and ye'll be tired a standin'."

His sarcasm caused no change to cross the girl's face; but Lem grinned broadly. He took the tacks from between his teeth and made as if to speak. After a few vain stutters, however, he replaced the tacks and hammered away at the old boot. Now and then the goiter moved up and down, each movement indicating the passage of a thought through his sluggish brain.

Fledra removed Snatchet and returned to the living-cabin, as Lon had suggested.

"I want to talk to you before I sit down," she said in a low tone. "What are you going to do with me?"

Just then the scow lurched, and the whistle of the tug ahead screamed a farewell to Tarrytown. Fledra heard the grinding of the boat against the landing as it was pulled slowly away, and she sprang to the window. She took one last glimpse of the promised land, one lingering look at the twinkling lights, which shone like glow-worms and seemed to signal sympathy to the terrified girl. Finally she turned a tearless face to Lon.

"I want to know what you're going to do with me when we get to Ithaca. Can I stay awhile with Granny Cronk?"

She glanced fearfully from Lon to the scowman, whose lips were now free of the nails. His wide smile disclosed his darkened teeth as he stammered:

"Yer Granny Cronk's been chucked into a six-foot hole in the ground, and ye won't see her no more."

Staring at the speaker, Fledra fell back against the wall.

"Granny Cronk ain't dead! She ain't! You're lying, Lem Crabbe!"

"Ask yer daddy, if ye don't believe me," grunted Lem.

Fledra cast imploring eyes to Lon.

"Yer granny went dead a long time ago," verified the squatter.

"Then I can stay with you, Pappy Lon, just for a little time. Oh, Pappy Lon," tears rose slowly, and sobs caught her throat as she advanced toward him, "I'll cook for you, and I'll work days and nights, if I can live with you!" She was so near him that she allowed a trembling hand to fall upon his arm. But he spurned it, shaking it off as he growled:

"Don't tech me! Set down and shut up!"

She passed over the repulse and sobbed on:

"But, Pappy Lon, I'd rather die, I'd rather throw myself in the water, than stay with Lem in this boat! I want to tell you how I've prayed—Sister Ann taught me to. I always asked that Flukey might stay in Tarrytown, and that nothing would ever hurt Mr. Shellington. I never dared pray for myself, because—because God had enough to do to help all the other ones, and because I never asked anything for myself till you found me. I want to stay right in the shanty with you, Pappy Lon. I hate Lem—oh, how I hate him!"

Lem coughed and wheezed.

"I guess we'd better shet her claptrap once and fer all," he said. "Lon, ye leave me to settle with Flea—I know how."

The squatter silenced Lem with a look and rose lumberingly. As he struck a match and made toward the steps, Fledra followed close after him.

"Pappy Lon, if you'll stay with me here on the boat till we get to Ithaca, then I'll do what you say when we get there. You sha'n't go and leave me now with Lem, you sha'n't, you sha'n't!" Her voice rose to a shriek, and her small body trembled like a leaf in a wind. So loud were

170

her cries, and so fiercely did she clutch at Lon's coat, that he turned savagely upon her.

"I'll do what I please. Shet up, or Middy'll hear ye. Git yer hands off en me!"

"Pappy Lon, if you leave me with Lem, then I'll jump in the river!"

She bit her lips to stifle the sobs; but still clung beseechingly to his coat.

Lon stepped backward from the chair, and whirled about so quickly that his coat was jerked from Fledra's grasp.

"Then I'll take Fluke, and what I won't do to him ain't worth speakin' 'bout." He glanced at her face and stopped. Never had he seen such an expression. Her bleeding lips and flaring eyes sent him a step from her.

"If you leave me with Lem," she hissed her repetition, "then I'll jump in the river!" Seeing that he hesitated, she went on, "You stay right in here with Lem and me, Pappy Lon, and when we get to the hut I'll do what you tell me."

Fledra heard Lem drop the old boot he had been mending and advance toward her. She turned upon him, and the scowman halted.

"I said as how I'd settle with ye, Flea," he said, "and now I'm goin' to."

But Lon glared so fiercely that Crabbe closed his mouth and retreated.

"It ain't time fer ye to settle yet, Lem, I'm a thinkin'," said Lon. "Ye keep shet up, or I'll settle with ye afore ye has a chance to fix Flea." Turning to the girl, he questioned her. "Did ye tell anyone ye was goin' with me?" Fledra nodded her head. "Did ye tell Flukey?"

"Yes, and Mr. Shellington. But I told them both that I came of my own free will. But you know I came because I wanted Mr. Shellington to live and Flukey to stay where he is. But I ain't going to be alone in this room with Lem tonight—I tell you that!"

Lon sat down and smoked moodily on his pipe. After a few minutes' thought he said:

"Ye can sleep in that back room where ye put the dorg, Flea, and if there's a key in the lock ye can turn it. You come up to the deck with me, Lem."

With a dark scowl, the scowman followed the squatter upstairs. He had reckoned that the hour to take Flea was near; but Lon's heavy hand held him back. When they were standing side by side in the darkness of the barge-deck, Cronk spoke.

"Lem," he said, "I told ye before that Flea ain't like Flukey. She'd just as soon throw herself into that water as she'd look at ye. She ain't

171

afraid of nothin' but you, and ye've got to keep yer hands offen her till I git her foul, do ye hear?"

"Ye ain't keepin' me away just fer the sake of that high-toned Brimbecomb pup, be ye, Lon?"

"Nope. I'd rather you'd have her, Lem, 'cause ye'll beat her and make her wish a hundred times a day that she'd drowned herself. I say, if ye let me fix this thing, ye'll come out on the top of the heap. If ye don't, she'll raise a fuss, and, if that damned governor gets wind of it, he might catch on that the kid be his. He'd run us both down afore ye could say jackrabbit. Ye let Flea alone till I say ye can have her."

"If yer dealin' fair—"

The squatter interrupted his companion with an angry growl.

"Have I ever cheated ye out of any money?"

"Nope," answered Lem.

"Then I won't cheat ye out of no girl; fer I love a five-cent piece better'n Flea any time. Now, shet up, and we'll go down to sleep!"

Fledra fled into the back room, and, closing the door quickly, slipped the bolt. She glanced about the cabin, which through the candlelight looked dirty and miserably mean. But it was a haven of escape from Lem, and she welcomed it. A large can of tobacco was on a wooden box. Fledra knew this belonged to the canal-man and that he would come after it. She picked it up, and, opening the door, shoved it far into the other room. She could bear Lon's muttering voice on the deck above, and the swish of the water as the tug pulled the scow along. Once more she carefully locked the cabin door, and then, with a sob, dropped to her knees, burying her face in the coarse blanket that covered the bunk. Long and wildly she wept, her sobs frequently stopping the utterance of an attempted prayer. Finally her exhaustion overcame her, and she fell into a troubled sleep.

CHAPTER THIRTY

When Fledra opened her eyes the next morning she could not at first realize where she was. When she did she rose from the bed fully dressed; for she had taken off none of her clothing the night before.

She drew a long breath as she realized that she would not be pestered by Lem during the trip to Ithaca. Peering through the small cabin window, she could see that they were slowly passing the farms on the banks of the river as the barge was towed slowly through the water. The peace of spring overspread each field, covering the land as far as the girl could see. Herds of cattle grazed calmly on the hills, and she could hear the faint tinkling of their bells above the chug-chug of Middy's small steamer ahead. At intervals fleets of barges, pulled along by struggling little tugboats, passed between her and the bank. These would see Tarrytown—the promised land of Screech Owl's prophecy, the paradise she had been forced to leave! The light of self-sacrifice shone in her uplifted eyes, and many times her sight was blurred by tears; but no thought of escape from Lem and Lon came to her mind. To reenter her promised land would place her beloved ones in jeopardy.

Her reverie left her at a call from Lon, and she unfastened the cabin-door.

"Come out and get the breakfast fer us, Kid," ordered the squatter.

Fledra left the little room and mechanically prepared the coarse food. When it was ready, she took her seat opposite Cronk, and Lem dragged a chair to the table by the aid of the hook on his arm.

"Ye're feelin' more pert this mornin', Flea," said Lon, after drinking a cup of black coffee.

"Yes," replied Flea faintly.

"And are ye goin' to mind yer pappy now?" pursued Lon.

"Yes, after we get to Ithaca," murmured Fledra.

"Tell me what ye said to Flukey in yer note."

"I told him he could stay with Brother Horace; but that I'd go with you, and—"

Her slow precise speech made a decided impression upon Lem; for he ceased eating and stared at her open-mouthed. But Cronk brought his fist down on the table with a thump that rattled the tin dishes.

"Don't be puttin' on no guff with me, brat!" he shouted. "Ye talk as I teeched ye to, and not as them other folks do."

Fledra fell into a resentful silence.

After a few seconds, Cronk said:

"Now, go on, Kid, and tell me what ye told him."

"If you won't let me speak as I like, Pappy Lon, then I'll keep still."

The girl faced him with brave unconcern, with such reckless defiance that Lon drew down his already darkened brow.

"Yer gettin' sassy!" Lem grunted, with his mouth full of food.

Cronk held his peace. He peered at her covertly, as if he would discover what had so changed her since the night before. Her dignity, the haughty poise of her head as she looked straight at him, filled him with something like dismay. Would Lem be able to subdue her with brute force? The scowman also observed her stealthily, compared her to Scraggy, and wondered. They both waited for Fledra to continue; but during the rest of the meal she did not speak again.

Miss Shellington was deeply surprised when the deputy met her with an open letter in his hand, and said:

"The court has called me away, Ma'm. I guess your troubles are all over."

For a moment Ann did not comprehend the meaning of his words. Then she laid a trembling hand on his arm and faltered:

"Possibly they'll send someone else; but I'd much rather you'd stay. We are—we are used to you."

"Thanks, Ma'm; but no one else won't come—the case has been called off."

Increasing excitement reddened Miss Shellington's cheeks.

"Oh, do you think they are going to leave them here with us?"

The deputy buttoned his coat and put on his hat.

"I'm sure I don't know; but I'd almost think so, or I wouldn't have got this order." He tapped his breast-pocket and made as if to go; but he faced the other once more instead, with slightly rising color. "You still have your doctor's orders, Miss, that nobody can take the boy away for sometime; so don't worry. And, Ma'm," the red in his face deepened, "you ain't prayed all these weeks for nothing. I ain't much on praying myself; but I've got a lot of faith in a pretty, good young lady when she does it. Goodby, Ma'm."

As Ann bade the officer farewell, the relief from haunting fears and racking possibilities almost overcame her. She went back to Floyd, resolutely holding up under the strain. She told him that the stranger had gone; but that, as she had received no communication, she did not know the next steps that would be taken.

It was nearly nine o'clock when Ann tapped softly upon Fledra's door. There had been no sign of life from the blue room that morning; for Miss Shellington had given orders that Fledra be allowed to sleep if she so wished. Now, however, she wanted the girl to come to the dining-room to welcome Flukey to his first meal at the table and to learn that the deputy had been withdrawn. When no voice answered her knock, Ann turned the handle of the door and peeped in. Fledra's bed was open, and looked as if its occupant had just got up. Miss

174

Shellington passed through to the bathroom, and called. She ran back hastily to the bed and put her hand upon it. The sheets were cold, while the pillow showed only a faint impression where Fledra's dark head had rested. Miss Shellington paused and glanced about, fright taking the place of expectancy on her face. She hurried to the open window and looked out. Then she rushed to the kitchen and questioned the servants. None of them had seen Fledra, all were earnestly certain that the girl had not been about the house during the morning. Ann thought of Floyd, and for the nonce her fears were forced aside. In spite of her anxiety, she had a smile on her lips as she entered the breakfast-room and took her seat opposite the boy.

"We'll have to eat without Sister this morning," she said gently to the convalescent. "She's a tired little girl."

"She'd be glad to see me here," said Floyd wistfully. "Sister Ann, what's the matter with Fledra?"

Miss Shellington would have given much to have been able to answer this question. Finally her alarm became so strong that she left her breakfast unfinished, and, unknown to Floyd, instituted a systematic search for the girl. Many were the excuses she made to the waiting young brother as the day lengthened hour by hour. Again and again he demanded that Fledra be brought to him. At length the parrying of his questions by Miss Shellington aroused his suspicions, so that he grew nervous and fretful. Five o'clock came, and yet no tidings of the girl. Ann's anxiety had now become distraction; for her brother's absence threw upon her shoulders the responsibility of the girl's disappearance, and the care of Floyd should he suffer a relapse. Her perturbation became so unbearable that she put her pride from her, and sought the aid of Everett Brimbecomb.

She called him on the telephone, and, when his voice answered her clearly over the wire, she felt again all her old desire to be with him; her agitation and uncertainty increased her longing.

"Everett, I'm in dreadful trouble. Can't you come over a moment?"

"Of course, dear girl. I'll come right away."

Not many minutes later Ann herself ushered Everett into the drawing-room, where she had spent such happy hours with him. But, when they were alone, her distrust of him once more took possession of her, and she looked sharply at him as she asked:

"Everett, do you know where Fledra has gone?"

"Who? Fledra Vandecar?" His taunt was untimely, and his daring smile changed her distrust to repulsion.

"No; you know whom I mean—Fledra Cronk. She's, not here. Horace has gone away for a few days, and I'm wild with anxiety. Will you help me find her, Everett? She must be here with us until it is decided which way the matter will go."

They had been standing apart; but the girl's words drew him closer, and he took her hand in his. He had truly missed her, and was glad to be in her confidence once more.

"Ann, you've never been frank with me in this matter; but I'm going to return good for evil. I really don't know where the girl is; still, anything I can do I will. But I do know that her father has seen her; for he told me about it. It was—"

Ann cut him off with a sharp cry:

"But he's seen her only the once, Everett—only that one afternoon when he first came."

This time Everett answered with heart-rending deliberateness:

"You're mistaken, Ann. Your paragon got out of the window when you were all asleep," Ann's sudden pallor disturbed the lawyer only an instant, and, not heeding her clutch on his arm or a pained ejaculation from her, he proceeded, "and went to her father. He told me this. Ann, don't be stupid. Don't totter that way. Sit down, here, child. No, don't push me away.... Well, as you please!"

"Oh, you seem so heartless about it," gasped Ann, "when you know how Horace loves her!"

Miss Shellington did not notice the smile that crossed his lips as he looked down at her, or the triumph in his eyes when he said:

"But, Ann, I've told you only what you've asked of me. I think you're rather unkind, Dear."

"I don't intend to be," she moaned, leaning back and closing her eyes. "Oh! she was with us so long! What shall I say to Horace?"

"Didn't you say he was out of town?"

"Yes, for four or five days," Ann put the wrong meaning to Everett's deep sigh, and she finished; "but I'm going to send for him."

"And, pray, what can he do? The girl is gone, and that ends it."

"But Horace might ascertain if she had been forced to go."

Brimbecomb laughed low.

"No one could force her to jump from the window of her bedroom."

"Everett, Fledra has always said that she hated her father, and that she never wanted to go back to him, because he abused both her and her brother."

"Yes, so you told me before, and I think I remember telling you that you were making a mistake in trusting in her truthfulness. It seems her brother told her that he did not wish to return with the squatter; so she left him here with you. For my part," Everett pressed closer to her, "I'm glad that she is gone. The coming of those children

176

completely changed both you and Horace. You'll get used to ingratitude before you've done much charity work."

Ann's intuition increased her disbelief in the man opposite her.

"Everett, will you swear to me that you had nothing to do with her going?"

Brimbecomb swore glibly enough, and supplemented his oath with:

"I've always felt, though, that you should not have them here; and I can't say that I shouldn't have taken them away, if I could, Ann. Don't you think we could overlook past unpleasantness, and let our arrangements go on as we intended they should?"

Ann rose hastily to her feet. She was sorely tempted to fall into his arms. How handsome he looked, how strongly his eyes pleaded with her! But her vague fears and distrust held her back. She sank again to the chair.

"No, no—not just yet, Everett," she said. "I've loved you dearly; but I can't understand Fledra's disappearance. Oh, I—I don't know how to meet Horace! He loved and trusted her so!" Again she looked at him with indecision. "Come back to me, Dear," she whispered, "when it is all over. I'm so unhappy today!"

CHAPTER THIRTY-ONE

Floyd raised his head when Ann bent over him. Agitation and sorrow had so altered her that the change brought him to a half-sitting position.

"Flea's sick, I bet!" he burst out, without waiting to be addressed. "Don't try to fool me, Sister Ann."

As his suspicion grew within him, his eyes traveled over her face again and again; then he put his feet on the floor and stood up.

"Ye didn't tell me the truth this morning, did ye?"

Miss Shellington forced him gently back on the divan, and sat down beside him.

"I'd hoped, Floyd, dear," she said tremblingly, "that we were all

177

going to be happy. You must be brave and help me, won't you? If you should become ill again, I think I should die."

"Then, tell me about Flea. Has Pappy Lon—"

"Fledra went back to him last night of her own free will."

With eyes growing wide from fear, Floyd stared at her.

"I don't know what you mean! Did she tell ye she was a goin'?"

"No, Dear. This morning Fledra was not in her bedroom, and for awhile I thought she had not heeded our cautions, but had gone out for a walk. But Mr. Brimbecomb has just told me that Fledra went back with your father, and that, she had not been forced to go."

"I don't believe it!" The boy's voice was sharp with agony. "Pappy Lon made her go—ye can bet on that, Sister Ann! Flea wouldn't go back there without a reason. I bet that big duffer of yours had a finger in the pie."

Ann flushed painfully.

"Floyd, dear, don't, I beg of you!"

"I'm sorry I said that, Sister Ann. But Flea didn't go for nothin'. Sister Ann, will you and Brother Horace find out why she went? I have to go, too, if Flea's in the hut. Pappy Lon and Lem'll kill her!"

He attempted to rise; but Ann's restraining hand held him back.

"Floyd, Floyd, dear, we don't know where she's gone; but my brother will come soon, and he'll find her. He won't let Fledra be kept from us, if she wants to come back."

The boy's rigid body did not relax at her assurance, nor did her argument lessen his determination.

"But what about Lem? You don't know Lem, Sister Ann. He's the worst man I ever see. I've got to go and get my sister!"

"Floyd, you'd die if you should try to go out now. Why, Dear, you can scarcely stand. Now, listen! I'll send a telegram to my brother, and he'll be right back. Then, if you are determined to go, and can, he'll take you. Why, child, you haven't been out in weeks!"

Three days crawled slowly along, and yet Horace made no response to the many frantic telegrams that Ann had sent. Never had the hours seemed so leaden-winged as those passed waiting for him to come. Ann had received one note from him, and three letters for Fledra lay unopened in the girl's room. His note to Ann was from Boston, and she immediately sent a despatch to him there.

On the fourth day after Fledra's disappearance, when Ann met her brother, one glance told her that he was unaware of their trouble.

"Oh, Horace, I thought you'd never get here! Didn't you receive any of my telegrams?"

178

"No! What's the matter? Has something happened to Floyd? Where's Fledra?"

"Gone!" gasped Ann.

"Gone! Gone where?"

His voice was filled with imperious questioning, and Ann stifled her sobs.

"I know only what Everett has told me. When we got up the morning after you left, she was gone. I called Everett over, and he told me she went with her father of her own free will. The squatter told him so."

"He's a liar! And if he's inveigled that girl—"

Ann's loyalty to Everett forced her to say:

"Hush, Horace! You've no right to say anything against him until you are sure."

Shellington took several rapid strides around the room.

"If I'd only known it before!"

"I've tried to reach you," Ann broke in; "but my messages could not have been delivered."

"Oh, I'm not blaming you, Ann," he said in a lower tone. "But those men in some way have forced her to go. I'm sure of it! Fledra would never have gone with them willingly. Did she leave no message, no word? Have you searched my room? Have you looked every where?"

"No, I didn't look in your room—it didn't enter my mind. Why didn't I think of that before? Come, we'll look now."

Under the large blotter on his desk Horace found the two tear-stained letters Fledra had left. With a groan the frantic lover tore open the one directed to him and read it.

"She's gone with them!" he said slowly in a hollow voice, and sank into a chair.

Miss Shellington took the note from his outstretched hand, and read:

"*Mr. Shellington.*—

"I'm going away because I don't like your house anymore. Let Floyd stay and let your sister take care of him like when I was here. Give him this letter and tell him I'll love him every day. I took Snatchet because I thought I'd be lonely. Goodby."

The last words were almost illegible. With twitching face, Ann handed the letter back to Horace.

In the man before her she almost failed to recognize her brother, so great was the change that had come over him. She threw her arms tenderly about him, and for many minutes neither spoke. At length, with a start, Horace loosened his sister's arms and stood up.

"Give Floyd his note—and leave me alone for a while, Dear."

His tone served to hasten Ann's ready obedience. She took the note for Floyd and went out.

Four times Horace read and reread his letter. He was tortured with a thousand fears. Where had she gone, and with whom? And why should she have left him, when she had so constantly and sincerely evinced her love for him? She could not have gone back to the squatters; for her hatred of them had been intense. He remembered what she had told him of Lem Crabbe—and sprang to his feet with an oath. Hot blood rushed to his fingertips, and left them dripping with perspiration. He fought with a desire to kill someone; but banished the thought that Fledra had not held faith with him. He called to mind her affection and passionate devotion, and knew that to doubt her would be unjust. But, if to leave him had made her unhappy, why had she gone? He thought of Floyd's letter, and a sudden wish to read it seized him.

When he entered the boy's room Floyd was lying flat on his back, staring fixedly at Miss Shellington, who was deciphering the letter for him. She ceased reading when her brother appeared.

"Horace," she said, rising, "Floyd says he doesn't believe that Fledra went of her own free will. He thinks she was forced in some way."

Horace stooped and looked into the boy's white face, at the same time taking Fledra's letter from Ann.

"Flea can't make me think, Brother Horace," said Flukey, "that she went 'cause she wanted to. Pappy Lon made her go, I bet! There's something we don't know. I want you to take me up there to Ithaca, and when I get there I can find her. Prayin' won't keep her from Lem. We've got to do something."

Horace shot a glance of inquiry at his sister.

"We prayed every morning, Dear," she said simply, "that our little girl might be protected from harm."

"She shall be protected, and I will protect her! Where's the deputy?"

"They called him away the morning Fledra left."

"May I read your letter, Floyd?"

"Sure!" replied the boy wearily.

Shellington's eyes sought the paper in his hand:

"*Floyd love.—*

"I'm going away, but I will love you every day I live. Floyd, could you ask Sister Ann to pray for everyone—me, too? Forgive me for taking Snatchet—I wanted him awfully. You be good to Sister Ann and always love Brother Horace and mind every word he says. I'm going away because I want to. Remember that, Floyd dear, goodby.

"FLEDRA"

After finishing the letter, Horace said to Ann, "I must see Brimbecomb at once." And he turned abruptly and went out. Ann followed him hurriedly.

"Horace, dear, you won't quarrel with him, for my sake."

"Not unless he had a hand in taking her away. God! I'm so troubled I can't think."

Ann watched him go to the telephone; then, with a premonition of even greater coming evil, she crept back to Floyd.

CHAPTER THIRTY-TWO

When Horace ushered Brimbecomb into his home, so firm was his belief that the young lawyer had been instrumental in removing Fledra that he restrained himself with difficulty from wringing a confession from the man by violence. For many moments he could not bring himself to broach the subject of which his mind was so full. Everett, however, soon led to the disappearance of the girl.

"I'm glad you telephoned me so soon after your arrival," said Brimbecomb. "I was just starting for the station. If you hadn't, I shouldn't have seen you. I had something to say to you."

"And I have something to say to you," said Horace, his eyes steadily leveled at the man before him. "Where is Fledra Cronk?"

Everett's confidence gave him a power that was not to be daunted by this direct question.

"My dear fellow," he replied calmly, "I don't exactly know where she is; but I can say that I've had a note from her father, telling me that she was with him in New York, and safe. I suppose it won't be necessary to tell you that she was not compelled to go?"

Horace whitened with suppressed rage. He was now convinced that the suavity of his colleague concealed a craftiness he had never suspected, and he felt sure that Everett had taken advantage of his

181

absence to strike an underhanded blow. Banishing a desire to fell the other to the floor and then choke the secret from him, he decided to ply all the craft of his profession, and draw the knowledge from Brimbecomb by a series of pertinent queries.

"May I see the communication you have received from Cronk?"

Everett seemed to have expected the question; for he made a brave pretense of looking through his wallet for the fictitious letter. He took up the space of several minutes, arranging and rearranging the documents. Then, as he looked at Horace, a paper fluttered to the floor, unobserved by him.

"On second thought," said he, "I think it wouldn't be quite right to show you a private letter from one of my clients. I have told you enough already. I'm sorry, but it's impossible for me to let you see it."

Everett mentally congratulated himself upon his diplomacy, while Horace bit his lip until it was ridged white. In his disappointment he cast down his eyes, and then it was that his attention was called to the paper Brimbecomb had dropped on the floor. He changed his position, and when he came to a standstill his foot was planted squarely on the paper. For a moment Horace was under the impression that Everett had seen him cover the letter; but the unruffled egotism on the face of the other betrayed no suspicion.

"Who ordered the withdrawal of the deputy?" Horace demanded.

Everett knew that the lies he told would have to be consistent; so he repeated what he had said to Ann.

"I don't know," Everett said. "I didn't."

Horace gazed at his companion for several seconds.

"Something tells me that you're lying," he said finally.

An evil change of expression was the only external sign of Brimbecomb's longing to throttle Horace.

"A compliment, I must say, my dear Shellington," he said; "and the only reason I have for not punching you is—Ann."

The other's eyes narrowed ominously.

"Ann is the one who is keeping me from thumping you, Brimbecomb. If you know anything of Fledra Cronk, I want you to tell me."

"I've told you all I know," Everett answered.

"For Ann's sake, I hope you've told me the truth; but, if you haven't, and have done anything to my little girl, then God protect you!"

The last words were uttered with such emotional decision that Everett's first real fear rose within him. With difficulty he held back a torrent of words by which he might exonerate himself. Instead, he said:

"Some day, Shellington, you'll apologize to me for your implied accusation. You have taken—"

"Pardon me," Horace interrupted, "but I must ask you to leave. I'm going to Governor Vandecar."

No sooner had his visitor closed the door than Horace stooped and picked up the paper from under his foot. Going to the window, he opened the sheet, smoothed it out, and read:

"Mr. Brimbecomb.—
"I told you I got the letter you wrote me, and you know I can't ever love you. I hate your kisses—they made me lie to Sister Ann, and I couldn't tell Brother Horace how it happened. I am going back to Lem and Pappy Lon to Ithaca because you and Pappy Lon said as how I must or they would kill Brother Horace. But I hate you, I hate you—and I will always hate you.
FLEDRA CRONK"

Like a brand of fire, every word seared the reader's brain. As his hand crushed the letter, Horace's head dropped down on his arm, and deep sobs shook him. The girl had gone for his sake, and was now braving unspeakable dangers to save him from an evil trumped up by his enemies. Tense-muscled, he sprang to his feet and rushed into the hall.

"My God! What a fool I've been! Ann, Ann! Here, read this!" His words, pronounced in a voice unlike his own, were almost incoherent. He threw the paper at the trembling girl, as he continued, "Brimbecomb dropped it on the floor. Now I think Governor Vandecar will help me! I'm going to Ithaca!"

With the letter held tightly in her hands, the woman read over twice the pitiful denunciation; then, tearless and strong, she went to her brother.

"What—what are you going to do for her first, Dear?"

"I must go to Albany and see the governor."

In the flurry of the departure little more was said, and before an hour had passed Horace Shellington had taken the train for Albany. He had instructed Ann to tell Floyd what had induced Fledra to leave them, and Ann lost no time in communicating the contents of the little tear-stained letter written to Everett.

Later in the day Ann received a telegram from her brother in which she learned that he had missed the governor, who was on his way to Tarrytown. Horace said, also, that he himself was starting for

Ithaca by way of Auburn. Ann sat down beside Floyd and read the message to him.

"Did he say," asked the boy, "that the governor was comin' here to Tarrytown?"

"Yes."

For many moments Floyd lay deep in thought.

"I'm goin' to Governor Vandecar's myself. If he's the big man ye say he is, then he can help us. Get me my clothes, Sister Ann."

"It won't do any good, Floyd," argued Ann. "Governor Vandecar has always thought that your father ought to have his children. He doesn't realize how you've suffered through him."

"I'm goin', anyway," insisted Floyd doggedly. "Get my clothes, Sister Ann. I can walk."

"No, you mustn't walk, Deary, you can't; we'll drive. But I wish you wouldn't go out at all, Floyd. Do listen to me!"

"But I must go. Please, get my clothes."

After brief, but vain, arguing, Ann yielded to Floyd's entreaties.

CHAPTER THIRTY-THREE

The governor, meditating in his library, was disturbed by a ring at the front door. The servant opened it, and he heard Miss Shellington's voice without.

In a moment Ann entered, white and flurried.

"I want you to pardon me, Floyd," she begged, "but that boy of ours insisted upon coming to see you. He would have come alone, had I refused to accompany him. Will you be kind to him for my sake? He is so miserable over his sister!"

Vandecar clasped her extended hands and smiled upon her.

"I'll be kind to him for his own sake, little friend. Mrs. Vandecar told me of her talk with Horace over the telephone, and I was awfully sorry to have missed him. But the little boy, where is he?"

Miss Shellington threw open the door, and Vandecar's gaze fell upon a tall boy, straight and slim, who pierced him with eyes that startled him into a vague apprehension. He did not utter a word—he seemed to be choked as effectually as if strong fingers were sunk into his throat.

Floyd loosened his hands from Ann's and stepped forward.

"I'm Flukey Cronk, Sir," he broke forth, "and Pappy Lon Cronk stole my sister Flea, and he's goin' to give her to Lem Crabbe to be his woman, and Lem won't marry her, either. Will ye help me to get her back? Brother Horace said as how ye could. Pappy Lon's a thief, too, and so is Lem. If ye'd see Lem Crabbe, ye'd help my sister."

Ann saw two pairs of mottled brown eyes staring at each other, and, as she listened to Floyd's petition, the likeness of the boy to the man struck her forcibly. The expression that swept over Governor Vandecar's face frightened her, and she held her breath. But quicker than hers had been the thoughts of the man. He staggered at the name of "Lon Cronk," and his mind coursed back to a heart-rending scene, to hear again the deep voice of a big-shouldered thief pleading for a sick woman. Again he saw the huge form of the squatter loom up before him, and heard once more the frantic prayer for a week's freedom. He had not taken his eyes from the boy's, and a weakening of his knees compelled him to grip the back of the chair for support. With a voice thickened to huskiness, he stammered:

"What—what did you say your father's name was, boy?"

"Lon Cronk, Sir—and he's the worst man ye ever see. I bet he's the worst man in the state—only Lem Crabbe! He beat my sister, and were makin' me a thief."

Governor Vandecar dropped into his desk-chair. For a space of time his face was concealed from Ann and Floyd by his quivering hand. When he looked up, the joy in his eyes formed a strange contrast to Ann's tearful face. Floyd, thinking the change in the governor boded well for Fledra, advanced a step.

"Sit down, boy," said the governor in a voice that was still hoarse. "Now, then, answer me a few questions. Did your father ever live in Syracuse?"

"Yep, me and Flea were born there."

"How old are you?"

"Comin' sixteen."

"And your sister? Tell me about her. Is she—how old is she?"

"We be twins," replied Floyd steadily.

The girl, watching the unfolding of a life's tragedy, was silent even to hushing her breathing. The truth was slowly dawning upon her. How well she knew the story of the kidnapped children! How often had her own heart bled for the tender mother, spending endless days in vain mourning! She saw Governor Vandecar stand, saw him sway a little, and then turn toward the door.

185

"Governor, Governor!" she called tremulously, "I feel as if I were going to faint. Oh, can't you see it all? Where is Mrs. Vandecar?"

"Stay, Ann, stay! Wait! Boy, have you ever had any reason to believe that you were not the son of Lon Cronk?" Through fear of making a mistake, he had asked this question. He knew that, should he plant false hope in the timid mother he had shielded for years, she would be unable to bear it.

"Nope," replied Floyd wonderingly; "only that he hated me and Flea. He were awful to us sometimes."

"There can be no mistake," Ann thrust in. "He looks too much like you, and the girl is exactly like him.... Oh, Floyd!"

Vandecar extended his arms, and, with a sob that shook his soul, drew his boy to him.

"You're not Cronk's son," he said; "you're mine!... God! Ann, you'll never know just how I feel toward you and Horace. You've made me your life debtor; but, of course—of course, I didn't know, did I?" Then, startled by a new thought, he realized Floyd. "But my girl!"

"Horace has gone for her," Ann cried.

"And I will follow him," groaned Vandecar. "Horace—and he could not interest me in my own babies! If I'd helped him, my little girl wouldn't have been taken away!"

In the man's breakdown, Ann's calm disappeared. Unable to restrain her tears, she fluttered about, first to Floyd, then to his father, kissing the boy again and again, assuring and reassuring the governor.

"Just remember," she whispered, bending over the sobbing man, "Horace loves her better than anything in the world. Listen, Floyd! He's going to marry her. Don't you think he'll do everything in his power to save her?... Don't—don't sob that way!"

Of a sudden Vandecar leaped to his feet. Brushing a lock of white hair from his damp brow, he turned to Floyd.

"Before I do anything else, I must take you to your mother."

"But ain't ye goin' for Flea?" demanded Floyd.

"Of course, I am going for my girl," cried Vandecar, "as fast as a train can take me!" He turned suddenly and placed his firm hands on the boy's shoulders. "Before I take you upstairs, boy, listen to me! You've a little mother, a sick little mother who has mourned you and your sister for years. I'm going to leave her with you while I'm gone for your sister. Your mother is ill, and—and needs you!"

Still more interested in his absent sister than in his newly found parent, Floyd put in:

"I'll do anything ye say, if ye'll go for Flea."

Ann touched the father's arm gently.

"Come upstairs now."

186

Mrs. Vandecar was alone when her husband entered. She was sitting near the window, her eyes pensive and sad. The governor advanced a step, thrusting back the desire to blurt out the truth. The woman glanced into his eyes, and the change there brought her to her feet. Her face paled, and she put out her slender, trembling hands.

"There's something the matter, Floyd.... What's—what's happened?... I heard the bell ring."

In an instant he crushed her to him, and in an agitated voice whispered gently:

"Darling, can you stand very good news—very, very good news, indeed?... No, no; if you tremble like that, I sha'n't tell you. It's only when you promise me—"

"I promise, I promise, Floyd! Is it anything about our—our children?"

"Yes—I have found them!"

How many times for lesser things had she fainted! How many hours had she lain too weak to speak! He expected her now to evince her frail spirit. He felt her shiver, felt her muscles tighten, until she seemed to grow taller as he held her. Then she drooped a little, as if afraid. Dazedly she brushed back her tumbled hair, her eyes flashing past him in the direction of the door.

"Bring—bring them—to—me!" she breathed.

Just how to explain her daughter's danger pressed heavily upon him. He dared not picture Lon Cronk or the man Floyd had described. To gain a moment, he said:

"I will, Dear; but only one of them is here. The other one—"

"Which one is here?"

"The boy, Sweetheart, our own Floyd."

Although she was shaking like a leaf, Vandecar saw that she was not fainting, and when she struggled to be free he released her. She staggered a little, and said helplessly:

"Then, why—why don't you bring—him to me?"

"I will, if you'll sit down and let me tell you something." He knelt beside her and spoke tenderly:

"Sweetheart, our children have been near us for months. They came to Ann and Horace—"

Fledra Vandecar gave a glad little cry.

"It was he, then, the pretty boy that prayed! Oh, Floyd, something told me! But you said he was here alone. Where is my girl?"

"That's what I want to tell you, Fledra. Look at me, dear heart."

The eyes, wandering first from his face, then to the door, fell upon him. They seemed to demand the truth, and he dared not utter a lie to her.

"By some crooked work, which Everett and the squatter—"

His words brought back Horace's story. A strange horror paled her cheeks and widened her eyes.

"That man, the one who called himself her father, took her back to Ithaca. Is that what you wanted to tell me?"

As she attempted to rise, Vandecar pushed her gently back into the chair and said:

"I'm going for her, Beloved, and Horace has already gone—Wait—wait!"

Vandecar was at the door in an instant, and when he opened it Ann appeared, leading Floyd by the hand. Mrs. Vandecar's eyes fastened themselves upon the boy, and, when Ann pushed him toward her, she rose and held out her arms.

Floyd was taller than she, and he stood considering her calmly, almost critically. He had been told by Miss Shellington that he would see his mother, and as he looked a hundred things tore through his mind in a single instant. This little woman, with fluttering white hands extended toward him, was his—his very own! He felt suddenly uplifted with a masculine desire to protect her. She looked so tiny, so frail! He was filled with strength and power, and so glad was his heart that it sang loudly and thumped until he heard a buzzing behind his ears. Suddenly he blurted out:

"I'd a known ye were mine if I'd a met ye any place!"

Governor Vandecar hurriedly left them and telephoned for a special train to take him to Ithaca. He entered his library and summoned Katherine. He talked long to her in low tones, and when he had finished he put his arm about the weeping girl and said softly:

"And you'll come with us, Katherine, dear, and help me bring back my girl? I shall ask Ann to go with us."

"Oh, uncle, dear, you know I will go! And, oh, how glad I am that you've found them!"

"Thank you, child. Now, if you'll run away and make the necessary preparations, we'll start immediately."

CHAPTER THIRTY FOUR

During the days of the passage through the Erie Canal, Fledra had remained on the deck of the scow when it was light. The spring days were beautiful, too beautiful to be in accord with her sadness. Yet only when they entered into Cayuga Lake did acute apprehension rise within her. They were now in familiar waters, and she knew the end would soon come. At every thought of Lem, Fledra shuddered; for never did his eyes rest upon her, nor did he approach her, but that she felt the terror of his presence—the sight of him sent a wave of horror through her. Much as she dreaded the wrath of Cronk, much more did she fear Crabbe's eyes, when, half-covered with squinting lids, they pierced her like gimlets. Snatchet was her only comfort, and she lavished infinite affection upon him. Night crowded the day from over Cayuga, and still Fledra and Snatchet remained in the corner, near the top of the stairs. The girl watched pensively the lights upon the hills lose their steadiness, as the scow drew farther away from them, until with a final twinkle they disappeared into the darkness behind. The churning of the tug's propeller dinned continually in Flea's ears; but was not loud enough to make inaudible the sound of a footstep. Lon came to the top of the stairs; but did not speak. He shuffled to the boat's bow, and with a mighty voice bawled to Burnes:

"Slack up a little, Middy! I want to come aboard the tug."

The words floated back to Fledra, and she half-rose, but again sank to the deck. Lon was leaving her alone with Lem! The tug stopped, and the momentum of the barge sent it close to the little steamer. When the gap between the boats was not too wide, Lon sprang to the stern of the tug, and again Middy's small craft pulsated with life, and again the rope stretched taut between the two vessels.

As the gloom of the night deepened, Fledra could no more discern the outline of the steamer ahead, only its stern light disclosing its position. For some moments she scarcely dared breathe. Suddenly a light burst over the crest of the hills opposite, and the edge of the moon's disk rose higher and higher, until the glowing ball threw its soft, pale light over Cayuga and the surrounding country. Once more the tug took form, and the deck of the scow was revealed to the girl in all its murkiness. Shaking with anxiety, she allowed her eyes to rove about until they riveted themselves upon two glittering spots peering at her over the top step from the shadow of the stairway. A low growl from Snatchet did not disturb the fascination the evil eyes held for her.

It seemed as if goblin hands reached out to touch her; as if supernatural objects and evil human things menaced her from all sides. The crouching figure of the scowman became more distinct as he sneaked over the top step and edged toward her. A sudden morbid desire came over the girl to throw herself into the water. She rose unsteadily to her feet, with Snatchet still clutched in her arms. She threw one appealing glance at the tug—then, before she could cry out or move, Lem was at her side.

"Don't ye so much as open yer gab," he muttered, "or I'll hit ye with this!"

The steel hook was held up dangerously near her face, and the threat of it rendered her dumb.

"Yer pappy be a playin' me dirt, and I won't let him. Ye're goin' to be my woman, if I has to kill ye! See?"

No sign of help came to the girl from the tug, nor dared she force a cry from her lips.

"Yer pappy says as how I can't marry ye," went on Lem, in the same whisper, "and I don't give a damn about that—-only, ye don't leave this scow to go to no hut! Ye stay here with me!"

Fledra had wedged herself more tightly into the corner, hugging the snarling Snatchet closer. As she backed, the scowman came nearer, his hot breath flooding her face.

"Put down that there dorg!" he hissed. Snatchet did not cease growling, and the baring of his teeth sent Lem back a step or two. "If he bites me, Flea, I'll knock his brains clean plumb out of him!"

With this threat, the scowman came to her again, stretching out his left hand to touch her. Snatchet sent out a bark that was half-yelp and half-growl, and before the man could withdraw his fingers the dog had buried his teeth deep in them. With a wrathful cry, the scowman jumped back, then lunged forward, wrenched the dog from Fledra's arms, and pitched him over the edge of the barge into the lake. The girl heard the dog give a frightened howl, and saw the splash of water in the moonlight as he fell.

He was all she had—a yellow bit she had taken with her from the promised land, a morsel of the life that both she and Floyd loved. With a shove that sent Lem backward, she freed herself and peered over the side. Snatchet had come to the surface, and in his vain effort to reach the scow his small paws were making large watery rings, which contorted the reflection of the moon strangely. He seemed so little, so powerless in the vast expanse, that Fledra, forgetful of her skirts and the handicap they would put upon her, leaped from the scow. Lem saw the water close over her head, and for many seconds only little bubbles and ripples disturbed that part of the lake where her body had sunk. An instant he stood hesitant, then he rushed to the bow.

"Lon, Lon!" he roared. "Flea's jumped overboard!"

The churning of the tug suddenly stopped, and the canal-man saw Lon's big body pass through the moonlight into the water.

The scow was soon close to the tug, and together Lem and Middy Burnes examined the lake's surface for a sight of the man and the girl. Many minutes passed. Then a shout from the rear sent Lem running to the stern of the scow which was now at a standstill. He looked down, and on Lon's arm he saw Fledra, pressing Snatchet against her breast. With his other hand the squatter was clinging to the rudder.

"Here she is!" Cronk called. "Grab her up, Lem!"

The scowman relieved Lon of his burden and carried the half-drowned girl below, whither the squatter, dripping with water, quickly followed. Snatchet was directly in his path, and he kicked the dog under the table. At the yelp, Fledra lifted her head, and Lon bent over her.

"What'd ye jump in the lake for, Flea?" he asked.

Still somewhat dazed, Fledra failed to answer.

"Were ye meanin' to drown yer self?"

The girl shook her head, and glanced fearfully at Lem. "Were ye a worryin' her, Lem Crabbe?" demanded the squatter hoarsely.

"I were a tryin' to kiss her," growled Lem. "A man can kiss his own woman, can't he? And that dog bit me. Look at them fingers!" Through the dim candlelight Lem's sullenness answered the dark look that Lon threw on him.

"I don't give a damn for yer fingers," Lon snarled, "and she ain't yer woman yet, and she wouldn't be nuther, if ye weren't the cussedest man livin'. Now listen while I tell ye this: If ye don't let that gal be, ye'll never get her, and I'll smack yer head off ye, if I has to say that again! Do ye want me to say that ye can't never have her?"

"Nope," cowered Lem.

"Then mind yer own business and get out of this here cabin! I'll see to Flea."

Fledra had faith that Lon Cronk would do as he promised. How often had there come to her mind the times when she was but a little girl the squatter had said when he would whip her, and she had waited in shivering terror through the long day until the big thief returned home—he never forgot his anger of the morning. Fledra winced as her imagination brought back the deliberate blows that had fallen upon her bare skin, and tears rushed to her lids at the memory of Floyd's cries, when he, too, had suffered under the strength of the powerful squatter. She was glad she could now at least rest free from Lem until the hut

191

was reached, and then, if only something should happen to soften Cronk's heart, how hard she would work for him!

The next morning the barge approached the squatter settlement, and Fledra was once more on deck. She wondered what Floyd had said when he received her letter, and if he believed that she had gone of her own free will. What had Ann said—and Horace? The thought of her lover caused bitter tears to rain between her fingers. But she stifled her sobs, and a tiny, happy flutter brightened her heart when she thought of how she had saved them all. Below she heard a conversation between Lem and Lon, and listened.

She first heard the voice of the squatter: "It's almost over, Lem, and then we'll go back to stealin' when ye get Flea. She can be a lot of use to us."

"But what ye goin' to say to that feller if he comes up tomorry?"

"He can go to hell!" growled Cronk.

"And ye won't give the gal to him?"

"Nope."

In her fancy Fledra could see Lon draw the pipe from his lips to mutter the words to Lem.

"If ye take his money, Lon," gurgled Lem, "ye might have to fight with him if he don't get Flea."

The listening girl crept to the staircase and strained her ears.

"I kin fight," replied Lon laconically.

When, next day, the tug came to a standstill in front of the rocks near the squatter's hut, Fledra went forward and touched Lon's arm. Her eyes rested a moment upon him, before she could gather voice to say:

"Will you let me stay with you, Pappy Lon, for a few days?"

"I'll let ye stay till I tell ye to go," growled Lon, "and I don't want no sniveling, nuther."

"When are you going to tell me to go?"

"When I like. Middy's gittin' the skiff ready to take ye out. Scoot there, and light a fire in the hut! Here be the key to the padlock."

Fledra's heart rose a little with hope. He had not said that she had to go with Lem that day. After she had been rowed to the shore, she went slowly to the shanty, with a prayer upon her lips. She had no thought that Horace would try to save her, or that he would be able to keep her from Lem and Lon. She prepared the breakfasts for Cronk and Crabbe and for Middy with his two helpers. During the meal four pairs of eyes looked at the slim, lithe form as it darted to and fro, doing the many tasks in the littered hut. Lon Cronk was the only one not to lift his head as she passed and repassed. He sat and thought moodily by the fire. At last he did lift his head, and Fledra's solemn gray eyes, fixed gravely upon him, made the squatter ill at ease.

"What ye lookin' at?" he growled. "Keep your eyes to hum, and quit a staring at me!" Fledra shrank back. "And I hate ye in them glad rags!" Lon thundered out. "Jerk 'em off, and put on some of them togs of Granny Cronk's! Yer a squatter, and ye'd better dress and talk like one! Do ye hear?"

"Yes, Pappy Lon," murmured Fledra, dropping her eyes.

"I ain't said yet when ye was to go to Lem's hut; but, when I do, don't ye kick up no row, and ye'd best do as Lem tells ye, or he'll take the sass out of yer hide!"

"I wish I could stay with you," ventured Fledra sorrowfully; but to this Lon did not reply. After breakfast she was left alone in the hut, and she could hear the loud talking of the tugmen and see Lem working on the scow.

Soon Middy Burnes' tug steamed away toward Ithaca, and Fledra knew that she was alone with no creature between her and Lem but Lon Cronk.

When Lon and Lem returned, the hut was tidy. Fledra had hoped that if she made it so Lon might want her to stay. She could be of much use about the shanty. Neither of the men spoke for awhile, and Fledra held her peace, as she sat by the low hut-window and gazed thoughtfully out upon the lake. In the distance she could see the east shore but dimly. Several fishing boats ran up the lake toward town. A flock of spring birds swept breezily over the water and sought the shade of the forest. Suddenly Lem rose up, stretched his legs, yawned, and said:

"I'm goin' out, Lon, and I'll be back in a little while. Ye'd best be a thinkin' of what I said," he cautioned, "and keep yer eyes skinned for travelers."

"All right. Don't be gone long, Lem," responded Lon. Fledra was not too abstracted to notice the uneasy tone in the squatter's voice.

"Nope; I'm only goin' up the hill."

Lem had decided to reconnoiter for Scraggy. He was filled with a fear that she might be dead; for he had left her in the hut unconscious. He climbed the hill, and, rounding her shanty, drew nearer, and peeped into the window. A piece of bread lying on the table, and a few embers burning on the grate bolstered up his hope that he had not committed murder. He drew a sigh of relief.

Presently, after the departure of Lem, Lon stirred his feet, dragged himself up in the chair, and turned upon the girl. Her heart beat wildly with hope. If he would allow her to stay in the hut with him, she would ask nothing better. His consent would come as a direct answer to prayer. How hard she would work if Floyd and Horace were safe! Cronk coughed behind his hand.

"Flea, turn yer head 'bout here; I want to talk to ye," he said.

The girl got up and came to his side. She was a pathetic little figure, drooping in great fear, and hoping against hope that he would spare her. She had dressed as he had ordered, and at her feet dragged a worn skirt of Granny Cronk's. With trembling fingers she hitched the calico blouse up about her shoulders.

"Flea," said Lon again, "ye came home when I said ye was to, and ye promised that ye'd do what I said, didn't ye?"

"Yes."

"And ye remember well that I promised ye to Lem afore ye went away. I still be goin' to keep that promise to Lem."

The bright blood that had swept her face paced back, leaving her ashen pale. She did not speak, but swayed a little, and supported herself on the top of his chair. Feeling her nearness, he shifted back, and the small hand fell limply.

"Before ye go to Lem," pursued Lon, "I want to tell ye somethin'." Still Fledra did not speak. "Ye know that it'll save Flukey, if ye mind me, and that it don't make no difference if ye don't like Lem."

"Wouldn't it have made any difference if my mother hadn't loved you, Pappy Lon?"

The question shot out in appeal, and Lon's swarthy face shadowed darkly.

"I never loved yer mother," he drawled, sucking hard upon his pipe.

"Then you loved another woman," went on Flea bitterly, "because I heard you tell Lem about her. Would you have liked a man to give her to—Lem?"

As quick as lightning in the smoke came the ghost-gray phantom, approaching from a dark corner of the shanty. Lon's eyes were strained hard, and Fledra saw them widen and follow something in the air. She drew back afraid. The man was staring wildly, and only he knew why he groaned, as the wraith in the pipe-smoke broke around him and drifted away. Fledra brought him back by repeating:

"Would ye have liked to have had Lem take her, Pappy Lon?"

"I'd a killed him," muttered Lon, as if to himself. "But ye, Flea," here he rose and brought down his fist with a bang, "ye go where I send ye! The woman's dead. If she wasn't, ye wouldn't have to go to Lem."

To soften him, Fledra knelt down at his feet.

"Pappy Lon," she pleaded, "you haven't got her, anyhow, and you haven't got anybody but me. If you let me stay—"

How he hated her! How he would have liked to bruise the sweet, upturned face, marking the white cheeks with the impressions of his fists! But he dared not. She would run away again—and to Lem he had given the opportunity to drag her to fathomless depths.

Fledra misread his thoughts, and said quickly:

"I wouldn't care if you beat me every day, Pappy Lon—only let me stay. I'll work for my board. And won't you tell me about the other woman—I don't mean my mother."

Then a diabolical thought flashed into the man's mind. He, too, could make her suffer, even before she went to Lem. A smile twisted his lips, and he said slowly:

"Yer mother ain't dead, Flea."

"Not dead!"

"Nope, she ain't dead."

"Then where is she?"

"None of yer business!"

Fledra clenched her hands and paled in terror. A mother somewhere living in the world, a woman who, if she knew, would not let her be sacrificed, who would save her from Lem, and from her father, too!

"Lon, Lon!" she cried, springing forward in desperation. "Do you know where she is? I want to know, too."

He flung her away, a grunt of satisfaction coming from his throat.

"And I ain't yer daddy, nuther."

"Then you're not Flukey's father, either?" she whispered.

"Nope; yer pappy and mammy both be livin' and waitin' fer ye. They've been lookin' fer ye fer years—and yet they'll never git ye. Do ye hear, Flea? I hate 'em both so that I could kill ye—I could tear yer throat open with these!" The squatter put his strong, crooked fingers in the girl's face.

A sudden resolution pumped the blood to the girl's cheeks.

"I'm not going to stay here!" was all she said.

Lon lifted his fist and stood up.

"Where ye goin'?"

"Back to Tarrytown."

She was standing close to him, her blazing eyes daring him to strike her.

"What about Flukey?"

"You couldn't have him, either, if—if he isn't yours."

Lon walked to the door and opened it.

"Scoot if ye want to—I don't care. But ye'll remember that I'll kill that sick kid, Fluke, and Lem'll put an end to the Tarrytown duffer what loves ye. I hate him, too!"

195

Fledra dropped to the floor as if he had struck her.

For some moments her senses were gone, and she opened her eyes only when Lon, vaguely alarmed, threw water in her face.

CHAPTER THIRTY-FIVE

Cronk entered the scow sullenly and sat down. Lem was sitting at the table, bending over a tin basin in which he was washing his bitten fingers. The steel hook and its leather strappings lay on the table.

"I told Flea," said the squatter after a silence.

"Did ye tell her she was comin' to my boat tonight?" asked Lem eagerly.

"Nope; but I told her that she weren't my gal."

"Ye cussed fool!" cried Crabbe, jumping to his feet. "Ye won't keep her now, I bet that!"

Cronk smiled covertly.

"Aw, don't ye believe it! She be as safe stuck in that hut as if I'd nailed her leg to the floor. Ye don't know Flea, ye don't, Lem. She didn't come back with us 'cause she were my brat, but 'cause we was goin' to kill Flukey and Shellington. God! how she w'iggled when I opened the door and told her to scoot back to Tarrytown if she wanted to! But I didn't forgit to tell her what we'd do to them two others down there, if she'd go. She floundered down and up like a live sucker in a hot skillet. What a plagued fool she is!"

Lon sat back in his chair and laughed loudly.

"Ye'll play with her till ye make her desprite," snarled Lem, "and when she be gone ye can holler the lungs out of ye, and she won't come back. If ye'd left her to me, I'd a drubbed her till she wouldn't think of Tarrytown. I says as how she comes to this scow tonight. Ye can't dicker with me like ye can with that kid, Lon!"

Cronk narrowed his eyelids to slits and contemplated the scowman.

"I want to have a little fun with her afore ye git her," he said. "I love to see her damn face go white and red, and her teeth shut tight like

196

a rat-trap. She won't do none of them things when you git done with her, Lem."

Crabbe rubbed the length of his short arm with a coarse towel.

"Yep, I can make her forget that she's got blood what'll come in her face," chuckled he. "'Tain't no fun ownin' women, if ye can't make 'em holler once in awhile. But ye didn't say as how she were a comin' here tonight."

"Nope, not tonight," answered Lon; "'cause when I showed her that it didn't make no difference 'bout her stayin' whether she were mine or not, she just tumbled down like a hit ox. My! but it were a fine sight!"

Lem lifted the steel hook in deep reflection and caught the clasps together.

"I'm a wonderin', Lon," he said presently, "if I'm to ever git her."

"Yep, tomorry," assured Lon.

"Honest Injun?" demanded Lem.

"Honest Injun," replied Lon. "If ye takes her tonight, she'll only cut up like the devil. That's the worst of them damn women, they be too techy when they come of stock like her."

"I like 'em when they're techy—it ain't so easy to make 'em do what a man wants 'em to as 'tis t'other kind—say like Scraggy. I love a gal what'll spit in yer face. God! what a lickin' Flea'll git, if she tries any of them fine notions of her'n on me! For every kiss Shellington gived her, I'll draw blood outen her hide!" Lem paused in his work, and then added in a stammering undertone, "But I love the huzzy!"

The other bent far forward to catch the scowman's words, delighting in the mental picture of Fledra's lithe body writhing under the lash. The proud spirit of the girl would break under the physical pain!

Fledra was still lying on the bed when Lon returned to the hut.

"Git up and git supper!" Cronk growled in her ear.

Mechanically she rose, sliced a few cold potatoes into the skillet, and arranged the table for one person.

"Put down two plates!" roared the squatter.

"I can't eat, Lon," Flea said in a whisper.

He noticed that she had dropped the paternal prefix.

"Put down another plate, I say!" he shouted. "Ye be goin' to Lem's tomorry, and ye'll go tonight if ye put on any airs with me! See?"

Fledra placed a plate for herself, and sat down opposite Lon. Choking, she crushed the food into her mouth and swallowed it with effort. For even one night's respite she would suffer anything!

After the dishes were cleared away Fledra knelt by the open window, and peered out upon the water. She turned tear-dimmed eyes toward the college hill, and allowed her mind to travel slowly over the road she and Floyd had taken in September. Rapidly her thoughts came to the Shellington home, and she imagined she saw her brother and Horace listening to Ann as she read under the light of the red chandelier. How happy they all looked, how peaceful they were—and by her gift! She breathed a sigh as the shadows crept long over the darkening lake.

She glanced at the clock, and counted from its dial the hours until morning. She wished that the sun would never rise; that some unexpected thing would snatch her from the hut before the night-shades disappeared into the dawn. Cronk moved, and the girl turned with a startled face. How timid she had grown of late! She remembered distinctly that at one time she had loved the chirp of the cricket, the mournful croak of the marsh frogs; but tonight they maddened her, filled her with an ominous fear such as she had never before felt. When Lon saved her from drowning, and had scathed Lem for his actions, she had hoped—oh, how she had hoped!—that he would let her fill Granny Cronk's place. She glanced at the squatter again.

Lon was staring out upon the lake with eyes somber and restless, eyes darkening under thoughts that threshed through his brains like a whirlwind. He was face to face with a long-looked-for revenge. Through the pain of Flea he could still see that wraith woman who had haunted him all the past-shadowed years. He believed with all his soul that then Midge would sink into his arms, silent in her spirit of thankfulness, and would always stay with him until he, too, should be called to join her; for Lon had never once doubted that in some future time he would be with his woman. If anyone had asked him during the absence of Flea and Flukey which one of them he would rather have had back in the hut, he would undoubtedly have chosen the girl; for well he knew that she was capable of suffering more than a boy. Still, he moved uneasily when he thought of the soft bed and the kindly hands that were ministering to the son of his enemy.

Suddenly the squatter dragged his pipe from his lips and said:

"Look about here, Flea!"

The girl turned her head.

"What, Pappy Lon?" she questioned.

"Keep yer mouth shet!" commanded Lon. "I'll do the talkin' fer this shanty."

Then, seeing her cowering spirit racked by fear, he grinned broadly. Fledra sank back.

"I've always said as how I were a goin' to make money out of ye,

198

and I've found a chance where, if Lem ain't a fool, he'll jine in, too. Will I tell ye?" Lon's question brought the dark head closer to him. "Ye needn't speak if ye don't want to," sneered he; "but I'll tell ye jest the same! Do ye know who's goin' to own ye afore long?" Fledra's widening eyes questioned him, while her lips trembled. "I can see that ye wants to find out. Does ye know a young fellow by the name of Brimbecomb?" Observing that she did not make an effort to speak, Lon proceeded with a perceptible drawl. "Well, if the cat's got yer tongue, I'll wag mine a bit in yer stead. Brimbecomb's offered to buy ye, and, if Lem says that it'll be all right, then I says yep, too."

Fledra found her voice uttering unintelligible words. She was slowly advancing on her knees toward the squatter, her face working into strong, mature lines.

"Jest keep back there," ordered Lon, "and don't put on no guff with me! Ye can do as ye please 'bout goin' away. I won't put out my hand to keep ye; only, remember, if ye go, what comes to the folks in Tarrytown! Now, then, did ye hear what I said about Brimbecomb?" Fledra nodded, her eyelids quivering under his stare. "Yer pretty enough to take the fancy of any man, Flea, and ye've took two, and it's up to 'em both to fight over ye. The man what pays most gits ye, that's all."

The girl lifted one hand dazedly.

"I'd rather go with Lem," she muttered brokenly.

"It don't make no matter to me what you'd ruther have. Ye go where yer sent, and that's all."

Only Fledra's sobs broke the silence of the next five minutes. She dared not ask Lon Cronk any questions.

Presently, without warning, the man turned upon her.

"He's a comin' here tonight, mebbe."

"Ye mean—oh, Pappy Lon! Let me go to Lem! I'll go, and I won't say no word!... I'll go now!" She rose, her knees trembling.

"Sit down!" Lon commanded.

Used to obeying even his look, Fledra dropped back to the floor.

"It ain't given to ye to go to Lem jest 'cause ye want to," he said. "As I says, that young feller is comin' here tonight to talk with me and Lem. I already told him, that he could take ye; but Lem hain't yet give his word."

Fledra glanced out of the window at the scow. Lem was there, arranging the boat for her reception in his crude, homely way. She was sure the scowman would not give her up. The thought brought Ann more vividly into her mind. If Everett came for her, and Lem held to his desire, Miss Shellington's happiness would be assured. The

199

handsome young lawyer would return to Tarrytown, back to the woman who loved him.

Fledra rose with determination in her face. Suddenly Lem had loomed before her as a friend. She moved uneasily about the shanty, Lon making no move to stay her. For awhile she worked aimlessly, with furtive glances at Cronk.

"Set down, Flea," ordered Lon presently. "Ye give me the twitches. If ye can't set still, crawl to bed till," he glanced her over, as she paused to catch his words,—"till one of yer young men'll come to git ye."

It was the chance Fledra had been longing for. She backed from him through the opening of Granny Cronk's room and closed the door. For one minute she stood panting. Then she walked to the window, threw back the small sash, and slipped through. Once in the open air, she shot toward the scow, and in another moment had scurried up the gangplank and into the living-room.

When he saw her, Lem's lips fell away from his pipe, and he rose slowly and awkwardly; but no shade of surrender softened the hard lines settled about the mouth of the panting girl.

"Lem," she gasped, "has Pappy Lon said anything to ye about Mr. Brimbecomb?"

"Yep."

"Are ye goin' to let me go with him?"

"Nope."

"Will ye swear, Lem, that when he comes to the hut ye'll say that he can't have me?"

Lem's jaw dropped, and he uttered a throat sound, guttural and rough.

"Do ye mean, Flea, that ye'd rather come to the scow than go with the young, good-lookin' cuss?"

"Yes, that's what I mean; and Pappy Lon says he's comin'."

Lem made a spring toward her.

"Don't touch me now!" she cried, shuddering. "Don't—yet! I'm comin' back by and by."

Before he could place his hands upon her, Fledra had gone down the plank. From the small boat-window Lem could discern the little figure flitting among the hut bushes; in another moment she had crawled through the open window into Lon's hut.

CHAPTER THIRTY-SIX

When Everett arrived in Ithaca he made arrangements with the conductor of the local train running to Geneva to have it slow down at Sherwoods Lane.

A sudden jerk of the engine as it halted at the path that led to Lon's hut brought Brimbecomb to his feet, and he hurried from the car with muttered thanks and a substantial consideration to the conductor. While the train rumbled away in the distance, he stood in the shadow of a large pine tree by the track and looked about to get his bearings. Suddenly he heard not far from him the faint, weird cry of an owl. Instantly he was on the alert; for there was something familiar in the melancholy sound. It took him back to a night in Tarrytown, when he had cast a woman into the cemetery, and he remembered that she had said she lived in Ithaca. Superstition sent him deeper into the shadow for a moment; but he recovered himself and, shaking his shoulders, went his way toward the lake with a muttered oath.

So dense was the woodland bordering the path, and so dark was the shadow of the bushes in the twilight, that he had almost to feel his way down the dark lane. He had not proceeded more than fifty yards when he saw a light gleaming through the underbrush from the opposite side of the gulch that ran parallel with the narrow road. He came to a path that branched in the direction of the light, and picked his way along it. Soon he crossed a primitive bridge and, climbing a little incline, paused before a dilapidated shanty. He knocked peremptorily on the door; but only a droning voice humming a monotonous tune made answer. Again he knocked, this time harder. The singing ceased, and after a shuffling of feet the door opened.

Standing before him, her hair bedraggled as it had been the first time he saw her, was the woman who had claimed to be his mother, the woman he had thrown into Sleepy Hollow Cemetery. Brimbecomb, in his astonishment, almost fell back into the gulch. But he quickly gathered his scattered wits and, forcing a face of effrontery, doffed his hat.

"Can you tell me," his agitation did not allow him to speak calmly,—"can you tell me, please, where Lon Cronk lives?"

Although his question was low and broken, Scraggy caught each word.

"Down to the edge of the lake, Mister," she replied. "It's a goin' to be a dark night to be out in, ain't it?"

In his relief, Brimbecomb drew a long breath. She had not recognized him! The dim light of the candle showed him that the same dazed expression still remained in her faded eyes. The smirk on her face, the crouch of her emaciated figure, about which the rags swirled in the wind, the dismal hut, and the loneliness of her surroundings, made such a picture of woe that Everett shuddered and hastened to get the information, that he might hurry away from the awful place.

"Is there a scow down there that belongs to—"

"That there scow belongs to Lem Crabbe," broke in Scraggy. "Yep, it comed in this mornin'. Lem be a good man, a fine man, the bestest man ye ever see."

Brimbecomb took some money from his pocket and, placing it in her fingers, hurried away.

Fledra heard Everett when he came to Lon's shanty door and knocked. She heard the squatter call him by name. She knew now that the only hope for Ann's love for Brimbecomb was that Lem would keep his word and insist upon Lon's holding faith with him.

Cronk ordered her roughly to come to him. When she appeared, the two men looked at her keenly. As she evinced no surprise at his presence, the lawyer knew that she had been told of his coming. He made an attempt to take her hand; but, as once before, Fledra flung her arms behind her.

"I 'low as she don't like ye, young feller," said Lon, with a laugh.

"Does it matter to you, Cronk?" retorted Brimbecomb.

"Not a damned bit!"

"Then go and make your arrangements with your one-armed friend and leave your daughter here with me."

"Ye be in too big a hurry, my fine buck! Lem ain't as willin' as I be; but I'll jest go down to the scow and speak with him."

"I want to go with you, Pappy Lon," cried Fledra.

"Ye stay right here, gal," commanded Cronk. Full in her face he slammed the door and left her alone with Brimbecomb.

Everett stood looking at her for fully a minute, and as steadily she eyed him back.

"I have come for you," he said quietly. "I could not leave you with these persons."

Fledra curled her lip scornfully.

"I lived with them a long time before I saw any of you folks," she said bitterly.

The girl did not reason now. She knew that she must send him back, that this was her only way to repay the woman who had saved her brother. So she went up to Brimbecomb appealingly, her eager eyes gleaming into his.

"I want you to go back to Tarrytown," she said, "and go to Shellingtons', and see Sister Ann. She's dying to have you back. And you belong to her, because you promised her, and she promised you. Will you go back?"

"When I wish to, I will; but not yet," muttered Everett. He had been taken aback at her words, and at that moment could think of no way to compromise with her. She was so near that he threw out his hands and caught her. Forcibly he drew her face close to his, his lips whitening under the spell of her nearness.

"Never, never will I let you go away from me again!" he was saying passionately, when Cronk opened the door and stepped in.

The squatter gave no evidence that he had seen Everett's action. He left the door open, through which the breeze flung the dust and the dead leaves.

"Lem'll see ye in the scow," he said. "I ain't got nothin' to say 'bout this—only as how Flea goes to one or the other of ye."

CHAPTER THIRTY-SEVEN

Not more than half an hour after Everett had reached Sherwoods Lane, Governor Vandecar's train came to a halt at the same place, and the party, consisting of the governor, Ann Shellington, and Katherine Vandecar, made ready to step out into the night.

"Please draw up to the switch," the governor instructed the conductor, "and I'll hail you as soon as we return. Keep an ear out for my call."

"Yes, Sir," replied the conductor; "but you'd better take this lantern—it's sure dark down by that lake, Sir. And you can signal me with the light."

Ann and Katherine clasped hands, and, aided by the light which Vandecar held high, slowly followed him. So stern did the tall man seem in the deep gloom that neither girl spoke to him as they stumbled down the hill. They halted with thumping hearts in sight of the dark lake. All three noticed a small light twinkling through the Cronk window, and, without knocking, Governor Vandecar flung wide the door of Lon's hut and stepped in.

The squatter sat on the floor, whittling a stick; Fledra crouched by the window. As the door opened, she raised her eyes wonderingly; but when she saw a tall stranger she dropped them again—someone had lost his way and needed Pappy Lon. Cronk looked up and, recognizing Vandecar, suddenly slid like a serpent around the hut wall until he was in touching distance of the girl.

"Ye'd better not come any closer, Mister," he said darkly. "I has this, ye see—and Flea's meat's as soft as a chicken's!" He raised his knife menacingly; but dropped it slowly at sight of Ann and Katherine.

"Sister Ann!" breathed Fledra.

Ann's fingers grasped Vandecar's arm spasmodically; but, without glancing back at her, he shook them off. His brow had gathered deep lines at Lon's words, and now his unswerving gray eyes bent low to the squatter. Under the steady gaze Cronk looked down and began to whittle.

In after days Ann could always conjure up the picture before her. Fledra looked so infinitely young and melancholy, as her eyes fixed themselves in wide terror upon Cronk. Out of the ragged blouse rose the proud, dark head, and the lovely face was almost overshadowed by two tightly clenched fists. Instead of falling into her arms, as Ann had imagined she would, the girl only sank lower to the floor, her face ghastly in a new horror. Miss Shellington's patience gave way as she stared at Vandecar—his delay was imperiling Fledra's life; for, if ever a wicked face expressed hate and murder, the squatter's did now. She turned appealing eyes to Katherine, and took a step forward; but the latter held her and whispered:

"Wait, wait a moment, Ann! Wait until Uncle has spoken!"

The whisper broke the silence, and Fledra turned her eyes from Lon. She wondered dazedly who the stranger was, and why he had come with Ann. She thought of Horace, and a pain shot through her heart. She was aware that his sister had come for her; but no thought entered her mind to give up the yoke that would soon be too heavy to bear. Then Governor Vandecar began to speak, and Fledra looked at him.

"I have come to take back my own, Lon Cronk," said he, "that of which you robbed me many years ago."

"I ain't nothin' that belongs to ye, and ye'd better go back where ye comed from, Mister—and don't—come no nearer!"

As the squatter spoke, his lips spread wide over his teeth, and he began picking up and laying down the bits of white wood. He did it deliberately, and no one present imagined how the sight of Vandecar tore at his heartstrings. Cronk could tolerate no robbing him of his revenge, no taking away his chance of soothing the haunting spirit of his dead woman.

Again Ann touched the governor's arm.

"Don't, Dear!" he said, pushing her back a little. "Lon Cronk—I want to tell you—a story."

Cronk made no response; only stooped over and gathered a few slender whittlings, and stacked them up among the others. There was an intense, biting silence, until the governor spoke again.

"Nineteen years ago, when I lived in Syracuse, there came to me an opportunity to convict a man of theft. Then I was young and happy; I knew nothing of deep misery, or of—deep love." The hesitation on his last words brought a shake from the squatter's shoulders. "This man, as I have said, was a thief, admitted his crime to me; but, at the time of his conviction, he pleaded with me that he might go home for a little while to see his wife, who was ill. But of course I had no authority to do that."

A dark shade flashed over Cronk's face, followed by one of awful suffering.

"Yep, ye had," he repeated parrot-like; "ye might have let him go."

"But I couldn't," proceeded the governor, "and the man was taken away to prison without one glance at the woman who was praying to see him. For she loved him more—than he did her."

"That's a lie!" burst from Cronk's dry puckered lips.

"I repeat, she loved him well," insisted Vandecar; "for every breath she took was one of love for him."

In the hush that followed his broken sentence, Lon moved one big foot outward, then drew it back.

"Afterward—I mean a few hours after the man was taken away—I began to think of him and his agony—over the woman, and I went out to find her. She was in a little hut down by the canal,—an ill-furnished, one-room shanty,—but the woman was so sweet, so little, yet so ill, that I thought only of her."

A dripping sweat broke from every pore in Lon's body, and drops of water rolled down his dark face. He groped about for another stick of wood, as if blind.

"She was too young, too small, Lon Cronk, for the cross she had to bear."

Lon threw up his head.

"Jesus! what a blisterin' memory!" he said.

His throat almost smothered the words. Ann began to sob; but Katherine stood like a stone image, staring at the squatter.

The governor's low voice went on again:

"She was sicker than any woman I'd ever seen before, and when I was there her little baby was born. I held her hands until she died. I remember every message she sent you, Cronk. She told me to tell you how much she loved you, and how the thought of your goodness to her and your love would go down with her to the grave. If I could have saved her for you, I should have done so; but she had to go. Then I wrote and asked you if I should care for her body."

An evil look overspread the squatter's face. The misty tears cleared, and he began to scrape again at the wood. He flashed a murderous look upward.

"Ye could have left her dead in the hut, as long as yer killed her!" said he.

Not heeding the interruption, Vandecar went on:

"But you sent me no word, and, because I was sorry, and because—"

The knife slipped from Lon's stiffened fingers, and a long groan fell from his lips.

"I didn't get no word from ye!" he burst out. "I didn't know nothin' till they told me she were dead." The man's head dropped down on his chest.

Relentlessly Vandecar spoke again:

"Because I could not give you to her when she wanted you, and because she had suffered so, I took her body and placed it in our family plot. I went to the prison to tell you this, so that you could go to her grave whenever you wished; but you had escaped the night before I arrived there, and I never associated you with my great loss."

The revenge Cronk had planned upon this man suddenly lost its savor before the vividly drawn picture. He did not remember that Vandecar had come for his girl; he had in mind only the wee, sweet squatter woman so long dead.

"Didn't the warden tell ye that I hit him, Mister," he groaned, "and that I smashed the keeper when they told me about her, and—and that the strait-jacket busted my collarbone when I was tryin' to get out to her?"

Vandecar shuddered and shook his head; but before he could speak Cronk wailed dazedly:

"Ye might have come and told me yerself, ye might a knowed how I wanted ye to!"

"I told you that I did come and you were gone," Vandecar answered emphatically.

"Ye didn't think how I loved her, how I'd a dreamed of huggin' my own little brat!"

Vandecar interrupted again:

"I took the baby with me, Lon Cronk." At the word "baby," Lon dragged his heavy hand backward across his eyes. "The baby," continued the governor, "was no bigger than this,—a wee bit of a girl, such as all big men love to father."

The squatter stood rigidly up against the wall, until his head almost reached the ceiling. His fierce eyes centered themselves upon Vandecar.

"If I'd a knowed, Mister," he mumbled, "that ye'd took my little Midge's hand in yer'n, that ye soothed her when she was a howlin' fer me, I wouldn't have cribbed yer kids—I'll be damned if I would 'ave! But I hated ye—Christ! how I hated ye! I could only think how ye wouldn't help me." He shuddered, wiped his wet lips, and went on, "After that I went plumb to hell. There weren't no living with me in prison, lessen I were strapped in the jacket till my meat were scorched. It seemed as how it made my hurt less for her to have my own skin blistered. Then, when I got out of prison, I never once took my eyes offen ye, and when yer woman gave ye Flea and Flukey—"

A cry from Fledra brought all eyes upon her save Lon's.

"When yer woman gave ye the two kids," he went on, "I let 'em stay long enough for ye to love 'em; then I stole 'em away. But, if I'd a knowed that ye tooked mine—" He moved forward restlessly and almost whispered, "Mister, will ye tell me how the little 'un looked? And were it warm and snuggly? Did ye let it lay ag'in' ye—and sleep?" The miserable, questioning voice rose in demand, but lowered again. "Did ye let it grab hold of yer fingers—oh, that were what I wanted more'n anythin' else! And that's why I stealed yours; so ye'd know what sufferin' was. If ye'd only telled me, Mister—if ye'd only telled me!"

Vandecar groaned—groaned for them all, no more for himself and for his gentle wife than for the great hulk of a man wrestling in agony. Tears rose slowly to his lids; but he dashed them away.

"Cronk," he cried, "Cronk, for God's sake, don't—don't! I've borne an awful burden all these years, and every time I've thought of her I've thought of you and wondered where you were."

"I were with my little woman in spirit," the squatter interrupted, "when I weren't tryin' to get even with you. Mister, will ye swear by God that ye telled me the truth about the baby?"

"I swear by God!" repeated Vandecar solemnly.

"And I believe ye. I could a been good, if I'd a had the little kid awhile. It were a bit of her, a little, livin' bit. I could a been, but I wasn't, a good man. I loved to lash Flukey and Flea. I loved to make the

207

marks stand out on their legs and backs. And I tried to l'arn Flukey to be a thief, and Flea were a goin' to Lem tomorry. It were the only way I lived—the only way!" Cronk trailed on as if to himself. "The woman camed and camed and haunted me, till my mind were almost gone, and I allers seed the little kid's dead face ag'in' her, and allers she seemed to tell me to haggle the life outen yer kids; and haggle I did, till they runned away, and then I went after 'em, and Flea—"

Vandecar stopped the speaker with a wave of the hand.

"Then you brought her back here, and I discovered that she was mine, and I came for her. Lon Cronk, you give me back my girl, and I'll," he whitened to the very lips, and repeated,—"and I'll give you back yours!"

With a sweep of the arm Vandecar pushed Katherine forward. The very air grew dense with anxiety. Ann clutched Katherine by the arm as if to stay her movement, as if to keep her from the dazed squatter. His confession of the kidnapping and his uncouth appearance forced Miss Shellington to try and protect her gentle friend from his contact. But Katherine loosened Ann's fingers in stony silence. Only a choking sound from Fledra broke the quietude. She was staring into Lon's face, and he was flashing from her to Katherine glances that changed and rechanged like dark clouds passing over the heaven's blue. He saw Katherine, so like his dead wife, bow her fair head before him. He noted her trembling fingers pressed into pink palms, her slender body grow tense again and again, relaxing only with spontaneous sobs. That he could touch the fragile young creature, that he might listen to the call of his heart and take her as his own, had not yet been fully forced upon him. The meaning of Governor Vandecar's words seemed to leave his mind at intervals; then his expression showed that he realized the truth of them. He swayed forward; but crouched back once more against the wall. Fledra rose silently to her feet, her ready intelligence grasping the great fact that she was free, that the magnificent stranger had come for her, that he claimed her as his. She was free from Lem, from Lon, free to go back to Flukey. Lem's menacing shadow had lifted slowly from her life, cast away by her own blood. For an instant there rose rampant in her breast the desire to turn and fly, before another chance should be given Lon to exert his authority over her. Then something snapped in her head, and, unconscious, she sank noiselessly to the floor. No one noticed her. She was like a small prey over which two great forces ruthlessly fought and tore at human flesh and human hearts.

Vandecar gently touched Katherine's arm; but her feet were powerless to move.

"Katherine," the governor groaned, "don't you remember that you cried over him and your mother, and that—"

"Yes, yes!" Katherine breathed. She was trying to still the beating of her heart, trying to thrust aside a great, revolting fear; yet she knew intuitively that the squatter was her father, and remembered how the recounting of her mother's death had touched her. In one flashing thought, she recalled how she had longed for a mother, and how she had turned away when other girls were being caressed and loved. But never had it entered her mind to imagine that her parents were like this. The picture of the hut in which the wee woman had died rose within her—the death agony had been so plainly described. The tall, shrinking, sobbing man against the wall was her father! Even that afternoon, when Governor Vandecar had told her of her birth and her mother's death, and of her father in the lake hut, she had not imagined him like this man. Yet something pleaded for him, some subtle, gentle spirit hovering near seemed to drag her forward. She shuddered, slipped from Vandecar's arms, and crouched down before the squatter. She turned a livid, twitching face up to his, her eyes beseeching his with infinite compassion. All that was beautiful in the gentle, soulful girl broke over Ann like a surging sea. This girl, who had been brought up in a beautiful home, always attended with loving kindness, was casting her lot with a man so low and vile that another person would have turned away in disgust. Miss Shellington's mind recalled her girlhood days, in which Katherine had been an intimate part. She could not bear it. She took an impulsive forward step; but Vandecar gripped her.

"Stay," came sternly from his lips, "stay! But—but God pity her!"

The next seconds were laden with biting agony such as neither the governor nor Ann had ever experienced. Katherine pleaded silently with the man above her for paternal recognition. Suddenly he drew away from the kneeling girl and shrank into the corner, pressing the wall with his great weight until the rotting boards of the shanty creaked behind him. Only now and then was his mind equal to the task of owning her. Gathering strength to speak, Katherine sobbed:

"Father, Father, I never knew of you until today—I didn't know, I didn't know!"

In her agony she did not notice the fierce eyes melt with tenderness; but Vandecar saw it with a tumultuous heart. He was waiting to claim the little figure on the floor, that he might take her back to her mother. In that way he would retrieve his own past errors and in a measure redeem the misspent life of the thief. He saw Cronk smooth his brow with a shaking hand, as if to wipe away from his befuddled brain the cobwebs of indecision and time-gathered shadows. His lips, drawn awry with intensity, opened only to drone:

"Pretty little Midge, I thought as how ye were dead! And ye've come back to yer man, a lovin' him as much as ever! God—God!" He raised streaming eyes upward, and then finished, "God! And there be a God, no matter how I said there wasn't! He didn't let ye die when I were pinched!" With a mighty strength he swept the girl from the floor and turned mad eyes upon Vandecar.

"She ain't dead, Mister—I thought she were! Take back yer brat, and keep yer boy—and God forgive me!"

So tender was his last petition, that it seemed but a breath whispered into the infinite listening ear of the God above. Katherine, like Fledra, had lapsed into unconsciousness.

"She's fainted!" cried Ann. "Oh, Katherine, poor, pretty little Katherine!"

"Help her, Ann!" urged Vandecar. "Do something for her!"

He did not wait to see Ann comply; but turned to Fledra, who, still wrapped in unconsciousness, lay crouched on the floor, her dark curls massed in confusion. Granny Cronk's blouse had fallen away, leaving the rounded shoulders bare and gleaming in the faint yellow light.

The father gathered the daughter into his arms with passionate tenderness. At first he did not try to revive her; but sat down and held her close, as if he would never let her go. Tears, the product of weary ages of waiting, fell on her white, upturned face, and again he murmured thanksgivings into her unheeding ear. For many moments only the words of Ann could be heard, as she tried to reason with Cronk to release Katherine for a moment.

"Lay her down, won't you? She's ill. Please, let me put water on her face!"

"Nope," replied Lon; "she won't git away from me ag'in. She's Midge, my little Midge, my little woman, and she's mine!"

"Yes, yes," answered Ann, "I know she's yours; but do you want her to die?"

With his great hands still locked about Katherine, Cronk looked down on her lovely face, crushed against his breast. She was a counterpart of the woman who had lived in another hut with him, and his dazed mind had lost the intervening years. Midge had come out of the prison shadows, and the big squatter had turned back two decades to meet her.

"She's only asleep," he said simply; "she allers slep' on my breast, Missus. She'd never let me put her off'n my arm a minute. And I didn't want to, nuther. She were allers afeared of ghosts—allers, allers! And I kep' her close like this. She ain't dead, Ma'm."

His voice was free from anger and passion. By dint of persuasion, at length Ann forced him to release Katherine and to aid her while she bathed the girl's white face with water.

Katherine was still limp and bewildered when, ten minutes later, Fledra opened her eyes and looked up into her father's face. The past hour had not returned to her memory, and she drew quickly away. Of late she had become timid, always on the defensive; and when Ann spoke to her she held out her arms.

"I'm afraid!" she whimpered. "I want to go to Sister Ann."

But Vandecar held her fast as Miss Shellington knelt on the hut floor at his side.

"Fledra, listen to me! This is your own father, Dear. Don't draw away from him. He came with me for you. We're going to take you back to your mother and little Floyd."

It seemed an eternity to the waiting man before Fledra received him. There were many things she had to reason away. It was necessary first to dispense entirely with Lon Cronk, to feel absolutely free from Lem. Until then, how could she feel secure? The eyes bent upon hers affected her strangely. They were spotted like Flukey's, and had the same trick of not moving when they received another's glance. Then Ann's exclamation seemed to awaken her lethargic soul, and she seized upon the word "mother."

"Mother, Mother!" she stumbled, "oh, I want her, Sister Ann! I want her! Will you take me to her? She's sweet and—and mine!" She made the last statement in a low voice directly to Vandecar.

"Yes, and I'm your father, Fledra," he whispered. He longed for her to be glad in him—longed now as never before.

Fledra's eyes sought Cronk's. He had forgotten her; Katherine alone held his attention. Timidly she raised her arms and drew down her father's face to hers.

"I'm glad, I'm awful glad that you're mine—and you're Floyd's, too. Oh, I'm so glad! And you say—my mother—"

"Yes, Dear," Vandecar murmured, deeply moved; "a beautiful mother, who is waiting and longing for her girl. Dear God, how thankful I am to be able to restore you to her!"

The governor held her close, while he told her of her babyhood and the story of the kidnapping, refraining from mentioning Cronk's name. It took sometime to impress upon her that all need of apprehension was past, that her future cast with her own dear ones was safe, and that Lem and Lon were but as shadows of other days.

Katherine, weeping with despair, was sitting close to Lon. She knew without being told that the father she had just found had lost from his memory all of the bitterness of the years gone by. He had gone back to his Midge, and now centered upon his newly found child the identity of this dead woman. It was better so, even Katherine admitted; for he was meek and tender, wholly unlike the sullen, ugly man they had seen earlier in the evening. The squatter's condition made it impossible to allow Katherine to be with him, and they dared not leave him alone in the hut. Later, when they were making plans for Cronk's future, Vandecar said:

"We can't leave him here, Ann dear. Can't we take him with us, Katherine?"

"It's the only thing I can see to do," replied Ann, with catching breath.

"You'll come with him and me, Katherine, and we'll take him to the car, while he is subdued. You, Ann, dress that child, and wait here for Horace. I'll come back directly. I must place Cronk with the conductor, for fear—"

"Don't be long," begged Ann. "I'm so afraid!"

"No, only long enough to signal the train and get them aboard. You must be brave, dear girl, and we must all remember what he has suffered. His heart is as big as the world, and I can't forget that, indirectly, I brought this upon him." He turned his glance upon the squatter, and Katherine's eyes followed his. The lines about Lon's mouth had softened with tenderness, his eyes were filled with adoration. Katherine flashed him back a sad smile.

"The little Midge!" murmured Lon. "I'll never steal ag'in—never! And I'll jest fish and work fer my little woman—my pretty woman!"

Vandecar rose and went to the squatter.

"Lon," he said, placing a hand upon the rough jacket, "will you bring your little—" He was about to say daughter, but changed the word to "Midge," and continued, "Will you bring Midge to my car and come to Tarrytown with us?"

Cronk stared vacantly.

"Nope," he drawled; "I'll stay here in the hut with Midge. It's dark, and she's afraid of ghosts. I'll never steal ag'in, Mister, so I can't get pinched."

Vandecar still insisted:

"But won't you let your little girl come back and get her clothes? And you, too, can come to our home, for—for a visit." His face crimsoned as he prevaricated.

But Lon still shook his head.

"A squatter woman's place be in her home with her man," he said.

Vandecar turned helplessly upon Katherine.

"You persuade him," he entreated in an undertone.

Katherine whispered her desire in her father's ear.

"We'll go only for a few days," she promised.

"And ye'll come back here?" he demanded.

The girl glanced toward Governor Vandecar, and caught the slight inclination of his head.

"Yes," she promised; "yes, we'll come back, if you are quite well."

Cronk stooped down and pressed his lips to hers.

"I'd a gone with ye, Midge, 'cause I couldn't say no to nothin' ye asked me." But he halted, as they tried to lead him through the door.

"I don't like the dark," he muttered, drawing back.

Fledra eyed him in consternation. Never before had she known him to express fear of anything, much less of the elements which seemed but a part of his own stormy nature. Never had she seen the great head bowed or the shoulders stooped in timidity. Katherine had Cronk's hand in hers, and she gently drew him forward.

"Come, come!" she breathed softly.

"I'm afraid," Lon whined again. "I want to stay here, Midge." He looked back, and, encountering Vandecar's eyes, made appeal to him.

"Cronk," the governor said, "do you believe that I am your friend?"

The squatter flung about, facing the other.

"Yep," he answered slowly, "I know ye be my friend. If ye'll let me walk with my hand in yer'n, I'll go." He said it simply, as a child to a parent. He held out his crooked fingers, and Vandecar seized them. Katherine took up her position on the other side of her father, and the three stepped out into the night and began slowly to ascend the hill.

CHAPTER THIRTY-EIGHT

To Horace Shellington it seemed many hours before the small, jerky train that ran between Auburn and Ithaca drew into the latter city. In his eagerness to reach the squatter settlement without loss of time, he hastened from the car into the station. He knew that it would be far into the night before he reached Lon Cronk's, and, with his whole soul, he hoped he would be in time to save Fledra from harm. At the little window in the station he hurriedly demanded of the agent a mode of conveyance to take him to the spot nearest the squatter's home.

"There's no way to get there tonight over this road," said the man; "but you might see if Middy Burnes could take you down the lake. He's got a tug, and for a little money he'll run you right there."

Horace quickly left the station, and, making his way to the street, found the house to which he had been directed. At his knock Middy Burnes poked a bald head out of the door and asked his business. In a few words Shellington made known his wants. The tugman threw the door wider and scratched his head as he cogitated:

"Mister, it'll take me a plumb hour to get the fire goin' good in that tug. If ye can wait that long, till I get steam up, I'll be glad to take ye." So, presently the two walked together toward the inlet where the boat was tied.

"Who do you want to see down the lake this time of the year?" asked Burnes, with a sidelong look at his tall companion.

"Lon Cronk."

"Ho! ho!" laughed Middy. "I jest brought him and Lem Crabbe up from Tarrytown, with one of Lon's kids. She's a pretty little 'un. I pity her, 'cause she didn't do nothin' but cry all the way up, and once she jumped into the lake."

"Did what?"

The sharpness of Shellington's voice told Middy that this news was of moment.

"Well, ye see, 'tain't none of my business, 'cause the gal belongs to Lon; but, if she was mine, I wouldn't give her to no Lem Crabbe. Lem said she jumped in the lake after a pup; but I 'low he was monkeyin' with her. Her pappy hopped in the water after her like a frog and pulled her out quicker'n scat."

With fear in his heart, Horace waited on deck for Burnes to get up steam, and it seemed an interminable time before the tug at last drew lazily from the inlet bridge, and, swinging round under Middy's experienced hand, started slowly down the black stream.

Ann closed the shanty door after seeing the governor and his two companions disappear up the hill, and smiled at Fledra with shining eyes. The wonderful events of the evening had taken place in such rapid order that she had no time to express her happiness to the girl. She opened her arms, and Fledra darted into them.

"It's all because you prayed, Sister Ann," she sobbed, "and

214

because you taught me how to pray. Does—does Horace know about my new father and mother?"

"No, Dear; he left Tarrytown before we ourselves knew. We received a telegram from Horace saying he had come on to Ithaca. We must wait here; for he'll arrive sometime tonight. We couldn't go and allow him to find this place empty."

"Of course not," the girl sighed impatiently. "Oh, I hope he comes soon!"

Her soul burned for a sight of him. He had been the first to fly to her rescue, even when he had thought her but a squatter girl. He had not shrunk from the dangers of the settlement, and, in spite of the peril of Lem and Lon, he had been willing to drag her away from harm for the love of her. The thought was infinitely sweet.

At length Ann brought her to the present.

"Fledra dear, can you realize that little Mildred is your own sister, and that Mildred's mother is yours? Oh, Darling, you ought to be the happiest girl in the world!"

"I'm happy, all right," said Fledra gravely; "only, I feel sorry for Katherine. Somehow, we changed Daddies, didn't we?"

"Yes, Dear, and I feel for her too," lamented Ann. "I can't see how she's going to bear it."

"Maybe she's been a praying," said Fledra, "as I did when I thought I was coming to Lem. It does help a lot."

"Dear child, dear heart," murmured Ann, "your faith is greater than mine! Katherine Vandecar is a saint, and—and so are you, Fledra."

"No, I'm not." The girl dropped her eyes and flushed deeply.

"Oh, but Fledra, you are!" Then a new thought entered Ann's mind, and she hesitated before she continued. "Fledra, will you tell me something about Mr. Brimbecomb? I mean—you know—the trouble you spoke of in your letter to him?"

Fledra flashed a startled glance.

"Did he dare show it to you?"

"No, no, Fledra; he dropped it, and Horace found it."

"Is that the way you knew where I'd gone?"

"Yes, and on account of it Floyd went to the governor's house."

"Oh, why did you let Floyd go out? He is so ill!" Her eyes were reproachful.

Ann, with a smile, kissed the girl.

"Dear, unselfish child," said she, "don't you understand that, if he hadn't gone, you wouldn't have your strong, big father, nor would little Floyd be now with his mother?"

215

"Maybe our mother'll make Floyd well," cried Fledra. "Oh, she couldn't help but love him, could she, Sister Ann?"

"And it will be impossible for her not to love you, Deary," exclaimed Ann, wiping her eyes. "But now you must dress. Have you still the clothes you wore away from home?"

"Yes, I have them; but they're all mussed. I fell in the lake, and got them all wet, and they're wrinkled now. They're up in the loft. Wait—I'll get them." She was scrambling up the ladder as she spoke, and her last words were uttered in the darkness of the loft.

Ann could hear the girl moving about overhead, and heard the dragging of a box across the floor. Then another sound broke upon her ears, and before she could move toward the door it opened, and a shabby, one-armed man shuffled in, followed by Everett Brimbecomb.

After Everett had disappeared across the little bridge, Scraggy closed the rickety door of her hut and went fidgeting about in the littered room. Long she brooded, sniveling in her bewilderment. Something hazy, something out of the past, knocked incessantly upon her demented brain. This something touched her heart; for she whimpered as does a hurt child when the hurt is deep and the child's mother is not near. She still missed Black Pussy, and when she thought of the loss of her only friend wilder paroxysms of frenzied grief filled the shanty.

After one of her raving fits of crying more vehement than those preceding, Black Pussy again came to her mind, and suddenly she was taken back to the wintry night she had lost him. Feebly she put the events of that evening together, one by one, until like a burst of light the memory of her boy came to her. Not once hitherto had she remembered him since his blow had sent her into unconsciousness. Now she recalled how roughly her son had handled her, and she did not forget his threat to kill her if she ever mentioned to anyone that she was his mother. She recognized, too, the identity of the stranger who had asked her the way to the scow but a little while before.

A sane expression came into her eyes, and she settled herself back to think. With her pondering came a clear thought—her boy was seeking his father! Still somewhat dazed, she tottered to one corner of the hut and fumbled for her shawl.

"He axed for Lon!" she whispered. "Nope, he axed for Lem, his own daddy. Now, Lemmy'll take me with 'em—oh, how I love 'em both! And the boy'll eat all he wants, and his little hand'll smooth my face when my head aches!"

Muttering fond words, she opened the door and slid out into the night. She paused on the rustic bridge, the sound of footsteps in the

216

lane that led to the tracks bringing her to a standstill. Several persons were approaching her. They came steadily nearer, passed the footpath that led to her hut, and she crept out. Two men and a woman were near enough for Screech Owl to touch them, if she had put out her hand. She remained perfectly quiet, and Lon Cronk's voice, muttering words she did not understand, came to her through the underbrush. Then, in her joy, Scraggy speedily forgot them, and, as she hurried down the hill sent out cry after cry into the clear night.

For a long time Miss Shellington stood staring at Everett, and the man as fixedly at her. The movements were still going on in the loft.

"How came you here?" cried Ann sharply, when she had at last gathered her senses.

"I might ask you the same thing," replied Everett suavely. "This is scarcely a place for a girl like you."

"I came after Fledra," she said slowly. "I didn't know—"

Everett came forward and crowded back her words with:

"And I came for the same person!"

Brimbecomb reasoned quickly that he dared not tell Ann the truth, and that so long as she thought his actions were for Fledra's welfare she would stand by him.

"I found out that these ruffians had taken her, and I came after her. I thought a good school would be better than this." He swept his hand over the hut, and did not notice the expression that flitted across Ann's face.

Lem uttered an unintelligible grunt, and growled:

"He's a damned liar, Miss! He wanted to buy the gal from me and Lon."

Everett laughed sneeringly.

"Miss Shellington would not believe such a tale as that," said he; "she knows me too well."

"I do believe him," said Ann. "I saw the letter you lost, which Fledra wrote you. You dropped it in our drawing-room. Horace found it."

Everett saw his fall coming. He would not be worsted by this woman, who had believed once that he was the soul of truth. To lose her and the prestige of her family, and to lose also Fledra, was more than he would endure. He bounded forward and grasped her arm fiercely.

"Where is that squatter girl? I'll stand nothing from you or that brother of yours! Where is he, and where is she?"

Ann stood silently praying for strength. So plainly had Everett shown his colors that she felt disgust grow in her heart, although her

217

eyes were directed straight upon him. She hoped that the girl in the loft upstairs would not come down until Governor Vandecar returned. Again she sent up a soul-moving petition for help.

"You can't have her!" she said, trying to speak calmly. "She is going to marry my brother, Everett."

Just then Fledra, robed in her own clothes, scrambled to the top rung of the ladder. She paused halfway down and glanced over the scene below with unbelieving eyes.

"Go back up, Fledra," commanded Ann.

"I don't think she'll go back up," gritted Brimbecomb. "Come down!" He advanced a step, with his hand upon his hip. "I've something to coax you with," he declared in an undertone. "It is this!"

Fledra saw the revolver, noted the expression on the man's face, and stepped slowly down the ladder. The silence of the moment that followed was broken by several loud hoots of an owl. The first one seemed in direct proximity to the hut; the last ones came faintly from the shore of the lake.

When she saw the gun, Ann whitened to the ears, and the threat in Everett's eyes caused Lem to gurgle in his throat, as if he would speak but could not.

"I told you," said Everett, with his lips close to Fledra's ear, "that I would use any means to get you.... Stand aside there—you two!"

He turned his flashing eyes upon the scowman and Ann, and, placing his arm about Fledra, drew her forward. The girl was so dazed at the turn of affairs that she allowed Everett to drag her, unresisting, half the length of the room. Then her glance moved upward to Ann. Miss Shellington's face was as pallid as death, and her horrified look at Everett brought Fledra to her senses. The girl looked appealingly at Lem. The scowman's squinted eyes and the contortions of his face caused Fledra to cry out:

"Lem, Lem, save me! save me!"

Crabbe drew his heavy body more compactly together, and, with his eyes glued upon the revolver, advanced along the wall toward Brimbecomb. His frightful wheezes and choking gulps attracted the lawyer's attention to him, and the gun was suddenly leveled at his breast.

"Stand back there, Crabbe!" ordered Everett. "You have nothing to do with this."

But, as the lawyer spoke, Lem sprang forward with the fierceness of a wild beast. Instantly followed the report of a revolver; but the bullet went wide and sunk into the opposite wall, for, as Everett aimed at Lem, Fledra twisted and struck his arm so heavily that his fingers loosened and the weapon clattered across the room.

The impact of the scowman's body bore the lawyer down, while Fledra was thrown away from the struggle by a sweep of Lem's left arm. Ann was petrified with fear; but this did not keep her from picking up the girl from the floor. In her terror she took in each motion of the fighters. She saw Lem lift his left hand, and heard the sickening thud as his great brown fist struck Everett full in the face. She saw the hook flash in the candlelight, then bury its glittering prong in the other's neck. Everett screamed once, then was silent; for with his unmaimed hand the scowman had grasped his enemy's throat and was shaking the body as a dog does a rat. In his frenzy, Lem threshed and tumbled Brimbecomb about on the hut floor, the sight of his rival's blood sending him mad; and always the sound of his gasps and chokes rose above the struggle. Of a sudden the gurgles in the throat of the scowman ceased, his face became purple black, and it seemed to Ann that his blood must burst through the thick skin. With one last movement he again buried his hook in Everett, then tried to throw the body from him; but, instead, he himself, fell in a heap on the floor.

Suddenly the door opened, and Scraggy Peterson staggered into the hut.

CHAPTER THIRTY-NINE

She sent no glance at Ann, nor did she see Fledra shrinking in the corner. No thought came to her weak brain save of the two men at grips with death. She staggered forward with a cry.

"Lemmy, Lemmy, ye wouldn't kill yer own brat?... He's our little 'un!... Lemmy!... God!... Ye've killed him!"

Scraggy put her hands on Everett, and saw Lem struggle to sit up, the lust of killing still blazing in his eyes. He had heard the woman's words, and as he slowly grasped the import of them he turned over and raised his head while pulling desperately at his throat.

"Oh, Lemmy, love," she murmured, "ye've killed him this time! He's dead!" She leaned farther over, and kissed the white face of her son. "Yer hook's killed our little 'un, Lemmy—my little 'un, my little 'un!"

219

"Oh, no, no, he isn't dead!" cried Ann. "He can't be dead!" She let go her hold on Fledra, and, with Scraggy, bent over Everett. "Oh, he breathes! But he isn't your son?"

"Yep; he be Lemmy's boy and mine," answered Scraggy, lifting her eyes once more to Ann. "Look! He were hurt here by the hook when he were a baby." She drew aside Everett's tattered shirt-front and displayed a long white mark.

Ann staggered back. Everett had said to her:

"My mother will know me by the mark on my breast."

So this was the end of Everett's dream!

"He didn't love his mammy very much," Scraggy went on, "nor his pappy, nuther; but it were 'cause he didn't know nuther one of us very well, and Lem didn't love him nuther. And now they've fit till he's dead! Lemmy's sick, too. Look at his face! He can't swaller when he's sick like that." She left Everett and crawled to Lem.

"Can ye drink, Lemmy?" she asked sorrowfully.

The grizzled head shook a negative.

"Be ye dyin?"

This time Crabbe's head came forward in assent.

"Then ye dies with yer little boy—poor little feller! He were the bestest boy in the hull world!" Here she placed an arm under Everett's neck; throwing the other about Lem, she drew the two men together before she resumed. "And Lemmy was the bestest man and pappy that anybody ever see!"

Screech Owl's last words were nearly drowned by the shrill whistle of a steamer. A minute later Ann and Fledra heard running footsteps coming from the direction of the lake. There was no knock; but a quick jerk of the latch-string flung wide the door—and Fledra was in Horace's arms.

"Thank God, my little girl is safe!" he murmured.

Then he glanced over her head, his horrified attention centered upon the group on the floor.

Scraggy looked up at him, still holding Lem and Everett.

"I'm glad ye comed, Mister. Can't ye help 'em any?"

For many minutes they worked in silence over the father and son. Once the brilliant eyes of Brimbecomb opened and flashed bewilderedly about the room, until he caught sight of Ann. A smile, sweet and winning, curved his lips. Then he lapsed into unconsciousness again.

"Oh, I want him to speak to me, Horace," moaned Ann, "only a little word!"

"Wait, Dear," said Horace. "We're doing all we can.... I believe that man over there is dead."

He made a motion as if to lean over the scowman; but Scraggy pushed him back.

"No, my Lemmy ain't dead," she wailed, "course he ain't dead!" She placed her lips close to the dying man's ear, and called, "Lemmy, Lemmy, this be Scraggy!"

The hooked arm moved a trifle, and then was still. The fingers of the left hand groped weakly about, and Scraggy, with a sob, lifted the arm and put it about her. Had the others in the room been mindful of the action, they would have seen the man's muscles tighten about the woman's thin neck. Then presently his arm loosened and he was dead.

Everett's eyes were open, and he was trying to speak.

"Is—Ann—here?" he whispered faintly.

"Yes, Dear, I am here, right close beside you. Can't you feel my hands?"

His head turned feebly, and his fingers sought hers.

"I have been—wretchedly—wicked!"

His voice was so low that Horace did not catch the words; but Scraggy heard, and crawled from Lem to Miss Shellington's side.

"Missus, will ye tell my little boy-brat that his mammy be here? Will ye say as how I loved him—him and Lemmy, allers?"

Her haggard face was close to Ann's, and the latter took in every word of the low-spoken petition. Miss Shellington bent over the dying man.

"Everett," she said brokenly, "your own mother is here, and she wants you to speak to her."

Brimbecomb partly rose, and, in scanning those in the hut, his eyes fell upon Screech Owl. The tense agony for an instant to leave his face, and it fell into more boyish lines.

"Little 'un—pretty little 'un," whispered Scraggy "yer mammy loves ye, and Lemmy loved ye, too, if he did hit ye!"

Screech Owl hung over him many minutes in a breathless silence; but when Vandecar came in Everett, too, was dead. Then, at last, Scraggy moved toward the door, and, with the same wild cry that had haunted the settlement for so many years, sprang out into the night.

From her hiding place in the gulch, Scraggy saw Vandecar and the rest mount the hill. When they had disappeared, she slunk down the lane and made straight for Lon's hut. With dread in her eyes, she stood for sometime before the dark shanty, and then swayed forward to the window.

221

When she reached it, superstition forced her back; but love proved stronger than fear, and she looked into the room. So dark was it within that she could see only the white mound on the floor—the mound made by the dead father and son. They were hers—all that was left of the men she had loved always! Scraggy tried the door; but found it locked. Then she attempted to move the window; but it, too, had been fastened. With a stone she hammered out the glass, making an opening through which she dragged her body. As she stood there in silent gloom, the very air seemed to hang heavy with death. In the dark Scraggy broke out into sobs, and was seized with spasms of shivering; she had no strength to move forward or backward.

But again love drove her on, and some seconds passed before she found matches to light the candle. When the dim flame lighted up the room, she turned slowly to the middle of the floor. Tremblingly she drew down the covering and looked upon her dead. They were hers— these men were hers even in death! Chokingly she stifled her sobs, and then the decision came to her that she would keep a night vigil until break of day. Of the two, Screech Owl knew not which she loved better.

"Ye both be dead," she moaned, looking first at Lem then at Everett; "dead so ye'll never breathe no more! But Scraggy loves ye.... God! ye nuther one of ye knows how she loves ye! There weren't no men in the hull world as good as ye both was.... Lemmy didn't know ye was his, little 'un, and ye didn't know Lemmy were yer daddy. I'll stay with ye both till the day."

Saying this, she crouched low between Crabbe and Brimbecomb, and, encircling each neck with an arm, thrust her face down close between them.

Lon Cronk's old clock on the shelf ticked out the minutes into the somberness of the hut. The waves of the lake, breaking ceaselessly upon the shore, softened the harsh, uneven croaks of the marsh-frogs with their harmony. Through the broken window drifted the night noises, and the wind fluttered the candle-flame weakly. Suddenly Screech Owl thought she heard a voice—a voice filled with tender sympathy and pathos. Without disengaging her arms, she lifted herself and searched with dim eyes even the corners of the hut. Misty forms shaded to ghost-gray seemed to steal out and group themselves about her dead. She took her arm from Everett and brushed back the straggling locks that blurred her sight.

The voice spoke again, pronouncing her name in low, even tones. Once more she wound her arm about Everett, and pressed herself down between her beloveds. Her eyes, protruding and fearful, saw the candlelight grow dimmer.

222

"Lemmy, Lemmy," she gasped between hard-coming breaths, "I'm comin' after ye and our pretty boy! Wherever ye both be—I come"

A film gathered over Scraggy's eyes, and her words were cut short by the pain of the intermittent flutterings of her heart. She fell lower, and with a last weak effort drew the heads closer together. Then Scraggy's spirit, which had ever sought her lover and her son, took flight out into the vast expanse of the universe, to find Everett and Lem.

Governor Vandecar bent over his wife.

"Darling," he murmured, "I have brought you back your other baby. Won't you turn and—look at—her?"

Fledra was standing at her father's side, and now for an instant she looked down into the blue eyes through which she saw the yearning heart of her mother. Then she knelt down with Floyd, and they rested their heads in tearful silence under the hands of these dear ones, who trembled with thankfulness.

The last fifteen years flashed as a panorama across the governor's mind. That day he had discharged his debt to Lon Cronk by placing the squatter where his diseased mind could be treated, and he had insisted that his own name and home should be Katharine's, the same as of yore. It was not until Mildred opened the door and entered hesitantly that he raised his head. Silently he held out his arms and drew his baby girl into them.

Horace's first duty when he returned to Tarrytown was to make Ann as comfortable as he could. She had borne up well under the tragedy, and smiled at him bravely as he left for Vandecar's. The governor met him in the hall and drew him into his library.

"I must speak with you, boy, before—"

"Then I may talk with Fledra?"

The governor hesitated.

"She is so young yet, Horace! I beg of you to wait, won't you? There are many things to be attended to before she can leave her mother and me. We've only just found her."

"I must see her, though," replied Horace stubbornly.

"You shall, if you will promise me—"

"I won't promise anything," said Horace, slowly raising his eyes. "After I have spoken to her, we'll decide."

Vandecar sighed and touched the bell.

"Say to Miss Fledra that I wish to speak with her," he said to the servant.

After a moment they heard her coming through the hall.

Vandecar placed his hand upon Horace's arm; but the young man flung it off as the door opened and Fledra came in. Her face was still pale and wan. Her eyes darkened by circles, testified to the misery of the days since she had left him. Horace spoke her name softly, held out his arms, and she fled into them. He pressed her head closely to his breast, smoothing the black curls, while blinding tears coursed down his face. The governor turned from them to the window. He stood there, until Horace asked huskily:

"Fledra, Fledra, do you still love me? Oh, say that you do! I'm perishing to be forgiven for my lack of faith in you. Can you forgive me, beloved?"

"I love you, Horace," she murmured, lifting bright, shy eyes. "And I love my beautiful mother, too, and—oh, I—worship my splendid father."

She held out one hand to Governor Vandecar, over which the father closed his fingers. Then she threw back her head and smiled at them both.

"I'm going to stay with my mother till she gets well. I'm goin' to help Floyd till he walks as well as ever. Then I'm goin' to study and read till my father's satisfied. Then, after that," she turned a radiant glance on both men, and ended, "when he wants me, I'll go with my Prince."

224

www.ingramcontent.com/pod-product-compliance
Lightning Source LLC
Chambersburg PA
CBHW011503170626
46812CB00008B/2955